KILLER ON THE LOOSE

"Is there any connection to your department?" Pauline asked. "Some kind of grievance against the police that may have instigated this attack?"

"The similarities between this case and the one last February would make that unlikely," September answered.

"Are you saying the two crimes are definitely connected, Detective?"

"The MO would suggest that."

"Not a copycat?"

"There are pieces of information that we purposely withheld that we believe only the same person would know. Our working theory is that it's one killer."

"And a woman."

"Yes."

"It's surprising that the killer is a woman," Pauline said in a voice that implied September was giving her a load of bull. "How is she attacking these men, and why?"

"As soon as we have some answers, we'll let the public know."

"Do we have some deranged serial killer in our midst once again? Should we be locking our doors against this woman?"

She was digging away. Trying to worm any information from September that she could. But there wasn't much more to say. Unfortunately, September was running more on feeling than fact, and how this woman targeted her victims was still a mystery. . . .

Books by Nancy Bush

CANDY APPLE RED

ELECTRIC BLUE

ULTRAVIOLET

WICKED GAME

WICKED LIES

UNSEEN

BLIND SPOT

HUSH

NOWHERE TO RUN

NOWHERE TO HIDE

SOMETHING WICKED

NOWHERE SAFE

Published by Kensington Publishing Corporation

Nowhere Safe

NANCY
BUSH

ZEBRA BOOKS
KENSINGTON PUBLISHING CORP.
http://www.kensingtonbooks.com

ZEBRA BOOKS are published by

Kensington Publishing Corp.
119 West 40th Street
New York, NY 10018

ISBN-13: 978-1-4201-2503-0
ISBN-10: 1-4201-2503-6
First Printing: September 2013

eISBN-13: 978-1-4201-3276-2
eISBN-10: 1-4201-3276-8
First Electronic Edition: September 2013

10 9 8 7 6 5 4 3 2 1

Printed in the United States of America

Prologue

The ground was hard, cold, and damp beneath him. He came to slowly, hearing the rustle of leaves around him and feeling a chill breeze against his arms that made his breath shake and his body quiver. He focused straight ahead, staring down the length of his own bare legs to his toes, now bluish in tone. As he registered his nakedness he watched orange and russet and gold leaves eddying away, a small tornado rushing up against the chain-link fence that separated the school yard from the street.

He was inside, looking out, and his surroundings came into full focus with a rush of recognition.

Twin Oaks Elementary School.

"Shit . . ." he whispered, cold panic flooding through his veins.

He tried to leap to his feet and smacked his head against the metal pole behind him. Yowling in pain, he momentarily saw stars and squinched his eyes closed. He heard something fluttering overhead and opened one eye to see a woven basketball hoop dancing in the stiff breeze. He was sitting on the concrete basketball court, he realized, and the ache in his arms was because they were bound behind him, around the pole.

His wrists throbbed from the pressure, his flesh pinched from the hard bindings.

Gulping in fear, he could feel his heart galloping inside his chest. He was *inside* the playground, *tied to a pole* . . . at the school where *he was employed.*

Blinking, jerking his body around, his eyes frantically searched his surroundings for an answer. He realized belatedly that he did have some clothing on. His boxer shorts. Nothing else.

That bitch. That bitch who'd zapped him with the stun gun! She'd done this. Tied him here on purpose. What had she said when he'd asked her who the hell she was? *What had she said?*

"I'm Lucky."

Christ. Oh, my God. Jesus Christ. Oh, God! If the kids saw him like this . . . the staff? How would he explain it? What could he do?

My God . . . my God . . .

He strained against the bindings and slowly got his feet under him with an effort, tiny bits of dirt and gravel digging into his soles. Straining, he slid his arms up the pole until he was at his full height. But that put his upper body above the hedge outside the chain-link fence and made him more visible to the street. Did he want to be seen? In the hope that someone would help him?

Hell, no.

He sank back down to the ground with a thud, jarring his tailbone. His teeth chattered spasmodically. He couldn't stop them. He was freezing and shuddering with fear.

There was a placard around his neck. With dread he looked down, knowing what it said, strangely hoping he had it wrong though he'd written it himself because she'd forced him to! Dipping his chin, he could make out the bottom words—I CAN'T HAVE—and it wrung a tortured cry from his soul.

That fucking bitch! She'd done this to him! She'd made him drink the drug that had knocked him out, and now he cringed inside, recalling the way he'd begged her to let him go, pleaded with her for mercy. She'd strapped him into the passenger seat of his own van when he'd been disabled by the shock, tying him down, and when he'd feebly fought her, she'd zapped him again. But he'd refused to drink her concoction. Wasn't going to let her take her damn abduction to another level. Wouldn't do it!

So she'd held up the gun and pressed the button and he'd heard the crackle, smelled the scent of dangerous electricity, seen the determination in her eyes. He'd babbled on and on, promising her things he could never deliver on, anything to be set free. He told her she had the wrong man. Whatever her deal was, he wasn't the right guy. There was some error here. She must realize that, right?

Her answer had been a hard, "No mistake, Stefan," and he'd gone slack-jawed at the sound of his own name. She knew him? She'd *specifically* targeted him?

She'd waited then, the drink in one hand, the stun gun in the other. He'd tried to reason with her once more and had screamed when she'd lost patience and hit him with the stun gun a third time. Everything he'd said to her fell on deaf ears. She wouldn't listen to him. She just *didn't care.*

So, he'd drunk the small cup of fluid she'd held to his mouth. All of it, because he believed her when she added coolly, "Spit it out and you're a dead man."

The bitch was capable of anything.

And now he'd woken up at the school—his school!—hours later. Who the hell was she? Well, fuck that, he didn't have time to care. He had to get out of this predicament. Before classes started. Before the sky grew any lighter.

Moving his hands, he realized the binding was plastic zip-ties. Like the kind his stepsister and brother—the god-damned cops—used as handcuffs if they didn't have the real thing, or they just needed another pair. Handcuffed . . . How the hell was he going to get free?

And then he thought of the young girls, coming to school in their little dresses and shoes, their hair shining, their faces soft and pink. He'd only wanted one . . . just for a little while . . . just to love her.

They couldn't see him like this!

He struggled once more, aware that the bitch knew of his secret desires. How? He'd been so careful. She was getting some kind of payback here, but he hadn't done anything. He hadn't. Yes, he'd taken those pictures of his stepniece in the bath, but he'd never touched her! Never.

Only because you didn't get the chance . . .

Cold tears collected in his eyes and he tried to blink them away. It wasn't fair. It just wasn't fair.

The bitch had assured him the drink wouldn't kill him, so he'd complied. What else could he do? But now . . . now he almost wished it had killed him. He couldn't have people know.

He started crying in earnest, sick with fear. And then he heard the footsteps. Someone jogging, nearing him, just on the other side of the hedge. He looked up urgently and saw a man in a stocking hat running by. As if feeling Stefan's gaze, he glanced over and nearly stumbled, his mouth dropping open in surprise, his breath exhaling in a plume.

"Hey!" the man called. "You okay?"

No . . . no . . . He was never going to be okay.

With every ounce of fortitude he possessed, Stefan put a smile on his trembling lips. "Stupid prank . . . Can't . . . get free. Can you . . . help?"

Immediately, the man turned back around and circumvented the wall of greenery that barricaded the school from the street. Stefan's back was to him as he approached, but he imagined him jogging up the sidewalk, crossing the grass at the front of the building, then looping toward the playground.

He could hear his pounding steps as he hit the concrete and then he was in front of Stefan, breathing hard, his hands on his knees. "Holy God, man," he said. "Whoever did this is no friend. You could freeze to death!" He stood up and dug a cell phone from a zippered pocket, his eyes drifting to the sign around Stefan's neck.

"Who . . . rrrrr . . . ya callin'?" Stefan chattered.

"Nine-one-one. Jesus . . ."

No. *No!*

But it was too late, the man had connected and Stefan wildly racked his brain for a possible explanation. He couldn't stick with the prank idea. He would have to come up with names if he did, some reason he felt it had all been done in "fun." That wasn't going to work. He had to come up with a Plan B.

Minutes later a Laurelton Police Department Jeep, light bar flashing in the gray light of morning, wheeled to a sharp stop in front of the school. Stefan was sweating. Fine. Good. Get here and get him the hell free because soon, soon, the kids would be arriving. *Hurry,* he thought, his new story in place, ready to tell. *Hurry.*

The jogger waved the cop over just as an ambulance came screaming up the road. An ambulance—shit. He didn't want to go to the hospital. Too much attention. Oh, God . . .

The uniform bent down and looked him in the face. He was young. Dressed in dark blue, his expression stern. "Don't worry. We'll get you out of here." He pulled out a knife to cut the zip-ties. "What happened?"

The jogger looked about to speak up.

"I was robbed," Stefan cut in, a very real quaver to his voice. "He knocked me out and took my clothes and my wallet and left me here."

The jogger's head jerked around. "Man, I thought you said it was a prank."

"A very dangerous one," the cop said repressively as he cut

through the ties. Stefan's arms flopped down to his sides, damn near impossible to lift.

The uniform helped Stefan to his feet, as two EMTs wheeled a gurney his way. Behind the ambulance Stefan saw a first car arrive at the school, its headlights washing the hedge and the ambulance and the cop car, still with its lights flashing. The EMTs helped Stefan onto the gurney. *Fine. Cover me up,* he silently begged, pulling the placard from around his neck with rubbery arms. Better for them to think he was ill.

"Not a prank, eh?" the uniform asked, taking the placard in his gloved hand.

The van? Where was his van? That fucking bitch took his *van*!

Sensing the cop's hard eyes on him, Stefan muttered, "He jumped me and took everything I had," as the EMTs pushed him toward the waiting ambulance. A flutter of worry arose in his chest as he thought of his cell phone. *She* had it. But at least the pictures he'd taken weren't on it any longer. He'd made prints, removed the images, and even the prints were gone now, too.

I WANT WHAT I CAN'T HAVE, the uniform read as the gurney rattled away from the playground, the words filling Stefan with dread, following after him like a bad smell.

How the hell was he going to explain the placard?

He had a momentary vision of being hauled down to the Laurelton Police Department and being grilled by September, or even worse, her twin brother, August—both cops.

A groan of pure misery erupted from his throat as the doors to the ambulance slammed shut behind him.

It just wasn't fair!

Chapter One

Someone other than Guy was manning the desk as September passed through the front doors of the Laurelton Police Department. Someone new who gazed at September a bit anxiously, as if knowing there was a tiny war going on between Guy Urlacher, the usual gatekeeper, and all of the department detectives as Guy was such a goddamn stickler for protocol that everyone wanted to throttle him. September's partner, Gretchen Sandler, who was currently on administrative leave for shooting the man who'd been in the process of stabbing September ten days earlier, was fierce enough that whenever she gave Guy the evil eye, he would back down and let her pass without showing her ID. Not so September, who was fairly new to the department and, well, a nicer person than Gretchen. Guy demanded her ID even if she'd just gone out for lunch. He truly was a pain in the ass.

"Where's Guy?" September asked the new woman, whose name tag read GAYLE.

"Sick with the flu, I guess," she answered. "It's my first day," she added unnecessarily.

Without being asked, September pulled out her ID and Gayle looked relieved that someone was going to be cooperative. But then September said, "Memorize my face," as she turned toward the hallway that led to the inner workings of the Laurelton PD. "Urlacher tries to make us show our ID every time we go by the front desk and it ticks everyone off."

"Detective Pelligree said it's department policy."

September paused before pushing through the door. "Wes is screwing with you. Trust me. Urlacher bugs him more than anyone."

"Oh."

Gayle looked like she didn't believe her and September let it go. She'd given the woman good advice. It was her decision whether to take it or not.

September went directly to the break room, found her locker, set down her messenger bag, which she carried like a briefcase these days because of her injury, and eased out of her jacket. The wound at her shoulder was healing fine but it still hurt like fire sometimes. She'd been told to take more time off, but after the past week of being a semi-invalid at her boyfriend's house, she'd thought she might go out of her mind. Jake knew better than to be too solicitous; she might just bite his head off. Still, she'd been relieved every time he left for work and she had the place to herself—which didn't bode well for their long-term living situation. Was she just too used to being by herself? Or, was it being under someone's care that she couldn't stomach?

She hoped it was the latter.

"Tell me you're coming back to work," Detective George Thompkins expelled in relief as he saw her enter the squad room, his chair protesting as he swiveled his bulk around.

"I'm coming back to work."

"My prayers have been answered," he said, watching a bit worriedly at the careful way she moved into her desk chair.

September sent him a reassuring smile. "You look like you haven't slept in days," she said, to which he gave a loud snort.

"I haven't."

No need to ask why. The detective squad was down in

numbers, and though Wes "Weasel" Pelligree, who'd been seriously injured on a job the previous summer, had just returned to work on a part-time basis, September had been out for the last ten days, and her partner, Gretchen Sandler, was going to be off for a while. Auggie, September's brother and another detective with the Laurelton PD, was currently on semipermanent loan to the Portland police. All of which left George doing pretty much all the detective work. Since he preferred sitting on his butt in front of his computer to any sort of fieldwork, September could just imagine how the days had been for him.

"Where's Wes?" she asked.

"Around. He got a call about some guy tied to a pole."

September had been looking at the jumble of papers on her desk, notes left by Candy in admin along with messages and papers that George had dumped there as well. There was even a memo from Lieutenant D'Annibal, asking her to check with him as soon as she got in, which looked like it might have been left yesterday. But her head snapped up at George's last comment. "Tied to a pole?"

"Yeah, I know. You were working on that other case."

"The postman who was stripped down and tied to a flagpole. Died of exposure."

George nodded. "Same thing with this guy but he was left at an elementary school."

She sucked in a breath. "What school?"

"Check with Weasel. He left about an hour ago to go talk to the vic."

September had already snatched up her desk phone and was punching in the numbers for Wes's cell. The line rang about four times before he answered, "Pelligree."

"Wes, it's September. You got a guy tied to a pole? At an elementary school?"

"Twin Oaks, but he's at Laurelton General being checked out now. Hey, September. How ya doing?"

"I'm back at work." *Twin Oaks,* she thought with a frown. She'd recently been at the elementary school herself, on a different case.

"How's the neck?"

"More shoulder than neck," she said. "Coming along. How's about you?"

"Coming along. Trying to put a full week in, this week. Y'know."

"Yeah, I do." It was annoying and a little scary how tired she felt. All part of the body's way of working itself back to health.

"You were working on that case earlier this year?" Wes said. "The guy tied to the flagpole outside the post office?"

"I inherited it from Chubb," she said, referencing the officer who had caught the case before September's time at Laurelton PD. Detective Carson Chubb had since moved on to northern California. "That vic's name was Christopher Ballonni. He worked for the postal service and was tied to the flagpole in front of his station. Happened last February. He died of exposure."

"Ahhh . . . yeah."

"He had a wife and kid. Teenaged boy named . . . I'll have to look it up. Chubb's report said they both sang Ballonni's praises in the initial interview. Until now, there's been nothing."

"Sounds like the same doer's at it again," Wes said. "Only this time the guy survived."

"So you're at the ER?"

"Yep. Better get down here. The vic's trying to leave."

She'd always liked Wes Pelligree, who had a lean, lanky build and a quick mind. He was unofficially known as the "black cowboy" around the department because of his slow-talking ways and penchant for cowboy boots. Until September had reunited with her high school crush, Jake Westerly, she'd harbored a secret interest in Wes, even though he lived with his longtime girlfriend, Kayleen. She'd since gotten over that, but she was glad to be unofficially partnering with him since Sandler wasn't available.

"Be right there. He was found at Twin Oaks?" September asked.

"Tied to a basketball pole. Lucky to be discovered before all the kids got to school."

"You said it. What time was he found?"

"Six-thirty, seven, maybe."

"Okay. I'm on my way," she said, slamming down the receiver as she slid from her chair.

"I'll hold down the fort," George told her.

"You do that," she said dryly as she headed toward her locker for her messenger bag and jacket.

Jake Westerly was emptying one of the drawers of his desk when the call came through. It was early and he'd been the first to make the coffee, the office's latest intern, Andrea, having not shown up for work yet. Not that either he or Carl Weisz were sticklers for anyone getting to work on time. Though they worked on the same floor and used the same general office space, they were separate, and rival, companies who shared an employee, the hallway that was their break room, and an abiding dislike for the conglomerate that swallowed up all the other rooms on the eleventh floor of their building: Capital Group Inc., or CGI.

Picking up his coffee cup, he took a swallow, his eyes on the scattering of pencils, pens, paper clips, notepads, extra staples, and other detritus that filled his top drawer. He was facing a job crisis of his own making as he'd decided to quit the investment business and find something else to do with his life. What the hell that was remained to be seen, and his clients were making the change difficult while Carl was standing back, rubbing his hands, ready to pounce on them.

Jake was gratified that his clients trusted him and wanted

him to stay in charge of their financial futures, but he'd become somewhat disenchanted with working with money in recent years. Yet . . . yet . . . on the other hand, he wasn't particularly gifted at doing anything else that he could see. Apart from his new relationship with September "Nine" Rafferty—or maybe he should say "renewed relationship" as they'd recently reconnected—he wasn't jazzed about much of anything.

So, he was cleaning out his desk. Slowly. Deciding whether this truly was what he wanted career-wise. His brother, Colin, ran the winery that they'd both inherited from their father, Westerly Vale Vineyards, but Jake didn't think he was really cut out for working there, either. The rustic somnolence of the winery was wonderful for a weekend away, but the idea of working there full time was enough to make him half crazy.

Maybe he did want to stay. He sure as hell didn't want Carl poaching his clients, or even worse, CGI.

His thoughts touched on his brother, Colin, who'd recently been released from the hospital. The psycho who'd targeted and attacked Nine had caught both his brother and his wife, Neela, in the crossfire, the two of them sustaining injuries, as well. Colin had been knifed in the chest and suffered a collapsed lung and nicked artery. Neela's injuries hadn't been as severe, and she'd been seen in the ER and released. Jake had tried to help at Westerly Vale while Colin was down, but Neela assured him everything was under control there even while she drove back and forth between the hospital and the vineyard. Colin had been home about a week now and under Neela's loving care, he was getting stronger daily, definitely on the road to a full recovery.

But it had been an awakening of sorts, or so Colin had said when he'd called Jake this morning, catching him just as he was pulling into his parking spot in the building's underground structure.

"Still going to the office, huh," Colin had said, when Jake switched off the engine.

"I told Neela I would help her," Jake had responded immediately. "She said—"

"Whoa," Colin cut him off. "That was just an observation. You're the one who said you were going to quit. Neela and I are fine. You know that."

"Okay."

"I just wanted you to know, we're on the baby train," Colin said, a smile in his voice.

"You're having a baby?" Jake responded, surprised.

"We're working on it. Life's short, y'know?"

"Yeah . . . but you just got out of the hospital."

"Last week. Some parts were injured, others are working just fine," he added dryly.

"Glad to hear it. Wow. That's great."

"You sound a little unsure."

"No. No, I mean it. It's great. I'm just thinking about you . . . a father."

"Well, it hasn't happened yet, but then, we've just begun."

"How is that, trying for a pregnancy?" Jake asked. "Seriously. I've always wondered."

"Pretty damn good," Colin drawled, again with a smile in his voice, and both of them had started laughing.

Jake had also felt a twinge of envy. His brother and Neela had fallen in love years earlier and they were eagerly heading down a life path together that was almost scripted: *First comes love, then comes marriage, then along comes a baby carriage.*

"Well, let me know when something happens," Jake said as they were about to hang up.

"You'll be the first," his brother had assured him.

Jake had shoved the drawer closed and leaned back in his swivel chair. He'd had an awakening of sorts, too. He wanted things to move faster with Nine. He didn't want to wait, and yet they'd barely reconnected. She wanted to go slower and it made him chafe with frustration, even though he'd been doing that same "commitment avoidance" dance for years with his ex-girlfriend, Loni. They'd been that couple that couldn't live with each other, couldn't live without, until Jake had finally ended it nearly a year earlier, once and for all. He'd been happily single since, until he and Nine ran into each other again this past September.

Meeting September in September.

Only he'd always known her as Nine, the month of her birth. She and her twin brother, August, were born on the opposite sides of midnight on August 31, and they'd each been named for the month in which they were born. But August was Auggie to those who knew him, and September was Nine. Nine Rafferty. She'd agreed to move in with him, but she was dragging her feet, and though he understood, or tried to understand, or at least made noise that he understood, he wanted their relationship to get going already. *Carpe diem.* Seize the day. He might not be ready for the baby train quite yet, but he sure wanted her.

That's when his cell phone rang, shattering his thoughts. It was lying atop his desk and when he glanced down at the screen, caller ID read: LONI CHEEVER.

"Jesus," he muttered, automatically straightening in his chair.

Was she a mind reader? His thoughts out there, available for her to see? She was calling him *now,* though they scarcely spoke any longer?

His hand hovered over the phone. Loni, his high school, college, and most-of-the-years-of-his-life girlfriend. The one he'd broken up with after years of relationship dysfunction. The one he'd gotten back with—foolishly—after that spring night his high school senior year when he and September had drunk wine coolers and made love in her family's vineyard. The one whose bipolar disease had worsened over the years.

He did not want to talk to her.

Chicken, he berated himself.

The cell phone sang away on his desktop. If he didn't answer she would call back. Or, her mother would. Loni had accepted their final breakup far more than Marilyn Cheever ever had. It was Marilyn who generally called Jake—and those calls came most often whenever Loni was hospitalized again.

At least it wasn't Marilyn this time. Unless she was using Loni's phone, which had happened before when she needed to reach him to let him know Loni was in the hospital from an overdose of pills.

"Hello?" he answered carefully, picking up the phone just before it switched over to voice mail.

"Hello, Jake," Loni said, sounding world-weary. "I just wanted to call and hear your voice. You're always so up."

Not a good sign. He knew better than to get sucked in to another drama, but he also understood how fragile she was at times. Until he was sure which Loni he was talking to, he had to be careful.

"Hey, Loni. How are you?"

"Well, I'm not in a hospital," she said on a short laugh.

"That's always good," he answered lightly. It hadn't been that many weeks since she *had* been in a hospital. He'd gone to see her when Marilyn had called him.

"I know . . . Umm . . . you're involved with Nine Rafferty. That's not why I'm calling. I just . . ." She sighed. "It's hard to lose a boyfriend and a friend at the same time. That's all."

Jake thought that over. They'd never really been friends, and since their last and final breakup they'd pretty much left each other alone, not counting that last bout with the downside of her condition and the pills that had sent her to Providence Hospital.

Before he could formulate a response, she asked, "How is Nine? I heard she was stabbed? Is that right? Is she okay?"

He tried not to let it bother him that Loni called September by her nickname. They'd all been in high school together. Everyone called September Nine. He did, so why couldn't Loni? "She's doing all right. I've been taking care of her."

"She's got a helluva scary job."

"Sometimes, yeah."

"But she's going to be okay?"

"Oh, yeah."

"She staying with you?" she asked casually. "You said you're taking care of her."

He kept his plan to have Nine move in permanently to himself and asked instead, "How are you? The last time I saw you, you weren't doing so well."

"I've been taking my medication, and it's evened me out, but you know the deal. Makes me feel dull. But it's given me a lot of time to think about how I've acted and I'm just sorry. For years and years of everything. I'm sorry, Jake."

"It's okay," he dismissed it.

"No. It's not okay. You always say that. But it's not okay, and I want you to know that *I know* it's not okay. But I really am better. I've gotten back into real estate, and things are turning around some in the market. I was showing this newlywed couple property before I . . . took that last trip to Providence. And they actually bought a two-bedroom house last week. Such a cute place."

"That's great," he said, aware that she'd skipped over saying "before I overdosed."

"It was hard, seeing them, y'know? The newlyweds. Thinking it could have been us. But that's not why I called. Well, maybe it is." She laughed again. "I just wanted to touch base, that's all. I'm not asking for anything. Really. I just wanted to talk to a friend."

"You can always call me."

"Yeah . . ." There was a sadness to her voice. "I'll try not to, okay? I don't want to be a bother."

"You're not a bother, Loni. It's good to hear you're doing well."

"Is it? Good to hear? Sorry. I sound so desperate. I just want everything to be cool between us."

"It's cool."

"I know it can't be like it was. Of course it can't. I was just thinking yesterday, y'know, while I was watching the newly-weds, that you and I used to have something really special. I know practically everybody says that about someone they loved, but we really did. I just started thinking about all the good times we had, and I forgot about the bad."

Jake realized his hand was clenching the phone and he slowly released the pressure. He never forgot about the bad, but he said, "I hear you."

"I'm going to be embarrassed about this phone call later. I can already tell." She huffed out a half laugh. "But it's worth it, just to talk to you. I know you don't want to hear this, but you're my touchstone, Jake. You always have been and you always will be."

"I don't know what to say to that."

There was a long hesitation, then she finished with false cheer, "Well, I'd better get going. We've got the home inspection today. Their house is over by Laurelton High. Every time I drive by I think about high school and that makes me think about you. Guess that's why I called." Before he could respond, she said, "Take care, Jake," and then she was gone.

Jake's gaze was on the contents of his top desk drawer but he didn't see any of it. He remembered Loni as she'd been: blond, beautiful, smart, spoiled. They'd been the couple mostly likely to break up, again and again and again, and they'd batted a thousand on that prediction. Her disease hadn't really grabbed hold of her until college or maybe sometime after, but now it was in full play, and though he'd tried, he couldn't save her.

With a feeling of desperation of his own, he placed a call

to Nine's cell. He might be Loni's touchstone, but September was his.

The Emergency Room at Laurelton General was fairly quiet this Tuesday morning. September saw Wes as she entered through the sliding glass doors. He was wearing a black shirt and blue jeans and the ever-present cowboy boots.

"Where's the vic?" she asked, looking toward the closed hydraulic doors behind which she knew were curtained, exam-room cubicles.

His gaze followed hers. "Through there. He called somebody to bring him some clothes, but they haven't gotten here yet. He didn't even want to come, but the uniform who found him and the EMT got him into the ambulance. He didn't have a car at the site. Name's Stefan Harmak, and—"

"What?"

Wes had been moving toward the hydraulic doors but now he stopped short, his dark eyes sweeping back to her. "You know him?"

"Yeah, I know him," September shot back. "Stefan Harmak was my stepbrother. Unless there are two in the area, which I strongly doubt, that's who our vic is."

"Wow." He shook his head.

"Stefan." She couldn't credit it. "What the hell was he doing?" From somewhere in her memory she recalled her ex-stepbrother had started working as a teaching assistant in the hopes of landing a full-time job.

"He told the guy who found him—a jogger—that it was a prank, someone tying him to the basketball pole. But he told Lennon, the uniform on the scene, that a guy had robbed him."

"Which do you think it is?"

"The second. He's got stun gun burn marks that he didn't mention. A number of them. When I asked him about them, he clammed up."

"I want to talk to him."

"Seeing as it's family and you should stay the hell away, I'll go with you."

"He's not family," September said succinctly.

"Tell that to the courts."

Wes pressed a button on the wall that allowed the hydraulic doors to slowly swing inward. No one stopped them, and they walked into a large rectangular room lined with a row of curtained cubicles, only one of which was being used—Stefan's, apparently. A nurses' hub occupied an adjacent wall and there were double doors that led to other hallways on the wall opposite the cubicles.

September walked to the curtained off area and said, "Stefan? You there?"

The curtain was pulled back by a nurse who stood on the other side. Beyond her, still in the bed, his hands folded over his chest and a look of angry determination on his face, lay her stepbrother. When he spied September color swept up his neck and suffused his face.

"What happened?" she asked him as the nurse replaced the curtain now that they were inside, collected a few items from the tray next to Stefan, then left them.

"Did Mom call you?" he demanded.

She shook her head. "I haven't talked to Verna."

"She was supposed to bring me my clothes." Anger flashed in his eyes.

Stefan Harmak had been a gangly teenager, and it had followed him into adulthood. His hands always looked too big for his arms. When his mother, Verna, had been married to September's father, Braden Rafferty, she'd placed a large picture of her son over the mantel in the living room of the sprawling Rafferty home—dubbed Castle Rafferty by Jake a name she'd adopted as well. But Stefan then, as now, had never been what you'd call portrait worthy. He wasn't actually all that bad looking really, but his attitude, which permeated everything about him, was petulant and secretive, and it came in flashes of meanness.

Stefan's portrait had been removed upon Braden's marriage to his third and current wife, Rosamund, who'd replaced it with one of herself when she was in her early stages of pregnancy. Rosamund's baby girl was due in January. While Rosamund insisted the child's name would be Gilda, all of the other Rafferty children were named after the month in which they were born, so September and her brothers, March and Auggie, and her sister, July, expected she would be named January, no matter what Rosamund wanted.

"Someone tied you to a basketball pole at Twin Oaks?" September asked Stefan when he subsided into silence. She felt rather than saw Wes come up beside her.

Stefan's beard stubble was just coming through. He was younger than September by two years but he seemed even younger now. He'd always been socially inept, kind of sneaky and hovering, and she'd stayed away from him as much as possible.

"Bastard drugged me so I couldn't fight him and stole my wallet and phone. Left me there damn near naked," he bit out, his face a dark glower.

"He drugged you in order to take your wallet and phone?"

His gaze flew to hers defiantly, apparently taking objection to her careful tone. "That's what I said. He drugged me and then robbed me."

"After he used a stun gun on you." September, too, could see the small marks. Several of them. Wes was right. Whoever had zapped Stefan had done it more than once.

"Jesus." Stefan's face was dark red. "Yes! Used a fucking stun gun, drugged me, and tied me up!"

In the Ballonni case, the man had been drugged as well, but there had been no stun gun marks. And though Ballonni's clothes and wallet were nowhere to be found, it hadn't really felt like a robbery, especially because the body had been staged with a placard around his neck that read: I MUST PAY FOR WHAT I'VE DONE. This didn't feel quite like a robbery, either.

"This thief left a placard around your neck?" September asked.

Wes said, "Crime techs have it now."

"Fucker thought he was funny," Stefan muttered.

"So, it wasn't a prank. It was a robbery," September said.

"It was both. Clearly!" Stefan snapped.

"Did he make you write it out himself?" September asked.

The color that had turned his face red now seemed to leach right out of his face. "What did it say?" she prodded when he didn't answer.

"I WANT WHAT I CAN'T HAVE," Wes told her when Stefan's silence continued.

"It doesn't mean anything!" Stefan's nostrils flared. "God! It's all just so fucked up!"

"What were you doing when he attacked you?" September asked.

"What do you mean?" Stefan folded his arms over his chest and glowered down at them, refusing to meet her gaze.

"Was it at the school? It must have been fairly early this morning that the robber found you," September prompted.

"Yeah, it was."

"What were you doing there so early?" she asked.

"What the fuck, Nine." He glared at her. "I was . . . I like to get to work early, and I was going to jog around the track."

"And he Tased you while you were . . . jogging?" Wes asked.

"Well, I stopped for a moment."

"So, he came up to you on the track, Tased you, then dragged you to the pole and tied you up," September said.

"Yes."

"Did he say anything to you?" she pressed.

"No."

"Do you jog often?" she asked. "So that he might know your routine?"

"No. I don't. . . . Jesus. You people—"

"Stefan?" a high-pitched voice called from beyond the curtain.

Stefan cut himself off short. Wes looked at September, then pushed back the curtain. Standing just beyond, her face taut with concern, was Verna Rafferty, Stefan's mother and September's one-time stepmother. Her blond hair was swept into a French roll and she wore a brown pantsuit with a white shirt, the collar of which was unbuttoned as if it had been hastily donned. She carried a gray duffel bag in one hand and when she saw Stefan in the bed, she dropped the bag as if her fingers had given way.

"Oh, darling . . ." She moved in quickly, arms outstretched, brushing past September without really seeing her, and then stopped short before giving Stefan the bear hug September had expected. Her arms dropped to her sides and it looked like she might cry. "What happened?"

"The clothes," he said through his teeth.

"What happened to yours?" she asked, half turning to the abandoned duffel that Wes had picked up and was holding out to her.

"They were taken by the bastard who drugged me and tied me up and stole my wallet," Stefan answered.

"Oh, baby." Ignoring Wes, she threw her arms around her son, who accepted the embrace in silence, his body language screaming his discomfort at the display of affection. "I've got your things right here." Now she accepted the duffel from Wes and placed it on Stefan's chest. It was at that point she noticed September and her mouth began quivering.

Drawing herself up straight and looking down her nose in that haughty way that was pure Verna, she demanded, "What are you doing here?"

Chapter Two

"I was called to the case," September told her ex-stepmother tightly. She'd recently learned that Verna and Braden's affair had begun while her mother was still alive, and that Kathryn Rafferty had intercepted a note from Verna that had subsequently led to the auto accident that caused her death. Was Verna responsible? No. Not really. But had circumstances been different September might still have her mother. And the truth was she'd never liked Verna all that much anyway.

"Leave me alone. All of you," Stefan said, ignoring the tension between the two women. "I want to get dressed."

September and Wes acquiesced by stepping outside the curtain, but Verna got barked at by her son when she apparently thought she would stay. By the time she flung the curtain aside, her cheeks were flushed with repressed anger—which she immediately took out on September.

"Who did this to him?" she demanded. "What kind of a sick person would leave my son out nearly naked in this weather?"

"This weather" was midforties, and though it wasn't exactly red hot, Stefan wouldn't have died from the elements like Christopher Ballonni had. "We don't know yet," September told her.

"I thought you were a detective, or something. Going after real crime."

"This is a real crime, ma'am," Wes pointed out.

Verna shot him a scorching look, then eyed him from head to toe. There was something inherently sexy about Wes that must have registered, because Verna turned back to September a little more distracted than before but still rattling down her own path. "Don't try to tell me you came here to help Stefan. I know how all of you think. You've never accepted Stefan like you should."

This was the song Verna had sung from the moment she'd married Braden. And though there was some truth to it, it was more that Stefan was just someone none of them wanted to know. It wasn't because he wasn't a Rafferty. It was because he was odd and remote and sullen.

Briefly, September thought about bringing up the Christopher Ballonni case; the story had been all over the news when it occurred and Stefan's placard suggested the crimes were by the same doer, as the MO was the same. But, as Wes had pointed out, Stefan was "family" in the loosest sense of the word, and as soon as her lieutenant learned of her connection to him, September might be yanked off the case.

Until that happened, she wanted to garner as much information as possible.

And, really, she didn't feel like offering any information to Verna anyway.

Stefan stepped from behind the curtain, dressed in dark slacks and a white dress shirt. "God, Mom," he muttered. "Couldn't you have found me a T-shirt?"

Verna turned her attention on him, her rigidity melting a little. "I brought your work clothes."

"You think I'm going to work after this?" he demanded.

"I didn't think. . . . You look so nice dressed up."

September assessed Stefan's white pallor and the flat line

of his mouth and decided Verna must see something that clearly wasn't there.

"Jesus, Mom," he muttered, attempting to brush by September.

Verna said, "We'll just go home, then."

"Are the two of you living together?" September asked. The last she'd heard Stefan had his own apartment.

He turned bitter eyes on her. "Just for a while."

"Stefan's going back to school," Verna volunteered stiffly.

"You work at Twin Oaks as a teaching assistant," September said.

"You know I do," he retorted.

Verna added quickly, "He wants to be a teacher. He's good with children, aren't you, Stefan?"

Stefan just gazed at his mother with burning eyes.

"You were on your way to work early, and then this robber came upon you while you were jogging," September pressed on.

"That's what I said."

"Jogging?" Verna stared hard at her son.

"Yeah, jogging, Mom. I know you don't think I do anything right, but I'm working on my body."

Verna frowned, opened her mouth, then clamped it shut again without speaking.

"I'd . . . walked to the school. We don't live that far. And he jumped me. Held a gun on me and made me drink that vile drink."

"A stun gun," September corrected him. Stefan looked as if he was going to deny it, then must have seen something in her expression that changed his mind, because he subsided into silence. "We can see the burn marks," she told him.

"Okay, fine. He zapped me. Hurt like *hell!*"

"While you were on the track, he ordered you to drink the drug and when you refused, he hit you with the stun gun, several times," she added, just in case he felt like lying some more. "Then he robbed you."

"Do I have to talk to you?" Stefan demanded. "I don't think so. You want to make a federal case out of it, go ahead. I drank the stuff because he was going to keep on zapping me, and the next thing I knew I was tied to the pole and it was damn cold!"

"I'm just trying to get the sequence of events straight," September explained.

"Well, now you know."

"You were going to say something?" September turned to Verna.

"I just don't see why you have to interrogate Stefan. He's the victim here," she reminded her.

Wes's gaze was on Stefan. "What did he look like?"

"He was, umm, wiry. Wore a baseball cap. Jeans and a jacket."

"Was he black, white?" Wes asked.

Stefan looked into Wes's dark eyes and then he glanced away, as if he were thinking hard. "White . . ."

"You don't sound too sure," Wes pointed out.

"It was dark. I couldn't really see. But shh . . . No, I'm certain he was white." He jerked away from them as if he couldn't stand in such close proximity to the police.

"Did you notice anything unusual about this guy? Some identifying mark?" Wes asked.

"No."

"Did he come from the parking lot?" Wes asked.

"No. I don't think so."

"Were there any cars in the lot?" September put in.

"I don't know! How many times do I have to say it? *I don't know.*"

"Was he carrying the drink in a cup, or a glass, or what?" Wes asked, ignoring the outburst.

"I don't think you should be harassing him like this," Verna said tightly.

"It was like a small thermos," Stefan said. "He just said, 'Drink it,' and he was the one with the weapon, so I did."

That's about the first thing he's said that really rang true, September thought.

"Are we done now?" Stefan demanded when both September and Wes went silent.

"Almost," she said. "It's just unusual, the way this went down. Most robberies at gunpoint are simply that: the doer points a gun at you and says something like, 'Give me all your money,' and faced with serious injury or death, most people comply. Using a stun gun on you, then forcing you to drink something and write out this message—all of that takes a lot of extra time and says something else about the crime."

"Maybe he's just screwed up and likes to drug people," Stefan muttered, his jaw working.

"Or, maybe he wanted you unconscious for some reason. To make sure you were found after school started?" September posed, figuring Christopher Ballonni must have suffered a similar fate at the hands of whoever had tied him to the flagpole. A complete autopsy had been performed and there were traces of Rohypnol in the man's system. She'd bet Stefan Harmak had been drugged with roofies, too.

"He just wanted to keep me down," Stefan said. "He didn't want me overpowering him, so he took care of that first."

"It looks like he wanted to humiliate you," September suggested.

September might have bought Stefan's theory more if her stepbrother was the kind of man who could physically scare someone, but he just didn't come off that way. He undoubtedly had some strength, but there was something so Jack Sprat about him that she doubted any adult male armed with a stun gun would consider him such a threat as to drug him.

There was definitely something else at play, and she also

suspected Stefan was deliberately keeping whatever it was from her. Maybe he was embarrassed, or maybe he was just being his usual asshole self, but he knew something.

She wanted to get a good look at the placard that had hung around Stefan's neck when the crime techs were through with it. Since Ballonni's placard read I MUST PAY FOR WHAT I'VE DONE, initially she and Gretchen had believed Ballonni must have been involved in a crime. They hadn't discovered anything in the man's past, however; Ballonni was a man who'd apparently been loved by his family and friends. The idea of suicide had been bandied about—an assisted suicide, given the zip-ties—but no one could believe Ballonni had been suicidal. He had a good job, a loving wife, a teenaged son who went hunting and fishing with him, a nice house with a low mortgage, credit card debt that was under control, and a social group with some good buddies.

September realized she knew next to nothing about her stepbrother's social life. "This attack seems personal."

"Bastard singled me out," Stefan muttered.

"He waited for you." She thought that over. "I'd like to talk to someone you work with."

"No!" Stefan practically gasped. "They can't know. It's too embarrassing."

"It's going to hit the news," September pointed out.

"Oh, *God.*" Stefan raked his fingers through his hair and Verna looked stricken.

"Who do you hang out with at the school? Maybe I can start with them," September suggested.

"Nobody. They're all married, old women." Stefan glared at her as if it were her fault. "It's just a job."

"I'll give Amy Lazenby a call," September said. She'd met the principal of Twin Oaks earlier in the fall.

"You know her?" Stefan burst out, as if he couldn't bear the thought. "Don't talk to her. She's a bitch."

September pointed out, "She's going to hear about this, so I can give her a heads-up before it hits the news."

"The news . . ." Stefan closed his eyes.

"It happened on school grounds," September said patiently. Stefan acted like the whole incident could just be swept under the rug, but that wasn't how these things worked.

Wes asked him, "Who should we talk to?"

"I don't know. No one." His chin dropped to his chest as if he were collapsing.

"Aren't you people the ones who figure that out?" Verna demanded, looking Wes over.

There wasn't much more they were going to get out of him now, September determined, so she said, "All right, Stefan. I'll give you a call later."

She and Wes left the hospital together and as they walked to the parking lot outside Emergency, she asked him, "So, how do you like my stepfamily?"

"Love 'em. Lucky you."

September smiled faintly. "You haven't met Rosamund yet."

"Do I want to know Rosamund?" Wes asked.

"Doubtful. She took Verna's place as my current stepmother. She's younger than I am, and she's pregnant, due in January. You know the whole deal with my family and the names."

"You're all months."

"My father's idea," September said. "My oldest brother's March, then my sister, July, then May, then Auggie and me. We do have a half brother who escaped the craziness, and although Rosamund thinks she's going to name her little girl Gilda, we're all betting on January."

"I thought my family had its issues," he observed, "but you Raffertys beat us all to hell."

"We beat everybody," September said on a sigh as she reached her silver Honda Pilot. "You know the fire at my father's house—the one that was done with gasoline and a match?"

"Have you got a suspect?" he asked with sudden interest.

"No, no. Not really. My father and half brother saw someone running away but they couldn't see who it was. My sister July wants to believe it was Stefan."

Wes had been peeling off toward his Range Rover, but now he stopped short. "Why?"

"Why does she think that? Because she doesn't like him. Or, why would he do it?"

"Why would he do it?"

September shook her head. "Why did someone make him write I WANT WHAT I CAN'T HAVE under the threat of being Tased by a stun gun, drug him, and tie him half naked to a pole outside the school where he worked?"

Wes shook his head slowly, then mused, "What does he want that he can't have?"

"What did Christopher Ballonni, professed all around great guy, do that someone made him write I MUST PAY FOR WHAT I'VE DONE?"

"I was waiting for you to tell Harmak about Ballonni," Wes said.

"Not until I talk to D'Annibal. There's a connection. Stefan's story parallels Ballonni's too closely, but I didn't feel like letting that out yet."

"It'll be on the news. There are leaks everywhere, and the Ballonni story was big."

"I'm going to talk to D'Annibal today," September assured him.

Wes nodded and headed toward his car while September climbed carefully into her SUV. She didn't relish talking to her lieutenant; she knew he would probably take her off the case and she was trying to come up with some excuse to stay on it.

Her cell phone rang and she pulled it out of her messenger

bag and read the caller ID. Sandler, her partner. Ex-partner, actually, until she was reinstated.

Smiling, September answered with, "How's that forced vacation going?"

"Like shit." Gretchen had never been known for holding back her thoughts. "Where are you?"

"Started back this morning and there's already been an interesting development in the Ballonni case."

"What?"

"Am I supposed to talk to you?"

Gretchen swore under her breath for nearly half a minute, and September grinned. It was so easy to rile her up.

"Meet me at Bean There, Done That, and you'd better be ready to talk," she growled.

"I can only stay a minute," September said, putting the vehicle into gear.

Bean There, Done That wasn't the closest coffee shop to the station, but it was the one used most often by September and her partner. It took her a while to find a parking spot and by the time she pushed through the door she found that Gretchen had snagged one of the prime booths.

"I had to jump on this or lose it," she said, "so you'll have to stand in line for a drink."

"No problem."

September walked to the back of the order line, standing behind a man in a business suit with a hurried manner, and a girl tuned into her smartphone so deeply that September practically had to push her forward when it was her turn.

She ordered a skinny latte and then waited to one side along with the other milling customers for it to be prepared. She glanced over at Gretchen, who was also studying her phone. September had been paired with the brash detective when she'd first joined the department and had been leery of Gretchen's reputation as a bitch on wheels. There was a reason she'd gotten that label, but September had learned early on that Gretchen knew her stuff.

Her name was called and she picked up her latte and slid across the booth from her partner. Gretchen had dark, curly hair and dark skin, a gift from her Brazilian mother, and slanted blue eyes, a gift from her father, who was, according to Gretchen, "as white bread as they come."

"So, what's with the Ballonni case?" Gretchen wanted to know.

"D'Annibal wouldn't like it if I talked about a case with you," September pointed out.

"You're going to anyway, so stop with the 'oh, I don't know if I should' shit. I'm only on administrative leave because I killed the fucker who was stabbing you."

"Eloquently put," September said. "And thank you."

"You're welcome. So, tell me," she urged her.

September relented, never really intending to keep anything from Gretchen anyway. They'd been on the Ballonni case together and were likely to be on it again as soon as Gretchen was cleared for duty. She told her about finding Stefan at Twin Oaks Elementary without mentioning his relationship to her at first, but she finished with, ". . . and here's the weird part—the victim, Stefan Harmak, is my ex-stepbrother."

"What?"

"His mother was my father's second wife."

"He's your *stepbrother?*"

"Was," September stressed.

"Is every case about you? Jesus, Nine." She frowned at her. "What the hell kind of thing is this?"

"I don't know."

"Who is this vigilante?" Gretchen said, gazing past September to the middle distance. "Making them write those signs? Who would do that? But your stepbrother survived."

"Maybe the guy didn't really mean to kill Ballonni. Gotta be the same guy, though, don't you think?"

"What did he look like?"

September related Stefan's description, finishing with, ". . . not much to go on. Stefan just wants to sweep it all under the rug."

"God, I gotta get back to the job," Gretchen chafed. "How long does it take?"

"It's pretty cut and dried. You killed him before he could kill me. It's not like there's any question about it."

She nodded. September wasn't telling her anything she didn't already know. "So, how's your love life?" she asked next.

"I told Jake I'd move in with him."

She picked up on September's careful tone. "Big step. How long have you known Westerly?"

"Years. You know."

"But, I mean, really known him. Like a month?"

"What about you and that bartender?" September shot back.

She made a face. "I didn't move in with him."

September glanced at the time on her cell phone. "D'Annibal's probably heard I'm semirelated to Stefan and wants me off the case."

"The Ballonni case is ours," Gretchen reminded her.

"Yeah, well, I've got to convince the lieutenant of that."

"God, I wish I was back."

"Me, too," September said, surprised that she felt so strongly about it. She liked working with Wes, but she missed Gretchen's abrasiveness. It was like being thrown into ice water and sometimes that's what it felt like she needed to sharpen her senses.

"When you talk to D'Annibal," Gretchen said as they were leaving, "tell him to get his head out of his ass and let you stay on the case."

"Yeah, I'll do that. Then we'll both be out of the department."

"So, what are you gonna do?"

"Pull up the Ballonni file and go over it again."

"I called the wife twice, but she wasn't interested in reviewing the case. She didn't like Chubb much," Gretchen said.

September nodded. And she hadn't liked Gretchen much, she would bet. Her partner's bullish style definitely took some getting used to. "But now there's been another attack. I'll meet with her, if D'Annibal lets me stay on the case."

"Keep me informed."

"I'll try," September said.

Chapter Three

Lieutenant Aubrey D'Annibal signaled for September to come inside his office, a cubicle of glass tucked into one corner of the squad room, almost the moment she returned from her locker. She'd intended to check the Ballonni file, but now that was going to have to wait.

"Close the door," he said as she stepped inside, and she did as he requested, then took a seat across his desk from him.

D'Annibal was lean, gray-haired, and his suits were sharp and neatly pressed. Everything about him was neat, in fact, and he'd intimidated September her first few months on the job before she learned that, though he strictly stuck to protocol, he was fair and listened more than a lot of men in his position did.

Now he gazed at her directly and asked, "How are you doing?"

"Fine."

"You could have taken more time off."

"I know."

"You're moving a little slowly. Maybe you should be part-time, like Pelligree, until you're at full speed."

"I'm okay. Really. I'll dial it back if it gets too hard."

He thought about that, then nodded. "All right. We're shorthanded around here and with the hiring freeze . . ."

She wanted to ask him when her brother would be back full-time from his gig with the Portland PD, but decided to keep her thoughts to herself. Auggie liked working undercover more than straight detective work, no matter what he might say differently. There was an even chance that he would be moving into a position with the larger police force full-time, and she didn't feel like facing that yet.

"What about this stun gun/robbery/kidnapping this morning?" the lieutenant asked her. He'd been standing, but now he seated himself across from her.

"The victim, Stefan Harmak, is my ex-stepbrother," she said. "I didn't know it until I was on scene, but I probably would have gone anyway. The MO is almost identical to the Christopher Ballonni case: victim drugged, tied up, left with a placard in his own hand. Ballonni's was I MUST PAY FOR WHAT I'VE DONE, and Harmak's is I WANT WHAT I CAN'T HAVE. We've never known for certain if it was a homicide, or possibly an assisted suicide, but Harmak says that the doer forced him to write the message, so I'd say Ballonni's death is a homicide."

D'Annibal steepled his fingers and said, "I agree. He died of exposure after being tied to a pole."

"Whoever did it let Stefan live."

"What does he have to say about it?"

September recounted her hospital conversation with Stefan and added what Wes had told her about the crime, too. "This man, this avenger, takes an awful lot of extra time just to make his point."

"Did you ask him if he knew why the doer wanted him to write on the placard?"

"Not exactly. He was reluctant to talk to me."

The lieutenant drew in a breath and let it out slowly. "I know you and Sandler were working the Ballonni case, but now that it involves your stepbrother, I think I'm going to hand it over to Pelligree or Thompkins."

"Let me stay on the Ballonni case, sir. I've been working on it since I got here. If Wes works the Harmak angle, I can stay off that part of it, but I don't want to stop on Ballonni, especially now that there's some traction on the case."

"But you have a personal connection to it now."

"Stefan Harmak's my ex-stepbrother," September said firmly. "He's really not a part of my family any longer."

"I saw how you walked in here. Like everything hurts. I'm only agreeing to have you stay because we're so short staffed."

"I'm just a little sore. I can spend most of my time at my desk making phone calls. I want to re-interview Mrs. Ballonni. See if anything's different since Gretchen called her last summer."

D'Annibal looked past her and through the glass surrounding his office. September turned to see what he was looking at. What was visible were the empty desks lining the squad room with George in the corner, tapping his computer keyboard, and Wes on the other side of the room, leaning back in his chair, deep into a phone conversation.

"Okay," he capitulated. "You can work the Ballonni angle, but stay out of the Harmak case. And send Pelligree in here next."

September was already to the door. When she crossed the squad room toward Wes, he looked up at her, still on the phone. She signaled for him to go in and see the lieutenant, and he nodded his understanding. Then she went to the file drawers that held current cases, searched through until she found the murder book on Christopher Ballonni, then returned to her desk.

A call came in and she glanced up to see who was answering. George was reaching for the phone and she was glad to let him be the point man. She wanted to review the Ballonni file while her meeting with Stefan was fresh in her mind.

George answered, listened briefly, and then said, "Rafferty, it's yours."

September glanced up from the file, then picked up her desk phone. "Detective Rafferty," she answered.

"Just checking in on you," Jake drawled. "How're you doing?"

September straightened as if caught in a nefarious act. "Fine. Why didn't you call my cell?"

"I did. Half a dozen times. Decided to come home from lunch and called you again and that's when I heard it singing away. It's here on the kitchen counter."

September swore silently. Despite what she'd told D'Annibal, she wasn't herself. She hadn't even thought about her cell phone once since she'd come to work, though normally she brought it with her to her desk.

"I'll come back and pick it up. Time to grab some lunch anyway."

"I'll pick us up some sandwiches at Wanda's. What do you want?"

"I don't know. Surprise me."

"How about a Reuben?"

"How about a turkey club?"

"See. I know better than to surprise you," he said.

She found herself grinning, amazed how glad she was to hear his voice. She'd just seen him this morning and yes, she'd been having a helluva time being his patient, but now that she was back at work she was missing him more than she would have believed. She shouldn't be this dependent on him, this fast. It didn't bode well for the future.

"I'll be there in twenty," she told him.

By the time September was pulling up to the rambler that was Jake's house, after battling some unexpected road construction, she'd actually chewed into thirty minutes of her lunch hour. Not that the department was a stickler for a punch card on its detectives, but it had been less than a year since September had been promoted to detective and taken a job with the Laurelton PD and she didn't feel comfortable abusing the unwritten rules too much. She'd already used up her weekly allowance by meeting with Gretchen and that didn't even count the information she'd revealed that she probably shouldn't have.

Jake opened the door, completely naked. He had her cell phone to his ear and was carrying on a bogus conversation. ". . . yes, she's here now. No, sorry, she's going to be busy for a while." A pause. "She's looking for the Johnson file," he said as September cried, "Jake!" and reached forward, ripping the phone from his hand, just to make sure he really wasn't talking to someone.

He was laughing as she said dryly, "I think I see the Johnson file." She checked the phone, then clicked off, relieved he was just joking around.

"Really? Where?" he asked innocently.

She pushed him through the door, shutting it behind them. "Good thing we don't have close neighbors."

"You're late. You gave me time to get the sandwiches and think up something fun for us to do."

"Uh-huh. And me being an invalid."

"Okay, we can just have lunch." He was grinning like a fool and she let her gaze slide over his muscled chest and lean torso.

"How fast are you?"

He'd been turning toward the kitchen, but now he glanced back, giving her a penetrating look. "Fast," he said.

"I only have about ten minutes and I'll have to take the sandwich to go."

"You sure?"

She tested her shoulder, feeling the pain but sick of being a slave to it. "Yessirree."

"Giddyup," he said, and with that he hurried her along to the bedroom as fast as he could, helped her out of her clothes, and then made good on his boast about speed.

"What are you smiling at?" Wes drawled as he stared across the squad room at September. He was leaning back in his chair, a grin playing on his lips also.

"What?" she asked.

"I don't think it's something in that file."

September glanced down at the pages of the Ballonni file, knowing she hadn't retained a word of what she'd just read. Her mind was full of images of Jake's body in rhythmic motion with hers. She could feel his body shake with silent laughter as she whispered, "Ride 'em, cowboy," before the mood changed and the only sounds were the rustle of the sheets and her own soft moans and his deeper growls of pleasure.

She slapped the cover shut and said, "The Johnson file."

It was Wes's turn to ask, "What?"

"Nothing."

She and Jake had only had a few minutes of actual talking time and even that was rushed. But he had managed to tell her that Colin and Neela were on the "baby train," and she'd looked at Jake and wondered what he thought about that. Their own relationship was so new that they were a long way even from marriage; babies were another world.

Not that she believed love, marriage, and babies had to come in that order. A case in point, her sister July, who'd recently let September know that she'd gone to a clinic, picked out her baby daddy's sperm, and now was pregnant. No one else in the family knew yet, so September hadn't told Jake, either. That news would all be self-evident soon anyway.

She'd left Jake at his house with a promise to come home

early, take care of her stiff and tender shoulder, and rest. He wasn't planning to return to the office as he was going to spend the afternoon shifting furniture around in preparation for her belongings.

Were they moving too fast? Yes . . . maybe . . . no . . . probably. But she also knew that she was sick of living alone and wanted to give it a try. If their relationship failed, which she sincerely prayed it would not, then she could always move out again. Still, she could feel that she was dragging her feet. She wanted to live with Jake. She really, really did. But she was suffering from a bad case of ennui. Was it because of her injury that she felt so tired and energy-less? Or, was this some kind of enervating dread that had infected her? Either way, whenever Jake talked about the upcoming move she wanted to lie down and put her arm over her eyes, classic ostrich behavior.

Now, she shook herself back to reality. She'd placed a call to the number she had for the Ballonni household and had reached their voice mail and Mrs. Ballonni's voice: *You've reached Janet and Chris; leave a message after the beep.* At first she'd thought Chris was Janet Ballonni's husband and she'd never changed the message on her voice mail or she'd simply wanted to keep her husband alive in this way. But then she'd glanced at the file and realized the Ballonni's son was named Christopher Jr. and figured the two names on the message were meant for Janet and her son.

She left her name and the department's number, just in case Mrs. Ballonni would need to verify her identity, then added her cell-phone number as an afterthought. George was on the phone at the same time September was and as she hung up, he suddenly slammed down his phone on an incoming call and barked out, "Woman's body discovered at Foxglove Park. Who wants to go?"

"I will," Wes said.

"I'll go with you," September said.

"We'll take the Rover," Wes said, getting up from his chair.

September had already eased herself to her feet. She could feel new and interesting tweaks and jabs inside that had nothing to do with the still healing knife wound. "Giddyup," she said under her breath, smiling some more.

As they headed out Gayle looked at them as they passed by her desk. Once outside, September said, "You've been messing with her."

"I just believe in Guy's attention to protocol."

"Bullshit."

Wes grinned, his teeth a slash of white. "All right, I'll leave the temp alone. Don't want to wish Urlacher back too soon." He hit the remote on his black Range Rover.

"Foxglove," Wes mused as they drove away from the station. "That's some kind of poison, isn't it?"

"Maybe you're thinking of hemlock."

"Nuh-uh."

As they drove to the park, which was about two miles west of the department on the outskirts of Laurelton and nearly to Winslow County, September's cell phone rang. Caller ID showed her father, Braden Rafferty's, cell number. He'd been calling her almost daily since she'd been stabbed, and she found it more annoying than helpful. They'd never been close and that gap had widened after her mother's death and then his subsequent marriages to first Verna, then Rosamund. When she and her twin had opted to become cops, he'd basically disowned them and his relationship with Auggie was still very tenuous. Recently, there had been baby steps toward a reconciliation but it was still a long ways off.

She debated on not answering, but it would only put off the inevitable. "Hey, there," she answered.

"Hi, September. I just wanted to check in and see how you're feeling."

"Better every day. I'm back at work."

"Already?"

"Yes." She heard how testy she sounded and changed the subject. "How are the renovations going?"

"Coming along. Rosamund's working with a decorator."

He sounded cautious, and September could well imagine why. The recent fire at the sprawling Bavarian-style house that was their family home, was the other reason her father kept phoning her. It had started in the garage and ruined Rosamund's lime green kitchen, which no one was mourning, least of all Braden, apparently.

"That's good," September told him. "Progress."

"Anything on the guy who did this?"

"Not so far."

Though her father and Dashiell, her half brother, had seen a shadowy figure running away, there had been no clues to whoever had set the fire, and therefore there was no knowing what the motivation was. Braden had made a fortune over the years in various financial deals and had earned himself enemies by the truckload, but was that behind who had started the fire? Someone who wanted payback? Or, was it the work of vandals? One of the ever-evolving group of disenchanted teenagers who seemed to bump from tire slashing to petty theft to vandalizing—and now maybe to arson?

Though, like her sister, July, September felt Stefan Harmak might be capable of anything, there was nothing to link him to the crime other than rampant speculation. He certainly could hold a grudge against Rosamund for usurping his and his mother's place at the house, but for all his character flaws, Stefan was more a griper than a doer, as far as September could see.

"If I learn anything you'll be the first to know, I promise," September told her father, who grunted an assent, then asked her a few questions about Auggie. September parried her father's probing remarks. Auggie was hard to get hold of at the best of times and damn near impossible for Braden as he actively tried to dodge his father. Finally, realizing he wasn't going to get anything further from her, Braden said good-bye and September clicked off with a sigh of relief.

"More family," Wes said.

"More family," September agreed.

Foxglove Park wasn't that far from the field where the body of another young woman had been discovered the summer before, September realized as they drove past. The Do Unto Others Killer had left the body of Emmy Decatur in a field about a half a mile west. September recalled meeting with the press—the scoop-monger, television reporter, Pauline Kirby—and going on camera at the site to try and keep the public calm and informed about the depraved serial killer whose MO included carving words into his victims' torsos, strangling them, and leaving their bodies in open fields. Looking out the passenger side window toward the field now, she thought about the man whose obsession with her had been a trigger to those killings, whose knife had been driven into her shoulder, a slice meant for her throat. She was lucky to be alive.

"Someone walk on your grave?" Wes said as she involuntarily shivered.

"Do you sometimes think about the guy who shot you?"

He thought about her question, but then slowly wagged his head from side to side. "Bullet caught my hip bone. Doctors took it out but had to scrape the bone to do it. When I move too fast, it jabs me, but the bastard who did it's in jail. That's what I think about." Wes turned onto a smaller road. "Here we are."

Although it was designated a park, Foxglove was actually a wetlands, an area designated by the city as a refuge for wildlife, a place adopted by some concerned citizens and glorified with its own name but little else to define it as a park. There were no paths or benches or water fountains. It was a shallow depression with cattails and dank maple leaves floating in shallow pools of water invaded by an overall scent of rot. The kind of place environmentalists love and germaphobes abhor.

There were already several cars parked alongside the road. Some lookie-loos and what appeared to be the bicyclist who'd apparently found the body, the uniform standing next to him. As Wes pulled to a stop they looked back to see the crime scene van heading toward them down the two-lane rural road, and behind it, the coroner.

The uniform introduced himself as Hadley and then said, "This is Mr. Morland," indicating the cyclist.

"I come by here every day," Morland said as soon as September and Wes introduced themselves. "Every day. Sometimes I walk into the park, if it's dry out. Thought it might be dry enough today and so . . ." He shook his head.

September looked past him to a spot where a flash of white showed on the soggy ground beneath a thin copse of maple trees. Skin.

"She's just lying there, peaceful-like," Morland went on. "Not a scratch on her, far as I could tell, but I didn't want to touch her. Well, except for checking her pulse, like. She musta taken something. Pills or something."

The tech team came through so September and Wes stepped back. They asked Morland some more questions, but the cyclist kept repeating the same information. Officer Hadley didn't know anything further, either, and the lookie-loos pressed forward, eager to talk, but they'd come after the fact and were no help.

September heard the light beep signaling a text coming into her cell phone and looked down at the screen. It was a message from Jake.

How about I pick up some soup at Zupan's and then we watch some bad TV and go to bed early?

Zupan's was a local specialty grocery store chain that also served five or six daily soup choices. She texted back: **Yes, please.** In truth, she was beginning to feel the effects of her first day back—no thanks to Jake, too—and the thought of collapsing into bed was enough to make her sigh.

One of the techs, Bronson, who was as prickly as a briar and loved to complain, made his way out to them as the rest of the team packed up their gear.

"So, have we got a homicide?" Wes asked him before he could open his mouth, which caused a line of irritation to form between the tech's brows.

"Could be suicide. Looks like she ingested something. Have to figure out what she poisoned herself with before we know."

"Foxglove?" Wes asked.

Bronson's frown deepened. "What makes you say that?"

"Oh, I don't know," Wes deadpanned.

"Could be," was Bronson's surprising answer as he headed to the van.

Wes turned to September, the look on his face causing her to break into a smile. "You don't think . . ." he started.

"That someone poisoned her with foxglove and then brought her to Foxglove Park? No."

"Bronson was fucking with me."

"That's what he does."

Wes stared down the tech as Bronson climbed into his van. "Maybe Foxglove Park's named for a reason, like it's full of foxglove. And maybe she ate some, thinking it was something else. Like eating the wrong kind of mushrooms."

"Seriously?"

"She probably overdosed on prescription drugs."

"And decided to die in parklike surroundings," September finished.

They both looked back at the chilly, damp, leaf-choked swamp and Wes snorted.

"Or, maybe it's a homicide," September said.

They watched as the woman's body was lifted onto a stretcher, carried from her bed of leaves and into the coroner's van.

First Stefan, and now this Jane Doe. It had been a full day already, September thought as Wes drove her back to the station. Even though there were a few more hours before her shift would be up, she checked with D'Annibal to make certain he was okay with her leaving early, and when he waved her away, she gathered her things and headed out to her silver Pilot. A lot of avenues to explore when she got to work tomorrow.

She moved her shoulder up and down as she drove up Jake's drive, assessing the amount of pain the movement caused. Not too bad. Sorta bad. Standable, anyway. But she didn't think it would take that long before she was back to her old self. It was the being tired, a natural part of the healing process, apparently, that surprised her. She looked forward to a bath and the soup Jake had promised, and an early night.

As she got out of the car, her thoughts turned to Stefan. He was probably a little stiff and sore himself, but at least he was alive.

Who had done that to him? Zip-tied him to a pole, just like Christopher Ballonni? Who was this kidnapper—or, this killer, in Ballonni's case—who'd gone to such lengths to make a point?

"I WANT WHAT I CAN'T HAVE," she said aloud. As she mounted the steps to Jake's front door she tried to picture the avenger who'd made Stefan write the sign, draped it around his neck, then had left him in front of his place of work for maximum humiliation.

Chapter Four

Leaves skittered beneath the tires of Mr. Blue's truck and blew into the deep ditches on either side of Highway 26. The tires spun at an even fifty miles per hour—well, as even as she could make it given the truck was a bucket of bolts with a small dent in the driver's side door and a rusted area along the top of the back tailgate. It had once been white beneath the layers of road grime, but now it was closer to dirty gray.

But she was lucky to have its use.

Lucky. Like her name.

She hit a pothole and bounced upward, slowing down to forty-five. She was anxious to get back. Anxious to put distance between herself and the scene of the crime. It had taken her most of the day to work her way from Twin Oaks to the mall where she'd left the truck, mainly because she'd been careful not to be seen by anyone and had spent more time whiling the hours away than actually walking or catching the west-side train during rush hour, when she'd be least remembered. Lying low was her best defense as she knew the police would be asking about anyone seen in the general vicinity of where Stefan Harmak had been left. She'd taken him to the school in the dead of night and then had driven his van to a residential area with a lot of cars parked along the streets, easing the van into a spot. It might not be found for days, if all went well. She turned off the overhead light before locking the van and slipping into the dark, moving like a wraith through the silent streets to a deserted commercial office building that she'd scoped out days earlier at the far end of the residential district. There, she went around the back side, dropped her backpack on the ground beside her, and simply slid down the wall and sat, her back against the side of the building until just before rush hour. Then, she hoisted the backpack over one arm and walked toward a street that was lined with fast food restaurants, a Red Roof Inn, and a couple of gas stations. She dropped the keys into a trash can filled with leftover food and cardboard boxes from a Burger King, then switched out her baseball cap for a straight, black, chin-length wig with bangs. Next she stuck several pieces of gum in her mouth, enough to keep her chewing like a cow, partly because she wanted to be remembered for the chewing, if anyone saw her, and less for her appearance, partly because she was hungry. And then she headed toward the main intersection. *Thank you, Christopher Ballonni*, she'd thought, remembering the mailman with the penchant for gum. Part of his shtick, but it worked for her in other ways.

At the intersection, she'd hit the WALK button. Across the highway was a Park and Ride for the bus and she could see commuters unlocking their cars, coming from the bus stop. She'd figured if the police got that far, the commuters would only remember the wig and the gum. She'd climbed onto the bus and then let it take her all the way into Portland, where she'd gotten off and hit a busy Starbucks, lined with customers. In the restroom, she removed the black wig and brushed her natural light brown hair down straight, tossing the gum in the trash. She put on a pair of slim-lensed glasses with no prescription, then left the restroom holding Stefan Harmak's cell phone, which she pretended to be rapidly texting into as she walked out of the coffee shop. She had her own fake cell phone, one she'd appropriated earlier in the year from a loud, rude asshole who'd been in a huge shouting match over politics at a different Starbucks in a different city. She'd taken it because he'd pissed her off and everyone else in the place, too. Later, she found the phone was useful as a prop.

But Stefan's phone was hot, so she'd carefully wiped it down and as she walked into Portland, tossed it into another trash can, before heading to another bus stop and eventually winding her way back to the mall. If they traced the phone, it wouldn't be connected to her.

Now, she held Mr. Blue's truck onto the road and tried not to pay attention to the internal clock that was always ticking inside her head. Before the event that had nearly killed her, she hadn't really noticed the passage of time. She hadn't cared. But since her recovery, time had been like a partner in her mission. She sensed she was heading toward a final showdown and it was sooner than she might like.

Lucky wasn't her real name, but it was the one she went by these days. Her name was Ani, if anyone cared, and they didn't, except maybe for that detective she'd been attracted to—more attracted to than she wanted to remember—and he would only care because he would use it as a way to find her.

And then, her sister might care, too—maybe—but Lucky had to stay far, far away from her as well.

The last time she'd seen her was when she'd been lashed to the pyre, feeling the scorching flames burning nearer . . . and nearer. . . .

The memory scratched across her mind and the tight scars on her back felt even tighter. Easing her shoulders like she always did, she tried to loosen the skin but the damage was too deep. To this day, she felt an abiding fear of fire. She was lucky to be alive.

Lucky.

Mr. Blue only knew her by Lucky. She never said who she

really was and he didn't ask. She was his guest, his ward, his friend, but only for the time being. They both knew, or maybe just she did, that their time together was destined to be brief. As she knew her time in this world was destined to be brief. She sensed it like she sensed many other inexplicable things, and her ability was what had earned her Mr. Blue's protection.

That and the fact that he liked her. Like a daughter. And she, who'd been used by her "father" every way in creation, felt the same way about Mr. Blue being her surrogate father. They liked each other and that was more than either of them could say about anyone else on the planet.

She hadn't told Mr. Blue that she was a fugitive, that the long arm of the law was after her, had almost reached her a time or two. He didn't ask questions on things he didn't want to know about. The less information the better, in this case. Occasionally, he requested that she go and get things for him as he rarely left his ramshackle house near the natural hot springs on his private property.

That was Lucky's job, too. To shoo trespassers from the hot springs, which were believed to be a rejuvenating treatment, a natural spa. Once in a while some enterprising asshole and his girlfriend would hike onto Mr. Blue's property and avail themselves of the hot springs and Lucky would deal with them while Mr. Blue stayed in the shadows. Yes, she was a fugitive, but a number of years had passed and her face wasn't as well known as it had been. With that inner sense that rarely did her wrong, she knew that she wasn't at the top of the Winslow County sheriff's hit list any longer. Other law enforcement agencies weren't paying that much attention, either, especially with the murder rate and increase in property crimes, hate crimes, personal crimes, and every other kind of crime. She got her information from Mr. Blue, who, though a loner and hermit by all accounts, had a satellite dish and Wi-Fi stick that allowed him to access the Internet and

God knew what else. He was a study in contradictions. A guy who knew a hell of a lot about a hell of a lot. Lucky considered him the first true friend she'd ever really had.

Now she turned off 26 to the long, rutted access road that wound to Mr. Blue's house and the hot springs beyond. She bumped along, mentally crossing her fingers that the old truck would make it. To date, it hadn't failed her, but vehicle maintenance did not seem to be Blue's priority.

When she reached the house, she parked on one side where several rusting appliances had come to die. She had a room that jutted out the back of the house from the garage, which had been turned into a greenhouse/storage room of sorts for Mr. Blue's various herbs and plants and other items for sale of varying degrees of legality. There was a bathroom just inside the main house from the garage that was mostly for her use; Mr. Blue's rooms were at the opposite end of the three bedroom ranch. Sometimes Lucky didn't see the man for days because he kept himself burrowed in his rooms with his books and computer. Other times, they met in the middle and shared meals together and short conversations about what he needed her to do, or what she might need from him. Neither of them was much of a conversationalist and they appreciated that about each other.

She literally owed Mr. Blue her life as he'd effectively saved it after she'd been brought to his doorstep, burned, feverish, and exhausted. Those weeks of him spoon-feeding her herbs and broths and then applying salves to her back were a misty haze of pain and gratitude.

She wasn't sure what he would think of her mission to rid the world of abusers and pedophiles who crossed her path. He might applaud her, but he might also think her methods too dangerous and turn her out. Once or twice it had been on the tip of her tongue to tell him about her special ability to sense an abuser, how brushing up against them sent her a message so loud it was almost as if the guy had blurted out his guilt in a scream. But she wasn't certain he would believe her, and she had no explanation for her "sixth sense," the same sense that told her time was running out. The hourglass had been turned over and the sands were slipping through. The showdown was coming. She was either going to die soon or be arrested, and if it were a choice, she would take the former.

To that end her mission was everything to her. Before she was through she planned to take out as many perverted bastards as she could.

Which was why she was still mulling over her decision to let the sick fuck who'd tried to nab the girl at the mall live. The weather wasn't cold enough for him to die. She'd left him with an admission of his guilt hung around his neck, but that was only part of it. The humiliation. There would be lots of questions directed at him, too many for him to come up with answers for.

But she should have killed him. She should have. She'd done it before, and she was undoubtedly going to do it again before her mission was complete. So, why had she left Harmak alive?

The scent.

Climbing out of the truck, the memory made her nose twitch. It wasn't a true scent exactly. It was more a feeling. She'd had to drag Harmak's dead weight to the basketball pole outside the school and she'd been glad it was pitch black because it was hard work and took longer than she'd suspected. With Ballonni, she'd just pulled up to the flagpole, dumped him out and tied him up, but with Harmak she'd had to traverse the basketball court and some grounds before she got him where she wanted him.

It was then the scent distracted her. She'd been tired and breathing hard and hurrying back to Harmark's van when she'd become aware of it. A feeling of . . . well, there was no other word for it: *evil.* It almost had an odor, something of rot and sickness. She'd turned her nose toward it and realized it wasn't from Stefan, though he certainly gave off the same vibe. But this one was different. More fully developed? And it was coming from around the school. If she'd had more time, she would have searched it out right then and there, but she couldn't risk it. And then it had dissipated and she'd had to jump in the van and leave fast, before anyone was about or Harmak woke up.

Now, she unlocked the man-door to the garage and crossed to her room, registering the musky and dry and sometimes pungent scents of the herbs, plants, mushrooms, and various substances inside that comprised the mainstay of Mr. Blue's stash. The deadlier plants were elsewhere. Mr. Blue didn't want anyone knowing about them unless there was a particular deal to be made, and then it was at his choosing. He also traded in illegal drugs like Rohypnol—roofies—to the right person and since Rohypnol was sold legally in Mexico, he had his own connections that were outside the traffic of the vicious drug lords of that country. Mr. Blue had his own rules, and he was more of a connoisseur of rare and exotic botanicals than your ordinary dealer who only worked for money could ever hope to be. You had to have a damn good reason to come to Mr. Blue for help, and then he might, or might not, deign to offer you what you sought.

She could smell chicken and herbs and realized Mr. Blue was making soup in the kitchen, so she removed her hand from the locked knob to her room and instead opened the door to the interior of the house, stepping inside.

Mr. Blue, whose real name was Hiram Champs, was stirring a large pot on the stove. He looked over upon hearing her and said, "I've made us dinner."

She looked into his blue face and said, "I've got the sourdough loaf."

"Cut it up and put the butter on the table. It's already set."

Lucky put the sack she'd carried from the car onto the counter, grabbed the bread knife and started slicing. At the last moment, Lucky had remembered she'd told him she would get some groceries and she'd pulled into a Safeway on the edge of Laurelton before turning west and heading home.

She glanced over at Mr. Blue, whose hair was a light gray but whose skin was blue. For years he'd drunk a concoction of colloidal silver that he made for himself, believing in its medicinal properties. The silver had settled into his skin and turned him permanently blue. Though he pretended not to mind, he rarely went out in public, preferring not to be stared at. The color added to his overall mysticism and he had followers and minions who attended to all his needs, just wanting to be near him. But the only person he allowed to stay more than a few minutes at a time was Lucky.

They ate in near silence, seated across from each other at the dining room table, which was placed in front of a picture window that faced out the back and onto his herb garden. Beyond that was a forest of Douglas firs, maples, and pine. Lucky's room could be seen through the window to the south and the eaves were hung with bird feeders. Hummingbirds hovered, even on the coldest day, and when Lucky was outside they sometimes whirred past so fast it felt like a huge insect zooming near her ear.

"Did you finish what you set out to do on this trip?" Hiram asked, ladling up the last of the soup in his bowl.

Lucky hesitated. Normally, he didn't ask questions that he might not want to know the answer to. "I was just thinking I've left some loose ends."

"Are you winning the battle?"

Lucky froze, her spoon in midair. This was as close as he'd ever come to talking about her mission. Maybe he knew more than she suspected.

She set down the spoon. "There's no real battle. Well, there is. I just find people that need to be . . . neutralized . . . and then I neutralize them."

"The police used the term 'neutralize' when they killed the

gunman who opened fire at Clackamas Town Center." He looked at her over his own soup spoon as he ladled the broth into his mouth.

"I'm on the front lines of a war that will never really end," she said, stepping carefully. "I'm just trying to keep ahead of the enemy."

"Sounds like an arms race." He put his spoon down and picked up his knife, deliberately buttering a thick slice of bread.

"What?"

"You're at war, but your enemy is evolving."

"Do you know what I do?" she asked.

He stared past her and out the window. "There's a particular type of newt that lives in this area. The Pacific newt. I've seen them in the back." He pointed to the garden outside the window, a garden shaded by the thick stand of Douglas firs that surrounded the property and led back into acres and acres of woods owned by the forest service. "Their skin is poisonous—highly poisonous. So if you pick one up you need to wash your hands. If ingested, the poison will kill most animals. It's highly toxic."

Lucky waited. Sometimes Mr. Blue went on about things that seemed to have no rhyme or reason, yet inside was buried sage advice.

"Do you know what a garter snake is?" he asked.

"Just a harmless, everyday snake?"

He nodded. "It's not poisonous, apart from a venomous quality to its saliva that may help with digestion as it eats its prey live. The garter snake is a predator of the newt and has developed a resistance to the newt's poison. So, over time, as a natural defense mechanism, the poison in the newts increases, becoming the new normal, as they say, and then the garter snakes die off until they develop a stronger resistance and can once again eat the newts with impunity until the newts' poison becomes more toxic. It's an arms race. I believe the garter snakes are currently on top." His gaze returned to hers. "Are you?"

"I'm not really in an arms race," Lucky protested.

"You might be and just don't know it. Be careful."

There was something about this conversation—a long one for him—that seemed to be telling her something. Should she tell *him* something? A little bit about her plans? Was this what he was asking?

"I don't intend for them to win," she said, purposely keeping her meaning vague.

"You can't often predict the outcome of an arms race."

Her heart beat heavily, almost hurting. She was rarely so honest with anyone. "I don't think I have much time."

He returned his attention to his soup, but she thought she sensed a sadness in him. "Is it enough to get done what you need to do?"

She thought of the sensation, the almost odor, at the school. After she took care of Harmak, once and for all, she intended on tracking the source of that feeling. Maybe he would be her last. "I hope so."

"If you need anything, just ask."

"I will."

She helped clean up the remains of the meal, then headed to her room. She needed to take care of Stefan Harmak soon. She should have given him enough to kill him, but she'd pulled back. The thought of those schoolchildren finding his dead body had influenced her. Now, she was going to have to catch him somewhere else, and the problem was, she'd put him on alert. Maybe she *was* in an arms race.

She shook her head, angry at herself, and gazed at her reflection in the old fly-spotted mirror above the ancient bureau. Once she was through with Harmak, she would figure out who was responsible for the noxious aura left behind at Twin Oaks, an invisible vapor trail.

She tilted her chin up. Could she play the part of a teacher, or a teacher's aide?

"I would like to apply for a job," she said aloud, forcing

her normally grim face to lighten with an almost smile. "I hear Twin Oaks Elementary is a great school. . . ."

September lay next to Jake in bed, her head tucked onto his chest while they watched a lineup of sitcoms. Jake's arm rested lightly around her, and she felt content and languid. "Sorry I've been such a bad patient," she mumbled sleepily.

"Nah, you've been fine." He was distracted.

"I've been a royal pain. You don't have to spare my feelings." She smiled. "Today was fun, though."

"Mmm."

Realizing he wasn't paying attention, she glanced up at him, her gaze traveling down the firm line of his jaw. "I'll move in this weekend as long as I don't have to do any heavy lifting."

"You will?" His attention came back to her with a bang.

"I've been delaying, I realize. We haven't known each other all that long." When he opened his mouth to protest, she corrected herself, "We've known each other, but it hasn't been that long since you and I got like this." She lifted a hand, to encompass the fact that they were lying in bed together.

"I spent too much time with Loni."

"We both were living our lives."

"I know, but a lot of it was . . . a waste." He looked down at her. "I can move your stuff myself."

"I have a queen bed. And your brother's laid up and making babies. I wish I could promise Auggie's help, but his schedule's too unpredictable."

"Don't worry. I'll figure it out." She could hear the smile in his voice.

"You're a happy camper now?"

"Very happy."

"We're not kidding ourselves, are we?" she asked suddenly. "Making all these plans too soon?"

"Nah."

"Okay. Good."

There was silence between them for a few minutes, and then the news came on. Jake had the television on channel seven and Pauline Kirby, in all her feral glory, came up, her attractive but sharp features making September's skin crawl a bit as she remembered how the relentless reporter had drilled her with questions during their interview about Do Unto Others. "Can you—" she started, but Jake had already switched the channel.

"A little of her goes a long way," he said, and he settled on a station with its reporter outside a post office.

September recognized the flagpole that the male reporter was standing by. "Oh . . . they've already made the connection."

"What?" Jake asked, as September hadn't filled him in on the case in detail.

She didn't answer as the reporter launched first into an account of Christopher Ballonni's death, and then, how the recent crime at the basketball pole mirrored Ballonni's.

"They don't have Stefan's name yet," she realized.

"Ah . . ." Jake said, as she'd told him over dinner about her earlier trip to the hospital to see Stefan and his story about being tied to the basketball pole. "You didn't say what happened to Stefan was part of a pattern."

"I'm not on Stefan's case. But they're letting me follow up again on Ballonni. I've put a call in to his widow, but I haven't heard back yet."

Jake nodded. September couldn't tell whether or not he was bothered that she hadn't told him everything. "It's not the only case we have," she reminded him, recalling the woman's body found in Foxglove Park. Wes was following up on that one, hoping to learn her identity.

"No, it's fine. I was just thinking that if Pauline Kirby

realizes Harmak is your stepbrother, she'll be after another interview," Jake said.

"*Was* my stepbrother. She'll learn it eventually, but it's not the first thing that'll crop up."

"You hope."

"Yeah, I hope. So, enough about me. Tell me about your work. How's the office move going?"

"Uh . . . slow."

"Slow, because . . . ?"

"I don't know. I don't know if I'm making the right choice."

She lifted her head to look at him. "Maybe you don't want to quit."

"Maybe I don't," he agreed, shaking his head.

"What changed your mind?" she asked.

His gray eyes glanced down at her. "You. Maybe. This." His gaze went to the gauze bandage on her shoulder, so close to her throat. "I thought it was the job that was the problem, but now I'm not so sure."

"You said you wanted to change your life. Maybe you mean . . . Loni," September suggested.

"No. That's been over for almost a year." He was frowning at the television, which had switched to a commercial.

"What's wrong?" September asked.

"Nothing's wrong. I'm just . . . figuring it out."

"You sure it doesn't have to do with Loni?" she asked carefully.

"What do you mean? No. That's over. You know that."

"Why are you so defensive?"

"I'm not defensive."

"No?"

"No." He heard himself and switched off the television with a snap of his thumb on the remote. "She's . . . not a part of my life. I don't want to see her anymore. It's over. And I just don't want to think about her."

"Okay."

He expelled a long breath. "She called me today," he admitted. "I was cleaning out my desk and she called and I just started feeling . . . bad . . . guilty, I guess. It's not about the job. You were right on that. It's about Loni and how I don't want to deal with her anymore, and that makes me feel like a shit."

"I know it's a cliché, but her problems are her problems, not your problems."

"I know. It's just that I'm happy, she's not, and I don't know that she will be, ever. So . . . yeah. Not good."

"Sounds like survivor's guilt," September said.

"Well, she's not dead."

"You know what I mean. So, you're staying with the job?"

"Is that a problem?"

"Not at all."

September snuggled back down against him, aware that her pulse had jumped raggedly but was now settling into a normal rhythm. She could talk big about Jake with Loni, like she understood everything about their years and years of a long relationship, but secretly it worried her a little. "Maybe I can rustle up Auggie to help with the move this weekend," she murmured, her voice muffled against the skin of his chest.

He leaned down and looked at her. She glanced up. "What?"

For an answer he kissed her on the lips. The kiss lingered and when he finally pulled back, he asked, "You won't back out?"

"No."

"Cross your heart, hope to die?"

A shiver slid down her bare back and Jake pulled her in closer. "Just cross my heart," she said.

"Any more interest in the Johnson file?"

"Tomorrow, bucko."

"Shucks."

Chapter Five

Stefan was hanging up his coat in the back of Mrs. Runderfeld's—Mrs. Run, to the kids—classroom where he was in the middle of a six-week training cycle when there was a knock on the open doorway. That bitch from the office, Lazenby's suck-up gopher, stuck her head inside.

"Mr. Harmak, could you come to the office, please?" she asked.

The second-graders were still coming in off the playground from the first bell, rushing to their seats, talking and bustling their way to their desks.

Stefan's heart seized up. "What for?" he asked.

"Principal Lazenby wants to see you." She ducked out and disappeared.

Mrs. Run had been talking to a kid's mother, a scatterbrained blonde with implants whose son ran in a pack of snotty little shits, entitled monsters with too much money and no discipline. Now, the teacher turned and lifted her brows to Stefan. So damn self-righteous he wanted to smack her.

"She probably wants to make sure you're over that flu," she said.

Stefan left the room, wading through the line of kids arrowing into the room. There was little Melissa with her sweet smile and little green dress. She was the best behaved of the girls, kind of forgotten in the back of the room. He tried to help her whenever he could.

Lazenby's office was toward the front of the building in a group of rooms behind the visitors counter. His heart was knocking as he entered the administration area and went to her office. When he looked inside, she wasn't there.

"Go on in. She'll be right back," Maryanne said. Her chair was right behind the counter and she greeted parents and kids by name.

She was a suck-up gopher, too.

He seated himself in one of the chairs opposite Lazenby's desk and anxiously waited for the middle-aged hard-ass bitch to return. Maybe it was like Runderfeld said and they were worried he would send another round of the flu through the school. They didn't know it was his excuse for being out the day before.

Lazenby bustled in. She was about five two with big breasts atop a barrel-shaped body, short, gray hair, and a pair of reading glasses perpetually on her nose. She shut the door behind her as she said, "Hi, Stefan. How are you feeling?"

"Better," he said.

She nodded as she took her seat behind her desk. "You called in with the flu yesterday about ten-thirty."

"Sorry. I kept thinking I would make it in." His palms were sweating. He wasn't even sure why he was keeping up the lie. Though he'd hoped he wouldn't be found out, he'd caught the late news last night, and though they hadn't named him, there was speculation all over the place that whoever had tied the teacher up at Twin Oaks had also killed a postman earlier in the year. Stefan vaguely remembered the incident. He hadn't once thought about it when he was tied up, and it wouldn't have come to him at all if he hadn't seen it on the news.

Jesus. Who was that bitch? What did she want? At least

she hadn't killed him like the postman, but she'd sure as hell taken his van, and his mother was all over him about that one!

"You should have told September that the psycho who did this to you took your van!" she'd declared as soon as they were alone.

"I'll tell her," he'd snarled back. "It's just so fucking humiliating."

"Language, Stefan," she'd responded, to which he'd started hysterically laughing and couldn't stop.

Amy Lazenby adjusted her glasses and said, "When I got here yesterday morning, the Laurelton police told me that a man was drugged and tied to one of our basketball hoops. Later, a detective called and said it was you."

September! Goddamned do-gooder! "I was sick," he defended himself. "After being left there all night . . ." The catch in his voice was very real.

"Do you think you should be here today?" she asked.

"Maybe not." He grabbed onto the thought as if it were a lifeline. He didn't want to be here. He wanted to be home, locked in his room.

"I've already taken a number of calls from newspeople. This is a media storm, Stefan, and I'd like to contain it as much as possible."

Stefan made an inadvertent sound of fear.

"Are you all right?" she asked, sounding sincere, but he knew better than to trust anyone. They were all on the other side.

No one had mentioned the sign yet, the one he'd been forced to write. But it was coming. The news was already talking about what the postman had around his neck: I MUST PAY FOR WHAT I'VE DONE. It was a goddamned nightmare!

"I feel sick," he said, his stomach roiling, and then he broke down and started crying. He covered his face with his hands and bent double.

"You shouldn't be here," she said, sounding surprisingly

kind, and that got Stefan wailing even more. He nodded behind his hands, and she said, "I'll get someone to take you."

He couldn't make himself drop his hands from his face. He wanted to disappear forever. That bitch. That fucking bitch. He was going to track her down and kill her. How could she do this to him? It wasn't fair. It just *wasn't fair!*

September put a second call in to her brother on her lunch break. She'd left him a message earlier and she'd tried texting him as well. When his voice mail answered again, she clicked off and sent another text: Need some muscle this weekend to help move my stuff to Jake's. You available?

She was walking back to her desk when her cell phone rang in her hand. "About time," she said aloud, lifting it up to see who was calling. But the number on the screen wasn't Auggie's and there was no name. "Hello," she answered at the same moment she realized why the number was so familiar: it was Mrs. Ballonni's.

"Is this . . . the detective who left a message yesterday?" Janet Ballonni asked, slowly picking her words.

"Yes, it is. I'm Detective Rafferty. I was wondering if I could talk to you about your husband."

"I already talked to that other woman detective. Twice," she stated flatly.

"I know, but we're investigating a new angle now. Would it be possible to meet with you and go over the case in person? At your house, or work?"

"I don't have a job anymore. Company downsized and I got laid off. Life's a bitch and then you die, right?" she added bitterly. "I don't think there's anything I can tell you that I didn't tell Detective Chubb or that other one."

"Detective Sandler."

"Yeah, her." She sniffed. "I said the same thing to both of them."

"I understand, but this new angle may help us in discovering who killed your husband. Would it be possible for me to come by today?"

"Oh . . . no . . . not today."

"Tomorrow?"

She sighed heavily, as if weighing her options, then said grudgingly, "Okay, tomorrow. You can come by the house in the afternoon. I've got Pilates in the morning. But make it early," she added suddenly, as if she'd just thought of something. "Twelve or one. No later."

"How about one?" September was inwardly jubilant that she'd at least capitulated.

"No later," she warned again.

"I'll be there right at one tomorrow."

Wes was on the phone when she hung up, and he signaled with his hand that he wanted to talk to her. George was staring into his computer. He'd been taxed with calling the houses nearest Foxglove Park and finding out if any of the neighbors had seen anything that would give them a clue into the name of the female victim left in the park.

Wes said, "All right," and hung up the phone. "Harmak's name's out there now. Bound to happen. I talked to Amy Lazenby, the principal, and either it went from there or somebody from the hospital or EMTs, whatever. Not that it's a secret, but it puts you one step closer to Pauline Kirby."

"I can handle her. I've got a face-to-face with Janet Ballonni tomorrow. Can you go?"

"What time?"

"One."

"Can you make it earlier? I've got a doctor's appointment." He lifted his hands and dropped them in frustration.

"She was pretty specific about the afternoon."

"Okay, well, then it's George."

Fat chance, September thought.

They both looked over at Thompkins. As if sensing their perusal, George glanced back at them, frowned, and then turned his attention to his computer screen. Ideally, the detectives investigated cases with their partners, but with all the budget cuts these were not ideal times. No one had assigned partners.

"I'm getting ready to track down your stepbrother and see if I can get anything else out of him," Wes added.

"Ex-stepbrother," September said automatically. "I'd go with you if D'Annibal would allow it."

Wes shook his head. "We're going to have to pry George out of that chair."

"Good luck with that."

Lucky drove Mr. Blue's van past the two-story daylight basement house where she'd followed Stefan Harmak home several weeks earlier. She circled the neighborhood and then parked down the street, wishing she had wheels that were less distinguishable. Once upon a time, when she'd first begun her mission, she'd appropriated vehicles from Carl's Hunk o' Junks near Seaside on a regular basis. But after nearly getting caught, and losing her life strapped to the pyre, she'd simply burrowed in at Mr. Blue's and accepted his goodwill, which included only the truck for transportation.

She had to make do with what she had.

Easing out of the vehicle, she glanced up and down the tree-lined street. The one advantage was the trees were evergreens, which were mostly overgrown, and the neighborhood didn't have curbs and sidewalks. It was one of those areas where the yards just meandered into dirt and gravel and then the blacktopped street, and the vegetation screened her progress somewhat as she walked down the road. The disadvantage was she had to walk on the street itself, but there was very little traffic in the middle of the day.

Harmak's house—where he lived with his mother, she'd learned later—was obscured by a rampant laurel hedge that made approaching it easier. She walked right by it, surreptitiously glancing down the driveway—the only view past the laurels to the house—seeing the way the ground sloped off the back, creating the lower level.

If she could get behind the house, it looked like the laurel hedge did not circle the back. If she came at night, she could approach from the rear, but she would have to move along the edge of one of the neighboring properties.

She walked past the house that lay to the east of Harmak's and realized there were very few windows on the side of the house closest to Stefan's. In dark clothes, she could probably sneak down the line of laurels on their side of the hedge and then come up behind Harmak's.

And then what? she asked herself. Two people lived at the residence. She had no quarrel with Harmak's mother. Hmm . . .

She took a circuitous route back to Mr. Blue's truck, climbed behind the wheel and drove away, careful not to go by Harmak's house again. She purposely wound through the neighborhood until she found where she'd left his van, still undisturbed, and then she headed away.

The first time she'd picked up on Stefan was at the same mall where she'd hit him with the stun gun, immobilized him, and then driven him to the elementary school. She'd been at the mall on a mission for Mr. Blue, picking up various supplies. Normally she made her forays into Seaside or some of the other beach communities, and when she did she wore a lot of makeup—darkening her eyes or covering them with shaded lenses if it was sunny, throwing on lipstick and blush with a heavy hand, making Ani look more like a caricature of herself than the real thing, so that when she went out as herself she would be less easy to identify. But on that particular day she'd gone as herself, Ani Loman, mostly known as Lucky, and had headed east toward Portland, passing by the town of Quarry, feeling the shiver that invariably slid down her back at the remembrance of her near-death experience each time she did, heading into the town of Laurelton. She'd still planned to go all the way to Portland but she'd taken a side trip to the mall.

She'd walked past Harmak and felt that aura, that godawful sensation, and she'd just kept on walking rather than have him get a look at her. She turned into a dress shop, stopped, then walked to the edge of the door and peered out. Harmak was just turning his face away from her, so maybe his gaze had followed her. She wasn't sure. But whatever the case, he wasn't looking at her any longer and she was bound and determined to find out who he was.

She watched him as he wandered the mall, staying far behind in case he should see her, but he never did. She observed him watching the shoppers, the girls that strolled by in flocks. His eyes betrayed him. He liked them young.

When he finally left the mall, she followed after him, watching as he climbed into a white van. Mr. Blue's truck was not all that far away, so she went to it and climbed inside. She had a pair of binoculars in the glove box and she pulled them out and leaned back and down in her seat until she could watch him with just the two eyes of the binoculars visible, though it was from far enough away and at an angle so that she was fairly certain he couldn't see her.

An hour went by and then a group of young tweens stepped out of the mall, the girls giggling and laughing and teasing with several boys. They moved through the crowd in a loose pack and Lucky could see the way Harmak's attention zeroed in, laserlike, on the youngest-looking girl, whose body hadn't made the leap into womanhood. As they all disappeared together, she also saw the frustration and longing on his face. Something about it made her feel better because she believed he hadn't acted on his feelings yet.

And she was bound and determined to stop him before he did.

When he drove away, she followed at a distance, all thoughts of shopping for Mr. Blue emptying from her brain. She watched him turn at the laurel hedge and she drove past as he was climbing from his van, which he'd parked in the driveway that ran alongside the house. He glanced her way, but she was pretty sure only the back of the truck was visible to him in the deepening twilight. Nevertheless, she was electrified with the sensation of his lust. It came to her in a pulsating wave.

She immediately began plotting her next move. She'd killed sexual abusers before. Several times. During her recovery at Mr. Blue's she'd told herself to stop playing with fire, so to speak. It was the only way to stay alive. But she'd disregarded her own advice almost immediately after she was well. She'd moved to Portland for a time, eventually making her way into the protection of Rick Wiis, a businessman who modeled himself after Hugh Hefner and offered employment to young women who might or might not be escorts, and might or might not be Rick's girlfriend du jour. Lucky had thought she could use Rick's place as a base, but she'd quickly learned that wasn't going to work. In his employ she was constantly put on parade under men's lustful stares and she didn't do well with that. Since there was no way she was about to entertain any of the men who roamed Rick's bar and back rooms looking for sex—even if she'd been able to, there was the problem of explaining the burned and scarred flesh on her back—her time at Rick's was short-lived and unlamented.

Besides, the sad and lonely losers who hung out there were not the pedophiles she sought. She left Rick's employ and returned to Mr. Blue's. It wasn't as handy a place to launch from, but Mr. Blue didn't ask questions and he had no expectations. It felt, for Lucky, as close to a home as she'd ever had.

Picking up Harmak was almost too easy. He'd been at that point of slipping into the dark side, and he was tired of waiting. She'd followed him home and then she'd followed him to work. Learning he was employed at Twin Oaks Elementary had stepped up her game. If he touched one hair on one of those children's heads she would kill him with her bare hands and screw the consequences.

From the early days when she'd nearly gotten herself killed taking out sick scum like Harmak, she'd learned to try and make their deaths look like suicides, if she could, inexplicable homicides if she couldn't. When she ran across Christopher Ballonni, the mailman with the searing eyes as he looked at any of the little girls along his mail route, she'd thought long and hard what she wanted to do with him. She'd run across him at the post office. She'd been walking back to the truck after picking up some packages for Mr. Blue—she never asked what—and Ballonni had whipped by in his mail truck. She was immediately enveloped in the stench of his intentions. She'd gazed at him hard and he must have felt the weight of her stare because he turned and narrowed his eyes on her before wheeling out of the parking lot.

She went back to Mr. Blue's and plotted what to do. The stun gun was his and she diffidently asked if she could borrow it. He nodded and said, "It leaves marks," and so she'd changed her mind, borrowing a .38 from Mr. Blue's cache of firearms. She'd picked out the cardboard for the sign, tied some twine to it so that it could loop around his neck, tucked a felt pen in her pocket, then wiped everything down so there were no fingerprints. She bought some zip-ties and thrust them in another pocket.

Then she made her concoction laced with roofies and put it in a thermos.

It was as cold as Ballonni's dark soul and she was wrapped

in a long black coat, wearing a fedora-type hat, sunglasses, and thin, flexible leather gloves. She timed it so she had the sign under her arm, the thermos in her hand, the gun in her pocket, and was walking across the parking lot just as he was finishing his route. As she approached, he glanced up. She smiled and, not immediately recognizing her for the threat she was, he smiled back, waiting to find out what she wanted. Even though it was freezing cold, she wore nothing under the coat and she flashed him as he was opening his driver's door, letting him get a good hard look at her body. She had too many curves to be his cup of tea, but it shocked him enough that she was allowed to draw close and press the muzzle of a gun under his ribs. "Get in," she whispered, reaching down and grabbing his flaccid cock through his pants.

"I don't—"

"Get the fuck in the car or I will shoot you dead right here."

He protested some more, but, with his eyes on the .38, he complied, scooting across to the passenger seat at her insistence. At gunpoint she drove him to a nearby park where, because of the frigid February weather, no one was around. It was a far riskier move than with Harmak; she could have been seen by other employees, Ballonni could have tried to overpower her, anything could have happened.

But all Ballonni wanted to do was protest his innocence. She had the wrong guy. He was a husband, a father. A *good* guy. She pretended to listen while she pressed the barrel of the gun against his temple and picked up the sign from where she'd dropped it behind the seat.

Reaching into her pocket, she pulled out the felt pen, handed it to him, and ordered, "Write this: I MUST PAY FOR WHAT I'VE DONE."

His blustering escalated and she put the index finger of her free hand against his lips. Gradually, he wound down and then he recognized her as the woman he'd seen earlier.

"Who are you?" he demanded, his voice quaking. "I didn't do anything! Nothing! You're dead wrong. I'm not that guy! I'm not!"

"You had sex with a child," she told him. She didn't know who. She didn't know how. She just knew it to be true.

"No! No! Never!"

"Write it."

"I can't. I can't. I can't."

She thought about just shooting him. She wanted to. Cold fury was running through her blood and she could probably get away with it. But as if he sensed her thoughts, he wrote out the words in a shaking hand, his pleading changing to a stuttered sobbing.

"Please," he said, handing the placard back to her. "I have a wife and a son."

"Shoulda thought of that before you hurt her."

"I don't know what you think you know. It's not . . . it's not . . ." he blathered, then his eyes widened in horror as she slipped the sign around his neck.

"Drink this," she said then, picking up the thermos.

"What is it? No. You're trying to kill me!"

She was implacable. Her finger tightened on the trigger.

He refused. He begged. He pleaded. He cried.

But she wasn't interested in negotiation. Finally, he took a few swallows, trying not to drink it all, but she eventually got him to finish it.

She drove him back to the post office, stripped him down, rolled him out, and zip-tied him to the flagpole.

Now, thinking back on it, she realized how many things could have gone awry. She was lucky he'd gone along so willingly. She then drove his car back behind the building and jogged down the road to where she'd left the truck.

No one had known what to make of it, according to the news. Was it murder, or assisted suicide?

After Ballonni's death, Lucky ran across another troller who wasn't as easily cowed and had tried to wrest the gun from her. She'd shot him in the process and was lucky to come out of that one unscathed. His death was put down as a case of road rage that had happened in the Portland city limits, so it wasn't being investigated by the same department that Ballonni and Harmak were.

She'd decided on the stun gun after that. It gave her an advantage in controlling her prey. Of course, the police would definitely know Harmak's death was a homicide, but then there was also a pattern now, too, so it was a moot point. Getting him to write in his own hand had been a trick. He'd been crazed with fear. Kept blubbering that his stepsister and brother were cops and they would crucify him. She told him she would zap him again, and eventually she got him to take the thermos cup and drink down the cocktail of drugs, pleading with her all the way. He practically wet his pants, he was so scared. And he started bucking wildly when she tried to loop the sign around his neck. She zapped him again and then the drugs finally took him out.

But she'd let Harmak live. Had been distracted by the other scent. Hadn't wanted the kids to find a dead body, but that just left him able to abuse some other child. She was pissed at herself. She would have to rectify that error and soon. Couldn't have him going back to work around all those kids.

Tonight, she thought. But how, with his mother there?

She thought about her own mother, a woman who'd given up her and her sister before spiraling down into madness. Her sister had fared better than Lucky, who'd been left in the care of a doctor, a surgeon, of sorts, who'd used and abused her every single goddamn night until that fateful day on the jetty when she'd lured him out to the edge and pushed him off.

Her life had been that of a vagabond ever since. She'd had a number of protectors and an even greater number of abusers. She'd learned to kill without compunction and apart from that time when she'd confronted her sister and her sister's lover, Detective Tanninger with the Winslow County Sheriff's Department, she'd steered clear of feelings and relationships and caring and *people*, ever since.

As she turned onto the road that led to Mr. Blue's, she determined that she would have to make sure Stefan Harmak's mother was away from the house before she could take him out.

But then he was hers.

Chapter Six

Janet Ballonni studied the young woman detective cautiously, one eye on the clock. One o'clock. Well, at least she'd come on time. But Janet didn't want her around by the time Chris Jr. got home, which should be around three-thirty, if all went according to plan. She didn't like the authorities messing in her life, and she really didn't like them messing in Chris's. Hadn't they suffered through enough pain already?

The young, auburn-haired detective was quite pretty with startling blue eyes and a slim, athletic build. Occasionally she caught herself up short, as if jabbed by some unseen pain. What had happened to her? And why, in God's good name, would anyone want to be a police officer?

"Can I get you something, Detective Rafferty? A soft drink, or coffee . . . ?" Janet asked cordially. She had to force herself to smile. She just wanted them all to go away and leave her and Chris Jr. alone.

"No, thank you," she demurred. "I don't want to take up too much of your time, so let me get to it, all right?"

"Thank you."

"I know Detective Chubb interviewed you, but I've taken over the case and I would like to hear your thoughts firsthand."

"Detective Chubb left months ago," she said, forcing herself *not* to look at the clock.

"There had been no movement on the case, but now we're looking at new leads."

"Oh?" Janet didn't really believe it. They always said something of the sort.

"I assure you, it's not been forgotten."

Janet hmphed at that. They all treated Chris's death like a suicide and she knew he would never kill himself. The idea! She'd heard law enforcement officers were more interested in job promotion than in actually solving crimes and she believed it. "I don't see how I can help you. I told Detective Chubb and the other detective the same thing."

"Could you lead me through the last few weeks before your husband's death?" the detective suggested.

Janet smoothed her apron. It was Thursday and she always baked cookies on Thursdays. Chris Jr. had always loved the ones she made with those tiny currants and oatmeal. He couldn't stand raisins, but the currants were his favorite. "I have no idea where to even start," she complained.

The detective had a file and now she picked it up and glanced into it. "Two weeks before your husband's death, there was a complaint lodged against him."

Wouldn't you know? The first thing out of her mouth was that. "Oh, that woman. She has one of those pit bulls and it came after Chris and he had to kick it. Barely slowed the beast down. It left teeth marks in his shoe and he warned her that it damn well better not bite him, or he would have it put down. I just don't understand people who raise animals like that. They say the breed is fine, but it's the owners who turn them into killing machines. Maybe that's just what she wanted—a killing machine."

"You're speaking of Mrs. Bernstein," she said, glancing into the file again. "I see that she had words with your husband before the attack."

"Well, she's a liar, then! Chris never had words with anyone. He was the nicest guy. Jovial, you know. Always had a smile for everyone."

"Mrs. Bernstein complained that your husband gave her daughter a stick of gum."

Janet could feel the color rise in her face. "Well, I'm sure he did. He gave everyone gum. That's just who he was. And Mrs. Bernstein's one of those women who hovers over her child like she's so fragile and lovely, but I can tell you, Missy Bernstein is a sly little imp. She loves to stir up trouble. My Chris gave all the kids on his route gum. He'd done it for years, and when Mrs. Bernstein complained, there were other people on his route who stood up for him. LeeAnn Walters and Marnie Dramur were right there. That better be in your file, too!"

"Yes, it's all documented. I'm just looking for anomalies."

"Are you going to interview Mrs. Bernstein? You should. Then you'll see what she's like."

"Was there anything else that occurred in the last few weeks before his death that seemed different, out of routine?"

"Detective Chubb asked me the same thing. No." Janet was firm.

"Your son is at school now?"

Janet's right hand clenched into the fabric of her apron. "Yes. Why? You can't talk to him. He's a minor."

"I would like to talk to him," the detective said. "With your permission."

"Well, I'm sorry. He's missing his father so much, it's all he can do to get himself up each day. It's so unfair. Someone did this to Chris and you people haven't done anything to find out who that is, and Chris Jr. is struggling so much. No, you can't talk to him. You'll just stir everything up for no good reason!"

The detective considered. Janet could practically hear

thoughts tumbling around in her head. "You've never felt your husband's death was a suicide," the detective said.

"Chris would never do that. Detective Chubb seemed to think that suicide was the likely answer, but he's wrong." She harrumphed again. "Not my Chris. And how would he have done it? He was drugged and he couldn't tie his hands behind his back by himself."

"Actually, Detective Chubb believed it was an accidental homicide. Detective Sandler agreed."

"They just said that because they knew I would never accept suicide. Accidental homicide—what does that even mean?"

"That whoever did this to your husband didn't mean to kill him."

Janet didn't like the way this was going. She hadn't liked it with the other detectives either. "You think he was playing some sex game with a woman and it got out of hand."

Detective Rafferty blinked. "I don't know about that. Your husband died of exposure and that was because the temperature sank into the teens that night."

"My husband wasn't the kind to cheat!" Janet declared. She knew what they were thinking. What they were *all* thinking.

"We don't know the reason he was tied up," she said.

"I know what it said in the newspapers," Janet retorted icily. "And I know what Gloria said. She's probably the one who said all those terrible things. Not that it's any of your business, but we had a healthy sex life. He wasn't into role-playing!"

"Who's Gloria?" she asked, searching her notes.

"Gloria del Courte. A coworker of Chris's. She always had a thing for him, but she didn't start making terrible remarks concerning him until after that scurrilous newspaper story about those weird sex acts, like autoerotic asphyxiation."

The detective frowned. "I'm not sure what newspaper article you're referring to."

"The *Oregonian* did a whole series of articles after Chris's death." She flapped her hands, waving the memory away. "It was just awful."

"There was a placard around his neck that read—"

"Yes, I know," she snapped. "I MUST PAY FOR WHAT I'VE DONE, or something. That's what they said in the papers. But he wouldn't cheat on me. I know it. Why won't anyone believe me! This wasn't role-playing. Someone killed my Chris!" Tears leapt to her eyes. They were all persecuting her. She was going to have to report them. Lodge a complaint at City Hall against the police. It was the only way to get them to leave her alone!

The detective hesitated a moment and Janet could tell she was considering what to say next. She braced herself. She didn't like this attractive young woman any more than she'd liked the older Chubb with his hangdog face and world-weary expression or the other woman detective who'd called on the phone.

Rafferty closed the file. "There's been another incident of a man drugged and tied to a pole. You may have seen it on the news."

Janet's mouth dropped open on a gasp. "What? I don't watch the news. I don't even read the paper anymore! Who is this man? What are you saying?"

"His name's Stefan Harmak and he was tied to a pole that holds up a basketball hoop on the Twin Oaks Elementary School grounds in Laurelton. Like your husband, he was stripped down to his boxer shorts, but the temperature's much milder now, so he survived."

"Oh, my *God!*" She pressed a hand to her cheek. "What does this mean? Who's doing this?"

"Mr. Harmak said a man accosted him, forced him to drink

something that had the drug Rohypnol in it, commonly known as roofies, or the date-rape drug."

"Rape?" Janet was horrified.

"Neither Mr. Harmak nor your husband was raped," the detective went on. "Mr. Harmak also had a placard placed around his neck. His said I WANT WHAT I CAN'T HAVE."

"Who is this man? Why is he doing this?" Janet could feel the hysteria rising in her voice.

"We believe someone targeted both your husband and Mr. Harmak specifically."

Something in her tone bothered Janet. Like she was blaming Chris for this. "I don't like where this is going."

"Excuse me?"

"You think this is my husband's fault. That he brought it on himself."

"I didn't mean to give you that impression."

"Didn't you?" Oh, they were all the same. She knew what they were thinking and it was like a hot needle in her brain. "I think I've answered all the questions I'm going to."

"I'm sorry you feel that way. This new case has opened up avenues into learning what happened to your husband."

The detective asked a few more questions, covering much the same ground, but Janet refused to answer in anything but monosyllables. She was also processing that this second guy tied up was going to throw more light on her husband's death. Hadn't they gone through enough? When did it ever end?

Finally, the detective made as if she were going to leave. Janet glanced at the clock. It was after two.

Go, she thought. *Get out.*

"I would really like to talk to your son."

"Out of the question," Janet snapped. "I don't want my son involved in any part of this. He's suffered enough."

"Our goal is to find out who did this to your husband," the detective reminded her, as if Janet were a schoolgirl.

"You want to sensationalize it! That's what you want. Chris

Jr.'s only thirteen. He doesn't know anything about this. Stay away from him," she warned.

The detective finally left after that and as the door closed behind her, Janet scurried to the front window and peeked through the curtains, watching her pull away from the curb in a silver SUV. Then she glanced down the street, wondering if anyone had seen the detective come to her door. Luckily, no one was around and the cop wasn't driving a squad car.

Damn.

She turned from the window and her eye caught the picture of her and Chris's wedding day, fifteen years earlier. They both looked so happy. She was all in white and her hair was long. She looked so incredibly young.

Touching her hair now, she wondered if she should grow it out again. She'd had gardenias in her hair for the picture, but she'd always worn headbands at that time. Headbands with bows had been Chris's favorite. And Mary Jane's with anklets. That had really turned him on and she remembered those times in the bedroom where he'd suddenly pushed her down and tickled her silly, ripping at her clothes until they were naked and he was driving into her and grunting like an animal. He never bothered to take off her shoes and socks.

A coldness settled into her lower back and she shuddered. Well, sex had never been her thing, really, despite what she'd said to that detective. Chris, too. They'd just loved each other a lot, though. They really had.

A tear slid down her cheek as she finished rolling out the dough for the cookies. She was just finishing up the last batch when she heard a car pull into her drive, then the front door flew open and slammed shut. "Chris?" she called.

She heard her son's heavy footsteps clomp down the hall to his room and then another door opened and slammed shut.

"Chris?" she called again, then with a sigh arranged the cookies on a plate and took them to his room. She knocked on the panels of his door, resenting his rule to knock before entering.

"Yeah?" he demanded, surly. He was always surly these days.

"I made you some cookies."

She tried the handle and he yelled, "Don't come in! I'm getting dressed!"

"Good heavens, Chris. I'm just trying to do something nice."

"Just . . . don't."

"Fine." She left the cookie plate on the floor in front of his room with a clatter. "I won't tell you about the female detective who came by earlier, then."

She was barely back in the kitchen before her son appeared in the room, staring at her through dark eyes so much like his father's—except Chris Jr.'s were open windows to his soul where his father's had been . . . opaque, harder to read.

"What detective?" he demanded.

"Detective September Rafferty with the Laurelton Police Department. She took over your father's case from that other one who didn't do anything. Frankly, I don't think she's much better."

"What did she say?"

"Oh, I don't know if I remember. You didn't want me to come into your room and talk to you. I see you're still wearing the same clothes you left in this morning."

"Mom, what did she say?"

"What's gotten into you?"

"What did she say about Dad?" he persisted. "Do they know who did it—and why?" He was so intense that Janet found herself sorry she'd said anything.

"Didn't you even try the cookies?" she asked.

"If I eat one will you stop stalling?"

"Christopher!" she said, hurt.

"Was it someone on his route?"

"What? No. What are you talking about?"

He turned away, thinking hard. "You were upset with Mrs. Bernstein."

"Good heavens, Chris. I was upset with her, but I don't think she's a *killer*."

"Not her . . . that other guy . . ."

"Who?" she couldn't help asking. Hearing herself, she said, unnerved, "They don't know who did it." She'd wanted Chris to come and talk to her, so she'd used the detective, but now she wished she hadn't said anything.

"What did the detective say?" he asked again.

With a sigh, Janet gave in. "There was another incident like your dad's, only that guy lived."

"What do you mean?"

Reluctantly, she told him about the man who'd been tied to the pole at the school. "His name's Steven Harmer, or something like that, but I suppose now they'll rake it all up again."

"Jesus, that's what Jamie meant."

Jamie was his girlfriend. A sneaky little junior high horror story, if ever there was one. "What did Jamie say?" she asked, trying to keep the snarl from her voice.

"She saw it on the news. Some guy zip-tied to a pole at Twin Oaks. Left in his boxers, like Dad. They said it was a prank."

"Well, the detective said they think both this Steven Harmer or Harner and your dad were *targeted* by the same person." She got some perverse satisfaction out of watching the color drain from her son's face. "You can tell Jamie it was no prank. There's some crazy man out there, randomly attacking people, and he killed your dad." She sniffled, calling up some real tears. She'd loved Chris. She really had. It just made her so mad sometimes that he hadn't gone for that promotion. He could have been the postmaster of the West Laurelton office if he'd just tried a little harder. Had she nagged him? A little, maybe, but Chris had always needed a push. And wasn't that what wives were for?

"Why?" her son asked her. "What's this other guy's name again? Steven what?" He was already turning away.

"I can't remember exactly. It started with an *H*." Then, as he pulled his cell phone from a pocket of his low-riding jeans, she said, exasperated, "You're going to go look it up on your phone, aren't you?"

"On the Internet," he answered.

She wanted to throw something. Chris Jr.'s last birthday gift had been a smartphone—his father's idea, and a bad one, as far as Janet was concerned. It gave him all the more reason to ignore her and half the time she wanted to snatch it out of his hands and throw it away. Except it was expensive.

"Don't step on that plate," she called after him. "And bring it back here."

Maybe she should stop paying his phone bill. She had a phone, too, but what junior high kid needed all that access? Just something to get him into trouble, and besides, without Chris's paycheck they had to be careful, despite the life insurance policy she'd taken out on him. Oh, sure, he'd laughed at her and made her feel stupid for getting such a big policy on him, but who got the last laugh, huh?

With that thought, she picked up her own cell phone and Googled Verizon. Clicking on the number, she idly picked up a cookie and munched away as she was waiting to be put through. My, but they were good! She could go into the business, if she had a mind to.

"Hi, this is Janet Ballonni, and I'd like to cancel my son's cell service," she began as soon as someone picked up, only to realize it was a recorded message.

"Sure, I'll hold," she snarled at the music coming through.

It took *forever* before she got through to the billing department, and what do you know, they wouldn't help her at all because she wasn't the primary account holder! She screamed at them that her husband was dead and then they had a helluva nerve asking her for a death certificate. "I'll bring it to your store tomorrow!" she shrieked, just as she heard the front door slam again. Hurrying to her post at the curtains, she saw her son walk rapidly down the driveway and then disappear down the street.

She was so angry, she hardly knew what to do. "I'll have to call you back!" she finally declared in frustration, slamming down the receiver and hurrying out the front door into a windy afternoon. She walked rapidly to the end of the drive and looked up and down the street.

Chris Jr. was nowhere to be seen.

"The Foxglove Park vic's name is Carrie Lynne Carter. She's suffered from depression on and off for years, according to her mother," Wes said as September entered the squad room.

George piped up. "Wes and I got the information."

"How?" September asked, dropping her messenger bag on her desk. She could take it back to her locker later.

Wes gave George a look. "I checked with the neighbors. Found out that one of them, Mrs. Debra Carter, was on vacation, but that she had a daughter about the right age and right description."

"So, I left a message at the Carter home," George said before Wes could go on. "Asked them to call and she just did."

"You didn't deliver this news in person?" September questioned George, a note of incredulity entering her voice.

"I did," Wes said. He turned from George but the look in his eyes revealed his disgust at the man. "Just got back. Mrs. Carter was in a state."

"I didn't tell her anything," George defended himself.

"You didn't have to." Wes's tone was cool. "She knew her daughter wasn't there."

"Okay," September said, hoping to ease the tension. "What did Mrs. Carter say?" she asked Wes.

"Carrie lives with her. She had a boyfriend who recently broke up with her, and Carrie was depressed. Her mother's pretty sure it's suicide but almost hopes it's foul play."

"Tox screen still not in?" September asked.

"Nah."

They knew Carrie had ingested some kind of antidepressant, but the finer details were yet to be determined. "Did Mrs. Carter say Carrie had been prescribed something?"

"Xanax, maybe. One of those. She wasn't sure, but Carrie was definitely taking something, so she probably overdosed on her prescription. There aren't any bottles around, apparently."

"Why aren't there any bottles?" September asked.

"She must have gotten rid of them herself. She was kind of sneaky about taking her meds."

"Her mom said that, too?"

"Yep."

"So J.J.'s ruling it a suicide," September said.

Wes nodded. J.J. was what everyone called Joe Journey, the county coroner. He was brusque and crusty, but September got along with him okay. Not so her old partner, Gretchen Sandler, who irked J.J. to no end and vice versa. But then what else was new?

"What happened with the Ballonni widow?" Wes asked.

"Nothing new," September answered. "She thought we were investigating a sex-role-playing angle. Something she saw on TV? Like a series that also ran in the newspapers?"

"It had nothing to do with the case," George said from across the room. Both of them looked at him but neither of them said anything. George, though, true to form, ignored their silent condemnation and said, "That was just one of those *Dateline*-like reports on sex games one of the local stations ran. Maybe it came out about the same time Ballonni died, but it didn't have anything to do with it."

"Mrs. Ballonni thinks one of Chris's coworkers, Gloria del Courte, was the one behind the story."

"Total bullshit," George said.

"Why would she think that?" Wes asked.

"She says del Courte had a thing for her husband. Her name's not listed anywhere, so I don't know if she was interviewed," September added, searching in her messenger bag for the file. "Janet Ballonni seems kind of . . . unwilling to believe anything bad about her husband." She related the part about the gum giving. "I'll talk to Mrs. Bernstein on his old route, and Gloria del Courte, see if there's anything there. I tried to get her to let me talk to her son, but she refused."

"How old is he?" Wes asked.

"Junior high-ish." September looked in the file. "Thirteen."

Wes thought about it a minute. "Was he there when you interviewed her?"

"He wasn't back from school yet."

"Try going to see her again when he's there. That age of kid . . . he could just override her and talk to you anyway."

"Or, run and hide from the law," George said.

Wes shrugged. "You never know what the hell you're going to get."

"Okay," September said. She would have liked to talk to Chris without his mother around, but there were rules about minors that needed to be obeyed. "Did you meet with Stefan?" she asked.

Wes shook his head. "Tried to, but he's a slippery kind of guy. Always putting me off. I went to his house and a news crew was camped outside."

"Uh-oh." September made a face.

"Had to call the home phone, since our doer stole his cell. Talked to his mother."

"Uh-oh, again."

"Yeah, well. She wouldn't let me talk to Stefan, though he was there, I'm pretty sure. The principal, Lazenby, sent him home, indefinitely it appears, as he didn't even attempt to go to the school today."

"She probably doesn't want the news vans at the school," September said. "Or, maybe Stefan needs more time off."

"A little of both, probably. Anyway, I told his mother to have him call me, but it hasn't happened yet."

"It won't," September predicted. "You're going to have to track him down."

"You know, there's no garage at their house, and there's only one car, a Chevrolet Impala."

"I think that's Verna's car."

"I was just wondering where his car was. It doesn't appear to be on the street anywhere, and it's not on the grounds."

"Good question," September said, reviewing her conversation with Stefan at the hospital. "He said he walked to the school Tuesday morning."

"Do you know what he drives?" Wes asked.

She shook her head. "We'll have to look it up."

"I'm going to ask him about it, among other things, but I gotta get in the door first."

"I'd offer to help, but he'd rather see me even less than you."

"And D'Annibal doesn't want you on the case."

"And D'Annibal doesn't want me on the case," she agreed.

"It's a white Ford van," George said, from across the room. He rattled off the license plate number and Wes went back to his desk, picked up the small notebook he carried at all times and wrote it down.

An hour and a half later, September packed it in at the station and headed to Jake's house. She was almost there when she turned around and veered toward her old apartment. She had a couple of months left on her lease and it had helped her drag her feet on the move over to his place. Not that she didn't want to go there. She did. She was doing it this weekend, come hell or high water.

But it didn't mean she wasn't deep down scared of the commitment. Jake's long-term relationship with Loni was something to consider. It was over now. Jake definitely wanted it to be over, but it had bounced back and forth between them for over a decade. And though September knew Jake really cared about her, loved her, even, she didn't trust that his feelings would last. Loni, for good or for bad, had burrowed a place in his heart that maybe even he didn't understand how deep. September had been jilted for Loni once already, back in high school. Maybe Jake was completely free of her, or maybe he wasn't. He thought he was; that was for sure, but September had spent a lot of years protecting her heart and she wasn't fool enough to ignore the possibility of a relapse. Some couples thrived on unhealthy relationships. Maybe Jake wasn't as immune to that as he thought.

She walked up the front steps. She still got a jolt or two of pain from her wound when she moved too fast, but she was getting better daily. She didn't have to move quite so gingerly. Another week and she might be damn near back to fighting form.

Inside her apartment, the place felt cold and damp. Quickly, she turned on some lights to dispel the twilight gloom. She looked around the kitchen and living room, then walked down the hall to her bedroom, staring at her queen-size bed. Jake wanted to move it to his spare room.

Moving in with him. . . . A shiver ran through her. She was thrilled and scared at the same time.

She walked back to the kitchen and then the living room. Opening up the square chest she used as an end table, she pulled out the quilt her grandmother, Meemaw, had made for her. It was the one possession that truly mattered to her, and she tucked it under her arm as she left.

In her Pilot, she pulled out her cell phone from her messenger bag and put another call in to her brother. Preparing herself for his voice mail, she swallowed back the complaint on the tip of her tongue when Auggie answered on the fourth ring. “Wow, you’re alive,” she said instead.

“Alive and able to leap tall buildings in a single bound, or move your bed to Jake’s, whichever comes first. How are you doing, Nine?”

“Fine. Good. Pretty damn good, actually,” she added with a smile. What was she so worried about?

“Liv’ll come with me on Saturday, and maybe we can go out and get something to eat afterward?”

“God, a double date? Have we ever done that?” she asked her twin.

“No. You didn’t date, remember?”

“Neither did you.”

“I dated,” he protested.

“You just ‘had women.’ Not the same thing.” Until Olivia Dugan had entered his life, Auggie had been the proverbial love ’em and leave ’em kind of guy, more interested in his dangerous career than romantic relationships, an adrenaline junkie, for sure, and in that he hadn’t changed much.

“How about that Thai restaurant right by your place. Where is it?”

“On Pilkington. But it’s a ways from Jake’s,” she reminded him.

“But it’s good.”

“Hey, I’m in. You’re helping me move, I’ll even buy.”

“Wow.”

Although Auggie seemed ready and willing to help her move, she knew deep down he thought she was moving too fast with Jake, someone they’d both known most of their lives, as Jake's father, Nigel Westerly, had worked for Braden Rafferty at one time, running the Willows for many years before he'd bought his own vineyard and had gone into competition.

"Thanks," she said.

"I haven't done anything yet."

"I know. Thanks, anyway. Did you know I'm back at work?"

"You think D'Annibal hasn't been screaming for me to finish up and get back there?"

"Well, you're still employed by the Laurelton PD, last I checked."

Auggie had been working on a joint task force with the Portland police off and on for months. He'd finished one assignment, then had been involved with the killings at Zuma Software, which had introduced him to Liv, who'd become his own live-in girlfriend. It was odd, a twin thing, maybe, that September and Auggie had both become involved in serious relationships about the same time when neither of them had done this before. Auggie had been an uninvolved dater when his job allowed it, and September had pretty much stayed away from romance in general. Apart from her one-night stand with Jake in high school, she'd removed herself from the dating/romance game.

"I'll be back as soon as I can," he said.

"And when's that?"

"Why? Miss me?" he asked.

"The entire department is me, Wes, and George. That's all I'm saying."

"George still riding the swivel chair?"

"And being a pain in the butt. He still hardly manages to leave the squad room, even with Wes and me recovering."

"Huh. Gotta get back there just to see that and make sure you're actually getting better."

"I am. I can almost rotate my arm in a full circle."

"Impressive."

"See you Saturday, and thanks again."

"Okay," he said. Then, "Glad you're okay."

"Me, too."

She hung up, switched on the ignition, and drove away from the apartment where she'd lived for the past three years.

"Is there any other car available?" Lucky asked Mr. Blue. The truck had been everywhere, and it had been left overnight at the mall where she'd taken Harmak. Though she changed the plates on it regularly, it was still too noticeable. If Stefan told the police where he'd been kidnapped, and they investigated diligently enough, there was a chance they would check the mall cameras and see the truck in the lot. The stolen plates wouldn't lead to Mr. Blue, but the police would have the truck's description and that made it too risky to keep driving.

She'd already used it too much.

Mr. Blue was seated at the table, staring into the backyard, his eyes on the hummingbird feeder, which was swinging hard in the wind that had sprung up. Now he looked at Lucky. "I see," he said, thinking about it for a moment before turning his attention back to the window.

Lucky waited a few moments, then headed for her room, her mind already seeking another plan. She'd gone back to Harmak's house the evening before, intending one more quick drive by before cementing her nighttime plans. She had still been working out how to get Stefan's mother out of the house when she encountered the news crew that was parked all along the road and had to quickly drive through, pretending she was a lookie-loo.

Unnerved, she'd driven in the opposite direction of where she really wanted to go—the highway that led to Mr. Blue's. Instead, she was suddenly near Twin Oaks Elementary and at seven at night, the parking lot was mostly empty as the school day was long over. But there had been a few people milling about and Lucky had worried that the truck was too recognizable, too memorable. That's when she'd determined that she had to get different wheels.

She'd intended to pass by the school without taking her eyes off the road. Just drive on by. But she looked over. A group of parents were standing in a knot by the front door and looking toward the playground and basketball court where Lucky had left Stefan.

Oh. Shit.

All the way back to Mr. Blue's she'd been in a daze of fear. They were talking about what she'd done and she'd driven right by! It had sent her scurrying to her room, locking the door behind her, and it had taken her most of today to pull herself together and go in search of Mr. Blue. But Hiram had spent the day in his suite of rooms and Lucky had been unable to talk to him until just a few minutes before, and that had been unsatisfactory.

Like him, she now stared through her own window at the swinging feeder, its red plastic bottom nearly touching her pane. She was kinda embarrassed she'd run like such a girl. They weren't going to catch her yet. She still had too much to do. Fear wasn't going to stop her from completing her mission.

She was going to get a few more of the sick bastards before she went.

That was a promise.

Chapter Seven

Wenches Night at Gulliver's. Graham looked around the room and his eyes settled on a young woman in a wench costume—a loose white blouse cut low at the neck and a full red and brown and orange skirt stuffed with petticoats—and he immediately grew hard. She was the youngest-looking one at the bar, with thick, straight, dark hair—maybe a wig?—and soft pink lips. She wore white stockings with bouncing red tassels that just covered her knees, allowing a tantalizing peek of smooth, taut thigh skin every time her short skirt flipped up and gave him a glimpse of kingdom come. Oh, mama. He could *burst.*

She didn't look old enough to be there, but he wasn't going to complain. She didn't have much of a bosom, which was a bonus. He hated that matronly cow look. Liked the lithe, tight bodies of adolescents . . . preadolescents, actually, but he COULD NOT GO THERE. Nope. He wasn't a pedophile. They were sick fucks who didn't know how to stay inside the lines. He liked them young, sure, but, well, there were rules in society and he needed to abide by them. He did abide by them. Hadn't he hooked up with HER just for that reason? He didn't love HER. Didn't even really like her, if he were really being honest—and he was an honest man. Maybe too honest.

Too real. She was middle-aged—well, late forties—and had short kind of spiked hair that was bleached and gelled and reminded him of someone trying to look younger, though it wasn't working. She might be mistaken for a school teacher with twenty years under her belt, but actually she was a motivational speaker, one he'd met while attending one of her seminars—How to Beat the Recession and Not Let It Beat You! He'd signed up for other reasons, hadn't really planned on listening to her, but she'd commanded the room with a strong voice and penetrating stare. He'd immediately known she thought she was all that and more. Like she knew jack shit about anything. Ha!

He'd gone to the seminar to meet young women and he'd met her instead. She was as hot for him as he was lukewarm for her. She'd thought their first round of sex was mind blowing; he'd thought it was passable. But he'd needed a place to live away from his father with his wandering mind, so he'd moved in with HER about a month earlier and now the arrangement was about to choke him. From passable, his sex drive had nose-dived and now at bedtime it was all he could do to get it up. He had to dig deep into his secret-most fantasies to replace HER with a nubile youngster and even then it was difficult to perform.

But now, looking at the sweet wench with the childlike body, he felt things were coming together pretty good. He was alone for the next few nights. SHE was on the road for the first time since they'd moved in together, sending him texts from Phoenix, and then she was on to San Antonio, and possibly Louisville. And though she'd said in that whiny way of hers he found particularly irritating, "I just don't want to be away from you so long," he'd managed to placate her.

"I'll be right here," he told her, hiding his jubilation.

She'd laid a hand on his chest and looked at him through limpid eyes.

It was enough to make him gag, and he'd turned away a

little sharper than he'd intended and asked, "Want some coffee?" as he walked to the good old Mr. Coffee.

"Graham . . ."

"You won't be gone that long. A few days. Absence always makes the heart grow fonder, you know."

She hadn't bought it. She'd pouted, which really was an ugly expression for a woman of her age. Shouldn't be allowed. In fact, her whole shtick had given him the heebie-jeebies and he'd felt a shiver go right down his spine as he poured them each a cup of coffee. He'd managed to make himself turn back to her as she'd taken the cup and checked her watch. Her flight was coming up, so she added a liberal dose of cream (which was going right to her hips) and then she slurped down half the cup as he sipped his own—dark, black, and strong—and waited. He thought he'd go crazy with the waiting and then finally, finally, she sighed, poured the rest of her coffee into the sink, leaned up and kissed him on the lips. Then, after making a huge fuss about her bag and ticket and laptop and God knew what else, she'd headed through the mudroom and out the back door to the detached garage and the waiting taxi. She had never taken her car to the airport since the time she'd returned from a trip and found there was a long scratch in the paint on her baby.

He'd waited and watched the taxi turn the corner of the long driveway, then made himself wait a full ten minutes longer, just in case she came shooting back for some forgotten item. But she was truly gone.

He spent the first night alone masturbating to porno flicks. When she called from Phoenix he asked where she was staying and when she gave him the name of her hotel he called it up and asked to be connected to Daria Johannsen's room. He was put through immediately but he hung up before she answered. He would call later again, just to be sure, even though he believed she was there.

You just couldn't be too careful.

"Want something to drink?" the bartender asked him, breaking into his thoughts. The guy was wearing a white shirt with blousy sleeves, pirate style.

"Black coffee." He never drank alcohol if he could help it. Dulled the senses whereas caffeine sharpened everything.

"Okay." The bartender's tone was slightly skeptical. The crowd on Wenches Night was always in a party mood and nobody, but nobody, stayed sober. The sexier the wench outfit worn by the women, the lower the cost of their beer and drinks. If they played their cards right, sometimes they even got them for free. The little one he had his eye on should be given a damn gallon pitcher for the way she looked.

She was over by the door, one hand on the suit of armor standing at attention by the exit, which was what everyone did for luck—but my, oh, my, this lass was actively stroking the metal and what was that? Did she dare to dart a hand between its legs?

She was laughing when she caught his eye. Looked at him hard and sashayed over. For a brief moment he wondered if she were a professional, but no, there was just something too innocent about her. He could already imagine himself hard inside her, pounding away.

His coffee came and he slid the cup toward him, sensing his hands were trembling slightly.

"Hey, there," the girl said. "I recognize you."

His heart lurched hard, hurt. "What?"

"You're the man of my dreams." She smiled coquettishly.

He was a lot older than she was. A lot older. But women liked him. They liked the way he looked—he knew that. And he liked the game she was playing. "Would that be a wet dream?"

"The only kind that matters." She leaned forward and he could look right down the front of her blouse to her navel. He lifted his hand and almost ran it inside the bodice. Would have liked to grab one of her tiny tits. She was goddamn perfect.

"What the hell are you drinking, sugar?" she asked, seeing the coffee.

"Want to be at my sharpest for you."

"A little of the good stuff can do it better." She lifted her empty martini glass. "And look at me, without a drink."

"You should be getting yours free."

"So I keep telling them, but no one's paying any attention. I could really use some more vodka . . . maybe a little cranberry. . . ."

He tried to get the bartender's attention. Someone had called him Mark, so he yelled, "Mark, over here! Gotta wet the lady's whistle." Mark was either ignoring him or it was simply too loud to hear. "Hey, MARK!"

Mark pointed a finger at him without looking up from the drink he was mixing. "Gotcha."

"Pooh," she said, wrinkling her nose. "Maybe I should just get on top of the bar and strip."

No. He didn't want that. Didn't want anyone to see her but him. "I wouldn't mind a private dance," he said.

She eyed him, and there was something mysterious in her look that did things to his gut. He was shocked when she laid a hand over his on the bar and wrapped her little thumb inside, stroking the inside of his palm.

"Can you put your thumb in your mouth?" he asked, the words wrenched from him before he could stop himself.

She smiled silkily, pulled back her hand and plopped her thumb between those pink lips, making little sucking motions. "I'm kind of little," she said. "Barely old enough to be by myself."

He was half turned-on, half horrified. She was into the game and he wasn't sure he wanted it so blatant. "Don't act," he said. "Just be."

"Wanna fuck me, Daddy?" she whispered in his ear in a sweet voice that was nearly the end of his sanity.

Mark appeared at that moment. Gave the girl a dirty look and said, "What do you want?"

"Vodka and cranberry, for my girl, here," Graham told him.

"Watch yourself, Jilly," Mark said to her before turning away.

She stuck out her tongue at him, then whispered in Graham's ear, "He only gives free beers to the girls with big tits. I'm gonna just have to buy me a pair, I guess." She cupped her tiny breasts and thrust them forward.

"Don't do that." The wave of revulsion that swept through him damn near knocked him off his stool. "Keep the ones you've got."

"You like 'em?" she purred, sliding up against him. Her small body was warm and tight.

"Yes."

The vodka drink came and Graham pulled out his wallet. It was HER money. She had a cache in the closet that she didn't know he knew about. He'd discovered it one day while she was on a conference call in the den and couldn't be interrupted. Bored, he'd decided to explore and when he'd found the cache he'd lifted a few hundreds just to see if she noticed. If she did, he would play dumb and never do it again. If she didn't . . . which was how it had turned out . . . he would keep lifting a few bills every week . . . which was also how it had turned out.

So now, that was how he paid for Jilly's drink, with a Benjamin. It hurt a little. He hated to part with cash, but his wide-eyed date raised her brows at the sight of the money. "Oh, sweetie . . ." Her mouth curved upward.

She downed the drink so fast it worried him a bit. "One more," she said, "and I'll be ready." So he signaled Mark again and with a dark scowl the bartender brought another cranberry and vodka. Graham finished his coffee, feeling the caffeine run through his veins like a hot drug, while his "date" took a little more time with her second martini.

"Gotta go tinkle," she said, swishing away with a half-hitch stumble.

Mark sidled over as soon as she was out of sight. "She's a vodka whore," he said in an aside. "Will do whatever you want for some alcohol. She's legal. Barely. But she's got a big problem."

"Thanks." Graham was chilly. He didn't need this fucker's advice.

Mark inclined his head and moved away, duty done.

The bartender's intervention cooled Graham's ardor a bit. He needed to get out of here *without* the girl. Didn't want to be remembered later. If SHE ever found out his dick would be in a vise. Couldn't have that. He was just getting used to the lifestyle she provided and though having sex with her was getting tougher, maybe he could get some of those little blue pills, just for the times with her. As they said on TV: *an erection lasting more than four hours was a problem*—no shit—but he'd be lucky to get one to last four minutes. He just needed to be able to get it up for HER without trying, that's all.

Other times, like tonight, he could indulge his fantasies, and the little blue pills could go fuck themselves.

So thinking, he climbed off his seat and straightened his jacket. Mark looked over and he nodded and left, acting as if he were taking the bartender's advice. But he had no intention of leaving the hot little bitch. Vodka whore, huh? Well, then he was going to ply her with it until she was damn near unconscious, if that's what she wanted, and then he was going to plunge inside her over and over again. That's what *he* wanted. That's what *he* had to have.

He went back out to HER car, the Lexus that smelled like cinnamon Altoids; she always popped them like candy before a meeting. Had to have that fresh, fresh breath. Now, he did the same, crunching on the spicy, cinnamon flat circles as he sat in his car and waited.

A steady line of people went in and out of the bar. It took

another couple of hours before Jilly came out on the arm of some douche bag with spiky hair and a blue jacket over an aqua T-shirt, *Miami Vice*–style. She was staggering; the douche bag had to keep pulling her up by her arms to keep Jilly on her feet. Then suddenly she doubled over and puked lustily into the bushes beside the front door beneath the tableau of corn stalks and jack-o'-lanterns, which gave the douche bag pause. Still, he waited, and while she wiped the back of her hand over her mouth, he led her to a silver BMW, dropped her in the passenger seat and tore out of the parking lot. Graham had already switched on his ignition, and now he smoothly followed them onto the road.

He didn't know what he was doing. He was in a heightened state of arousal and he had the flagpole to prove it. He'd never done anything like this before, except in his dreams. In those, he was always riding some sweet piece of ass—an image of lovely Molly instantly popped into his head, though she was off limits and he fought it back—and she was moaning and crying and he was telling her to shush, that he loved her, that everything was going to be perfect but she just couldn't tell.

He followed Jilly and the douche bag to a swank apartment complex with open wrought iron gates and a glass workout room where he could see men and women in sleek workout gear, running on treadmills in front of the windows. So Douche had some money, maybe. Graham would bet there was some illegal enterprise in there somewhere.

He pulled into the lot and parked in a visitor's spot. Across the way, he could see Douche getting out of the BMW and Jilly staggering out of the passenger side. Douche yelled something at her, and Graham realized they knew each other this was more than a single night's hookup. "I'm not carrying you!" he snapped at her, and turned on his heel toward the door to the stairs. In a moment he was gone, but the girl was kneeling down at the side of the car, her ruffled colored skirts a bright sun around her.

His heart started a dull pounding. For a few moments he sat with his hands on the wheel, telling himself not to go there. But she was irresistible, and feeling like he was in a dream, he slid open the driver's door and moved toward her, his eyes scanning the surrounding area. Were there cameras? He didn't see any, and he was pretty careful about those things. He didn't want HER car, or anything he was about to do, captured on film.

"Hey," he said, kneeling down to her.

She was half crying, and when she looked up, her mascara was streaked. It was a complete turnoff, but Graham wasn't ready to give up, so he reached over and rubbed off the smudge with his thumb. "What are you doing here?" she mumbled.

"Who's the guy you're with?"

"Oh . . . Thomas. He's an *ass*." She sniffled some more.

"Do you live here?"

"No . . ." She waved an arm and let it slap down to her side.

"Can I give you a ride?"

She gazed up at him and blinked a couple of times. "Would you?"

For an answer he helped her to her feet.

"What's this?" Jake asked, picking up the quilt with its blocks framed in lavender from where September had laid it across the back of his couch.

"It's mine," she said, narrowing her eyes at the way he held it away from himself and snatching it away from him. "My Meemaw made it for me."

"Your Meemaw?"

"My grandmother."

He held up his hands in surrender at her militant tone, then slid a look at the colorful blanket that September had folded over her arms. "Did she choose those colors?"

September looked at the lavender and smiled. "No, that was all me. Third grade I wanted everything lavender, so Meemaw used it as the main color."

"Hmm."

"What are you, an interior designer?"

"I just can't picture you with such girlish tastes." Jake's gray eyes sparked with amusement. "You were always a tomboy with scraped knees and a bad attitude."

"Untrue! I didn't have a bad attitude. I just was competitive with my brother, and as an extension, all boys. But I liked lavender. And hot pink."

"And now all you wear is black and gray."

"Lavender and hot pink just don't scream authority, if you know what I mean. Besides, by fourth grade I was totally into my tomboy persona and liking army green."

"Ah, yes. That's what I remember."

He drew her into his arms and she closed her eyes and inhaled his scent. They'd shared hamburgers and fries he'd picked up from a local burger spot and had just finished cleaning up the kitchen together. She'd told him Auggie and Liv were on for Saturday's move, and that's when he'd looked around and noticed that she'd done some minor redecorating.

As they were settling down on the couch to watch television, his cell phone rang. It was on the counter and September was nearest to it, so she picked it up and looked down at the screen. "Loni," she read, trying to keep her tone neutral as she handed him the cell.

Jake had been reaching for the phone but now his hand stopped in midair.

"You don't want to talk to her?"

"No," he stressed. "Maybe I'll just let it go to voice mail."

They stayed frozen for several more rings, then with a

growl of frustration, Jake finally grabbed the cell and pressed the TALK button. "Loni?" He listened a moment, then clicked off. "She hung up."

Secretly September was glad. She was really trying to be adult about the whole Loni thing, but she'd never liked Jake's ex all that much when he was dating her, and she wasn't sure what she felt about her now that she was dating Jake. When she'd learned that Loni had been diagnosed with mental issues—bipolar being the most frequent label, though Jake seemed to think there might be something more at play—September had felt a twinge of regret that she'd had such mean thoughts about her. While she'd always kept her distance from Loni, not that it was a problem since they'd been classmates but never friends, now her relationship with Jake had kind of thrown her back into the ring with her.

She and Jake watched the television in silence together. A comedy with canned laughter was on, and when it ended, September wouldn't have been able to tell what the plot was about for the life of her, if called upon.

"What do you think I should do?" Jake asked after long minutes had elapsed.

"About Loni? I don't know."

"Her mother'll call me, if there's a problem. She always does."

He looked over at her and September gazed into his face and thought about how much she loved him. She didn't say it. It wasn't the time. He knew it anyway. But the way his eyes smiled, and the curve of his jaw and the sandpaper feel of his face all combined to fill her with awe at how much he meant to her.

"I'll call her tomorrow," Jake decided. "Tonight, I just want this." The arm that had been draped loosely around her shoulders suddenly tightened.

"Me, too," September agreed, aware that Jake's ex was probably desperately missing moments just like these.

"Here," he said, pulling the quilt down over them both as they stretched onto the couch together with Jake on his back and September half lying on him. Snuggled close to him and under Meemaw's quilt, September felt secure and safe, but she had to fight a niggling feeling in the back of her head that something awful could happen to steal away her fragile happiness.

I won't let it happen, she told herself firmly.

She just wished she believed herself.

Chapter Eight

As they wound down the long driveway to HER house, Graham looked over at his hot little babe. Not so hot now. Just silent and staring through the windshield and looking about twelve years old. Maybe ten. Or nine, if you didn't look too closely and just thought about the tightness of her flesh . . .

"Where are we?" she asked, when he'd parked and come around to her door, chivalrously helping her out.

"My place."

"God, I should go home."

Graham's jaw tightened, but he said, "I thought we could have some more martinis . . . vodka. The bar was getting damn loud."

"The bar . . . ? I was with Thomas. . . ." She was struggling to process. Alcohol had muddled the events of the evening.

"Thomas didn't look like he was being nice to you."

"He's a prick." She looked like she might cry again, and Graham half walked, half carried her to the back door, through the mudroom and kitchen to the hall bath. "Thought you might want to freshen up while I get the drinks."

She nodded a couple of times and closed the bathroom door.

Graham quickly went to the liquor cupboard and found the vodka. He grabbed a pitcher of grapefruit juice from the refrigerator and then scavenged HER glassware until he found two martini glasses. Jilly would probably hardly notice the change of mixer, he decided as he poured two drinks, filling hers with vodka and a splash of grapefruit juice, pouring just grapefruit juice into his own glass. Longingly, he threw a glance at the pot of strong coffee still in its stainless steel carafe, leftover from breakfast. There was a cup or two left, but he thought it would be better if he at least pretended they were drinking together.

She came out of the bathroom looking a thousand times better. She'd scrubbed off the makeup and her face looked fresh and young.

"You saved me," she said on a hiccup as Graham pressed the stem of her glass into her hand and picked up his own.

"A damsel in distress," he said, clinking the edge of her glass to his. The sharp *tink* as they touched sounded like a promise. She heard it, too, and some of her earlier sassiness returned.

"What do you wanna do?" she asked, sliding him a look out of the corner of her eyes. She sipped at her drink.

Graham thought about what she would look like without her clothes and he felt almost light-headed. "C'mere," he said, moving into her space. He put her free hand on his hard-on through his pants and she kept on drinking but her eyes sparkled. She reached out to set the martini onto the counter, but the glass hit so hard the stem shattered and most of her drink spilled over the edge and onto the floor.

"Whoops," she said, eyes wide, but he leaned forward fast and kissed those plump lips, smashing his own mouth down on hers. "Slow down, Daddy," she mumbled against his lips, but meanwhile she was unbuckling his pants and before Graham could think he was ripping off her clothes and his own and they were on the kitchen floor and he was pounding into her tightness just like he'd imagined, his mouth on her tiny tits.

He came so fast it was almost embarrassing. No little blue pills needed here!

She started giggling and it kinda put him off. "Couldn't make it to the bedroom, huh?"

He pulled out of her and looked down at her childlike form. It was so good. So tight. Dragging her to her feet, he half walked, half shoved her toward the master bedroom. "Be a good girl. Get on the bed."

"Like this?" she asked, crawling atop HER bed, her smooth ass waggling in front of his eyes. He had a vision of his semen leaking out of her onto HER comforter and he was instantly hard again. He jumped on the little bitch and took her from behind, one hand running up and down her narrow back. He threw back his head and grunted and groaned. She was so young. He couldn't get enough.

Finally, he collapsed on her. Vaguely, he realized she wasn't even breathing hard and a niggling doubt filled his mind. She wasn't into it, and she should be.

Wriggling beneath him until he was forced to pull out of her, she then flopped over and looked up at him through slitted eyes. "Got a smoke, Daddy?" she asked.

Her drunkenness had passed, apparently. She'd puked up most of her last drinks and had come out sober. And she'd only had a few sips of the martini he'd fixed her before she'd broken her glass.

"No smoking," he growled, feeling possessive of her. His mind was crowded with all kinds of wild ideas. He wanted to keep her for his very own. To have whenever he wanted. He couldn't let Daria find out. He wanted to stay here. After he'd lost his money and had to move in with his father, he'd damn near been suffocated by the old drab house and the neediness. Luckily Dad had a part-time nurse now, so he didn't have to do anything for him.

"I've got some smokes in my . . . oh, shit. I bet my purse is in Thomas's car." She looked dejected, then suddenly regarded him through eyes that were too knowing. "Or, maybe you've got something . . . smoother?"

"Like what?"

Lazily, she lifted one hand and brushed back her hair. "Oh, I don't know. Cocaine would work."

"I don't do drugs."

"I figured. You never were the type. Although you musta followed me to Thomas's. That's crazy, man!" she laughed.

"What do you mean, 'I was never the type'?"

"You don't remember me, do you?" she asked. When he just stared down at her, she said, "Mr. Harding, you were my sixth-grade teacher."

His whole body went numb. Cold. Frozen with fear. He couldn't breathe. Couldn't think! "You must have me mixed up with someone else," he managed in a tight voice.

"It's okay. I turned twenty-one last May. No one has to know I'm fucking my teacher!"

And she started laughing like a hyena, braying and braying.

So, he slapped her. Hard.

He hadn't meant to. It just happened. The laughter ended on a cry and she gazed at him in horror, one hand flying to her injured cheek.

"You hit me," she said in shock, her eyes wide with sudden fear.

And then she jumped off the bed and *ran*. Graham scrambled off himself, chasing her. She was naked and so was he, but she was screaming now. "Get the fuck away from me! Get *the fuck* away from me!"

He caught at her arm and she jerked away. She ran back through the kitchen to the mudroom but he grabbed her as she tried to yank open the back door. He spun her around and crowded her into the door panels. Her chest rose and fell in short, rapid gasps.

"Don't hurt me. Please, Mr. Harding."

"Don't call me that!"

"Please . . ."

"I'm not going to hurt you. I'm sorry."

Her eyes were wide. She wanted to believe him. She raised a trembling hand upward and he caught it and held it tight.

"I never want to hurt you," he gritted out, pushing her hand down toward his dick, which was already at attention again.

And she grabbed hard and yanked with all her strength. He yowled and threw her off him and then she was scrambling past him, running toward the living room, toward the entryway and the front door.

He stumbled after her, slamming a shoulder into the fireplace as he lurched around the corner from the kitchen toward the living room. One hand swept upward, to catch his balance, and he encountered the Maori figurine atop the mantel, a bronze piece of HER favorite aborigine art. Without thinking he snatched it up and ran with it held high. He got her as her hand twisted the doorknob, slamming the figurine into her skull. It made a satisfying *thunk* sound and then she went down in a heap on her back, jerked around for a few seconds, eyes open and staring upward, and then she went still.

Graham stared down at her in shock. Blood began pooling onto the entryway traverse beneath her cloud of dark hair.

Oh. Shit. *Fuck!*

He was frozen. Stunned.

"Oh, God . . ."

He didn't know how long he stood there. A moment. An eternity. But then his mind was working again, and he ran to the mudroom and into the garage, grabbing the tarp on the shelf near the door, the one Daria used to cover the bottom of the trunk every time she went to a nursery and brought home new plants or mulch or whatever for her garden.

In fact . . . Graham slid to a stop at the edge of the kitchen and the nook, casting an eye out the French doors to the backyard and beyond, to the garden. Daria's raspberry vines stretched outward toward the acreage behind her house. There wasn't another house for a good half mile or more in that field behind them.

He would bury her. How hard could it be? There were shovels and rakes and hoes and shit in the garden shed. He would bury the little cunt and no one would know.

Quickly, he went to the closet and grabbed his oldest jeans and a dark brown shirt, threw them on. His boots were in the garage and he ran back for them, slipping them on, aware that he was going to have to really clean them before Daria got back because she knew he never used them.

He went back to the entryway and stared down at her. He didn't like the way she was looking at him, so he closed her eyes. Then, carefully, he wrapped her body in the tarp and hauled it onto his shoulder. He carried it toward the sliding glass door that led to the back, swiveling around to make sure she wasn't leaving a trail of blood. Nothing. Good. He was safe. The tarp held all the blood.

He toted her out to the yard and the garden beyond, his hair lifting from the wild, spurting wind that seemed to be playing with him. He spent the next hour digging a grave deep enough that Daria wouldn't find her, then another half hour covering the body and trying to make it seem like the ground was undisturbed. The wind could be a help, he decided, and he moved some other dirt around, trying to make it look as if the top layer of soil had been blown around.

"No one has to know that you fucked your teacher," he said to the ground where she lay when he was finally finished. He was breathing hard and sweating like he'd been in a cardio workout.

Back inside he washed up in the shower, changed into sweats and a T-shirt, then grabbed paper towels and wiped up the blood on the entryway traverse, examining it closely when he was finished. Was there any trace left? Probably. Worried, he went into the kitchen and pulled a bottle of bleach from underneath the sink, then he took the bottle back to the entry and poured a circle onto the tiles. Carefully, paper towels in each hand, he wiped down the small space again, making sure he didn't get the bleach on the living room carpet that butted up to it. When he was finished he examined that edge of carpet fibers with critical eyes, recalling when he'd slammed the figurine into Jilly's head she'd gone down by the far wall. There was no blood spatter on the walls, as far as he could see, but he wiped them down, too, just in case.

The figurine was another matter. He took it to the kitchen sink and poured water over it. He wasn't sure what bleach might do to the finish, so he left that alone. He dried it off, then carefully put it back on the mantel.

Next, he went out back and turned on the hose, rinsing off the boots that he'd left by the sliders. He then wiped them down with more paper towels and put them back in the garage.

What to do with the bloody paper towels? They were the only evidence he needed to get rid of. Daria had a fireplace, but it was never used. In fact, she'd placed candles on a metal framework inside the firebox as fucking art.

He wasn't going to put them in the trash. No way. He had to get them far away from the house. So thinking, he pulled out a gallon-sized plastic bag and shoved the paper towels inside. He would take them to some public trash can. Take them out of the plastic bag to hasten decomposition, before tossing them in. Better yet, spread them out. One or two at one place, another somewhere else.

No way to trace them back to him.

Letting his breath out slowly, he suddenly felt better. He'd wait until the dead of night, when there was no one about, then he'd hit a couple of parks where people walked their dogs and put all that dog shit they collected in baggies into the trash cans. He'd shove the paper towels in there, too.

With time to kill, he decided to brew a pot of coffee. As he watched the dark fluid drip into the pot, he tried to remember the girl's full name. Jilly? Short for Gillian? Or, was she just Jill, and Jilly was a nickname? She was twenty-one, so it had been about ten years since she'd been his student. He felt he could almost remember her, but it escaped him. He was sick with relief that he hadn't left the bar with her. No one could know.

With faintly shaking fingers, he poured himself a large cup of coffee. His mug was the biggest in the house and Daria often teased him about it. As he drank it down, there was a little hum running under his skin, like an engine that hadn't been shut off. Adrenaline working overtime.

Vaguely, he realized he was recalling the moment that he'd slammed the figurine into her head. Screwing her had been delicious, but killing her had been, well, better. He couldn't stop thinking of how he'd felt when the statue had connected with her skull, the power that coursed through him as she collapsed. The scenario ran over and over in his mind, and for just a moment, he let himself think about having another girl. . . . Maybe this one could be just a little bit younger. . . . *Molly!*

No, not Molly. Never Molly.

But someone . . . that he could maybe keep around for a while. Just for a while.

His blood ran cold when he thought about what would happen if he were ever found out. Maybe he wouldn't keep her around after all.

Dead girls told no tales.

Chapter Nine

A rap on Lucky's bedroom door sent her shooting to wakefulness, the wisps of a recurring nightmare—where she was running from a burning pyre—evaporating into smoke.

"Mr. Blue . . . Hiram?" she called, afraid. He'd never knocked on her door before and if it wasn't him, then who was it?

"Come on out," he said through the panels.

Quickly she looked at the sky through her window and realized the gray light of dawn was edging out the blackness, giving faint visibility to the evergreens beyond the garden. She hurriedly grabbed the clothes she'd thrown on the floor the night before: a pair of jeans, black socks, a tan jog bra, and a black sweater. Padding sock-foot across the floor, she unlocked her door and peered into the garage. Mr. Blue was nowhere to be seen, so she shut her door and headed into the kitchen.

She'd expected him to be seated at the dining table, contemplating the outdoors, but he was in the kitchen, drinking from a mug of tea. She could smell the deep, loamy scent of the herbs he used to steep it.

This time his gaze was through the window over the sink, which looked out to the front of the house. He turned her way, then nodded toward the window. Lucky moved up beside him and looked out. In the front of the house was an older model champagne-colored compact sedan. A Nissan, she thought, though she couldn't quite tell from her angle of sight.

"Juan brought it up from California," Mr. Blue said.

Juan was Mr. Blue's contact who bought and sold up and down the West Coast and into Mexico many of the items Mr. Blue asked for. Lucky didn't know Juan's last name. She'd scarcely actually ever seen him, nor he her, which was all to the good. The less connections, the better. And every deal was made in cash. Maybe once upon a time Mr. Blue had trusted banks. She suspected he still had an account or two somewhere, but his dealings in herbs, narcotics, and various other illegal ventures were strictly in US dollars that were kept somewhere on the property.

"Thank you," Lucky said.

"The plates are good. Be careful." Then he handed her the keys and headed back down the hall to his rooms.

"The tox screen came back on Carrie Carter," Wes said when September arrived at work on Friday morning. "Looks like she died of an overdose of several different narcotics, Special K being one of them."

"Special K . . ." September repeated.

"Ketamine hydrochloride. Big in the nineties," George called from across the room.

"Big at raves, I know. I was just wondering where she got the stuff." September shot George an annoyed look.

"Some dealer in date-rape drugs," Wes said with a shrug as she continued on her way to the break room and her locker.

Ketamine hydrochloride was commonly used in veterinary clinics to anesthetize animals before surgery. Administered intravenously, the drug worked instantaneously, but it could also be taken orally—put in someone's drink, for instance—

and within minutes, the person would be dissociated from reality or completely out, depending on the amount ingested. Roofies and GHB were the two drugs September had encountered most often, roofies being what had been used on Chris Ballonni and probably Stefan.

When she walked back into the squad room with a cup of coffee, she asked, "So is J.J. leaning toward homicide now?"

"Results are inconclusive. I'm going to go talk to Carrie's mom again. See what shakes loose. She's convinced it was suicide, but there was no note. Can you come along?"

"Yeah. I've got a call into Rhoda Bernstein, one of the people on Chris Ballonni's mail route. She complained about Ballonni. He gave her daughter a piece of gum, which was something he did all the time, apparently."

"Not smart. Handing out gum to kids."

"Yeah, I know. She says he handed out gum to everyone. She doesn't see why anyone would object."

"She ain't living in the real world, then," Wes said.

"I'm hoping Mrs. Bernstein calls me today. I plan to talk to other people along her husband's route, and also his coworkers. But for now, I'm yours." She smiled.

"Let's go."

Wes went to grab his coat and September did the same. There was rain in the forecast but currently it was dry, though a sharp wind was hitting in surprisingly hard bursts. Half an hour later they were pulling up to the Carter home, a two-story saltbox that had seen better days. Originally painted dusty blue with white trim, the blue had faded unevenly and the white trim had yellowed and chipped. It was located about two miles from Foxglove Park.

Wes and September walked up to the front door together and Wes pressed the bell. He had to push it a second time before the door was opened by a woman with dark circles under her eyes and wearing a bathrobe that was as faded as the house.

"Mrs. Carter?" Wes asked. She nodded, silently opening the door as she stepped back to allow them entry. Wes had called and alerted her that they would be stopping by, so she'd been expecting them, but she hadn't gotten dressed in the meantime. Grief zapped energy, and there was no doubt that she was grieving.

"I'm Detective Rafferty," September introduced herself.

Debra Carter shook her hand limply. "Have a seat," she said, gesturing toward the living room before letting her arm drop. "Can I get you something to drink?"

"No, thank you, ma'am," Wes said. There was a slight drawl to his words that intensified his unconscious, cowboy-ish manner.

They sat down in two occasional chairs while Debra dropped onto one end of the couch, leaning above the overstuffed arm as if it were her total support.

"A reporter called me," she said. "They wanted to do an interview. . . ."

Wes looked to September and she realized he wanted her to take the lead. She rarely had while Gretchen was her partner because Gretchen just bulled right into the questions and damned the consequences.

Diffidently, she said, "Mrs. Carter, in your initial statement you indicated that you felt your daughter had committed suicide."

She had a box of tissues on the table beside her and she reached over and grabbed one up, crumpling it in one fist. "Carrie Lynne was heartbroken after Dan broke up with her. I didn't like him much, but she thought she was in love. When he left and moved to California, she quit her job and planned to go after him, but he told her not to. He was just moving on."

"How long ago was that?" September asked.

"About two months."

Wes had told her that he'd tried to contact Dan Quade, the boyfriend, but the guy was hard to find.

"Where did she work before she quit?" September asked.

"T.J. Maxx. I sent her to Dr. Rolfe. I told you that, didn't I?"

She was looking at Wes, who nodded and reminded her, "You said Dr. Rolfe prescribed the antidepressant found in her system."

"There's who killed her," she said sorrowfully. "The doctor."

"Mrs. Carter, there were other drugs found in her system, too," September said. "Ketamine hydrochloride was one."

"What's that?" She asked the question with no real interest.

Wes said, "It has a lot of street names: Special K, or just K, or OK, Vitamin K. It's a legal drug used for anesthesia but it's also a date-rape drug."

She focused on him, a line between her brows. "You think someone gave her a date-rape drug?"

"We don't know how it got into her system," September said.

Debra Carter sighed and wagged her head back and forth. "You know, I didn't want to go on vacation, but Charles, he loves Mexico, loves the sun. I knew Carrie wasn't doing well after Dan left. He was such a bad influence. If she had Special K or whatever it's called in her system, you can be sure he got it for her." She opened the tissue and smoothed it out. "I'd like to blame him, but she probably used it on herself. She was like that." She thought for a moment, and then added hopefully, "Unless Dr. Rolfe prescribed it for her . . . ?"

"That's unlikely. It's used by veterinarians to sedate animals before surgery," September explained.

She blinked several times. "It's for . . . animals?"

"Does that mean something to you?" September asked.

"The Stafford Animal Clinic is right across the parking lot from T.J. Maxx. That's how Carrie met Dan. His brother worked there at the clinic."

September looked at Wes, who had pulled out his notebook and a pen. He asked, "Do you know his brother's name?"

"No. Ben, maybe?" she tried, then shook her head. "I don't think he's there any longer. But maybe he got the drug for Dan and then Dan gave it to Carrie."

They asked her a few more questions, but Debra couldn't add anything further. She got up from the couch a few minutes later and walked them to the door, saying sadly, "I know it's your job to make sure this wasn't something else, but in the end, I think she just couldn't stand to be here anymore, so she found a way out."

When they were back in Wes's Range Rover, September said, "She blames herself for not being around when her daughter committed suicide."

Wes nodded. "Think she's going to forgive Charles for taking her away when her daughter needed her?"

"Not a chance. Let's go check with the Stafford Animal Clinic and see what they have to say."

"And then Dr. Rolfe."

"And Stefan," September reminded Wes. "When you interview him again, I want to know what he says."

"Your stepbrother doesn't want to talk to the police. No way, no how."

"Ex-stepbrother."

He snorted. "Yeah, right. I keep forgetting."

"I don't," September said, thinking about Stefan's secretive ways and sour disposition.

They were almost back to the station when her cell phone sang a familiar tune, *Hawaii Five-0,* which she'd assigned to her sister, July, more an homage to cop shows rather than because it had any real meaning for her sister. Once Auggie had sneaked *Dragnet* onto her phone as her default ring-tone, which she'd immediately taken off as soon as it rang and her brother collapsed into fits of laughter. Now, she kind of didn't care.

"Hey, there," she answered.

"September, my God. What the hell's up with Stefan?" July asked.

"Yeah, I know. First he said he was tied to the basketball hoop pole as a prank, then he recanted and said he was attacked."

"It's just like that other one, right?"

"Christopher Ballonni. Definitely looks like the same MO, but it could be a copycat."

"I always said he was a creep," she declared fervently. "But I kind of expected him to attack somebody, not the other way around."

"Stefan's too much of a coward," September heard herself say. She hadn't really thought of him in those terms—mainly, she didn't think about him, period—but once the words were out, she realized how true they were.

"Who's doing this?" July demanded.

"Don't know yet. We're following up." September couldn't keep her sister informed, but at this juncture there wasn't much to say anyway. "How are you feeling?"

"I should be asking you that," July said. "How's the neck?"

"More shoulder than neck. Fine. How's the baby?"

"So far so good."

Her older sister had determined that she was going to have a baby whether there was a father in the picture or not. To that end, July had gone to a fertility clinic and had been artificially inseminated with her daddy-of-choice's sperm. Originally, she'd thought her little girl was due in May, and she'd planned to name her after their sister, May, who'd been killed when September was in her early teens. But recent tests showed that the baby was further along and it looked like the little girl would be coming in April. The last September had heard, her sister was torn between still naming her baby May, in honor of their sister, or April, in keeping with the family tradition of naming children after the months of the year in which they were born. Not that July was really in love with that idea, but she'd admitted she liked the name April. Still, like September and Auggie, July scoffed at their father's strange obsession. Braden had just been lucky Auggie was born in August and September in September. If it had been the other way around, would he have kept with the tradition?

Whatever the case, July's daughter would be born in April.

"Have you talked to Dad about the fire?" July asked now.

"Over and over again. There's been no movement."

"What's that mean?"

"No new information. No new clues. It's still an open case."

"You know what I think."

"About Stefan? Yes," September said.

Though July wanted to believe Stefan was responsible for pouring gasoline in the garage at Castle Rafferty and setting fire to it, there was still no proof. It was all well and good to believe Stefan capable of such an act, but just not liking him wasn't reason enough to lay the blame at his feet. This was the same thing she'd told her sister damn near every time they spoke, so now she decided to go the other way. "Let's say you're right. Then why? Why would Stefan set the fire?"

"To destroy evidence," July responded promptly.

"What evidence?"

"Of a crime."

"You gotta be more specific."

"Maybe it was drugs," July said, grasping at straws. "Or computer files, or something, that incriminated him. God, it could be anything."

"The fire was set in the garage and it burned into the kitchen," September reminded her.

"And it burned up all those boxes of our stuff that Rosamund dragged back from the storage unit after you nailed her about tossing them out."

"Dad got on her, too," September reminded her.

"As well he should," she said roundly. "Don't get me

started on Evil Stepmother Number Two. Rosamund can't just erase everything Rafferty from the house. But back to my point: some of those boxes were filled with Stefan's old stuff."

"And Verna's. Which she had a fit about losing. None of us likes Rosamund much, but Verna can't stand her, and she won't forgive Rosamund for helping destroy her things. Verna's said that enough times for me to believe it. And as I recall, you blamed Rosamund for the fire first, before you blamed Stefan."

"I was just talking," July said airily. "Verna might have been upset about losing her things, but Stefan wasn't. You remember? He was just silent. Like he was afraid to open his mouth and give himself away. And Dad and Dash saw *a man* running away."

"They saw a figure running away," September corrected her. "Look, I really don't want to play devil's advocate, here. I just need more than a feeling before I can lay the fire at Stefan's feet."

"But now, there's this other thing, too. Someone tying him to a pole, almost naked, leaving him there? There's something going on with Stefan. I can't be the only one who feels that way."

She wasn't. September sensed something was up as well. She just wasn't as quick to rush to judgment. She couldn't afford to in her job.

"My partner's talking to him some more," September said, sliding a glance toward Wes as he drove. He wasn't exactly her partner, but it was going to be a while before Gretchen was back and she had an actual, bona fide one again.

"*You* need to talk to Stefan, Nine. You know him."

"Yeah, well . . ." She wasn't going to go into the whole problem about being semirelated to him.

"Call Dad," July suggested. "He wants to know more about the fire. Tell him about Stefan."

That was the last thing September planned to do, but she

hedged on the phone with July in order to end the conversation. She didn't want her father suddenly believing Stefan was responsible before there was any proof. That would be the worst, and it would give Braden another reason to be more in her life than he already was, something she absolutely did not want.

When she was off the phone, she ran through the previous conversation she'd had with her father before taking his call yesterday. It had been several days earlier. He'd reached her on her cell phone, and when she'd answered, he'd said, "Hello, September," in that stiff way of his that never ceased to put her on edge. "Thought I'd see how you are."

"I'm fine, Dad," she'd told him.

"Have, uh, you talked to August recently?"

This was damn near a mantra with her father. "If you want to talk to Auggie, you should call him yourself."

"I've tried calling, but he never seems to be available."

Of course he knew Auggie was avoiding him; Auggie was always avoiding him. She diverted him by saying, "Since you asked, Jake and I are doing fine. We're moving my furniture into his house this weekend."

"Oh? That's good, if it's what you want."

"Yep, it's what I want."

"You're giving up your apartment?"

Since she hadn't known he even knew she lived in an apartment, September had to mask her surprise. "Can't see any reason to hang on to it."

Her father had then made noise that it was okay that she was seeing Jake Westerly, but he certainly hadn't felt that way in the beginning of their relationship. Jake's father, Nigel, had once worked for Braden, and they'd had a falling out over September's mother, with the result being that Nigel had been abruptly fired. Not that Nigel and Kathryn had been involved. They hadn't been. But Nigel had been first on the scene of the single-car accident that had killed Kathryn and he'd been unable to save her. Based on his own tendency toward infidelity, Braden had assumed they'd been together as the accident had happened near the Willows, the Raffertys' winery, where Nigel worked.

After he was fired, Nigel had then purchased a vineyard and winery of his own, which he renamed Westerly Vale Vineyard, that was just down the road from the Willows. This had created even more conflict between the two men and their families. Recently Nigel had turned Westerly Vale over to Jake's brother, Colin, to run, and Braden had put July in charge of the Willows. Both sides were trying to get over the past, it seemed, with Braden making nice with the Westerlys ever since September and Jake had become a couple. She was glad for the thawing of hard feelings and she hoped the trend would continue. Because of the enmity between their families, September had never told her father how she'd hooked up with Jake for one night in high school. In fact, she'd never told any of her family except Auggie, who, it turned out, had known all along.

But there was no question that the accord between the Raffertys and the Westerlys was a work in progress, as was the continuing drama the Raffertys played out among themselves. After a recent family dinner that actually drew Auggie in, and where September dating a Westerly wasn't even the biggest news, Braden had been trying very hard to tear down the fences he'd erected himself in a fury of patriarchal control. Years before he'd almost lost Auggie completely in the process, and September had just been hanging around the fringes herself. Because she worked for their father, July had come to an uneasy peace with him, but even she had her issues. Their older brother, March, was the only one who seemed to have no problem with their father, but that was because he was a chip off the old block—autocratic, stern, and unrelenting to a fault—and he worked directly with Braden in his myriad of other financial endeavors.

That recent dinner had also been the scene of another revelation: the introduction of their half brother, Dashiell Vogt. July had brought him with her and initially they'd all thought she was dating him. Instead, they found out Dash was Braden's son through his affair with the family's one-time Rafferty housekeeper, Anna Marie Vogt. Anna had left her job without ever telling anyone, Braden included, that she was pregnant, but after his mother died Dash decided to look up his father. He'd introduced himself, and his claim, to July first, and then July dropped the bomb on the family all at once, which did not go over well with Evil Stepmother Number Two, Rosamund, among others. Braden had immediately denied Dash's existence, but in the end, DNA didn't lie.

Now, September felt Wes's gaze on her and she looked his way as they pulled into the parking lot of the strip center mall that held the Stafford Animal Clinic. She could see the sign for T.J. Maxx on a wing of the building set at a right angle to the clinic.

"This is it," she said as Wes parked.

"Yep."

They both climbed out of the car and headed inside.

Chapter Ten

Lucky circled the parking lot of Twin Oaks Elementary in the Nissan, searching for the source of that noxious aura. She'd left the California plates on the car as Mr. Blue had said they were good, but knew they would be more memorable than Oregon ones, in case anyone was watching. Still, the Nissan was a better choice than the truck, which was definitely too identifiable. If a cop ever attempted to pull her over, however, no matter what vehicle she was in, she was going to make a run for it for all she was worth. Her fake ID wouldn't hold up for long; technology was just too advanced. Right now, she had Mr. Blue's .38 in her glove box, too, so, with all those strikes against her should she be caught, she was one of the safest drivers on the road.

She'd dressed in a pair of black slacks, her only pair as she tended to wear jeans, T-shirts, and casual jackets or jogging gear as a rule. She'd had to buy herself a blouse, light gray and conservative, at Macy's. She'd thought about how she would approach the school and had changed her mind. She wasn't going to apply for a job, after all. She was going to present herself as a parent who was moving to the area and wanted to preview the school. No worry this way that someone might actually try to look up her employment record.

She gave a last check to her appearance in the rearview: the swept up light brown hair, fake pearl earrings, heavy face makeup, eyeliner and mascara, pale pink lips. She forced a smile at herself and recognized the cautiousness in her hazel eyes. She didn't think that could be helped.

On her way to the school, she'd turned down the street that would take her past Stefan Harmak's house. Maybe tonight she could find a way to sneak in with the .38. The thought of shooting him in cold blood bothered her more than she cared to admit. She didn't mind taking the sick fucks out, but she definitely preferred a more indirect method. Not that she couldn't do it. She could . . . she had . . . but generally only if they attacked her first.

As she'd drawn close to the Harmaks, she'd seen that the newspeople had dispersed for the moment. More pressing stories were always developing. Didn't mean they wouldn't be back, though. Stefan's mother's car was in the drive and as Lucky drove by, her heart jolted a bit to see the woman herself come outside with Stefan walking behind her, head down, in jeans and a sweatshirt, both of them heading toward her vehicle.

As soon as Lucky could, she turned onto the nearest street, pulling into one of the driveways, then backing out. She'd then faced back in the direction she'd come just in time to see Stefan's mother's car shoot past. Were they going to Twin Oaks? That was the direction they were taking. Even with her different look, Lucky had worried that she might run into Stefan at the school, so she'd followed them, hoping that wasn't the case.

It wasn't. Stefan's mother turned before she reached the school and, at a distance, Lucky had followed them. Stefan and/or the police hadn't found his van yet, apparently, as she'd had the impression he didn't want to be anywhere near his mother and yet they were carpooling.

They drove to a nearby Albertsons grocery store. Lucky had stayed back, watching through her windshield. Stefan's mother climbed out of the car and stared back in at her son through the open driver's door, clearly pissed. It appeared she wanted him to get out of the car and go in with her, and she wasn't moving until he did. With great reluctance and a slamming of the passenger door, Stefan stalked after her but stayed about ten feet away.

Lucky had smiled faintly, pulled out of the parking lot, and driven directly to Twin Oaks, reasonably sure that Stefan was otherwise engaged for the time being.

Now she walked toward the front of the school, mentally practicing what she would say. There was a guard at the door as she entered, which made her heart flutter a bit, but he just smiled at her as she made her way to the front counter and offices.

A woman at the desk with flyaway dyed brown hair and a harried look glanced up at her. "May I help you?"

Lucky launched into her rehearsed tale. "My name's Alicia Trent and my husband and I are moving to the area. Our son, Joshua, is a fourth grader, and he'll be finishing up at his school in Phoenix in December. I wanted to learn something about each elementary school."

"What would you like to know?" She shot a worried look toward the guard and there was something about it that made Lucky realize he was a new addition. Possibly because of what had happened to Stefan.

"Could you tell me a little about the principal and your teaching staff?"

"Amy Lazenby, our principal, is absolutely great. Everybody loves her. But I'm not sure she could see you right now. She's really busy. . . . Umm . . ." Her eyes tracked back to the guard again. "Our assistant principal, Dave DeForest, might be available. He could tell you about the fourth-grade teachers."

She swiveled around in her chair and looked at one of the closed doors behind the counter. "Just a minute," she said, then got up from the chair and, walking as if her knees seriously hurt, moved with an effort to the door and gave it a light knock. There was a soft rumble from an impatient voice within and the woman shot Lucky a smile, holding up one finger, before disappearing inside the room.

Lucky wasn't picking up the noxious sensation she had earlier. Maybe her quarry wasn't even here today. Maybe it had come from one of the kids' fathers instead of a teacher. All she knew for certain was that it had emanated from a man bent on ill deeds; she knew that feeling—scent—well.

Her eyes traveled over the flyers and posters and notes stuck into the bulletin boards that lined the walls surrounding the central desk. She realized a "Fun Night" was scheduled that very evening, a fund-raiser of some kind with a Halloween theme. As the woman made her way back to the counter, Lucky read the nameplate on her desk—MARYANNE.

"Would Joshua's potential teacher perhaps be at this 'Fun Night'?" Lucky asked her as she reseated herself with a long sigh.

She glanced at the poster. "Oh . . . yeah . . . Most all the teachers attend, if they can. The kids love it. We're just, umm . . . It may have to be canceled."

"Oh?"

But Maryanne didn't elaborate. Instead, she said, "I'm sorry, Dave is busy right now, too. You could wait . . . or maybe come back later?"

"Do you have some paperwork I could look at? A listing of staff, maybe . . . or a calendar of events . . . ?"

"Oh, sure." She yanked open a drawer and fingered through some files. "I might need to print off another yearly calendar." Muttering to herself, she slammed the drawer closed, got up again, and made her way slowly toward a back room whose door was open. Lucky could see a bank of file cabinets as Maryanne disappeared within.

Dave DeForest's office door suddenly opened and he called out impatiently, "Maryanne?" Then louder, "Maryanne?" When his gaze fell on Lucky he stopped short.

"Could I help you?" he asked, his whole manner changing as he came toward her with a smile.

Yeah, asshole, Lucky thought, knowing the paunchy man with the receding hairline liked what he saw. "Are you Mr. DeForest? I'm Alicia Trent. I'm doing a little research on your school in case my son goes here."

"Ah, yes." He, too, looked at the guard, a line drawing between his brows. Thinking a moment, he stuck his hands in his pockets and rocked back on his heels slightly. "I've got a little bit of time, as it turns out."

"Wonderful." Lucky smiled with an effort. He wasn't the man she sought. She was reading nothing from him other than the fact that he found her attractive and suddenly had lots of time to spend with her. But he was just the kind of male she couldn't stand: bullying, self-important, convinced he was God's gift to women. She didn't need her sixth sense to pick that up.

Once more she launched into her tale about her mythical husband and fourth-grader, finishing with ". . . so, we're deciding between two houses, and one of them's very close to Twin Oaks."

"Well, whichever house you decide on, you can still choose us as your son's elementary school. We're all part of the same school district and we have some flexibility. On this side of town, Twin Oaks and several other elementary schools feed into Brandyne Junior High and Rutherford High School. All great schools. On the other side, the elementary schools feed into Sunset Junior High and Laurelton High. The only issue is the bus route. If you buy on the other side of town, and want to come here, you'll have to drive your son."

"So, it doesn't matter where we buy, as long as it's in Laurelton."

"Well . . . we like to think Twin Oaks is the best, of course," he said with a slow smile.

"Of course."

"May I say, you don't look old enough to have a fourth-grade son," DeForest said.

Lucky eyed him sharply, worried for a moment before she realized he was just paying her a compliment, awkward as it sounded. Before she could respond, Maryanne trundled back with a sheaf of papers. "Gotta have that surgery or I'll be in a wheelchair before Christmas," she muttered. "Here's the school calendar. I don't have a full staff listing at hand, but I wrote down the names of the fourth-grade teachers. All of them are wonderful." She slid a look DeForest's way. "Your conference call is finished?"

"Yes. I was looking for you," he said coolly.

"I was getting Mrs. Trent what she asked for. My knees, you know."

DeForest didn't look like he much cared, though his gaze practically caressed Lucky. *Horny old dog,* she thought. She'd been down this road too many times to count, but sometimes horny old dogs could be useful to her.

"Can anyone attend Fun Night?" Lucky asked. "If it comes off?"

"Oh, it's definitely on," DeForest declared, shooting Maryanne a dark look. "We're very old-school here, so to speak. It's one of our primary fund-raisers, along with our silent auction in the spring, but the kids just love Fun Night. You can buy tickets at the door," he told Lucky. "Bring your son, and husband," he added as an afterthought.

"We don't know that it's really going to—" Maryanne began, looking at the guard.

"We had a strange thing happen," DeForest cut her off, his attention on Lucky, "and it got some parents worried. There was talk of postponing Fun Night."

"What happened?" Lucky asked, her pulse running light and fast.

Maryanne and DeForest exchanged looks and then he said reluctantly, "Someone pulled a prank on one of the aides. Tied him to a basketball pole, out in the playground."

"It was on the news," Maryanne said.

"That was at this school?" Lucky asked, pretending to be shocked.

"It was a prank. Nothing more," DeForest assured her quickly.

"Do they know who did it?" she asked.

Maryanne shook her head and rubbed her knees. "That's why we have the guard now. Amy wanted to be sure everyone was safe. You know, with the way things are now. If one of those psychos should come in here, I'd be a sitting duck with these knees. Couldn't help myself, let alone the kids!"

"Let's not get hysterical," DeForest said. "It was just a prank. We brought the guard in just to calm fears so we could still have Fun Night. I hope this doesn't put you off, Mrs. Trent."

"No. It's all about protecting the kids," she said with a nod.

"Here, here," DeForest said.

"Let's face it. There are some dangerous sickos out there," Lucky added, getting into her role.

"You can say that again," Maryanne declared.

"I hope you'll come," DeForest said.

"I might. But I'd be by myself. My husband and son are still in Phoenix."

A smile spread across DeForest's fleshy face. "Don't let that stop you. I'll be by myself, too."

Maryanne's head jerked around and she murmured, "I thought Patti was coming with you."

"She's not sure," he said stiffly.

Lucky left them eyeing each other like adversaries. She hadn't picked up any vibes, but maybe her quarry was still in the building, just too far away for her to feel him. Or, maybe he was a parent. Either way, she thought she might show up for Fun Night and see if she could pinpoint him. If Stefan Harmak decided to attend, of course, things could get too risky. *You have to get rid of him once and for all,* she reminded herself. From the news reports she'd seen, it didn't appear that he'd revealed that he'd been abducted by a woman, which gave her extra camouflage—except if she were to come face to face with him.

Climbing into the Sentra, her gaze traveled to the closed glove box and the gun that she knew lay within it. Though shooting him wasn't her preferred way to kill Harmak, it might be the most effective way to get the deed done.

Tonight, she thought.

The girl behind the circular counter at Stafford Animal Clinic had long brown hair tucked behind her right ear to show a line of silver studs marching along the inside shell of her ear. There was another stud beneath her lower lip that glimmered under the floodlights above the counter. "Can I help you?" she asked, just as loud, frantic barking broke out somewhere in one of the back rooms.

September and Wes showed her their identification and the girl's eyes widened. Wes said, "We'd like to speak to someone about an ex-employee named Ben Quade."

"Umm . . . there was no Ben Quade. We had a Bill Quade for a while, but he quit. Well, actually, he was kinda let go."

"Do you know why?" September asked.

She looked behind her, to the closed doors beyond. "Umm . . . I don't want to get anybody in trouble, but . . . he was caught trying to steal something."

"Ketamine hydrochloride?" September tried.

"Oh, you know." The girl relaxed. "Good Dr. Amato caught him and told him to get out. Bill was pretty pissed and dropped some F-bombs and left."

"Dr. Amato is one of the vets here?" September asked.

"Uh-huh."

"Is he here now?" she pushed.

She nodded, said, "I'll go get him," and went through the door to the back offices. A few minutes later an Asian man came through the door, wearing blue scrubs and a white lab coat. "Can I help you?" he asked, frowning.

Wes said, "We have a victim who died from a mixture of drugs, one of which was ketamine hydrochloride. She was dating a man named Dan Quade whose brother apparently worked here."

"Bill?" The doctor's face flushed scarlet. "I caught him in the act. He never got away with any of it. Believe me, I checked the inventory afterward and nothing was taken, so it didn't come from our clinic."

"You're certain," September said, which made him nod at her fast and hard.

"Bill was verbally abusive when he left. Said he knew where to get the stuff without having to steal from me. He kicked a hole in the wall on his way out! Luckily, he didn't hurt any of the animals."

"Did he ever mention his brother?" September asked.

"I didn't listen to him much," the doctor said.

"Did you know what he meant about where he would get the 'stuff'?" Wes asked.

Dr. Amato drew a deep breath through his nose. "He was a bad hire. If Zach hadn't recommended him, I would have never allowed him to be a part of our staff, even for the short time he was here."

"Who's Zach?" Wes asked.

"Dr. Swanson," the girl put in. "He's nice."

Dr. Amato's lips tightened. "My partner," he bit out. "His son was friends with Mr. Quade, apparently."

"Could we speak to Dr. Swanson?" September asked.

"When he gets back from Barbados, I'll have him call you," Amato said tightly.

Clearly, the doctor was nursing some seriously bad feelings. "Do you have an address or phone number for Bill Quade?" she tried.

"In his file, unless he's moved. I'll get it," he said.

He left and then returned a few minutes later with a Laurelton address and a cell phone number. They thanked him for his help, and as soon as they were out of earshot Wes said, "Think the doc was telling the truth?"

"Why?" September asked. "Did you think he wasn't?"

He shrugged as he pulled out his cell phone and plugged in the number Dr. Amato had given them. "He sure didn't want the blame blowin' back on him, but he seemed like the type who would know his inventory." He listened for a few moments, then clicked off. "Didn't go through," he said. "Maybe a prepaid that he ditched."

"Should we go to the address?" September asked.

"Yeah."

The apartment building was a *U* shape with three levels, all of the doors opening to the outside like a motel. They parked in a visitor's spot, then walked up the stairs to the second level, reaching the door that had been Bill Quade's unit and finding it ajar. Wes knocked lightly on the panels and the door swung inward on its own. "Hello? Mr. Quade?"

They could see through the living room to a hallway, and there was the sound of a toilet flushing. Then a man stepped into the hallway and glanced at the two of them standing in the doorway. "Hey," he said.

"Are you Bill Quade?" September asked.

He stilled, as if suddenly connecting on who they might be. "Who's asking?"

"I'm Detective Rafferty and this is—"

"Fuck!" he yelled. "I didn't take the goddamned stuff. Ask that fuckhead Dr. Amato! I didn't kill her!"

"You're talking about Carrie Lynne Carter?" September clarified.

"I didn't kill her. I didn't even get the stuff!"

"How did you know what killed her?" Wes asked.

That stopped him and he looked scared.

"May we come in?" September asked.

"No. Hell, no." He grabbed a coat off the couch and came toward them fast. They moved back to allow him onto the balcony. He looked to be in his early twenties with tousled, curly brown hair and a scruffy beard. He wore a pair of dirty jeans that looked like they were about to fall off his hips, a T-shirt that said *I Hate You,* and was shrugging into the jacket, which was giving him some trouble.

"How did you know what killed her?" Wes asked again.

"The K, man. The ketamine. You found it in her system, right?"

"Yes, but it hasn't been on the news," September said.

He looked confused for a moment. "Well, shit. Okay. Carrie wanted some, right? Dan wanted me to get it for her, but that was when they were together and they were going to just take some. Recreational drugs, man. You know how it goes. But I got caught by that shit Amato, and he fired my ass."

"So, how'd she get the ketamine in her system?" Wes asked.

"I don't know, man."

"Did your brother get it for her?" September asked.

"Ahh . . ." He sighed dolefully. "You think either Dan or I killed her? That's wrong, man. I'm sorry she's gone. I really am. I saw it on the news and just freaked. But she was too unstable, too into Dan, and he couldn't take it. But nobody killed her. She did it to herself, man."

"Where did she get the ketamine?" Wes pressed.

"Wasn't me. I didn't get it for her," he said with certainty, wagging his head back and forth. "Okay, I tried. I admit it, but I couldn't do it. I'm tellin' you, talk to Dr. Amato at the Stafford Animal Clinic. He'll tell ya."

"It was your brother who got it for her," September said.

Bill suddenly looked like he was about to cry. "No, man . . ." he said, but there wasn't much conviction in his voice.

"Where is your brother now?" September asked.

"I don't know. California . . . south . . . Tustin area, y'know?"

"I know Tustin. About an hour south of LA," Wes said.

"I guess. He just had to leave, y'know. She wasn't supposed to kill herself."

"Can you get us in touch with Dan? You got a phone number?" Wes pressed.

"Nah, he got rid of his phone. I don't know how to get ahold of him right now. I've called his friends, but he's like vanished. He does that sometimes. He probably doesn't even know about Carrie. He did like her a lot."

"Where did Dan get the ketamine?" September asked.

"I didn't say he got it for her."

"He got it for her," she said firmly. "He didn't mean for her to die from it, but he got it for her."

Bill ran his hands through his hair. "Man, this sucks," he said. "It was supposed to be *fun*."

"We're going to need to talk to Dan," Wes said.

"I don't know how. He's like in the wind, man."

"Where would Dan get the stuff?" September tried again. She was pretty sure they'd about wrung Bill dry, but it was worth a try.

"Not from me . . ." He trailed off, frowning.

"It would really help you if we had some other place to look, y'know?" September pushed.

"There's this guy Dan talked about. . . ." He looked over his shoulder, as if afraid to be overheard.

"What guy?" Wes asked quietly.

September knew Wes's brother had died from an overdose and that he was particularly invested in getting drug dealers off the street, so she let him take over the questioning.

"I don't know. He's myth, y'know?"

"Myth," Wes repeated.

"He's like a procurer, y'see? But his skin's all screwed-up like an alien, or something. Dan told me about him, but I don't know. It's kinda far-fetched." He emitted a short laugh.

"He has some kind of skin disease?" September asked. She was picturing this mythical drug dealer with a distorted face.

"No, he's just blue, man. Like I said—an alien. That's what Dan told me, anyway, but then Dan's full of shit most of the time."

"If Dan should contact you, you need to get in touch with us right away," Wes told him, holding his gaze.

"He's my brother, man."

"Dr. Amato said you tried to steal drugs," Wes reminded him. "We could be looking at you for years to come."

"Aww, man . . ."

They tried to get more information out of Bill, but he was both tapped out and worried sick that the law was after him. They left him on the balcony, pondering his options.

In the SUV Wes was quiet for a while, then said grimly, "I wanna get this 'procurer.'"

"I know."

By the time they were heading back toward the station it was almost past lunchtime. Both hungry, they took a trip through McDonald's.

"Kayleen took the doctor's orders to heart," Wes muttered around a bite of Quarter Pounder with cheese. "I've been eating soup and rice for way too long."

"You're not doing anything bad to yourself, are you?" September asked with a smile.

"Don't care if I am."

She looked at his flat stomach as they sat in the car. The bullet he'd taken in the abdomen had missed his stomach, but had played havoc with his intestines, from what she'd heard. "Glad you're okay."

"Back at 'cha," he said.

As they headed back to the station September said, "What about Carrie's psychiatrist? Dr. Rolfe?"

"Hasn't called me back yet," Wes said. "Nobody wants to talk to us about nothing."

"You got that right."

"I'm gonna call him again," Wes said determinedly. "This thing is looking like a suicide more and more, and I want the doctor to tell me what went on with Carrie Lynne. Jesus, they're sticky about giving out information, even when the patient's dead."

September said, "If we find this 'alien' dealer, we might be able to charge him with something."

"You think any of that's true?"

"Some of it." September shrugged.

They entered the station through the main entrance and encountered Guy Urlacher, back from sick leave. He immediately asked to see their identification and Wes just gave him a "don't fuck with me" look and headed for the door.

"It's policy," Guy said, a wheedle in his voice.

"You're making me wish for more Gayle," Wes said.

September broke down and showed him her ID and he reached under the counter and hit the release button. "You look kind of peaked," she told him as the door unlocked and Wes bolted through.

"Damn norovirus." Hearing himself, Guy looked shocked.

"Norovirus?" September asked.

"It's going around and it's . . . bad."

It was the most conversation September had ever had with Guy. Maybe it was the start of a new dawn, she mused, as she followed after Wes into the squad room.

She set her cell phone on her desk and it rang before she could go hang up her coat and messenger bag. Glancing down at it, she thought the number seemed familiar so she picked it up and clicked on. "Detective Rafferty."

"This is Rhoda Bernstein," a sharp, female voice greeted her. "You left a message that you wanted to talk to me about Christopher Ballonni."

"Yes, Mrs. Bernstein. Thank you for returning my call. I've taken over the investigation, and some new evidence has come to light in the Ballonni case."

"What does that mean?"

"There's been a second kidnap victim who was tied to a pole and left."

"Oh, yes. I saw that on the news, Detective," she stated flatly. "All this time since Christopher Ballonni died and now you're investigating. I guess nothing happens with you people until somebody else gets tied up."

"Yes, well . . ."

"I know he was a victim, but he wasn't the good guy everyone said he was. I suppose I should just be glad that you're finally doing something about it. That other detective that came and saw me . . ."

"Detective Chubb."

"Yes, him. Well, he didn't take me seriously, either."

September saw she was going to have to work around the enormous chip on the woman's shoulder. "Could you just go over it again with me? What happened between Mr. Ballonni and your daughter?"

"Nothing happened, because I was there," she snapped. "Missy was on the sidewalk when he pulled up to our mailbox. She knows better than to talk to strangers. But that day, she wasn't minding me, and she ran right over to his window.

She knew I would have a fit. And what did he do? He gave her a stick of gum! I came flying out of the house, I'll tell you. He told *me* I was overreacting. It was just wrong. You don't offer candy or gum to children. What is that teaching them, I ask you? I took that gum out of Missy's hands and threw it into the trash before she could open it. I probably should have saved it as evidence, or something. Anyway, all of a sudden, *I'm* the bad guy! Missy was crying and screaming at me. Totally out of control. I had to put her to bed right then, and it was only three o'clock in the afternoon!"

"And you placed a formal complaint against Mr. Ballonni that day?"

"You bet I did."

"Do you remember how long it was before Mr. Ballonni's death that he offered Missy the gum?" September asked.

"Three weeks to the day," she said with conviction.

"Had there been any other incidents where you felt Mr. Ballonni had been inappropriate with Missy?"

"He was always too friendly. I said so to LeeAnn Walters and Marnie Dramur over and over again, but they wouldn't do anything." She sniffed in derision.

The names were familiar. September glanced over at the row of files and wished she had the Ballonni file at hand. As it was, she had to dig through her memory. "Mrs. Walters and Mrs. Dramur live along your same mail route?"

"That's right."

"Did you ever witness Mr. Ballonni being inappropriate with anyone besides Missy?" September asked, dropping her coat and messenger bag on her desk and heading to the bank of files.

"You don't believe me, either, do you, Detective?" she demanded.

"I'm just gathering information."

"You sound just like the other detective." September could hear the disdain in her voice. "All careful and suspicious. I know what you're all thinking. That I'm an overprotective helicopter parent. I know. I've heard the term. Hovering over their kids too much. Well, I say kids don't get enough discipline these days. I don't mean being too harsh, but just making sure they do what they're told. How are they going to learn respect if we don't teach them, huh?"

September said, "Mrs. Bernstein, how old is Missy now?"

"She just turned seven. Why?"

"I was wondering if I could talk to her and—"

"Not on your life! I can't believe you people."

Holding on to her cool, September asked, "Do you know if she ever had any further contact with Mr. Ballonni?"

"She did not. After the gum incident, I watched for him to drive by. Whenever I saw him drop off the mail, I made sure Missy was inside the house. I can't say I was brokenhearted to learn someone killed him. Assisted suicide?" She made a sound of derision. "I always knew it was murder. It didn't take the incident with this new guy to tell me that. If you ask me, they're both pedophiles. Mark my words."

There was silence after that. September couldn't think of anything more to say, so she just thanked the woman and hung up. Wes was on the phone when she looked over at him, but George was sitting back in his chair, his gaze on her, a slight smile on his face.

"What?" September asked.

"Your voice got colder and colder. Who was that?"

"One of the mothers on Christopher Ballonni's mail route believes he was a pedophile. He tried to give her daughter, who's now seven, a stick of gum."

"What do you think?"

"She's hard to listen to, but . . . I don't know, maybe. I agree with her on one thing—somebody killed him. If someone believed he'd abused their child, I can't think of a better motive."

"Huh."

"She gave me the names of two other women in the file, so I guess I'll check with them. Chubb canvassed the neighborhood, interviewed most of them already, but maybe I'll learn something new."

"What does that say about your stepbrother?" George asked, his brows lifting.

"Nothing good," September admitted. What *did* that say about Stefan? "I've never liked him, but before I start down that road I want to be sure. And George?"

"Yeah?"

"He's my ex-stepbrother. I would really appreciate it if somebody around here could remember that."

Wes hung up at that moment and swung around. "Just got off with Dr. Flavel Rolfe. Too early to tell, but all signs point to Carrie committing suicide."

"Kinda what we thought. What did he say?" September asked.

"It's what he tried not to say. Didn't want to reveal anything about her that could help us until I went on about us believing her ex-boyfriend had killed her on purpose."

"You mean you lied," September said.

"Oh, yeah. Laid it on thick. Couldn't tell me anything until he thought we were railroading Dan Quade. Then, he started defending the man. He said Carrie went from crying her eyes out about Dan dumping her, to wanting to get back at him. What's the best way? The old 'you'll be sorry when I'm gone' stuff. Sounded like he felt Carrie played that card."

"Wouldn't she leave a suicide note?" September questioned him.

"Don't know." Wes shook his head. "I'll talk to D'Annibal. See what he wants to do."

"Jesus Christ!" George suddenly exploded.

Both September and Wes looked over at him. He was sopping up coffee he'd knocked over on his desk, but his eyes were on the computer. "That goddamn Pauline Kirby's ahead of you guys. I got headlines here. She's already saying exactly what you just decided, that Carter's death was a suicide. Bet it's on the five o'clock news."

"How?" Wes asked in disbelief. "I just talked to Rolfe."

"Debra Carter," September said. "She told us newspeople wanted interviews. She probably took the next call and told them what she thought."

"Did Kirby mention the ketamine?" Wes asked, looking at George.

"Shit, yeah." George finished sopping up his coffee.

Wes made a grumbling noise and then stalked across the room with purpose, turning toward the break room.

"Are you leaving?" September called after him.

"Yep. I'm going to interview your stepbrother again, one way or another. Let's get some traction going before Pauline Kirby does our job for us on that case, too."

September watched him leave, then slid a look over to George, who raised his hands to ward off what was coming. "He said stepbrother. I didn't," he reminded her.

Chapter Eleven

Fun Night started at six P.M. and ran until nine. The school parking lot was jammed as Lucky eased to a stop a little after six. She'd never gone to school herself, having been home-schooled, if you could call it that, by her adoptive father, bastard that he was. After his death, she'd wound up in foster care for a very short time, as she didn't trust either of the families who had taken her in, and she ran away from both of those homes as quickly as she could, disappearing into a world of street kids who lived a vagabond existence in and around Oregon coastal towns.

She recognized there were huge gaps in her education but didn't care. She wasn't like other people. Tonight all she wanted was to find the source of the scent she'd picked up, and then she'd get the hell out. Stefan Harmak was at home; she'd cruised by his house first in her black Lycra jogging suit and had been lucky enough to catch him walking by the front window of the house. It just didn't look like he was leaving. If he showed up, hopefully she would catch his aroma before he saw her. And she also hoped Dave DeForest wouldn't become too much of a problem, either, but if he did, she would just disappear into the night and he would probably assume her family hadn't moved into the area after all. There was no way he would connect her with what happened to Stefan earlier . . . or what she had planned for him later tonight.

She was now wearing the same outfit she'd worn when she'd gone to the school this morning. In between her trips to the school she'd changed in a restroom at the train station to her baseball cap, a heavy sweatshirt, and baggy pants to use as a disguise while she bought a disposable cell phone at a Portland convenience store. She'd also teamed that outfit with a pregnancy pad she'd purchased a while back, which she hoped, under the sweatshirt, gave the impression that she was overweight rather than with child. The disguise worked well enough because the guy behind the counter barely looked at her. She'd ditched that outfit and was back to looking like professional Alicia Trent.

Just before she climbed out of the Nissan, she threw another glance at the glove box where she'd stowed not only the .38 but also the stun gun, a pair of binoculars, and another small thermos of sweet dreams, her name for the roofie-laced concoction she'd learned to make. She hoped she would be able to use her preferred methodology on the man she was after, but there were always contingencies.

The cool wind whipped at her hair, which was pulled into a sleek bun. She didn't want to go inside the school just yet. She'd kind of hoped she could pick up her quarry when he was either going in or coming out, but so far that hadn't happened. She'd waited until the bulk of the people had arrived in order to stay in her car and just watch without anyone wondering why she didn't get out. If enough people went by and looked in at her, however, she would have to enter the school, just to keep from drawing too much attention to herself.

Exhaling a long breath, she decided to wait a few minutes more.

Come on, bastard. Show yourself.

* * *

"If you aren't going to call the police again, I will," Verna stated flatly, turning away from Stefan and toward the house phone.

Stefan felt his blood pressure rise. His mother had been on him all week. He'd told her he'd reported the theft of his van, but though she'd believed him in the beginning, she didn't anymore. Being stuck together in the house had eroded communication between them. Gone was the Verna who fawned over him. In her place was this other Verna, the one who'd blighted his childhood with mercurial moods that zipped from zero to sixty in one second, his mother changing from sickly sweet over-attention to a fulminating rage so fast it damn near made him dizzy.

"Leave it alone!" he demanded.

"This man took your van. They need to find him AND your van! I can't believe you're so complacent!"

"I'm not complacent. You think I want to keep riding in the car with you?"

"You should have told that detective who called. Pelligree."

"I'm seeing him tomorrow, okay? I told him I would." Stefan was already trying to think of ways out of that. He couldn't talk to the police again. They were too knowing. Too searching. And the media was just as bad, but he didn't have to talk to them if he didn't want to.

"I'm calling September tonight," Verna said with conviction. "They all still think you walked to school that morning. Let's give her the facts."

"I *did* walk to school," he said, but it sounded weak even to his own ears. Of course the reason the van was missing was because the bitch had taken it. He'd told Verna that someone must have stolen the van from the driveway at the same time he was being tied up, but that was way too much of a coincidence for her to believe. Over the last few days she'd gone from wanting to believe him to being annoyed and bullying. She just wouldn't leave him alone. But no matter how much she nagged he'd stuck with the lie rather than admit that he'd been taken at the mall and driven to the school.

He just wanted it all to go away.

And goddamn it, he wanted his van back, but not from the police. He didn't want them searching through it, maybe finding something he didn't want them to discover. What if the bitch who'd drugged him had planted some evidence inside? *God.* She would. She'd made him write those words. Who knew what else she was capable of?

"You can't call September," Stefan said.

"She's a member of the family," Verna snapped out. "I could call August, if you prefer."

Stefan didn't like September much, but he distrusted Auggie and March and all the rest of the Raffertys even more. They all had those blue eyes that looked so much alike and stared at him in silent judgment. He'd felt their disdain. He knew how much they detested him, and he detested them right back.

"The Raffertys aren't family," he muttered between his teeth.

"Oh, yes they are. And they can help you."

She swept up her cell phone from where she'd left it on the kitchen counter. He watched as she placed the call and put the cell to her ear.

Then he leapt forward and yanked it away from her, shutting it down.

"Stefan!" She was shocked and dismayed, her mouth opening like a fish.

"Just fucking leave me alone!"

With that he grabbed her keys off the table and slammed outside, breaking into a run for her car.

By six forty-five Fun Night was going strong. Lucky had gotten back in her car, half afraid to go into the school. She'd cracked her window and had listened to the faint blur of noise from within the school walls. Pulling out the binoculars, she'd lifted them to her eyes only occasionally, afraid someone would spy her. She could see the guard near the door and the table that was set up just inside with several women manning it, selling strings of tickets to . . . what, she wasn't sure. Games? Food? Prizes? Maybe all of the above.

Headlights washed over her car as another vehicle suddenly entered the lot. She barely had time to drop the binoculars, and feeling exposed, she got out of the Sentra again, pretending she'd just arrived. The car, a black Volvo sedan, circled around the lot, looking for a spot.

Her breath caught when he pulled up behind her as she pretended to be locking the car in preparation for going inside. She'd pulled on her black raincoat and the hood covered her head and obscured the sides of her face.

"Are you leaving?" the man behind the wheel asked hopefully.

"Sorry." She remote locked the car until it beeped at her.

He lifted a hand and moved on, but Lucky didn't think she could risk getting back in her car one more time, so she walked on leaden feet toward the school. As she approached, the hairs on her arms lifted. *He's here,* she thought. *In the school.*

If she got close enough, brushed against him, she would know who he was for certain, though she preferred to keep her distance until she was ready to make her move. Sometimes, she got too close too early. If that happened and he noticed her too much, she played off the feeling as if it were a mutual attraction, something they both felt. She would stare at her mark with wide, eager eyes, trying to seem more childlike and naive, attempting to tap into their sick desire. She was way too old for them, but she sure would catch their attention. That generally allowed enough time for her to put a plan into action.

But at the school? How was this going to work?

The women selling tickets looked up at her with big smiles as she entered the school. "Hello, there," one said. "How many tickets do you want? Twenty dollars worth?"

"Sure," Lucky said. Beside the table was a poster on an easel that depicted a big red thermometer with lines where numerical amounts were listed. The bulb at the bottom was full, but the neck of the thermometer was still empty, stopping short of the ten-thousand-dollar mark.

"Our goal is twenty-five thousand before the end of the year," the other woman said as the first one took Lucky's twenty-dollar bill and handed her a string of tickets. "This and the spring auction are our biggest fund-raisers."

"Be sure and go to the cakewalk," the first woman urged. "One of our families owns Laurelton Bakery and all the cakes come from there."

"It's one of our most popular attractions," the other one chimed in.

"Cakewalk," Lucky repeated, mystified.

"Just go straight on down to the end of the hall and turn right. It's in the west wing."

Lucky did as she was told. She felt naked and exposed in the sea of parents and children clogging the hallway. The parents were talking in clumps, and the kids were running from room to room, being constantly told to slow down.

Her whole being was alert. The sensation that had lifted the hairs on her arm hadn't dissipated, but neither had it increased.

Pop rock music emanated from the room where the cakewalk was held. Lucky paused in the doorway and watched adults and children moving in a circle, stepping from one numbered, plastic footprint stuck on the floor to another. Other people stood by in a line, waiting their turn apparently. Suddenly the music stopped and everyone jumped on a footprint and expectantly looked at the man in front.

"Okay," he yelled. He had fine wisps of hair covering a mostly bald head and he wore a huge smile. Reaching into a deep, cylindrical metal jar, he pulled out a ping-pong ball with a number on it. "Seventeen," he cried, and a little girl with pigtails started jumping up and down and shrieking, "It's me! It's me!"

"Well, go on and pick somethin' out," he said to her.

The girl ran forward, abandoning the number seventeen footprint, and raced to a long table where an array of cakes stood by. "That one!" the girl cried, pointing to a cake in the shape of a jack-o'-lantern with a candy corn mouth and black gumdrop eyes.

"Good choice," a woman said, from behind the table. She quickly boxed up the cake and handed it to the child. "Better take this to Mom or Dad," she said. As soon as the child was gone, she pulled out another box from a stack against the back wall, set it on the table and pulled out a cake from inside, placing it in the space left by the jack-o'-lantern one. This one was a square sheet cake with a skull on it in black icing.

"I want that one!" a boy declared, as the people who'd been walking in the circle departed and the people waiting in line took their places.

On their way out, the people who hadn't won were each handed a small plastic toy, apparently as a consolation prize. Lucky moved forward with the next round, intending to sit out the game, but another young girl said, "Get on your number or they won't do it!"

She opened her mouth to protest and felt heads swiveling her way. Feeling like she was having an out of body experience, she walked around the circle as the up-tempo music played. Suddenly the music cut out. She looked down and was standing on number twenty-six.

She watched the man in front plunge his arm into the metal cylinder and wondered if she could just leave her footprint.

"Number twenty-five!" he yelled.

The woman in front of Lucky let out a shriek of delight and danced her way to the table, picking up a cake with pink and lavender flowers, while Lucky felt her jumping pulse slowly return to normal. This was too much of an attention-getter.

She filed out with the rest of the losers, a little rattled. If she'd won it would have been a disaster. This was what came from walking in unprepared. She needed to go back outside and hope she could pick up her quarry's trail from the safety of her car. She was picking up her consolation prize, a little green alien, when she heard, "Hello, Mrs. Trent."

Sucking in a breath, she turned to see Dave DeForest. He was smiling at her, but there was a tightness to it that worried her until she saw that a woman was clinging to his arm. Ah, the wife had made it after all.

"Hi," Lucky said.

"How do you like Fun Night so far?" he asked as his wife's grip tightened.

Lucky almost felt sorry for her. "It's—fun." She felt her own smile freeze. She'd never been good at this kind of thing.

But DeForest didn't seem to notice. "PTA got rid of it, for a while. Kept the jog-a-thon, and the wrapping paper sale, you know, and of course, the silent auction."

"Mmmm," Lucky said.

"Fun Night's a lot of work, and everyone thought the kids would want to just stay home and play video games, that kind of thing. But it's turned out to be really popular."

His wife was practically digging her nails into her husband's arm. "After what happened this week, we really needed to come together," she said, her eyes sharply cataloguing everything about Lucky. This was no good.

"That's why we have the guard," DeForest told her, his jaw tightening a bit.

"Good," Lucky said, for lack of anything else to say.

The wife asked, "You have a boy, or a girl?"

"Patti, don't grill Mrs. Trent."

"I wasn't," she protested, but Lucky smiled and moved through the doorway into the hallway again.

Trying to pick up on the man's aura, she wandered the halls for another half hour, peeking into the rooms but staying well out of them. She watched kids shoot suction-cup darts at a bull's-eye, and drop a fishing line over a curtain that adults were clearly behind, slipping toys they'd caught onto the plastic hook at the end.

She couldn't get a trace of his scent, so she headed back toward the front door and stepped outside, afraid she'd taken a big chance for no good reason.

Pushing through the door, the odor hit her like a choking wave.

She looked up sharply. Across the lot, a man was just climbing into a black sedan. Lucky moved behind one of the posts that held up the portico over the front door, just in case there was any chance he might notice her and remember her later.

As he turned from the lot, she bent her head and walked rapidly to her car. He was in a black Lexus. And damn. He was moving fast.

She ran the last few yards. Jumped in the Nissan. Stuck the key in the ignition, fumbling a bit, swearing. Then she was after him. Pulling out to the street in the direction he'd taken, driving as fast as she dared within the speed limit.

At a cross street she glanced left, then right. She saw taillights far ahead. Had to be him. Driving carefully, but racing like a madwoman inside, she took off after him.

But when she got there, the taillights were wrong. Not the Lexus.

"Shit!"

She gazed frantically around. Ahead of the car she was following were familiar taillights. The Lexus! Chafing, she tried to figure out how to get around the loser driving like a turtle.

Damn, damn, damn! She couldn't lose him. She didn't want to ever go back to Twin Oaks again. She'd overplayed that hand. She needed to find him *now!*

And then, achingly slowly, the car in front of her took a left-hand turn and she hit the gas, watching the speedometer needle rise five miles above the speed limit. Even that was dangerous, but she had to risk it. Had to.

The Lexus wasn't waiting around. Her nerves were screaming as she followed after him, not closing the gap, but not falling behind. When he hit the freeway she was ten car lengths behind him and she breathed a little easier.

Where are you going, fucker?

A police siren suddenly wailed behind her. Her heart leapt to her throat. Oh, God! Oh, *God.* She was going to have to run for it. She couldn't be stopped. Not with the guns. Not with sweet dreams.

The lights flipped on behind her. A swirl of red and blue.

"Shit!" Lucky thought she might faint. No. Nope. Couldn't do that. Had to draw from her courage, rely on adrenaline, recognize that this could be her last hurrah.

Mouth dry, she touched her toe to the accelerator.

Woo-woo-woo-woo! The police car suddenly zoomed around her in a flash of color, its siren blaring.

Lucky gasped in shock and relief. The Lexus suddenly slowed down as if encountering a wall of water. She came up on him fast and had to tromp on the brakes. *Damn!* She drew back slowly, wondering if he'd noticed her abrupt rush toward him, her heart rate out of control, feeling slightly sick from the backlash of adrenaline.

But he was just as shaken by the police as she'd been, apparently, as the Lexus kept a slow, even pace after that, making it easy to follow him.

When he turned off the freeway onto a main artery into Laurelton, she eased even further back and then made the turn after him. When he slowed for the entrance to Bad Dog Pub, she drove around the corner and pulled to the curb on a side street with a view of the parking lot. She wasn't sure she should face him just yet. Too dangerous. She definitely needed a little more intel on the guy.

And she needed to go check on Stefan Harmak. Living with his mother was helpful, as it made it harder for him to lead a secret life. And leaving him tied to the pole had gotten him some unwanted notoriety. Still, she didn't trust him. Once more she kicked herself for not giving him an overdose when she had the chance. In fact, if she found that he'd managed to attack someone in these few days, she would feel completely responsible. She should have killed him. She should have—

Her thoughts shut off as she saw him walking back to the Lexus alone. He hadn't stayed at the pub long. What was that about? Had he made some kind of connection? It wasn't the kind of place for a pickup of the nature he was looking for.

Hmm . . .

Keeping way back in his rearview, she followed after him through traffic that grew lighter as he hit a residential neighborhood. When he turned into a long drive with landscaping that obscured the house, she drove on past and zigzagged up and down several streets until she felt secure in parking. She hadn't had time to change her clothes yet, so she just threw the bulky sweatshirt on over her blouse and grabbed her sneakers, running barefoot as she had no time to put on the shoes, skirting puddles that had formed from a light rain.

There was a brick wall that ran alongside the property, dividing it from the neighbors. On the neighbor's side, she moved cautiously through wet, cold grass, hugging the brick wall, hoping to God they didn't have a dog. The bricks changed to chain-link about two-thirds of the way down, and then the neighboring property ended at a chain-link section that branched out perpendicularly and encircled their property in a wide rectangle. Beyond the fence lay open field and the house at the end of the long drive that her quarry had turned into. The chain-link was the neighbor's fence because her target's property was not fenced past the perimeter of this fence. She could see a ranch style house with a detached garage. The garage door was down; presumably the Lexus was now inside, though there was a station wagon parked outside. A Chevrolet, she thought.

Light filtered from the living room, but she couldn't see anything from her angle. Quickly, she tossed her sneakers to the ground and squinched her cold feet inside, lacing them up.

Grabbing hold of the fence, she carefully climbed up, glad it wasn't so high that she couldn't work her way over. Dropping down, she slipped a little on the wet field grass, catching her sleeve, hearing the sweatshirt tear.

No time to see if she'd left any threads. Carefully, she made her way to the front of the house, staying to one side of the driveway, moving just near enough to see inside the window.

To her surprise she caught her quarry in a warm embrace with a middle-aged woman. She was just pulling back and smiling and talking in an animated way. He was stiffer, his body language hard to read.

Lucky had a moment where she wondered if she'd picked up on the wrong guy. She memorized his features. He was cruising into middle-age himself, she thought. Had a strong jaw and even features and all of his hair. Looked fairly handsome, as far as she could tell.

Then he suddenly looked straight out the window and she held her breath in shock. Nope. This was the right guy. She could *feel* it. She didn't know what the hell was going on with his female companion, but her radar never failed her.

From faraway she heard the mournful howl of a coyote and it raised the hair on her arms. When the woman suddenly grabbed his arm and led him away, out of sight, Lucky faded further into the shadows. Carefully, she slid along the shrubbery that lined the drive, ran lightly along the curving blacktop to the street, then slowed to a walk as she worked her way back to the Sentra.

The clock inside her head suddenly ticked loudly. The seconds of her life rapidly flying past.

Not much time left.

Time to take care of Stefan Harmak, she thought, and turned the nose of her car back toward his mother's split-level home.

Chapter Twelve

September sipped at the glass of red wine and watched Jake as he barbecued steaks in the rain. It was more a light drizzle, really—regular Oregon rain—but it was still wet and dark, and he wore a gray hoodie that obscured his face.

A few moments later he slid open the door from the back patio, a flurry of wind and rain following him inside. "Almost done," he said, picking up his own glass.

"Don't overcook mine. Please, God," September said.

"Not a chance." He smiled and she lifted one brow because the last time he'd barbecued they'd gotten distracted and her steak had turned into the proverbial shoe leather. Jake didn't mind his meat well done, but September felt medium rare could maybe have been left on the grill too long.

"So, tell me what Pauline Kirby said," he prompted her.

"Not until after you finish the steaks."

"Huh."

September didn't really want to talk about the voracious reporter who'd called her just as she was getting ready to leave work. Kirby had wanted information on Stefan Harmak and had called September, who she felt was her liaison within the department, a situation Lieutenant D'Annibal had actually set up as a means of fostering good relations with the press.

To that end, he'd given her September's name, making her the sacrificial lamb.

"I threw Wes under the bus," she admitted through the crack in the door Jake had left open. She watched him fork the steaks onto a platter before coming back inside, shutting the slider firmly behind him.

"How'd you do that?" he asked.

"I told her that Wes was investigating the attack on Stefan. Didn't mention that I was working the Ballonni angle."

"Wes can handle it."

"I know, but his surgery wasn't that long ago. The last thing he needs is Pauline climbing up his ass."

"There's an image."

"It doesn't matter anyway," September said glumly. "She only wants to talk to me."

"You're her favorite," Jake said with a grin.

"D'Annibal's fault. He threw *me* under the bus and now she thinks she can only talk to me." September reached into the refrigerator for the bowl of "salad in a bag" she'd mixed together. She set it on the table as Jake refilled their wine-glasses. It was after nine by the time they were seated at the kitchen table. September cut into her steak, forked a bite into her mouth that felt like it was melting on her tongue.

"Mmm. You're getting the hang of this," she said with a sigh.

"Yeah?"

"Yeah."

She could feel some of the tension dissolve from her shoulders. She hadn't told Jake everything about the call from Pauline Kirby. It wasn't just D'Annibal. The pushy reporter seemed to think they had some special bond since September had done the on-camera interview for her. Or, at least that was the tack Kirby took whenever she wanted something, and today she'd wanted information about Stefan Harmak. September had braced herself, expecting Pauline to have made the connection between herself and Stefan, but that hadn't happened. Maybe she didn't know yet, or maybe Pauline was playing her, which wasn't above the woman's tactics.

"She started out asking me a lot of questions about the fire at my dad's place," September admitted. "I thought, wow, really? The fire? Maybe there is something to July's theory. But it was just to show some interest. Like we're buddies and she had to ask."

"Ahh. What was she really after?" he asked.

"What they all want now. Information to connect what happened to Stefan with what happened to Christopher Ballonni. Like I said, I tried to give her to Wes, but she wouldn't go there. When I stalled her, she even moved on to questions about the suicide victim, Carrie Lynne Carter."

"That's definitely suicide?" Jake asked.

"It looks that way. Carrie Lynne's mother's convinced her daughter committed suicide, and maybe she did. Pauline was just fishing around, asking me any questions she could think of, but the real story she was after was Stefan's."

"Does she know yet that you and Stefan were related?"

"Nope. She didn't bring it up, and she probably would've if she had known. And I sure as hell wasn't going to tell her. Verna, Stefan, and I are not friends." She finished up her plate and picked up her glass of wine, heading toward the sink. "She's going to think I was purposely holding out on her when she does find out."

"You are." Jake followed and helped her clean off the dishes and load the dishwasher. Then September wiped down the table while Jake went at the grill with a steel brush.

Afterward, they moved into his family room with their wineglasses. September eased herself onto the couch, lying the length of it, while Jake took the recliner in front of the massive television. Once settled, they looked at each other and laughed, and Jake said in mock horror, "My God. We're like an old married couple."

"It's only because of my shoulder," September disagreed firmly. "As soon as I'm 100 percent I'll prove you wrong."

"Yeah?"

"I'll wrestle you for the recliner."

"You're going to have a fight on your hands," he warned her.

"Just so you know, this is all an act. I'm tougher than I look."

"Yeah, sure."

"You don't believe me?"

He was looking at her, his eyes full of amusement. September felt her breath catch a little as she smiled back. Sometimes she could hardly believe she and Jake were together and she was moving in. Actually, she was moved in already, really. Tomorrow they were just bringing in the final pieces of her furniture.

The wine created a pleasant lethargy and when Jake turned on the television her thoughts wandered to her work, her mind reviewing all the pieces of the cases that she'd been working, picking at loose threads. She was drifting off to sleep when a cell phone started ringing somewhere, and she jumped awake before she realized it was Jake's, not hers.

His phone was still in the kitchen, so he made a sound of annoyance as he got up to answer it. While he was gone, she eased onto her side and faced the television. Jake had turned the sound down low, probably when she started to fall asleep, and she could hear him as he answered his cell.

"Hello," he said in such a cautious way that September's ears pricked up. He was silent for a few moments, then he said, "Loni, I really can't talk right now." A pause. "Well, I'm kind of tied up this weekend, but maybe next week."

Jake's tone was polite but disinterested. It was clear he was just trying to put her off. September tried to tamp down her anxiety about Loni; Jake and his ex-girlfriend had been together too long for her to consider it nothing whenever Loni contacted him. But she could tell Jake didn't want to talk to her and it wasn't because September was in the other room.

Loni, apparently, heard it, too, because after another long silence, Jake's voice remarked, "I'm not available this weekend. That's all I said." Another pause while Loni spoke, then, "Sure. Just call. I'm around." After several attempts at trying to say good-bye, he was able to finally hang up.

A few minutes later he returned with a full glass of wine. "Did you hear that?" he asked.

"Loni wants to see you."

"Man . . ." He shook his head, then seeing her empty glass, said, "I'll get you another."

"No. No, thanks." She pulled herself to a sitting position. "I don't think I can handle another glass. I'm already passing out."

"Go ahead and pass out. Get some rest because we have a big moving day tomorrow." He came over to her and leaned in and kissed her, holding her tight. "Don't let her bother you."

"It doesn't bother me," she denied.

"Yeah, it does."

"Don't put words in my mouth."

"Okay, it doesn't bother you." He pulled back to look at her.

"Well, shit," September muttered, which made him laugh.

"One of these days she'll get the message," he assured her.

"Yeah."

"I'm serious." He kissed her on the mouth, then said lightly, "But I might have to marry you to get it across."

"Who says I'd marry you?"

"Will you marry me?"

She looked at him sideways. "No."

"Yes, you will."

"You're an arrogant son of a gun," she muttered.

"Oh, come on. When it's time, it'll be a yes, right?"

"What are you saying? Is this something I should be worrying about?" she asked.

"Worrying," Jake repeated on a groan. "That's not the word. *Anticipating*."

"Is this something I should be anticipating?" she asked.

He gazed at her hard, the smile slowly disappearing from his lips. "Yes," he said, and then he studiously ignored her while he channel-surfed, and September tried to tamp down the sweet feeling spreading through her like a hot wave.

Graham was sick with fear and excitement and a kind of latent desire left over from Jilly that he was seriously trying to channel toward Daria, though he was afraid if she pushed things, he wouldn't be able to perform. It was a delicate balance with him trying to trick his mind into believing she was something she wasn't, and he was afraid he was getting worse at it.

She'd come home unexpectedly and had damn near given him a heart attack. What if he'd been scoring with another girl and brought her home? God, he could just imagine Daria walking in on *that*!

The vision of what could have happened had left him on edge from the moment he'd walked in the house to find her already home. Her bags were on the dining room floor and he'd asked in a voice pitched much too high, "How did you get back?"

"I called a taxi." She'd come toward him then, but he'd turned to the living room, needing some space. She'd caught him in front of the window and embraced and kissed him.

"I meant, how did you get back so soon?" he said.

"I'll tell you later. I see you've been driving my car instead of your old station wagon," she added, a soft rebuke.

The Chrysler wagon was one of his dad's cars that Graham had appropriated. It wasn't that old, really, but it was a *station wagon*. He wanted a sports car, and he was determined to have one. He just didn't have the money right now. He'd been sucked into an investment that had turned out to be a Ponzi scheme, and he was still fighting his way out of it.

"C'mon," she'd said, clasping his hand and dragging him forward.

His pulse had fluttered in his head when he saw she was dragging him toward the bedroom—would she see the semen stain he'd quickly wiped off the cover? He'd dropped her hand, made some excuse and headed for the kitchen instead. A few moments later she'd returned, questions in her eyes, and for a moment he'd thought the gig was up. But then she'd said, "I'm hungry. Anything in the refrigerator?"

"Uh . . . some leftover pizza?"

"Good. Anything." She flopped a slice of pizza on a plate and put it in the microwave, then pulled out the stainless steel pot from the coffee maker and began making some of the horrible coffee she brewed.

Then his throat tightened when she said, "Something sticky here on the floor."

He didn't answer. Pretended he didn't either hear or care.

But she persisted. "What spilled?"

"Huh. Oh, some lemonade."

"Since when do you make lemonade?"

He shrugged. "I was thinking of making us some lemon drops. . . ."

"Well, look at you," she said, amused, which got under his skin.

After the pizza, he kind of thought he was home free, but suddenly, as if drawn by a magnet, she'd walked over to the mantel and picked up the Maori figurine, fingering it lovingly for a few moments.

Shit. *Fuck!* He'd thought he might die. He'd actually stumbled toward the entry hall, his gaze frantically searching for any telltale sign that would give him away: a drop of blood, a strand of long hair, *anything* he'd forgotten.

His movement only drew her closer to him, closer to the

scene of the crime. He'd stiffened when she'd suddenly wrapped her arms around his waist and drew herself against him, purring, "I missed all this, and you most of all."

She'd been gone less than three days.

"I missed you, too," he lied, his eyes traveling to the entry hall floor.

Then she was nuzzling his neck, but his mind was traveling. The one who hadn't been missed, apparently, was Jilly. There'd been nothing on the news about her disappearance. Maybe no one would report her. Maybe the douche bag she'd been with would just think she went home, wherever that was, and not worry about her. He sure hadn't seemed all that interested in having her around. Maybe she lived alone and it would be weeks, or months, before anyone thought about her again.

But no. That was fantasy shit talking. He couldn't lie to himself. Too dangerous. She'd been a student in his *sixth-grade class,* for God's sake! She'd gone to Twin Oaks ten years earlier. My God. *Ten years.* It made him feel old and now, being with HER, just made him feel older.

And Jilly . . . someone would realize she was gone and it could happen as early as tonight, twenty-four hours after he'd picked her up. Then what? They would trace her back to the guy with the BMW and probably then to Gulliver's. Mark, the bartender, would remember him, but *he'd left without her.* He'd made certain of that. She'd driven off with her boyfriend, or whatever he was, and no one knew about *him,* so he should be safe, he really should, but if they believed the boyfriend's story that he left her in the parking lot, and Mark talked too much, and the police started looking around, and—

"Graham," Daria said, breaking into his frantic thoughts.

"What?" he bit out. Everything about her just put his teeth on edge.

"I'm talking to you. Good heavens, where are you?" She

snapped her fingers in front of his face, smiling, but though she was teasing, he wanted to smash his fist into her mouth.

"Right here. What do you think?"

"No need to bite my head off. I just thought you'd be a little happier to see me."

She'd looked at him suggestively and had waggled her brows, letting him know she was ready to get laid. Graham had deliberately ignored all that, asking instead why she was home so early, both because he really wanted to know and to gain himself some time to work up some enthusiasm, since she clearly expected him to perform.

"Louisville canceled," she said, pursing her lips. "Not a big enough turnout, they said, but that just means the promoters didn't do their job. So, I just turned around in Phoenix and came back to surprise you."

"What about San Antonio?"

"No, that's next week, honey," she chided him. "You have to open your ears."

Open his ears? Bullshit. He kind of thought she'd purposely misled him. Maybe to check up on him? If that was the game she was playing, the stakes were getting higher by the minute.

Which made his dick suddenly jump up and now he found he *did* want to fuck her. Good. He would be able to perform and then she would get her trained circus animal to go through all his tricks.

But he didn't want to go to the bedroom. He wanted to throw her down in the entry hall, right *there,* where Jilly had fallen down. With that in mind, he grabbed her, sliding his hands up her arms.

"Oh, my," she said, in a kittenish tone that nearly turned his stomach, and he had to concentrate on the memory of Jilly's body, recalling the way it fell in a heap, the crunch of her skull cracking.

When he tried to move Daria from the window to the entry hall, she murmured, “What are you doing?”

“Shhh . . .”

“The bedroom’s that way,” she said, inclining her head in the other direction.

Like he didn’t know that. His anger leaped upward and it took all he had to keep from hitting her. With an effort, he said tautly, “Just go with me, here. And shut up,” he added, trying to make it sound light when his nerves were screaming at the sound of her metallic voice.

“Well, let me just get the blinds, Romeo.”

Easing out of his arms, she drew down the blinds over the front window. It gave him a moment’s pause when he thought about how he’d grabbed the Maori figurine and slammed it into Jilly’s head in full view of anyone looking in. But Daria’s house was down a long, winding private drive, and there was no way anyone had seen him.

But what if they had?

A ribbon of fear ran like ice through his veins, yet it only served to make him harder. He grabbed Daria again as soon as the blinds dropped and spun her around.

“Hey,” she said, surprised.

Before she could protest further, he pushed her into the entry hall and up against the wall, pressing his hot body against hers, letting her feel his rock-hard cock.

“Baby,” she whispered, thrilled, and he couldn’t . . . listen . . . anymore. He practically yanked her off her feet and onto the floor. She went down like wax, melting along the wall, and he climbed on top of her and shimmied up her skirt, running a hand up her leg. There was a moment of tangle with the pantyhose but he got them down to her ankles and undid his own zipper.

Then he was on her, grabbing her ass and pulling her hips upward. She gasped when he slammed into her and he had to close his ears to the sound.

Jilly . . . Jilly . . . Molly . . .

She was moaning and thrashing and clawing at him and he wanted her to stop being so aggressive.

"Ulysses," she breathed.

His first name. The one he detested and never used. Placing his hand over her mouth and pressing down, he pumped hard and fast and it was Molly who filled his vision with her soft green eyes and ponytail and he came with a loud groan of pleasure as he spilled into her. . . .

Into HER.

Just as that ugly thought penetrated, she bit the flesh at the base of his thumb.

With a howl of pain he jerked out of her. "You bit me, bitch!" he cried.

She struggled to her feet, ripping off the remnants of the pantyhose. "You damn near suffocated me!" she cried in return, and then she burst into tears. "Get out! Get the hell out of MY house!"

"Oh, baby . . ." Graham was instantly contrite, sick with worry that she meant it.

"No. Don't call me that. Get away from me." She staggered toward the kitchen and Graham quickly pulled up his pants and stumbled after her.

"I'm sorry," he said, pretending he was talking to Jilly. "I'm sorry. I didn't want any words. Just sighs . . ."

"I couldn't BREATHE!"

"I know. I'm sorry."

Her face was red and blotchy from her tears and she gazed at him through wounded eyes. It made him feel impatient, but he studiously kept the concerned look on his face.

"That wasn't what I meant to do."

"What did you mean to do?" she asked, partially mollified.

"Love you," he said, the words ashes in his mouth.

Slowly, he watched the transformation. She went from being ready to toss his ass onto the street, to getting all wet and ready for him again. He could practically see the transformation. "Then show me," she said, grabbing hunks of his shirt in both hands and marching him backwards down the hall to the bedroom. "Show me how much you love me."

She kicked the door shut behind them and threw him onto the bed. This wasn't going to work, Graham knew. She couldn't have control. The circus animal wouldn't be able to perform.

But then she pulled down his pants and wrapped her mouth around his cock and he closed his eyes and thought of Jilly . . . and then Molly . . . and then that girl in Mrs. Pearce's class with the rosebud lips . . . what was her name . . . ?

Chapter Thirteen

Stefan drove around the mall aimlessly in his mother's car. It was Fun Night evening, he realized, and his chest hurt that he wouldn't be able to go for fear they would all stare at him. He felt weak and angry and trapped. That detective—Pelligree—wouldn't let up. Kept calling and calling and calling, and the media people were relentless, too, though at least they'd stopped camping out on his doorstep, trying to make more of it than it was. But then his mother kept on bitching and bitching and bitching about the van. Jesus. It was enough to make him suicidal.

He couldn't go back to the school and have everyone stare at him, and anyway that bull dyke Lazenby didn't want him there, either. He could just tell. And he'd seen the way the rest of the staff, DeForest and Maryanne in particular, had looked at him, too. Like he was repugnant. Like there was something wrong with him. That he'd brought this all on himself.

Who was the bitch who'd zip-tied him? Why had she done this to him? If he found her, he'd kill her. Flat out. He'd grab her and throw her against a wall, or snap her neck, or lock her in a dark room and starve her to death. Something to inflict the same kind of pain she'd inflicted on him.

Why? Why? He hadn't *done* anything!

I WANT WHAT I CAN'T HAVE.

She'd read his mind, he thought with cold fear. She'd looked into his heart. She'd stopped him from having one of the beautiful girls, and now he was branded. They all knew he'd been kidnapped and forced to write those words and now everyone was speculating as to what they meant.

Oh, God.

He found he was crying and he swiped at the tears as he parked the vehicle, climbed out into a blustery night, heading toward the mall doors. It was damn near closing time. Maybe it was after closing. He didn't expect there to be any pretty girls around and there weren't, but he wandered the corridors anyway until the overhead speakers told him the mall was closing.

Outside again, he got back in his mother's car and drove along nearby streets, not caring which way he went. Fun Night was over by now, too, but though he wanted to drive by and see the kids standing outside the school, waiting for their parents or walking to their cars with them, he knew he couldn't. She'd done this to him and she was going to have to pay.

Why? Why?

It wasn't like his life was so great to begin with. He didn't know his father. Cecil Harmak was little more than a well-worn story to him, a story Verna pulled out about when she was young and working as a part-time model/dancer/actress. According to Verna, which might be just another big lie, she'd met him in Vegas where he was a high roller and she was a dancer. Stefan kinda thought she might have been with an escort service, but Verna refused to answer any in-depth questions. She married Cecil and they apparently tried living together just long enough to conceive him. After that, they stayed married but had separate residences until Cecil found a new, younger showgirl and finally decided to cut his ties with Verna and his son for good.

So, Verna had moved them to Los Angeles where she worked as a receptionist for a commercial real estate firm and left him with a string of babysitters. She hit the jackpot when she met Braden Rafferty, who was in town looking at potential real estate investments. His mother and Braden started a torrid affair that lasted until the day Braden's wife was killed in a car accident. Stunned and grieving, he broke it off with Verna only to have it start up again a few months later when Verna moved to Laurelton, Oregon, to be near him. Verna had her hooks in him but good by that time and wasn't going to let go. After they were wed, Stefan had moved into the sprawling Rafferty home with not only his mother and Braden, but also May, September, and Auggie Rafferty as well. Braden's eldest children, March and July, had already moved out, but it was still a houseful, and then May was killed while working at a fast food restaurant. It was just more drama, to Stefan's way of thinking—he didn't really even know May to care—and there was plenty enough drama already.

Stefan had tried to stay in the shadows during that time, but his mother took over the household as if all of it were her divine right. She even had him sit for a portrait that she then hung over the fireplace in the living room. God, that was embarrassing. Even he could admit he wasn't much of a subject.

The only good thing was that March and his wife, Jennifer, went through a divorce and March got partial custody of Evie.

Evie. Sweet, sweet Evie with the soft blond hair and easy smile. While he lived with the Raffertys, Stefan watched her grow from a toddler to a young girl. During those years he tried not to think about her too much, but March would bring her over and there she was, the only child in the big house.

He spent as much time as he could with her. At first no one paid attention. They even let him babysit her once and, heart in his throat, he took his camera into the bathroom while she was taking a bath. He managed to get several pictures before she really noticed, and then he hid the camera from her, hoping she would forget.

Later, he couldn't keep from touching her. Nothing wrong with smoothing his hand over her hair, was there? It nearly killed him when she started sidling away from him and he worried she would say something to her father. He told himself to stay back, act cool, but it was like he was possessed by an evil genie who whispered in his ear and told him to brush up against her in the kitchen, or the hallway, or the doorway to the garage. Anywhere that got tight enough for him to pretend to squeeze through at the same time she did.

She got wise to that, too, and started hanging back whenever he was around. Once, when her dad barked at her to get in the car, waving at her to follow him through the door at the end of the kitchen and through the garage, she looked directly at Stefan and asked, "Are you going outside now?" He'd shaken his head and frowned at her, like he didn't know what she was talking about, but Verna had been in the room and she'd glanced over sharply.

After that he'd had to content himself with his pictures. Evie's photos were tucked into a zippered book with a tiny lock on it along with a few other ones he'd taken of various little girls around a neighborhood pool one summer. One of the moms had started looking at him funny, though, so he'd had to leave there, too. But the pictures remained in a special box that he'd kept in his closet, tucked under a raft of old memorabilia from his elementary school days.

Then that cunt Rosamund Reece Rafferty caught Braden's eye and it was all over for Verna. In like *one hour* she and Stefan were out of the house. A screaming fight between Verna and Rosamund ensued with Rosamund practically pushing Stefan and Verna out the door. Verna swore she would never set foot inside that bastard's house again and that was just fine with Rosamund, who demanded their keys back.

But Stefan held on to his, swearing he'd lost it. He was afraid she would change the locks before he could get his belongings without his mother helping him retrieve them. He just couldn't let them find those pictures!

His worst fears were realized when Rosamund boxed up Verna's and his belongings and shipped them over to their new home, but when the boxes arrived, the one with the pictures was missing. Verna didn't get all her stuff either. Rosamund had been sloppy and didn't give a shit and just shoved their things around.

Verna had done a similar purge when she moved in, shoving the first Mrs. Rafferty—Kathryn's—personal items into boxes and storing them in the attic or garage or wherever, so she didn't care that some of her stuff was missing. She was almost glad there was something of hers still at the house.

Not so Stefan. He imagined over and over again what would happen were the pictures of Evie ever to be discovered. He lay awake night after night in a cold sweat, trying to think of a way to sneak into the house and get his things back. When he finally had an opportunity, the boxes were gone. Missing.

He'd finally gotten the courage to ask Rosamund where the boxes were, but it was to no avail. "There's nothing here," she told him, folding her arms over her chest. She was pretty and young and acted so high and mighty she could have been royalty. "I sent everything back to you," she insisted, and either she was a better actress than he would have ever imagined, or she really believed she had.

He'd wanted to throttle her on the spot but he'd had to stay back and seethe and worry in silence.

Time passed and after a couple of years the animosity passed between Rosamund and Verna, mainly because Verna wanted to make nice with Braden and to do that she had to put up with his new wife. Verna kept hoping Braden would provide for her beyond the alimony she lived on. Stefan thought she was being stupid and naïve, but at least the tensions started to ease up a bit and he and Verna could be around some.

Over time, he managed a few quick searches. Even took a trip to the attic and tiptoed around, scared shitless someone might hear him above them. But though there were boxes of other people's things, his weren't among them.

Then, at a recent Rafferty dinner, one which he and his mother were invited to, it came out that Rosamund had shipped the rest of Verna's and his belongings to a storage unit. It was September who, looking for some of her own childhood schoolwork, discovered Rosamund hadn't wanted any trace of Verna and Stefan, or any of Braden's children, around. September got all over Rosamund so she brought the boxes back.

Then, suddenly, things were worse. What if someone went through the boxes before he had a chance to find the pictures? Controlling a rising panic, Stefan had sneaked over to the house at his first opportunity, intending to rake through the boxes for his precious treasures, but when he got there Braden was at the house, talking with his bastard son, Dash. They damn near trapped him in the garage, and so he'd sneaked into the house and taken the fireplace lighter that was kept on the mantel above the fireplace. With a baleful look at the huge portrait of Rosamund with her baby bump, the one that had taken the place of his own, he'd hurried back to the garage and grabbed the gasoline can that had sat against one wall for years.

He could hear Braden and Dash come outside, saying good-bye to each other, ostensibly, but then loitering by the front door. He waited, breathless, in the dim interior of the garage. To his dismay, they walked back into the house together. Damn! He couldn't get caught in the garage.

There was no time. And there were too many boxes for

him to dig through. There was no other option but to douse them with gasoline, and he poured the entire can over anything he could find that looked combustible. His heart sank a bit at the loss of the pictures, but there was no other answer he could see.

Lighting the starter, he saw the little flame appear at the end like a beckoning finger.

He touched the flame to the gas.

Whoosh! It went up with a *bang!* A curtain of fire! He'd already opened the man-door to the outside and air swept in, feeding the flames, turning the place into an inferno so fast he damn near was singed and burned. When he staggered to the open door he was blown outside.

Stumbling to his feet, he ran across the wide yard and toward the road beyond. He heard someone yelling at him, either Dash or Braden, but there was smoke and fire and the roar of the flames. He ran and ran and ran, cutting through fields and across roads and through neighborhoods. By the time he collapsed he was three miles away. He'd left his car a long way back in the opposite direction, parked in a McDonald's lot that was about a half mile from the Rafferty property.

He finally slowed to a walk, exhausted, and it took him a couple of hours to circle back and find his way to his car. He really hadn't wanted to burn the place. He'd just wanted what was rightfully his. But in the back of his mind he'd known he might have to destroy the pictures, and sadly, that's what had happened.

And now . . . now *that bitch* had ruined him. Just when he'd thought it was the right time to take a few steps to find someone to love. If only she'd just left him alone!

It was so goddamned unfair!

He drove back to the house in a dark fury, his mind filled with injustice. As he pulled into the drive he could see the glow at the back of the house from Verna's bedroom. He hoped she was in bed. He didn't want to see her, maybe ever again. He didn't want to see anyone. He was going to have to leave the area. That was the truth of it. He couldn't stay here any longer and be a pariah.

Unfortunately, when he walked in the front door, Verna was standing right there in her bathrobe with that cold look on her face.

"I heard you come back." Her mouth was pinched. "Where did you go?"

"God, do I have to tell you everything?"

"You took my car," she pointed out, turning toward the kitchen. When he didn't immediately follow her, she stopped and whipped back, her voice a razor. "I put a call in to September and told her you hadn't been truthful."

"What?"

"That's right. I told her about your van. We have to find it, Stefan," she said, her tone changing to one of insistence. "I don't know what the hell you're hiding, but it's got to stop right now!"

"Fuckin' leave me be!" he screamed, and then he ran down the stairs to the basement level, racing to the sliding glass door and yanking it open, tearing into a rain-blasted night where the wind slapped at him in harsh gusts. He had no coat and he didn't give a goddamn.

Bitch. He hated her. *Hated* her. *Hated them all!*

He ran across the backyard with its crabgrass and weeds, to the back of the property where a sagging, dilapidated fence defined their property from the neighbors. Laurel hedges ran along both sides of the property line to his left and right. Braden had given Verna a "going away" settlement and there was the alimony, but it was a hell of a comedown from the life they'd led. His mother was stingy and careful, too, so they rented this cheaply built house while she hung on to her money like a miser. Stefan hated her for that, too.

She'd called *September*? He'd rather die first than admit he lied!

He was breathing hard, his head crashing with the fury of it. Slowly, he surfaced to realize he wasn't alone.

"Who's there?" he demanded, sensing another being in the dark shadows. He could just make out the intruder over by the edge of the laurels. In the gap between the hedge and the neighbor's fence.

He gasped and staggered back when a body materialized from the darkness, and then he realized it was *her*!

Holding a fucking *gun,* aimed at *him*!

"What!" he cried, holding up his hands, warding her off. "What the fuck?"

All his bravado disappeared. He broke and ran for the house, screaming. "Mom! Mom! *Mom!!*"

He'd left the sliding door open about a foot. He raced toward it.

Bang!

He shrieked and leapt forward. If he'd been hit, he couldn't feel it. He misjudged the door, slammed against it, struggled through the opening, then caught his ankle on the step and went sprawling forward onto the tile floor.

And then she was on him. On his back. Her fingers digging into his neck.

"Get up," she grated through her teeth.

"You shot me. You shot me!" He was scrambling across the tile, trying to throw her off, but she clung on hard.

"You just—"

He twisted away from her, flopped onto his back, saw the gun in her hand, grabbed for it. *I'll kill you,* he thought jubilantly. *I'll kill you!*

They fought for control. He could hear her breathing, hear his own. She was half on top of his legs while he shimmied backward. His eyes were on the gun.

"Fuck you, bitch!" he snarled, wresting the gun from her grip.

Bang!

This time he felt the shock of the hit. More like a slamming punch to his chest.

She scrambled backward, stunned. "You did it. You did it," she said in a shocked voice.

"I—I—" He was lying on his back. Tried to sit up. The gun slipped from his grasp, clattered to the floor. He watched her climb to a crouch, then to her full height, reaching over him, bending to pick it up.

He didn't feel pain, really. He felt . . . weird. His hand explored the front of his chest but there was nothing.

"Stefan?" His mother's voice called from above.

He tried to call back to her. Tried to talk. He watched blankly as his assailant walked backward, still holding the gun on him. She reached the slider door and backed out, disappearing into the night. He wanted to stop her. Shoot her like she'd shot him. Yell for help.

Only he couldn't do any of it.

"I heard something loud," his mother said.

The bullet had gone into his chest under his right armpit. With his left hand, he reached over and explored the small hole. He had trouble breathing. Pain filled him. His heart was racing. He'd wrenched the gun from her, yanked it away, pulled the trigger at the same moment.

And fucking shot himself.

He was laughing silently as Verna moved into his line of vision, looking down at him, frowning. "What's the matter with you?" she demanded.

"I've been shot," he managed to whisper.

"Is this some kind of joke?" she asked suspiciously.

And then he felt lethargy stealing over him, knew it for the seductive danger it was. "Don't let me die," he said, or maybe it was all in his head.

The last thing he remembered was his mother's mouth in a black oval as she opened it to scream his name.

Chapter Fourteen

September eased out of her shirt and looked in the bathroom mirror at the bandage that ran from the base of her neck and along the line of her collarbone. She might be able to get away without it. The incision just felt sore underneath it.

Coming from the bedroom, Jake glanced her way. "Why didn't Stefan tell you his van was missing?" he asked.

"I have no idea. Verna just wanted to report it stolen."

"Just by coincidence?" His eyes met hers in the mirror. He sounded as disbelieving as she felt.

"She just called, told me that and hung up. Stefan must have been in his van when he went to the school. His story's never added up. Maybe his kidnapper stole it. I don't know."

"Why would he lie?"

"God knows. But he's been lying from the get-go, that's for sure. Maybe I should go over there and talk to him tonight," she said. "He's avoided Wes for days and I don't give a damn anymore that he was my stepbrother. If I'm in his face, he'll have to talk to me."

With that she headed back into the bedroom with Jake at her heels. "You sure you want to go tonight?"

At the dresser she swept up her cell phone, unhooking it from its charger. "No, I'm tired. But I want answers."

"You planning to go in your bra?"

She gave him a look. "I was going to put my shirt back on."

"All right. Let's go."

"You don't need to go with me."

"I'm going."

"This is a police matter, Jake. We've talked about this."

"I'm not going to sit around here tonight while you're meeting with your unstable *ex*-stepbrother."

"I didn't say he was unstable." September picked up her shirt from where she'd tossed it across the bed and put it back on.

"Close enough."

"Well, I'm driving, then. I had one glass of wine to your three and it was hours ago."

"One and a half, but who's counting?"

"Jake, seriously. This is my job and I don't need your protection or help."

"Bull. Shit," he said succinctly.

Her cell phone rang in her hand. It was her default tone, so she looked down to see if she recognized the caller. "It's Verna again," she said, surprised, clicking on. "Hey, Verna, I was just—"

"He's been shot! He's been shot! He came back and shot him!" She was shrieking.

"Stefan? Stefan's been shot?"

"Yesssss!!!" She was full-on crying.

"Who shot him?"

"That man who tied him up. He came back and shot him!"

"Where are you?"

"At the house." Her voice was quivering. "I called 9-1-1. They're coming."

"Is Stefan okay?" September was terse.

"NOOOO!!!"

"Okay, Verna, I'll meet you at Laurelton General. If they take him somewhere else, call me and let me know."

"He shot him. . . . Why . . . ? Oh, God, why . . . ?"

"I'll see you as soon as I can. Remember to call me if plans change."

"Hurry . . . !"

It was all Lucky could do to keep from pressing her foot to the accelerator. She wanted to pour on the speed and put as many miles between her and Harmak as was humanly possible. Without really thinking it through, she headed toward Highway 26 and Mr. Blue and she drove for miles in a state of almost suspended animation.

The turnoff to Hiram's house and the hot springs came up on her right but she kept on going. The beach wasn't all that much farther. The western end of the North American continent. Nothing beyond that but salt water and lots of it. The Pacific Ocean lay black and uncaring and stretched to the horizon and Lucky wanted to see it, to drive right to it, to stare into its vast watery depths like she had when she was a little girl.

She'd thought of suicide a time or two while growing up. It had seemed like an answer, an end to the sexual abuse from her adoptive father, the much revered doctor who drank and used pills and was old enough to be her grandfather but had turned out to be no blood relation at all. The sea had beckoned to her then, but she'd resisted. Instead, she'd run to the end of the jetty one dark afternoon with the wind ripping at her clothes, half bent on throwing herself off the end, half hoping instead that the doctor would follow her out, that he would believe he could save her.

Her memory had failed her for years about the true events of that night, but it had slowly come back. Now she could recall the scene in sharp relief, remembering every moment, every emotion, her fear and her relief.

She'd begged him to take her to the jetty, had coaxed him, swore she would help him with his pills and be a good little girl. He'd acquiesced reluctantly, but he'd loved it the rare times she went along with him and so he did as she wanted.

She recalled the way the headlights from his car, two yellowy orbs, cut through the afternoon's gloom. At first she'd jumped out and run away, stumbling along the rocky crest of the jetty.

"Ani!" he'd yelled, getting out of the car but not coming after her. "Come back right now! It's not safe! The wind is . . ."

She'd run even faster, toward the end of the jetty.

"Ani!"

Then she'd tripped and half fallen, crying out.

"ANI!" he'd cried, growing frantic, moving slowly toward her. Unable to hurry to her aid. Either too high or too old to help.

And that's when her young mind had decided it was he who should die.

She'd returned to him, stumbling along, bleeding from the cut on her knee through her ripped jeans. She'd slipped her hand in his and tugged him toward the end. "I just want to go to the edge," she said. "Please."

"No . . ."

"Please."

If he hadn't been so inebriated, he would have resisted, but she'd given him several pills and made sure he washed them down with alcohol. He stumbled and swore as she tugged him forward, but she kept up the pressure, inexorably pulling him away from the car and safety and toward the end of the jetty. She'd read his emotions that night in the same way her sister could—a dark skill they both possessed, though Ani hadn't known of her twin until years later—and had seen how he planned to abuse her as soon as they were alone again. But she'd had her fill of *that,* so she led Dr. Parnell—as the local townspeople, who she believed now had turned a blind eye to his sexual abuse, had called him—toward the sea. As they got to the edge she took one last look at him, at his head and shoulders bent to the wind, his raincoat flapping around his pant legs, and thought, *And now you die.*

"This isn't safe," he muttered. Beyond, the ocean was a restless, black roar with curving lacy waves that rushed in and hit the jetty with a *boom* as it sprayed upward in a frigid plume.

His hand ran down her arm. He was silhouetted in the golden glow of the headlights, an old man with a black soul and a foul temper when crossed.

This isn't safe?

She'd looked down with one eye into the foaming, slapping waves that were reaching upward. She was drenched from the water tossed by the wind. Her teeth began to chatter and he made the mistake of pulling her closer, away from the edge.

Isn't *safe*?

She leaned away from him, as far as she dared, testing the bonds of gravity above the sea, knowing she could plunge into those depths herself, hit a submerged rock or simply smash into the boulders that made up the jetty itself.

But none of that happened.

"Ani," he cried one last time at the same moment she wrenched away, out of harm's way, sticking out her foot and overbalancing him. For a moment he teetered, arms pinwheeling. Then with a screeching wail he went head first over the edge, landing with a smack onto the boulders far below, lying there like a large, fallen black bird, his mouth a wide *O* of surprise. A greedy wave reached out and grabbed him, shaking him free from the rocks, turning him over as he was dragged into his watery grave.

She'd stared into his sightless eyes and felt a sense of satisfaction.

"Hey!" a voice had called out.

She'd turned in shock and saw a man hurrying toward her. Had he seen? Immediately, she hid her feelings and protested when he grabbed her arm and dragged her away from the edge. She'd been sick with fear until she realized he blamed the doctor for being drunken and foolish and putting both their lives at risk. Only then did she relax.

She heard later that the doctor's body had washed up about a week afterward, but by then she was already planning her first escape from her first foster home.

Now, she drove onward, her eyes drifting restlessly toward the glove box and the handgun inside. She had to get rid of it. It was Mr. Blue's, not hers, but now it had been used in a crime, and though she hadn't actually pulled the trigger and shot Harmak, who would believe her? No one. The gun had to go.

Her teeth were chattering. She'd left some loose ends, but it couldn't be helped. She hadn't expected Harmak to come shooting out from the house and when he had, she'd debated only a moment before deciding to confront him, regardless of the fact that his mother was still inside. But then he'd cut and run back toward the house and she'd shot at him, wildly, missing him entirely. She wasn't going to let him get away again, so she'd chased him inside and tackled him. She'd been running on pure instinct, fueled by adrenaline. She'd wanted to kick and hit and scratch and kill. He deserved to die. They all deserved to die.

But he'd turned the tables on her, grabbed for the gun, even managed to rip it from her hand. For a moment, her life flashed before her eyes. Truly. A clear picture of what she'd done and where she was going. But her only thought was: *I haven't had enough time yet!* Then Harmak jerked his arm back hard and pulled the trigger at the same time. Lucky half turned, expecting to be hit, but it hadn't happened.

Harmak made a grunt of surprise, then there was silence.

She'd looked at him then, staring down at his right side where the bullet had entered beneath his armpit.

"You did it," she sputtered. "You did it." She was more amazed than scared, and with his mother calling and calling she'd had the presence of mind to pick up the gun and her baseball cap, which had fallen off her head when she'd tackled him, then back quickly out of the room. Had she left fingerprints on the tile floor? A sample of her hair? Maybe. But those weren't the most pressing of her worries. When she'd run into the night, back across the Harmaks' lawn and to the edge of the laurel hedge, crossing to the next-door neighbor's property, she'd thought she was home free. She'd smashed the cap back on her head, then looked down at the gun in her other hand, the evidence of what she'd done. Immediately, she started stuffing it into the pocket of her jacket, running lightly, and was almost back to the road when she nearly ran smack into a couple in an embrace.

"Shit!" the guy said, when Lucky stumbled toward them from the depths of the backyard. At that moment a riot light came on from the top of the neighbor's house, blasting the area with near daylight illumination.

"Who are you?" the girl cried. "What are you doing?"

Lucky turned from the light. It hadn't been on when she'd sneaked along the hedge, but it was sure on now. It glowed blue white and Lucky could count the freckles on the girl's face. The boy wore a baseball cap backward but she could see his face as well, his dark eyes and open mouth and scruffy goatee.

She ducked her head, hoping the bill of her own cap would give her a shield, then she simply ran. Not to the car. The opposite direction and then around the block the long way, circling back to where she'd parked. She jumped in the car and turned on the ignition, already moving before the door was completely shut. Because it was the easiest route away, she drove in front of Twin Oaks Elementary where, through the front doors, she could see the janitor sweeping up the last bits of paper and decorations that had fallen to the floor.

How well had the couple seen her face? The house must have been where one of them lived. Were they now telling one of their parents about the woman who'd come from behind their house? Were the parents thinking about the popping sounds next door?

She shivered uncontrollably and couldn't stop.

More time. Just a little more time. That's all I need.

September pulled into the parking lot outside Emergency at Laurelton General, wheeled into an available spot, stamped on the parking brake and climbed out of the car. Jake jumped out of his side and soon they were hurrying toward the Emergency Room doors in tandem.

"I'm looking for Stefan Harmak. He was brought in by ambulance," September said to the first person she saw in scrubs, a nurse or nurse's aide. She flashed her ID.

"Oh . . . uh . . . Can you check with Maura? She's in admissions." The young woman waved vaguely in the direction of the cubicles along the west wall as she headed toward an outer hallway and elevators that led to the interior of the hospital. Most of the admittance cubicles were empty but there was a middle-aged woman inside one, helping a man who was sitting on the opposite side of the desk from her.

"Excuse me," September interrupted, earning her an annoyed look from the woman until her eyes focused on September's ID. "I'm looking for a gunshot victim, Stefan Harmak."

She nodded. "Go right on through the double doors. There's a button to push on the wall that—"

"I know the drill. Thanks."

As they moved toward the double doors, Jake murmured, "You're kinda good at being a hard-ass."

"Act like you're my partner." She punched the large, square button and the doors swung outward.

"You want me to be the good cop?"

"I want you to be the silent cop."

For the second time this week September was looking for Stefan in one of the curtained rooms, but she didn't have to look far. There was a flurry of activity at one of the rooms at the far side of the ward, closer to the doors that led to the OR. They were clearly prepping him for surgery.

Verna stepped out, her hand to her mouth, staring at what was presumably Stefan behind the curtain.

"Verna," September said, and the older woman whipped around at the sound of her name.

"Nine," she gulped. Her face was ravaged and her jacket and pants looked hastily donned. She threw herself into September's arms and started bawling, acting as if they were old friends when in reality they'd barely tolerated each other. It was the first time in September's memory that she'd called her by her nickname. "He's not doing well. There's internal damage in . . . in his chest. . . ."

"Is he awake?" September asked.

She nodded and then pulled back, clasping September's hand and dragging her closer. Stefan was on his back staring at the ceiling and the doctor was talking to him, telling him they were about to operate.

"Stefan," Verna said, a catch in her voice. "September's here."

Stefan's gaze moved to her.

"I'm going to find who did this," she told him.

"She took my van," he said, forming each word with an effort.

"She?" September questioned.

". . . at the mall and . . . she came over . . . got in the van."

"At the mall?" she repeated as he exhaled heavily. Mind racing, she asked, "This person—*woman*—got into your van at the mall, and then . . . you drove to Twin Oaks?" September didn't bother hiding her surprise.

". . . have to get her . . ." Stefan's tongue rimmed his lips.

"Excuse me," the doctor said firmly. "We need to get him to surgery."

"This woman who kidnapped you . . . she's the one who shot you tonight?" September pressed as they started to wheel Stefan away.

"Lucky," he said, his voice drifting back to her.

"What?" She wanted to follow them in but the doctor gave her a forbidding look and Stefan was pushed through doors that swung back against the wall and led to the operating rooms.

It was two hours almost exactly from Laurelton to Deception Bay, the little town on the Oregon coast where Lucky had spent her formative years, if you could call them that. She drove down Highway 101, which bisected the town and was its main street. She didn't recognize many of the businesses; it had been years since she'd been here. She'd mostly lived along the coast north of here, the Seaside area mainly, though one of her foster families had been even further north, Astoria and across the bridge to Long Beach, Washington. Mostly, however, she'd been on her own. Running away had been her go-to move for self-preservation, and by the time she was thirteen she had learned to stay under the radar with ease. Of course, she'd made the mistake of relying on a series of men who'd turned out to be users and abusers as well, but she'd learned from them. More than one had tried to rape her, even the seemingly friendly car thief and mechanic who'd shown her how to hot-wire cars. She'd thought they were friends and had stopped by his place after their last lesson, and he'd thrown her onto the bed and ripped off her clothes and was pushing her thighs apart while she screamed for him to stop. Clearly, he did not believe that no meant no. His determination fueled her own rage. With a strength built from boiling fury, she yanked out the table lamp and wrapped the cord around his neck. Ezekiel hardly even noticed, as he was busily pulling out his dick and, she suspected later, he was roiding out. She pulled and pulled and *pulled* on the cord until his face was dark red, his eyes were bugging out and he was burbling and spitting saliva, wrenching at the cord to no avail.

It took twenty minutes for her to believe he was really dead and release her grip. She rolled out from underneath him, wiped the place down for fingerprints, grabbed up the lamp and cord, hoped there wasn't any DNA evidence she'd missed, and walked out.

She'd pitched that lamp into the ocean, and that's what she planned to do with Mr. Blue's gun.

It was dark and the wind was slapping rain at the car in hard smacks as Lucky drove onto the jetty and bumped toward the low gate that kept cars from driving the entire length. The jetty was constructed of boulders with crushed rock on its top surface and it was wide enough for a car to drive all the way to the ocean, hence the gate.

Before she got out of the Sentra, Lucky turned off the interior light, then she stepped onto the heavy gravel, shut the door behind her and remote locked it. The gun was heavy in her pocket, and she held her elbow tight to her body to keep its appearance secret in case there was anyone about.

But there wasn't a soul. Not on a night like this. Bending her head to the wind, shrieking at her as if she were committing a heinous act, which in a way, she was, she moved to the end of the jetty and the dark waters below. She inched as close to the edge as she dared, pulled the gun from her pocket, wiped its surfaces with the hem of her jacket for good measure, then stretched her arm back and hurled it out as far as she could with as much strength as she could muster. It might come right back to shore. It might get sucked out never to be found again. Salt water would erase her identity from it, though she supposed the police could get a bullet match to it if it were recovered.

With that last thought, she huddled into her coat and hurried to her car, backed onto the highway and turned around in the direction she'd come. She didn't want anyone finding her here, seeing her make and model. Nope. It was time to return home to Mr. Blue's and the relative safety of her room, and hope to hell that the bullet that had entered Stefan Harmak's chest had killed him.

Then she could think about the man from Twin Oaks. The one she'd followed. The sexual abuser. He hadn't seemed like a parent. She just hadn't gotten that vibe. So, maybe he was a teacher, or a teacher's aide like Stefan.

Either way, she was going to take him out, though she would have to come up with a new plan. No more leaving them zip-tied to poles nearly naked, hoping to humiliate them as well as hasten their demise. No sweet dreams. No more fooling around. She didn't have that much time, so as soon as she lured him into a trap, she was going to have to kill him.

Chapter Fifteen

September rolled out of bed, bleary eyed. It was early Saturday morning, and she was scheduled to have the day off, but after last night's shooting, she knew she was going to have to go in. And she wanted to. She wanted to know who this woman was who had kidnapped Stefan and stolen his van.

Jake flopped an arm her way. "Where ya goin'?" he mumbled.

"To the station. Lots to be done."

"Come back . . ." He rolled onto his side, then squinted his eyes open to slits.

"Later." She smiled and ducked into the bathroom and the shower. When she stepped back into the bedroom fifteen minutes later in her bathrobe, combing her wet hair, she saw the bed was empty.

"Hey," he said from the hallway, and September jumped as if goosed.

"You scared me!"

"Sorry." He looked anything but repentant. "You want me to come with you?"

"To the station? No, of course not. Besides, I need you to move my bed here."

"I don't want you to be alone."

"I won't be alone. D'Annibal will be there and Wes and George. We're all going in today. Doesn't matter that it's Saturday with all this going on." She paused. "You're gonna drive me crazy, Jake. You know that, right?"

"I just keep seeing him attacking you with the knife."

For a moment she, too, was taken back to that moment when she was on the ground, fighting for her life. "We're both going to have to get over it," she told him soberly. "And I am really, really okay."

"I liked being with you at the hospital last night," he admitted.

"I liked having you there, too. Did I tell you how much I appreciated you keeping your mouth shut?"

"Hardest thing I ever had to do."

She leaned up and kissed him lightly. "Go back to bed. Maybe I can make it a half day. I just gave D'Annibal the basics last night, and I've got to fill Wes in further, too. This is really his case and I just ran with it."

"Your stepmother called you," he reminded her. "Not the other way around. Ex-stepmother," he corrected himself before she could.

"That's what I told the lieutenant, but he still wants me off the case. Either way, I need to write up a report. I also want to see if Wes found out anything on the boyfriend and his ketamine 'procurer.'"

"You don't have enough people working at that place," he complained.

"I know. But at least I'm clocking overtime."

"Tell your lieutenant to hire somebody and give you all a break."

"You sound like Gretchen. She told me to tell D'Annibal to get his head out of his ass and leave me on Stefan's case. Needless to say, I didn't follow her advice."

"Not sure how I feel about being compared to Gretchen."

September smiled. Jake and her previous partner circled each other like feral dogs, neither trusting the other. "And then, I also want to check with some people along Christopher Ballonni's mail route."

"Thought you said you didn't believe helicopter mom's complaints about Ballonni and her daughter."

"Ahh, yes . . . I told you about Mrs. Bernstein," she said, more to herself than him.

"Who am I going to tell?"

"I don't know. Loni?"

Jake pulled back and skewered her with a *look*. "Not likely."

"Forget it." September was embarrassed at showing her insecurities. She'd made it a rule to keep her feelings about his ex to herself, a rule she seemed destined to break over and over again.

"You just want to get out of moving today," he accused her lightly, letting her off the hook.

"My master plan." She smiled again. "I put a BOLO out on Stefan's van. Maybe it's turned up."

"BOLO . . . is for?"

"Be on the lookout."

Jake pulled her into his arms for a deeper kiss, which went on for a while and damn near turned into something else. She was teetering on the fence between desire and duty when he finally broke the kiss and pushed her gently away. "Fine, go," he said. "The earlier you get there, the sooner you'll be back."

"I'll call you," she said, fighting down the stirring in her own blood. He could get to her so fast.

Quickly, before she changed her mind, she stripped off her robe and threw on her work clothes—a dark shirt and slacks—as fast as she could, grabbed her messenger bag and a piece of toast and headed out.

* * *

There were very few cars around as September pulled into the department forty minutes later. She parked in the rear lot, but the back door, which was used to bring in all manner of people under arrest, was generally locked, so she didn't bother even trying it. She circled the building instead and entered through the front. Guy Urlacher was back at his post, eyeing September as if he'd never seen her before, so with an inward sigh she pulled out her ID.

"You're working weekends now," she observed.

"The temp's sick, so I said I'd come in."

"Overtime?"

Though she'd meant it more like a commiserating party because yes, she was working on her day off, too, he glared at her like she'd insulted him. "I was out with that virus the first part of the week."

Guy was a difficult conversationalist at the best of times, and September sometimes wanted to bang her head against the wall just for trying to deal with him.

Luckily, he let her in without another word and she entered the squad room to find she was the only one around. She sent a look toward D'Annibal's office, but the curtains were open and the room was dark and empty. She'd expected to see either Wes or George already here, but their desks looked as if they hadn't been touched since the day before.

Huh.

After dropping off her messenger bag in her locker, she poured out the cold coffee from the night before and set up the coffee machine to brew a new pot. Then she checked the break room vending machine for anything edible and seized on a packet of peanut M&M's, which she munched on the way back to her desk. She could have gone further down the hall to see who else was around, but instead she picked up her desk phone, throwing a glance at the clock to check the time. Nine o'clock.

She called Wes's cell first. When he didn't answer, she

grabbed up her own cell phone, which she'd laid on her desktop, and quickly texted him. **Where are you?**

She waited a couple of minutes, but when he didn't immediately get back to her she made a call to the hospital about Stefan and was put through to the nurses' station. After explaining who she was, she was told that the doctor would be in later and could give her more information but that the patient was in CCU, the critical care unit. She asked if he'd been put there because there were complications, or whether this was standard procedure after surgery, but the nurse maddeningly just told her the doctor would call her when he was in.

Fine.

She thought about phoning Verna, but scratched that idea in favor of calling Janet Ballonni again. She wanted to ask her once more about Mrs. Bernstein. Clearly there was no love lost between the two women. Rhoda Bernstein thought Christopher Ballonni Sr. had crossed the line with her daughter and it kind of sounded like she was right. But Janet Ballonni didn't feel that way. She was defensive about her husband, but September hoped to get her to open up a little more. Be a little more friendly.

And then, maybe she would gain permission to speak to Chris Jr. It was a long shot, but she wasn't going to get anywhere unless she massaged the woman's feelings.

Checking the clock again—nine-thirty—she wondered if it were too early on a Saturday morning to call her. If she wanted to become the woman's "friend" maybe she should wait till after ten.

"Hello?" a drowsy, young male voice answered, blowing her thoughts to smithereens.

"Hello," September said, thinking fast. "This is Detective Rafferty with the Laurelton Police Department. I'm sorry to call so early. Is this Chris Jr.?"

"Umm . . . yeah . . ."

"I was actually hoping I could talk to you," she admitted.

"Yeah? I saw you were the police department on caller ID."

"Oh."

"My mom isn't here. She's got Pilates, or something."

"I see." She pretended to consider. The tricky issue of parental consent wasn't something to be ignored. Still, she didn't want to lose this tenuous connection.

"I—umm—kinda want to talk to you, too. That's why I picked up the phone," he said.

"You mean you want to talk about your dad?"

"Mom told me that you came by. It was you, right?"

"Yes."

"I don't wanna screw things up, y'know. But my dad, he wasn't—umm—he kinda lied about stuff, I think."

"What kind of lies?"

He didn't answer for a few moments and September waited, holding her breath. "There was this girl at school," he carefully launched in again. "A couple years ago. We weren't really friends but we knew each other."

"You were in the same class?"

"Uh-huh. But . . . her family moved away. But I kinda knew her. She knew my dad because they used to live on his mail route."

The route.

When it didn't appear he was going to continue, September prompted, "Did this girl say something about your dad?"

"No . . . no . . . not really."

"What do you mean, 'not really'?"

"It's just that she wanted to talk to me but I didn't want to talk to her."

"About your dad," September tried.

"My girlfriend, Jamie? She doesn't like my mom and Mom doesn't like her, either, but she thinks my dad lied about a bunch of stuff, too. She kinda thinks my dad did something. I don't think so. I mean, no. He wouldn't."

There were questions in the words, as if he hoped September would rush in and agree with him. "What did Jamie say about your dad?"

"That he was a perv. But she says mean things all the time."

September's pulse was running light and fast, like it did when she was closing in on a breakthrough. In this case, she sensed it was more a confirmation of her own amorphous thoughts and feelings. "Do you know why she said that about your dad?"

"It's all kind of screwed up, y'know? Jamie didn't like my dad, either, but she was nice after he was dead when everybody else was looking at me weird." A tremor had entered his voice.

"Why did Jamie think your dad lied?" September asked.

"He got killed, didn't he? She said somebody probably knew what happened with Shannon and they tied him up and left him there."

"Is Shannon the girl on the mail route who moved away?"

"I—I gotta go."

The hunter had scared the deer. "Wait, Chris. Just tell me—is Shannon the girl?"

A pause. "Yeah."

"That's her first name?"

"Yeah . . . I really gotta go."

"Last name. Chris. Just give me that, and I'll talk to her."

"She's the liar!" he burst out. "Jamie just wanted to believe her 'cause she doesn't like my parents."

"Last name," she pressed.

"Kraxberger. But . . . don't . . . If my mom asks, I just didn't talk to you."

"What's Jamie's last name?" she tried, but he was already gone.

September stalked toward the filing cabinets and grabbed

up the Ballonni folder from where she'd refiled it. There was a list of all the people on Ballonni's route that September had scanned enough times to almost know by heart. She didn't think the name Kraxberger was among them, and as her eye moved down the list she realized she was right. There wasn't a name that looked even close to it, but then Chris had said Shannon's family had moved away. She would need to look up the property records and find out which houses on the route had sold over the last few years and which ones were rentals.

She gazed a long time at the list of names, thinking hard. Had Ballonni been inappropriate with Shannon Kraxberger? Chris Jr. was implying something of the sort, and his girlfriend, Jamie, seemed to think so, too. Rhoda Bernstein certainly believed he'd been too familiar with her daughter, Missy. There was definitely a thread of sexual impropriety running through the fabric of this story.

Was that why the vigilante—possibly a woman, per Stefan's comments the night before—had targeted both Ballonni and Stefan? The placards strung around their necks suggested it. Ballonni's read: I MUST PAY FOR WHAT I'VE DONE. And in Stefan's scrawl: I WANT WHAT I CAN'T HAVE.

As she thoughtfully closed the Ballonni file, September considered her ex-stepbrother. She'd never seen him with a woman, or a man, for that matter, in any romantic sense in all the time she'd known him, and he was now in his late twenties. But was Stefan truly a pedophile? Her gut reaction said no, but she knew it was because she just didn't want it to be so. Didn't want to think about all the hours he'd lived at her father's house, all the times he'd been around Evie, her brother March's now ten-year-old daughter. Or, maybe he was interested in boys. . . .

September resisted making the leap just yet. She had to be careful. If she were wrong, even with all the circumstantial evidence, it would be so damaging and downright ugly that it would taint everything in Stefan's life from here on out.

She needed to find Shannon Kraxberger and hear her story. And maybe she needed to talk to Missy Bernstein as well. Undoubtedly she would be faced with a blockade of parents who wouldn't want her speaking to their children, but if the Kraxbergers, by any chance, had moved out because of Chris Ballonni Sr. . . . they might be willing to talk.

The file had been scanned into the computer system, so September put it back in the drawer and inputted her code to gain access to all the pages and notes listed under *BALLONNI, Christopher*. She printed off the list of people who'd lived on the mail route, pulling the sheet from the printer in the alcove off the main room.

Picking up a pen, she quickly added the name of Ballonni's coworker, Gloria del Courte, to the list, the woman Janet Ballonni was convinced had been hot for her husband.

She wondered if there was any connection between any of these people and her ex-stepbrother. Maybe a woman they both knew somehow . . . ?

She shook her head. Was it really a woman who'd zip-tied Ballonni and Stefan to poles outside their places of work? A woman who thought they were child abusers and was trying to stop them, even if it meant killing them, to keep them from inflicting any more harm?

Who the hell is this vigilante? she asked herself.

Lucky woke up early and stayed in bed, staring through her window at weak fall sunlight slanting onto the hummingbird feeder and the herb garden beyond. She felt weirdly powerless, as if she had no ability to make choices any longer, as if she were merely acting out some long-ago scripted scenes.

Climbing out of bed, she pulled a white T-shirt and a plain black jogging suit out of her drawer, picked up her well-worn sneakers, then carried the lot out of her bedroom and into her bathroom. She took a quick shower, then ran a towel over her hair and brushed her teeth, naked. Looking at her face in the mirror, she rolled her shoulders forward, easing the tightness of her scarred back before she got dressed.

Back in her room she looked at her image in the dresser mirror. Her hazel eyes glowed, hit by a stream of sunlight from the garden window that turned them more green than brown. Quickly, she put her still-damp hair into a ponytail and grabbed up her baseball cap, tucking it into the waistband of her sweats. Today was Saturday and her quarry would not be at school, but she might be able to stake out his residence and jog around the neighborhood for a while, her own method of reconnaissance. If he took out his station wagon, she could follow him in her car, if she didn't jog too far and wide and find herself unable to get back in time. She would jog just enough to look as if she belonged in the area, then she would return to her car to wait for him as long as she dared.

She headed into the kitchen, but there was no sign of Mr. Blue and she wondered if he would make an appearance today. She really needed to talk to him. To tell him about the gun, for certain, but she also wanted to discuss a few other things with him as well. Maybe it was time to take him fully into her confidence, even if he didn't quite want it. Better to be forearmed than taken by surprise.

She waited fifteen minutes, then, when he still hadn't come out of his rooms, she scavenged through the cupboards and came up with some cornflakes. Grabbing the milk from the refrigerator and a bowl from another cabinet, she settled herself down at the table. Just as she poured the milk over her cereal, she saw Mr. Blue coming from the woods beyond the garden, holding something small and brown in his blue hands. He circled around the side of the house and came in from the garage.

She saw that he was holding a salamander.

"The Pacific newt," he said.

The little creature was alert and staring with bug eyes at Lucky. She was going to ask Mr. Blue what he planned to do with it, but he answered her question before she even opened her mouth as he raised the sash on the window over the sink and let the newt escape.

Then he thoroughly washed his hands.

"There are a lot of them in the garden and around," he said. "I suspect we'll have a thriving population of garter snakes soon."

"What were you doing outside?" Lucky spooned up some cornflakes.

Mr. Blue deliberated for a while. He, too, made himself a bowl of cornflakes, then scraped back a chair opposite Lucky. "There's something I need to show you."

"Okay."

"It's in the woods. Do you have boots?"

"Umm . . . no. I have sneakers."

"That'll do."

As soon as they finished their meal they headed out through the sliding glass door, skirting the rows of herbs and plants, and passing by his grouping of pitcher plants, carnivorous plants that caught insects in a sticky gel on their blossoms, which looked like dew.

He took the path that led toward the hot springs, but when they grew near the pools, he turned into the woods instead, in an area where there was no designated footpath. She followed behind him, her feet sometimes sliding a bit in the slippery muck beneath the leaves and sticks and undergrowth that surrounded the boles of the firs, maples, and scrub oaks.

Finally, he stopped and, breathing a bit hard, said, "My house is over there." He waved to the east, from the general direction they'd come. "It's closer to just run out the back and head straight west to come to this spot, but I don't want to leave a trail unless I have to."

"A trail to what?" Lucky asked. She didn't see anything besides the forest.

He took a step to one side and then looked down at the

ground where he'd been standing. Lucky realized she was looking at a moss-covered wooden hatch.

"It's a root cellar," he explained. "Or, it was until I modernized it."

"A root cellar out here?"

"There was a structure here once. A shed. I took it down because I didn't want to mark the spot."

He bent down and lifted the moss-covered lid. A ladder led down into a dark cavern and Lucky could smell the dank odors of must and earth. She immediately shied away from heading down. What she feared more than anything was being trapped in any way. She'd spent too much of her youth being caged by others, if not physically, then by rules of society and law. It was why she knew she would die before letting herself be caught and sent to prison.

But Mr. Blue headed down the ladder to the belly of the hole and he disappeared into darkness. She waited anxiously for several moments, and then the yellow glow of a lantern reached up to her. "Come on down," he invited her, his voice sounding hollow.

If it were anyone but Hiram she wouldn't have. Not in a million years. But it was Hiram, and she trusted him with her life.

Swallowing her misgivings, she descended down, gripping each rung with hands wet with sweat. At the bottom, she turned and looked around. Three battery-operated lanterns were lit, revealing shelves lined with canned goods, bottled water, a battery-operated radio that also had a hand crank, several rolled up sleeping bags, a small, portable latrine that was basically a bench with a basin. There were kitchen implements scattered at the end of one of the shelves and there were several folded up lawn chairs inside their fabric sleeves hanging on the other one.

"What's this for?" she asked.

"Hiding."

"I mean . . . what do you use it for?"

In the uncertain light his bluish skin looked gray and alien. "There may come a time when one or both of us needs to hide from the police for a while."

Her heart fluttered. She didn't like that idea at all. "I had to get rid of your .38," she confessed. "I threw it in the ocean."

"Why? Did you fire it?"

"Well . . . it was fired, but not actually by me. It was taken from me, and the person who took it pulled the trigger and shot himself."

"Is he dead?"

"I hope so."

He thought about that for a long moment, then nodded for her to ascend again. "Let's go back to the house."

After turning out the lanterns, Mr. Blue followed her up the ladder and they retraced their steps through the woods until they reached his house again. Once inside, he moved into the little-used living room and invited her to take a seat. The room was dark and curtained and he had to turn on a floor lamp as he sank into a recliner. Lucky perched on the edge of one of the occasional chairs, which looked like it could use a thorough cleaning.

"I received a call from someone I've done business with in the past," he began. "Someone I should never have trusted, and now I think there could be some—blowback."

"Who is this person?"

"He first came to the hot springs, but he was looking for me. He'd heard rumors about a man with blue skin who dabbled in herbs and poisons. I ignored him at first, but he became a nuisance. A friendly nuisance," Mr. Blue admitted. "He was the one who found you wandering from where you'd driven your car off the road and brought you here."

She only knew that a good Samaritan had found her, dazed, burned, and delirious, and brought her into Mr. Blue's care. She knew, too, that she'd absolutely refused to let him take her to a hospital.

"But he's untrustworthy," Mr. Blue went on. "He helped you, but altruism is not in his nature. He always wants something in exchange. Different drugs, mostly. Recently, I sold him something, and he used it unwisely. Now the police are on his trail and that could lead them to me."

Lucky's heart started pounding heavily. "Oh."

"You're sure the gun won't be found?" he asked now, sounding tenser than she'd ever heard before.

"Is it registered to you?" she asked.

"It was acquired in a trade with the same young man I just told you about. It was registered to him, and I was . . . holding it for him until I got payment."

"Oh, no. I'm sorry. I didn't know."

"It doesn't matter. I'll get him another one. It was just all I had in firearms at the moment."

"Who is this man?"

He shook his head. "Better you don't know. But if something should happen, if the police should show up here and you don't want to be seen, go to the bunker. It's out of range."

Lucky nodded. Several cameras were mounted high in the trees that flanked the long drive that led to the hot springs and his house. He was both technologically advanced and living in another age.

She'd wanted to talk to him about her mission, had been on the verge of confiding in him, but now she suspected that it would be better to keep him in the dark as well. The less they knew about each other's business, the less chance they would give the other one away. She didn't want to be an additional problem and if he knew her plans and she was caught, he could be an accessory to murder.

A few minutes later he returned to his rooms and Lucky decided it was past time to hit the road and start surveillance again on her latest target.

The clock was ticking down to what could be her last showdown.

Chapter Sixteen

George wandered in at eleven looking like death warmed over.

"What's wrong?" September demanded. She'd briefly talked to Wes, who was on his way, but wasn't feeling all that sharp, either.

"Sick. That stomach flu thing. Urlacher poisoned us all with it, the bastard."

September immediately backed away from him. She'd finally walked down the hall and looked in the administration offices and the main rooms used by the uniforms and had realized how low the staff was there, too. "Go home," she told him.

"Somebody's gotta be here." He gave her a look through red-rimmed eyes. "I was up all night puking my guts out."

"You get me sick, Thompkins, and I'll kill you."

"Death doesn't sound that bad right now."

"Go away. Get the hell out."

"Oh . . . shit . . ." He jumped up and ran for the bathroom.

Immediately she picked up the phone and called Wes again. "Have you been puking?" she demanded as soon as he picked up.

"Hey, Nine," he greeted her dully. "Not yet, but my stomach's kinda jumpy." She could tell he was driving.

"Damn it," she muttered. "Don't come in. George just got here and he's already in the bathroom. I don't want to catch the flu."

"Winter vomiting disease," Wes corrected her. "Norovirus. Not the flu."

"Whatever the hell it is, stay away."

"Okay. The idea of puking my guts out with my surgery . . ."

"Take care of yourself," she said quickly, feeling a bit like a selfish heel.

"Yeah. I'm turning around. What about you?"

"I'll manage." Then, "What about D'Annibal? I've called him and he hasn't called back. He doesn't want me on the case, but it's like he's gone dark since I talked to him last night."

"Could be the bug," he admitted. "One thing. The bullet pulled from your ex-stepbrother is at ballistics. Came from a .38."

"Yeah, thanks. I'm going over to the hospital later."

"I gotta go, Nine."

"Get well . . ." She hung up, lost in thought. One of the uniforms, Maharis, was working his way up to detective, handling robbery/burglaries and missing persons and the like whenever the other detectives were overrun with work. Homicides took priority, unless a missing person was at imminent risk.

September was walking down the hall when she thought of her brother. If he was free to move her queen bed today, then it stood to reason that he should be able to come in. It wasn't her job to scare up more recruits, but currently she felt like the only man standing, so she pulled up Auggie's cell number on her call list. Punching it in, she thought fleetingly of Gretchen. How she would love to have her old partner off administrative leave, but that was outside the legal bounds of the department.

When Auggie didn't answer she swore through her teeth and tried again, once more to no avail. Having reached administration, she asked the girl at the desk, a newby she didn't recognize, "Is Maharis around?"

"He was . . ." She looked around, a little lost.

"Thanks. I'll find him."

But she didn't find him, and after a ten-minute search she was back at her own desk. Maybe he was out on a call, or maybe he was home sick, or God knew what else. She had his cell number and she phoned it but, like her brother's, her call went straight to voice mail.

"Damn. It," she stated succinctly.

She sat down quietly for a moment, letting her thoughts travel along different avenues. The call she'd put in to Verna hadn't gone so well. Her ex-stepmother alternately cried or yelled at September that the police weren't doing enough to find the crazed woman who'd targeted her beloved son. She'd damn near been impossible to talk to, but September had managed to wring out of her the name of the mall that Stefan generally frequented. She'd then put a call in to mall security to see if they could pull up the videotape of the parking lot the night Stefan was kidnapped. If this vigilante had appropriated his van and driven him to the school, then she most likely had come in some kind of vehicle that she'd left in the lot, unless she lived nearby, which felt like too much of a convenient long shot. Alternately, someone could have dropped her off, but September didn't like that scenario either. This crime read like a personal vendetta.

Now September rolled that idea around in her head. If the crime was sexual, if both men had targeted children, was the female killer one of Stefan's or Christopher Ballonni's past victims? Or a victim of both men? And if Stefan were at the mall, wasn't that a perfect place to troll for unsuspecting tweens and teens? A place an attacker could lie in wait?

Maybe a place at which this woman had once unfortunately met up with either Ballonni or Stefan?

She needed to talk to Stefan. She needed him to be honest with her. She wasn't sure quite how she was going to go about that, but if September had to bully him for answers, she was fine with that.

"Sick bastard," she muttered, gathering up her cell phone.

George stumbled back into the room as a call came to his desk. "Thompkins," he said in a weak voice. A moment later, he glanced over at September. "Uh, yeah. We're on it." He hung up as September was turning out of the room, heading toward the lockers. "Possible homicide on Monroe," he called. "Domestic. Uniforms are on their way, but they want us to come down."

"Us?" she asked dryly.

"Well . . ."

"Go home," September ordered again.

"Will you go, then?" he called after her.

She ground her teeth together and yelled over her shoulder, "Sure. I got nothing else to do."

Lucky sat in the front seat of her parked car, lifting her arms over her head and closing her eyes, catching her breath. She'd sat outside her quarry's driveway and down the road for a couple of hours, then she'd gone on her jogging run, returned a few minutes earlier, climbed back in the car, and now she was worried that she might have to give up for the day. She'd been here too long already.

Her thoughts drifted to Stefan Harmak. She'd tuned to a news station for a while, but hadn't heard anything about the shooting. Was he still alive? She sure as hell hoped not. If he decided to confess the full story, which she didn't think he had yet, that or something would be on the news, then her time table would be compressed.

Vaguely, she imagined what the authorities might do if Stefan confessed the truth, and her insides grew cold with fear.

She needed him to be dead or die.

She needed time to finish this last mission.

"Come on, bastard," she whispered, opening her eyes and staring at the end of the driveway. "Come on . . ."

Graham felt suffocated. Every time SHE spoke his skin felt like it was covered in insects crawling all over him. How had he come to loathe her so much? he marveled. She'd been almost attractive in the beginning, for a woman her age, or at least that's what he'd told himself when he'd watched her as she'd gone on and on about the economy and money and how to make it with a shrinking income, blah, blah, blah. Now, the only thing shrinking was his erection whenever he thought of HER. In the pit of his gut, he could feel his hate distilling and compressing into a hard, black ball that made him seethe inside, a cancer that had to be eradicated.

There was only one way to cure himself. He knew for a certainty he had to kill her.

But how? When?

"Darling . . ." Her sickly sweet voice reached for him from the kitchen and he felt the hairs on his arms lift in repulsion. The kids in his class called it being "icked out" and he sure as hell was all that.

"Come on in, I've made some coffee."

Like she even knew how to do *that*. Weak-ass shit.

But he had to play the game. At least for a little while longer.

With leaden feet, he met her in the kitchen where she was

pouring him a cup from the carafe. He could see how pale the fluid was. The ball in his stomach grew harder.

Her cell phone buzzed and skittered a little atop the counter. She picked it up, frowning down at the screen, etching ugly lines between her brows. "It's the San Antonio people," she said.

She handed him his coffee and placed a quick peck on his cheek as she headed away from him, down the hall. He stared into the light brown depths and thought, *Please get the fuck out. Please get the fuck out. Please go to San Antonio. Please.*

She returned a few moments later. "Well, what do you know. It's back on for Monday."

"Really?" He could scarcely hide the jubilation that welled up inside him. "You're going?"

"No . . . I don't know. I said I'd think about it. They can't jack me around that way, although I suppose I should check with Louisville, too." She sighed. "We could really use the money, so maybe I should work out a new deal with them."

Graham's mind was traveling ahead. If SHE were gone, he could go through the school day on Monday and then a bar that night. Maybe pick up on somebody new . . . Dangerously, his thoughts cruised to Molly and he felt almost ill with wanting. Molly, in his last period class. So alone and forgotten while her other classmates were shooting out breasts and hips like the cows they would eventually become. That hadn't happened to Molly yet, and by the looks of her mother, who was small and petite and as flat chested as a board, it might not at all.

"Is that for me?" Daria cooed, looking down at his pants. Then she reached forward and grabbed his hard cock and he jerked in surprise, sloshing his coffee onto her. She jumped back and cried, "Shit, Graham! Didn't you even drink any of it?"

He put the cup on the counter, his vision of Molly shattered by her sharp rebuke. He looked at her down-turned mouth and felt fury rise in him, a volcanic tide.

"What?" she asked, recoiling a bit.

"Nothing."

"Darling, you looked mad enough to *kill.*"

"Nah. Just sorry that I ruined your blouse."

She glanced down at the brown stain on her fat breasts. "Well, you should be, you bad boy. Now, where were we . . . ?" And she reached back to his now flaccid member and started stroking.

When she bent down to his zipper Graham stared over her head and thought about Molly and Monday and how he would take care of her. She was his little girl. She was his.

And he grew hard again.

September arrived at the site of the domestic violence case to learn that a woman had shot her husband in the chest, a wound from which he'd died. The woman was weeping and shaking and saying that he was the one with the gun and she'd just tried to take it from him. From the early signs of the destruction around the room it looked like her story might be correct. The tech team was there and September let the uniforms take the woman into the station to get her full statement.

Blake Maharis had finally gotten back to her as she was driving to the hospital to check up on Stefan. He was out on a missing persons case: a girl had disappeared from her boyfriend's car on Thursday night and hadn't been seen since. He'd taken down the information and was back at the station and September asked if he would take a statement from the woman who'd shot her husband when she got there, which he agreed to. He was young, dark haired, and swarthy skinned with a set of white teeth—too good looking for his own good—about her same age and eager to move up to detective full time.

The guy from mall security called her back as she was parking her car, but her initial hopes were dashed when he said he was sorry, but there were no videos of the parking lot on the night September had requested. In fact there were no videos from the past month. Some screw-up in their system that hadn't been fixed, apparently. From his tone, September wondered if he were lazy or inept or both; she could tell he wasn't going to lift a finger to help.

With thoughts of calling the mall owners and ratting him out to see if he was telling the truth, she forced herself to shut down her phone and forget it as she drove to the hospital. The doctor still hadn't called back, so she was going to him.

As she walked toward the front doors, pulling her coat close against a biting wind, her cell phone sang the ringtone she'd assigned to Auggie. "Wonder of wonders," she muttered, clicking the green ANSWER button. "Hello, there. Nice of you to get back to me."

"Hey, I moved your bed for you," Auggie defended himself.

"And thanks for that. Now get your ass back to work. I'm dying out here. Everybody's sick." She brought him up to date on Wes's, D'Annibal's—who'd finally phoned and related that he was sick as a dog, too—and George's conditions.

"Food poisoning?" Auggie said.

"That stomach virus, most likely. Guy was sick with it first and it's a bitch."

"What guy?"

"Guy Urlacher. Have you forgotten all of us already?"

He grunted his remembrance. "You want me to just leave the rest of this move to Liv and Jake?"

"*Yes*. I don't mean to sound ungrateful, but Jesus H. Christ, Auggie. I had to bring in Maharis. Everybody else is out sick."

"Except you."

"So far."

"All right. Things seem to be under control around here. I can come in. Where are you?"

"About to go into Laurelton General." She quickly brought him up to speed on Stefan's condition, as far as she knew, and then hit the high points about the Ballonni investigation. Finding Dan Quade, Carrie Carter's boyfriend, the would-be source of Special K, was free-falling off her priority list, though she knew Wes wouldn't let it go as soon as he was able.

"Nine, I need to talk to you about something later," he said, sounding serious.

September felt her frustrations boil over. "Today is not the day to hit me with something else."

"I said 'later.'" He sounded as irked as she felt.

"I've changed my mind. If it's bad news, spit it out and let's get it over with."

"I'm moving to Portland permanently. That's all."

That's *all*? she wanted to scream. She hadn't realized how much it meant to be working in the same department as her twin. Sure, she'd scarcely seen him since she'd been promoted to detective, but she'd felt him with her, at least. A partner, a friend, an ally.

"Well, good luck with that," she said, then she clicked off, knowing she was being an ungrateful bitch and not caring—much. Okay, she cared, but he was really pissing her off.

As soon as she hung up she remembered she'd wanted him to connect her with Jake. She hadn't talked to him since she left this morning and she really wanted to hear his voice. If she couldn't depend on her brother, she could at least depend on her boyfriend. *Boyfriend,* she thought. She detested that term because it didn't say enough about their relationship. Fiancé said too much, but goddammit, why wasn't there something in between?

She walked into the hospital with a dark cloud hanging over her head. Everybody and everything was bugging her, and yes, she knew, probably, that it was mostly coming from inside herself, but that didn't mean she wasn't *pissed off.*

"Detective Rafferty with the Laurelton PD," she said tersely to the woman behind the curving front desk. "I'm checking on a surgical patient who's now in recovery: Stefan Harmak."

Behind the woman, carved out of wood, was a hand-hewn plaque with the image of three Douglas firs chiseled into it and the words LAURELTON GENERAL HOSPITAL.

New art, she decided, grudgingly admitting to herself that it was better than the plain metal letters that had spelled out the hospital's name without any adornment.

The woman checked her computer, then asked, "Did Dr. Rajput call you?"

"No one's called me. I was here last night when Mr. Harmak was brought in and taken to surgery. I've asked to be updated, but so far that hasn't happened."

"Let me put in a call to the doctor."

You do that.

September walked to the windows that looked out on the front parking lot while she waited to hear something. She knew she was on the verge of stepping off the ledge, going from merely acting irritated to becoming totally unreasonable. Taking a breath, she told herself she just needed something to go right. One break to fall her way.

"Dr. Rajput will be right down," the woman called to her, then looked away quickly, as if she expected September to bite her head off.

She heard the elevator bell *ding* and looked over to see an Indian man in a white lab coat step off the elevator. She turned toward him and there was just something about his demeanor that telegraphed the news to her before she even had to ask.

"Detective Rafferty?" he asked with a slight accent.

"He's dead, isn't he? Stephen Harmak is dead."

He blinked several times, then nodded gravely. "Yes, that is what I was going to say."

Jake looked at the queen-sized bed in his spare bedroom with satisfaction. He liked seeing it there, liked knowing September was almost completely moved in. Feeling Liv Dugan's gaze on him, he glanced over at Auggie's girlfriend, seeing the smile that quirked at the corner of her mouth. "What?" he demanded.

"You're happy. That's all."

He didn't know Liv that well. She and Nine's brother had hooked up the previous summer before Jake had reconnected with the Rafferty clan. But he sensed that she approved and that was enough for him. "Well, yeah," he told her.

"Living with a Rafferty . . ." She lifted a brow. "Be careful what you wish for."

"I don't see you complaining."

"No." The smile grew.

Auggie had left a few minutes earlier and now Liv gathered up her purse and headed for the door herself. She and Auggie had come in separate cars because he planned to go to his job with the Portland PD afterward. But then September had called him, and she'd asked—make that demanded—that he come help her, and Jake was all for that. Whatever it took to get September home earlier.

Liv and Jake had been left to wrestle the mattress on the bed and set up the nightstand. The rest of September's furniture was dumped in Jake's garage. Sometime in the future they would go through the pile together and sort out what she wanted to keep. There were still some smaller items at her apartment that she needed to box up and haul over, but the bulk of the heavy work was done.

Jake said good-bye to Liv, then dialed September. He could tell from Auggie's conversation with her that she was a bit overwhelmed, but he was hoping to talk to her for a few minutes and tell her about the canceled dinner plans, although when Auggie caught up with her she would know. In truth, he just wanted to talk to her.

Her cell went straight to voice mail. Figured.

"You've reached Detective Rafferty," her voice said on the message. "Leave a detailed message and a number where you can be reached."

After the beep, Jake drawled, "Detective Rafferty, this is Jake from Apartment to Home Delivery Service. Your belongings have been left in good order. Unfortunately two-thirds of my team had to leave before the agreed upon payment—Thai food, I believe—was delivered and therefore the debt is still outstanding. I'm sure some other arrangement can be made to . . . fill the bill, and I hope you can offer recompense later this evening. I've put the invoice in the Johnson file. Please open it as soon as you return."

He was grinning as he clicked off. Hearing the dryer buzz, he realized the sheets were dry and he headed out to the laundry room off the garage. He was returning with the wad of sheets in his arms when he heard his cell phone buzz on the table.

Dropping the pile, he swept up his phone, but the ring-tone was his default, not September's assigned song. Looking at the screen, he saw the number had no name attached to it but he recognized it all the same: Marilyn Cheever, Loni's mother.

He said one choice word and debated on not answering. He didn't want to talk to Marilyn or Loni or anyone in the Cheever family ever again. He was, in fact, sick to the back teeth of all the drama and endless conversations and hand wringing.

He actually walked away from the phone, but it kept on

buzzing. “Damn it,” he finally said through his teeth, striding back to sweep up the cell. “Hello,” he said coolly.

“Jake? Oh, God, Jake. It’s Marilyn.” Her voice was unsteady.

“What’s happened?” he asked without enthusiasm. This scene had played out too many times for him to be nice.

“It’s Loni.”

“Uh-huh.”

“She’s . . . she’s missing. She took off and she left a note.”

“A note?” His heartbeat accelerated. A *suicide* note? Loni had never actually gone that far before.

“Could you—could you help me? She needs you. *I* need you.” And she started softly crying.

Loni’s parents had divorced years earlier. Her father had moved away and Loni had never been close to him. When her disease had become a serious problem, Marilyn had tried to turn to him for help, but he’d grown even more distant, not less. Jake had been the one who was there for both of them.

“What can I do?” he heard himself say.

“Help me find her.”

He looked at the pile of sheets on the table, sighed, and said, “Okay.” September wasn’t going to be home for a while anyway.

“Oh, thank you, Jake. Thank you.”

Lucky’s quarry rolled out in the station wagon late in the day. She waited until he was out of sight, then followed behind him at a good distance. When he pulled into a grocery store, she drove into the same lot a few minutes later, parking several rows back. She wanted his name, but wondered if this was the time to get close to him. So many people around.

When he went into the store, she climbed out of her car, squared the baseball cap on her head and walked across the lot toward him. She thought he was going to the grocery store but he turned into the cleaners beside it.

She slowed her steps, following his movements through the large, plate glass window at the front of the store. It was a small space with a counter. If she were inside with him, he would immediately notice her, and this was not the place to make his acquaintance. Besides which, what would she say to the Hispanic woman behind the counter? Ask her for prices?

No, it was better to just wait outside and so she walked past the store, darting a quick look inside. Her target was dropping off a woman's blouse, pointing out what looked like a coffee stain to the clerk. Lucky kept on walking, turning before she reached the end of the strip mall where Dizzy's Pizza stood, a local chain that had become both a place for tweens to play video games, hang out, and eat pizza, and for adults to sit in the bar area and watch sports on the lines of TVs suspended from the ceiling, and hang out and eat pizza as well.

Lucky had just turned around and was walking back when she saw her guy heading her way. Ducking her head, she kept on going, nearly overwhelmed by the scent of his desire. She dared to look back once and saw that he'd entered the restaurant. She could see him hesitate for only a minute before heading to the tween side.

She ground her teeth together. Bastard was escalating. She could feel it.

What should she do? She wasn't dressed right to lure him in. There were too many people and cars circling the parking lot for her to hit him with the stun gun here. It was just all around the wrong place to be, at this time of day.

But she didn't want to leave him alone with the unsuspecting tweens.

After a moment she walked into the restaurant. One look and she saw his attention was already lasered on a young girl who was playing a video game while her mother stood by observantly. Lucky decided to take a minute to use the restroom and when she returned she had a bad moment when she saw the girl, the mother, and her quarry were all gone.

But then she saw the mother and girl heading to a car and her quarry loitering by a newspaper box with change in his hand. However, his attention was really on them. Lucky dared to walk past him and toward the cleaners, but when the mother and child pulled out of the lot, he headed straight for his car.

She stopped and stared straight at the window of the cleaners, all the while watching his reflection. When he was in his car, she moved quickly toward her own, racewalking the last few steps. He was pulling out of the lot as she jumped into the Nissan.

She managed to find him easily enough. He was stopped at the light and through the rear window she watched him slam his palm down on the steering wheel in frustration.

"No luck, huh, fucker."

He drove back toward his house. Just before he made the last turn to the side street that led to his driveway, Lucky pulled alongside him in the left lane. She kept on heading forward, stealing only a small look, watching his tail lights turn red as he slowed for his driveway. He'd been thwarted in his hunting. Probably because the only girl he wanted—the youngest one—had been under her mother's watchful eye and he couldn't approach her. Or, maybe the woman she'd seen him kissing in the window kept him on a very short tether.

Whatever the case, she sensed her hunting was over for today. Nevertheless, she reparked her car along the street, further back now and flanked front and rear by different cars, which might make her less noticeable. She would wait a few more hours and see what developed. Then she would go back to Mr. Blue's and see how things stood there. If the situation were getting hotter, he might ask her to leave. She didn't want to go, but she didn't want to get caught, either. Hiram wasn't known for exaggeration, and so she had to believe the police might come to his door, asking questions. Better for her not to be there when that happened.

So . . . she might as well keep up her vigil.

Switching off the ignition, she popped open the glove box, withdrew two energy bars, then pulled the baseball cap down over her eyes and leaned back, unwrapping the first bar and settling in for a long wait.

Chapter Seventeen

"This isn't a suicide note," Jake said with some relief.

He glanced over at Marilyn Cheever with a sense of growing frustration. There was no denying that Loni had serious problems, but her mother's fears were set off by a hair trigger these days, and they always included phoning Jake.

Marilyn dabbed at her nose with a tissue, staring down at the unfolded page Jake now held in his hands. They were standing in her kitchen where Loni had propped her message in front of the salt and pepper shakers, so Marilyn had told him as she'd been holding the paper between shaking hands when he arrived at her house. Recently, apparently, Loni had moved back in with her mother, and though the arrangement seemed to suit Marilyn, Jake wasn't sure how well it was working for Loni.

Maybe that's why she had started calling him again.

"It's for you," she said, a little testily. "And it's full of sorrow."

He gazed down on the note again.

Jake, I'm sorry for everything. I shouldn't rely on you like I do, and I'm going to try not to in the future.

I love you. You know that. If you want to find me, you know where I am.

It was full of Loni's special brand of manipulation, guilt, and sadness, meant to pull at his emotions, but he wasn't about to tell Marilyn that. Surreptitiously, he checked the time on the microwave clock, but she caught him at it.

"You just can't wait to get back to your life, can you?" she said bitterly.

"Loni does this when she's feeling low. You know that. It's when she reaches out to me."

"She's bipolar. She can't help herself."

Jake almost said, "Bipolar and maybe something more," but again, he kept that to himself. Loni's problems, which had seemed manageable once upon a time, felt as if they were gathering speed like a boulder down a hill. He was certainly no doctor, but he knew her very well. Marilyn knew her, too. Though she said all the correct, clinical terms and espoused belief in medical treatment, Loni's mother had made herself believe that her mentally ill daughter would be all right if Jake would just play his part.

He'd done that for far too long.

"What place is she talking about?" Marilyn asked. "I'll go get her." *Since you won't,* her tone added.

"I'm not sure," Jake said.

"Well, where does she mean?"

"Marilyn, I don't know."

"Is it some place you used to meet?" she pressed.

He spread his hands. "There was an Italian restaurant in downtown Portland that we used to go to, but it closed."

"Come on, Jake."

His frustration mounted. "If I knew, I would tell you. Believe me."

She gazed at him, determination in her set jaw, but as he

met her stare that determination fell by degrees until her chin was quivering and her eyes were welling with tears.

"Won't you help find her?" she asked.

He wanted to say no. He really did. He wanted to tell her he couldn't keep spinning on this merry-go-round with Loni. He did have a life he wanted to get back to. Very much. A life with September.

Instead he said, "All right," and headed for the door. Later, he knew, he would mentally flagellate himself for giving in, again, but he couldn't callously walk out on Marilyn Cheever when she was so brokenhearted and sick with worry.

He checked the time on his cell phone. God knew what Loni was up to. He sure as hell hoped he would find her quickly.

The pain in September's shoulder, mostly a jolt whenever she moved too suddenly, started in as a dull ache about the time Auggie and Verna appeared at the hospital, walking in from the parking lot together. Verna had gone home to take a shower as she'd spent the night in the hospital despite everyone's attempts to shoo her out, and now she hurried inside and found September waiting for Auggie. By coincidence, the elevator door softly *dinged* as September was greeting both Verna and Auggie, and Dr. Rajput stepped out. He came over to them, sober and quiet, and Verna, who initially turned expectantly toward him, took one look at his face and went white.

"Oh, no," she said, staggering backward.

"I'm sorry, Mrs. Harmak," the doctor began regretfully, but Verna waved him off, warding off the words she sensed he was about to say.

"Oh, God." Verna's knees wobbled. Auggie swiftly moved to catch her the split second before she collapsed.

He carried her to a nearby chair where she began to wail and shake. Dr. Rajput sat next to her and asked her to come with him to a private room. If she heard him, September couldn't tell, but Auggie and the doctor managed to get her to the elevator, and on the third floor several nurses helped usher the group of them into a small, unmarked waiting room apparently designed for this purpose.

Verna was inconsolable, shaking and crying.

"The bullet did too much damage to his lungs and heart," the doctor told her.

While Verna cried, September felt a headache build inside her skull. Verna was given a sedative and Auggie offered to drive her home.

"I can't go back there," she cried. "I can't ever go back there."

Stepping completely out of his own comfort zone, Auggie called their father and said he was bringing Verna to Castle Rafferty, and Braden, apparently so bowled over at having his younger son call him, agreed.

"What are you going to do?" Auggie asked September as they both walked across the parking lot to their respective vehicles with Auggie helping Verna to his car.

"My car . . ." Verna said weakly.

"I'll drive her car to Dad's," September said, "but I'm not staying."

"Me neither." Auggie was clear on that. "I'll bring you back to your Pilot."

September nodded. She wanted to ask Verna some more questions about Stefan, but she didn't have the heart or the energy right now.

They caravanned to the house, then September climbed into Auggie's Jeep and they returned to the hospital and collected her SUV. "You going home?" he asked her as he dropped her off.

Her headache hadn't dissipated. "We're so short staffed I should check in at the station, but I really don't give a shit."

"I'll meet you there," he decided.

By the time she wheeled into the department lot, this time choosing the front of the building and damn the visitors who might use the spots, the rest of her energy had leaked away and even the thought of a few extra steps felt like too much.

She passed Guy Urlacher with her ID raised and her eyes focused on the door, willing him to buzz her in without speaking, which, for once, he did.

Auggie came into the squad room a few minutes later and said, "He's a putz."

"I thought Guy never asked for your ID."

"He did this time."

"Serves you right for abandoning us."

Her brother gazed at her through knowing, Rafferty blue eyes. "You okay?"

"Hell, no. I'm overworked and tired and probably getting sick."

"What do you need?" he asked.

September hardly knew where to begin. It wasn't often these days that she had her twin's undivided attention, and in the future, at least work-wise, it didn't look like she was going to have it at all.

"Start with Stefan," he suggested, as she sank into her desk chair.

"Stefan . . . You know, he lied about what happened to him from the beginning," she said, then told him how he'd initially said he'd been attacked at the school, but just before going into surgery he'd said he'd been accosted at a mall by a woman who'd hit him with a stun gun, driven his van to the school, forced him to write the words on the placard they'd found around his neck and to drink down a concoction of drugs, then left him tied to the basketball pole. ". . . the van's still missing. Verna called me with that information last night, and the next thing you know, he was shot."

"A woman."

September nodded. "So, maybe it was a woman who killed

Christopher Ballonni, too." Quickly, she reminded him of the similarities to the Ballonni case. How Christopher Ballonni had also been tied to a pole outside his place of work. How he'd also been wearing a placard around his neck written in his own hand. How he'd been stripped down to his boxers and left to the elements.

"Ballonni died, and maybe Stefan was meant to, but when that didn't happen she attacked him at his house," September added, then she went on to tell him about Rhoda Bernstein's complaint, her conversations with Janet Ballonni and Chris Jr., what Chris Jr. had said about Shannon Kraxberger, and how she planned to interview Gloria del Courte, Ballonni's coworker, as soon as she had some time. She finished with, "The two cases are tied together and even though Stefan was Wes's, the Ballonni case is mine. Now that Stefan's dead I think I can be on both. Wes plans to continue investigating the apparent suicide of Carrie Lynne Carter. He wants to backtrack and find who supplied Carrie Lynne's boyfriend with ketamine. And we had another homicide today—a wife shooting her husband, maybe in self-defense. I put Maharis on it because there's nobody here, including D'Annibal. They're all sick."

"Wow," Auggie said.

"That's why I wanted you here," she added with more energy. "I could use some damn help."

He lifted his hands. "D'Annibal has my resignation already, but I've got about an hour before I have to be in Portland."

Her mouth dropped open.

"I told you I took the other job," he reminded her.

She clamped her lips together again. She'd just expected he would help her. "Maybe I should have taken up Jake's offer," she said, fighting anger. "He wanted to come with me to the station."

"You look like hell, Nine," he said softly. "You're not a one-woman show. Let Maharis and some of the other uniforms fill in for you."

"I can't."

"Being stubborn isn't going to help."

"There's the pot calling the kettle black."

"And Stefan's death is a shock, whether you want to admit it or not."

A long silence passed between them as September assessed his words. She did feel like shit, and learning of Stefan's death only added to it. "I didn't like him," she admitted.

"None of us did. Don't feel guilty about it. He was weird. It's a fact."

"Do you think he was a pedophile? That's the direction we're headed."

"The investigation will go where it goes."

"Don't get all wise on me," she said on a sigh, but she knew what he meant. "Whoever this *woman* is who tied Stefan and Ballonni up, she must have a damn strong reason. From what she had them write on the placards, it sounds like Ballonni acted on his perversion, but she stopped Stefan before he could."

Auggie nodded and September realized that none of the phones were ringing. "Calls aren't being sent to the detectives?" she said, straightening at the realization.

"That's because you're all sick."

The Laurelton Police Department was small to medium sized and the uniforms were always eager to fill a vacationing, or "on administrative leave" detective's job. That was exactly how September had felt and she'd worked hard to move up.

"What's the connection between this woman and her victims?" Auggie posed, bringing her back to the case. "How did she meet them? How did she get close enough to them to figure out their deviancy?"

"Suspected deviancy. I don't know. Maybe she worked with one of them . . . ?"

"But not both of them," Auggie pointed out.

"Did she date them?" September made a face. If this woman had dated Ballonni, it was a secret affair outside his marriage, and if she'd dated Stefan . . . wouldn't Verna have some idea? "I'll make that talk with Gloria del Courte a priority. And I'll check in at Twin Oaks Elementary. I already know the principal, Amy Lazenby."

"When will Wes be back?" Auggie asked.

"God knows," she muttered. "That's the problem."

Maharis came into the room at that moment, frowning down at a piece of paper he was carrying. He looked up, saw Auggie and grinned. "Hey, Rafferty. Where ya been?"

"Moving on," he said. "Nine could use some help with the workload since everyone's down with the plague."

"That's what I'm here for," he said. "Mrs. Calgary's waiting for arraignment, and then I'm ready."

"The wife who shot her husband," September said for Auggie's benefit.

"I got this missing girl, too." Maharis glanced down at the paper again. "Gillian Palmiter. Twenty-one. Her roommate said she went out to a bar called Gulliver's last Thursday and never came home."

"I know Gulliver's," September said. "Gretchen and I were there on the Do Unto Others case."

"Did she go by herself?" Auggie asked Maharis.

"The roommate wasn't feeling all that great. She drove Gillian—Jilly—to the bar and then went home. Said Jilly was supposed to call her but never did. At first the roommate was glad she didn't have to go pick her up because she was praying to the porcelain god. Thought Jilly went home with one of the guys she dates. Then she got worried when she hadn't heard from her by this morning. Jilly's not answering her cell."

"The roommate have the norovirus?" September put a

hand to her stomach. Was it just the pain in her shoulder and all of the talk of the virus making her feel a bit queasy, or was she really coming down with it?

"Huh?" Maharis asked.

"The plague around here," Auggie said.

"Ahh . . ." Maharis nodded. "I didn't ask, but that's all you see on the news. Everybody sick. They said to wash your hands a lot. It lasts like—hours—on surfaces or something."

"Great," September muttered. "How many guys does Jilly date?"

"I got a few names." Maharis handed the page to September to look at. "I was going to make a few phone calls." He glanced around the room and picked Gretchen's desk to settle into. "I've got a picture from the roommate to broadcast."

September nodded. "Good."

"Go home," Auggie said to September again. He inclined his head in Maharis's direction. "You got a replacement."

"Yeah, one person."

The truth was, though, that September was leaning toward Auggie's suggestion. "Can you follow up on the dealer for Wes?" she asked him.

"Sure you don't want me on the Ballonni case?"

"I've got it," she assured him.

After getting all the information he needed to move on the Carter case, he gave September a guy hug, side by side with an arm around her shoulder, then he was gone. September felt slightly bereft afterward. She was close to her brother in that indefinable way twins were, but he had a different life now, one of his own choosing, and she was moving in another direction as well.

She pulled out the list to the Ballonni case and put a call in to the post office where Ballonni had worked, asked for Gloria del Courte and was told she no longer was employed by them. She searched out Gloria's home number and left a message on her voice mail.

After that, she drove back to the house, expecting to find Jake, but he wasn't around. Her sheets were in a pile on the table, so she peeked her head into the second bedroom where her bed was set up but unmade. Wondering where he was, she pulled out her cell and realized she'd missed a call from him while she was at the hospital with Verna and Auggie and Dr. Rajput. She clicked the VOICE MAIL button and listened, her smile growing as he finished with, ". . . the debt is still outstanding. I'm sure some other arrangement can be made to . . . fill the bill, and I hope you can offer recompense later this evening. I've put the invoice in the Johnson file. Please open it as soon as you return."

"I wish," she said, attempting to call him while she poured herself a glass of water. It also went to voice mail, and she just hung up, knowing he would see the missed call. She headed for the bedroom she shared with him, stripped off her clothes and pulled on some sweats and a T-shirt. She was shivering and thought, *Peachy,* just before she bolted for the bathroom and her own ignominious vomiting into the toilet.

It was dark by the time Jake, frustrated and ready to chuck in the whole damn thing, finally had an inkling of where Loni might have meant she would be. He'd already been to the real estate office where she worked and talked to several women there, one of whom recognized him. She'd printed a page off her printer with all of Loni's listings and he'd driven by each one on the off chance she would be there. He'd also driven by all the restaurants that he could remember where they'd eaten, places they'd once deemed special, and he'd continually checked her cell phone, which went straight to voice mail over and over again.

He'd damn near called Nine's cell a dozen times, but he kind of wanted her to pick up his message and phone him first. She would call him when she could. She'd told him that enough times for him to believe it. And she'd made it pretty clear this morning that she had a job that he wasn't invited to help her with. He was lucky she'd allowed him to go with her to the hospital last night.

But he was losing steam and interest and he was about to break that rule and call September anyway. How long was she going to stay at work anyway? The sun, such as it was behind all those gray clouds, had set.

And then he knew where Loni would be. She'd told him when she'd mentioned the newlywed couple whom she'd sold a house to.

He drove to Sunset Valley High and immediately saw the vintage Chevy Malibu parked at the back of the senior parking lot behind the sprawling brick building. It was the car she'd had in high school, and it hadn't been new then, either. Seeing it bothered Jake, because, though she hadn't sold it, Loni hadn't driven it in years. She was taking some dark trip down memory lane that didn't speak well to her state of mind.

He pulled his Explorer up beside her, then went around to her driver's door and tapped on the window.

She was slumped in the seat, staring straight ahead, and wouldn't look at him.

"Loni," he said loudly. For a moment he was scared, she was so still. But then he saw the rise and fall of her chest.

"Loni," he called again.

She swiveled her head and looked at him, then leaned over and popped the lock on the passenger side door.

Jake hesitated. This didn't bode well at all. He thought he heard his cell ringing inside the Explorer and he almost grabbed it out and answered it. It sounded like September's ring-tone. But then he looked at Loni again, at the defeated way she sank into the seat, and instead he did as she apparently wanted, walking around the back of her car, opening the passenger side door, and ducking his head inside.

She was wearing a pair of gray slacks and a pink blouse

with a string of fake pearls at her throat, a gift Jake had given her when they were still in high school. "What are you doing?" he asked her cautiously.

"Remembering."

"It's dark. Maybe we should get home. Your mom's worried about you."

"I can't." To his consternation her eyes welled with tears that rolled slowly down the hills of her cheeks. "Our best times were here."

"I know, but . . . high school's long over. We dated through college, too, and beyond," he reminded her. "We have a lot of history."

"But high school was before everything went to shit."

"There were good times after high school, too."

"Were there?" She finally turned to look at him just as the skies opened and rain began to fall in a deluge. "Get in," she ordered.

He complied, slamming the door shut against suddenly pounding rain that ran over the windshield like honey, steamed the windows and was loud enough to damn near drown out his voice as he shouted, "We should call your mom."

"Just give me a minute with you, okay?" she shouted back.

Jake sat silently, staring ahead, waiting for the rain to abate. It went on for several long minutes and he could sense Loni's gaze on him, a heavy weight. It worried him, but not as much as when Loni's hand stole over his.

As soon as the rain started to abate, he turned to her and said, "At the risk of being a real bastard, I need to say a few things." She yanked her hand back as if she'd been burned. "I'm no psychologist, but I'm pretty sure it's not me you want. You're looking for something that isn't there anymore." He gestured toward the building in front of them. "You want the past, and it's over for us."

"Don't you remember when we went to that playground at midnight and you pushed me in the swing?"

What Jake recalled was Loni insisting they go down the slides even though it had rained and he'd gotten his pants soaked. He'd only humored her on the trip to the nearby park because he'd really been thinking about breaking up, again, and was trying to feel his way through it. It was spring, senior year, and he'd had his one and only night with Nine amid the grapevines of her parent's winery and all he could think about was the feeling he'd had making love to her.

"Loni, don't do this," he said.

"Jake, this is me you're talking to. For God's sake, I'm not going to break into a thousand pieces!" Then, "What's Mom been telling you?"

"She just wants to be sure you're safe."

"I am safe!"

"Okay."

"Fuck you, Jake." She turned her face away from him and he could see her shoulders begin to shake with silent sobs.

"The last time I saw you, you were in the hospital," he reminded her. "This isn't good, you being here."

"Yeah, well, I don't have somebody who *loves* me. I don't have somebody who's *moved in* with me. I don't have somebody I've been screwing since high school when I was supposed to be *faithful!*"

"I wasn't with Nine—"

"Who the fuck cares? You are now!"

"Jesus, Loni. You've got to let it go."

She hauled off and slugged him in the arm. "I hate it when you're so rational. I just *hate it*. And I'm sick of being placated. *I fucking hate it*."

"I'm going." He reached for the door handle.

She switched on the ignition and roared the engine.

Jake's head jerked her way. "What?" he asked.

She suddenly smashed her foot onto the accelerator. The back wheels spun and they were shooting forward.

"Loni!" he yelled.

The brick wall rushed toward them and Jake braced himself, throwing up his arms to shield his face. "Stop!" he screamed, or at least he thought he screamed, but then they rammed into the wall at thirty miles an hour. One moment dark red bricks were rushing toward him, then *Blam!*

The hood crumpled up like tinfoil.

Then blackness.

Chapter Eighteen

September was lying on the bathroom floor, feeling like hell, when her cell phone rang, skittering along the tile floor where she'd placed it after trying to call Jake again. He wasn't picking up and she was mystified at where he could be but was too damn sick to do anything about it.

She caught the phone with one outstretched arm as it was heading toward the open door, squinted at the number and realized it was the department. Damn. "Rafferty," she answered, clearing her throat when she heard how raspy her voice sounded.

"Detective, it's Maharis. The vehicle registered to Stefan Harmak has been found. It was parked in the same neighborhood as Harmak's residence."

"Good. Good work." She tried hard to infuse her voice with the enthusiasm she felt. "Is it being processed?"

"It's on its way to the crime lab."

"Maybe we'll learn something." She drew a careful breath and let it out slowly.

"Detective . . . ?" His tone was tentative.

"Call me Rafferty, or September, or Nine. Whatever works for you. Have you heard from my brother . . . or Wes, er, Weasel?"

"Umm . . . I have some information for you."

"Well, spit it out, for God's sake." She didn't have time to play nice.

"There's been an automobile accident and one of the victims is someone you know, I believe. Jacob Westerly."

September sat up so fast she nearly fell over from the wave of dizziness that slammed into her. "What? Where? Victims . . . ? Is he okay?"

"Both of them are on their way to Laurelton General."

"Oh, God."

"I knew . . . I heard you were dating someone with that name, so I—"

"Is he okay?" she screeched.

"I don't know."

It felt like her brain was on stall. "Who's the other victim?" she asked. She rose to her feet on wobbly legs, but her heart was pounding, her body flooded with adrenaline.

"A woman . . . Loni Cheever. Her next of kin was called."

"Jesus."

The phone clattered to the floor, slipping out of her hand and smacking onto the tile. She bent to pick it up and nearly fell over, grabbing the towel bar to steady herself. She realized her eyes were leaking fluid, tears of fear.

"Maharis?"

But he wasn't there. She'd been going to tell him to call Jake's parents but someone probably already had.

Stripping off her T-shirt, she put her bra back on, then a new black shirt and jeans. Her stomach was jumping around and she stopped briefly, holding on to each side of the bedroom door jamb, heart pounding, trying to get her body under control.

Was she fit to drive? She did a quick check and decided, yes, she could do it. Laurelton General wasn't that far. The accident must have taken place nearby.

As she was getting into her car, her cell rang again—Auggie. She wasn't the only person Maharis had called.

"Nine," he said in a heartfelt, worried tone.

That was all it took. A sob fought its way up her throat. "What happened?" she managed to get out.

"I'm on my way to Sunset Valley now. I'll let you know."

"Sunset Valley?"

"Didn't Maharis tell you? That's where she drove into the school."

"Loni drove into the school?"

"Yeah."

"With Jake in the car?"

"That's what it looks like."

"On *purpose?*"

"Nine, I don't know. I'm going to check it out." He paused. "You going to the hospital?"

"Yeah."

"You don't sound good."

"I'm not," she said. "Keep me informed." And then she hung up because she couldn't hear anything more right now. Not now. Not yet. Not until she saw Jake and made sure he was all right.

That's where she drove into the school.

"Oh, Jake," she whispered, so scared that her teeth started to chatter.

Laurelton General ER was bustling when September arrived, the waiting room filled to capacity. She looked around wildly for help and realized that people were lined up to check in with the nurse. Someone was coughing and she looked over to see a young man who looked pale and sweaty.

"Ma'am." A nurse grabbed her arm and she realized she'd been teetering on her feet.

"I'm fine," she said, but the nurse tried to steer her to the only empty chair.

She realized belatedly then, that she thought she was here as a patient. "I'm a detective," she explained. "There was a car accident at Sunset Valley."

"Why don't you take a seat and someone will be right with you."

As the nurse moved on, September headed toward the square button that operated the hydraulic doors that led to the inner sanctum.

"Ma'am, you can't go through there," another nurse told her sternly. "You don't look well and you could jeopardize the health of others."

That stopped her. And the fact that her stomach was sending her messages of imminent need. "Bathroom?" she asked.

With a pinch of her lips, the nurse managed to take pity on her and show her to the nearest restroom. September half ran inside and into a stall, heaving over the toilet, but there was nothing left to come up. She'd hardly eaten anything and it was currently to her advantage.

But she was sick with worry, desperate for help. Pulling out her cell, she phoned Auggie. He answered immediately and she confessed, "I'm sick. I made it to the hospital but I've got that goddamn bug and they won't let me near him. I need help."

"I'll be right there."

The next hour was a blur. Auggie found her curled into a chair in the waiting room. She was too sick to do more than feel angry and miserable, though she'd made a pest of herself and gotten some minimal information about Jake. "He's unconscious. They're running tests," she told Auggie.

"You should be in bed, Nine."

"I can't leave. I just can't. Tell me what happened at Sunset Valley."

He squatted down beside her chair and gave her as much as he knew. "Jake was looking for Loni because her mother asked him to," he told her. "Mrs. Cheever is in with Jake now. Lennon's the uniform who caught the call and he said that Mrs. Cheever told him Loni left some kind of note for Jake and he went looking for her. He found her at the high school and got into her car. His Explorer's at the school. Loni drove straight into the side of the building. The vehicle was old enough that there were no air bags." He paused, watching September with concern as she absorbed the news.

"And Loni?" September asked. She'd been so worried about Jake she hadn't asked.

"They brought her here, too. That's all I know."

"She did this to him."

Auggie squeezed her arm. He knew Loni well, too. Though they'd all run in different circles, they'd been in the same grade at Sunset Valley. "I'll go see what I can find out," he said. "And then I'm going to take you home. You look like shit."

"I feel like shit," she muttered. But she couldn't leave no matter what he said. Not until she knew Jake was going to be okay.

Lucky drove back to Mr. Blue's. Her quarry was in for the night, she was pretty sure. He'd been thwarted from connecting with the girl at the restaurant and was back again with his middle-aged woman, possibly his wife.

His hunger was overtaking him and he was getting desperate, she'd decided. He was stopping into places and looking around for something to quench his need and then leaving in frustration.

She wondered how she could learn his name. She couldn't

go back to the school again. She couldn't risk being seen by DeForest and Maryanne. Too much hanging around would be suspicious. Of course, there was the option of breaking into his car and checking his registration—the station wagon was parked right outside the house and she was pretty sure it was his—but if she were caught she would lose the power of secrecy.

Tomorrow was Sunday. And the next day was Monday and school would start again and he would likely be back at Twin Oaks.

As she drove home, she turned on the radio and had the satisfaction of learning that one Mr. Stefan Harmak had died of a gunshot wound from a home invader who was still at large.

Auggie took September to his house, and though she protested all the way, she was grateful to be able to burrow into the bed in their spare bedroom, though she didn't touch the tea and toast Liv brought to her bedside table. She hadn't wanted to leave Jake. She'd damn near wanted to flail and scream and make Auggie carry her to the car, but in the end she'd acquiesced. He'd assured her that they would get her SUV on Sunday, and so she'd allowed him to tuck her into bed and she'd drifted off into an uneasy sleep.

She woke up in the middle of the night as if an alarm had rung, but she was really awakened by the worries scratching away inside her mind. Jake. And Loni. *Damn her for doing this.* Yes, she had mental issues. *Yes, yes, yes.* But she'd hurt Jake and that was unforgivable.

September's stomach felt calmer, but then it was dead empty. She used the bathroom and then climbed back into bed. Auggie had not gone to his job with the Portland PD after all, at least while this crisis was on.

She lay awake in the dark for what felt like hours, thoughts of Jake circling her brain. She wanted to call the hospital in the middle of the night but knew it would do no good. The only way to get information was to get her strength back and go there tomorrow with her identification and determination.

Finally she fell into a deep sleep and didn't awaken until there was a light tap on her bedroom door. She didn't know what time it was. Someone had closed the shades and the room was dark. Outside, she could hear the incessant rain.

"Come in," she invited, and there was Liv, fully dressed and carrying another tray of tea and toast.

"I didn't touch the last one," she admitted.

"Don't worry about it." Liv exchanged the new tray with the old, then asked, "How are you doing?"

"Better. Where's Auggie? My car's still at the hospital. What time is it?"

"Auggie went in to work and it's ten."

"Ten!" September fairly shrieked. She threw back the covers and scooped up her cell phone, which was dead. "I don't have my charger. I've got to call work. And I need to get to the hospital."

"I can drive you to the hospital, and you can use my cell, if you want."

"Thanks."

Liv went to get her phone and September placed a hand to her throbbing head, glancing at the tray of food. Carefully, she picked up a piece of toast and nibbled at it, then swallowed down some tea. So far so good. Encouraged, she gathered up her clothes from where she'd tossed them on the floor the night before and headed for the bathroom. After a quick shower, she was thrilled to see a tube of toothpaste and a toothbrush, still in its packaging, laid out on the counter beside the sink. She unwrapped the toothbrush, squirted some toothpaste on the bristles and brushed her teeth long and hard. Then she looked at herself in the mirror. Good. God. Could she be more pale?

Dressing as fast as her aching head would allow, she returned to her bedroom to find Liv's phone waiting for her on the nightstand. Silently blessing her brother's girlfriend, she snatched it up and then was stumped. The only number she had memorized was the station's main desk. She couldn't recall anyone's cell but her own and Auggie's, and a fat lot of good that would do her.

Dialing the number, she said, "Hi. It's Detective Rafferty. Can you put me through to Lieutenant D'Annibal?"

"He's not in today, but Detective Pelligree is."

Thank you, God. "Good. Put me through to him."

Wes answered the phone, "Detective Pelligree."

"Wes, it's September. Jake's at Laurelton General, and I've got the damn bug, but I feel better and I'm going to the hospital. So glad you're at work. What's the story around there?"

"I came in to help. Still feel god-awful, but like you said, better. D'Annibal called. Wanted to talk to you. He's still in the shits, if you know what I mean."

"Only too well. What about George?"

"Don't know. Maharis is here."

"Good. I'll be in after the hospital."

"What happened to Jake?" he asked.

"Car accident. He's . . . going to be all right."

There was a moment of silence. She didn't want Wes to say anything more about it in case she fell apart. He must have picked up on her feelings because he changed the subject and asked, "What are you thinking about Harmak's murder?"

This was easier to talk about. "Stefan said a woman was behind the crime. I've got some work to do on the Ballonni part of the case. Some interviews. If you want to look at the file . . ."

"I'm on it."

"Okay, thanks. I gave Auggie what I had on Carrie Lynne's

boyfriend. He's going to see what he can find out. Try to trace the ketamine back to the dealer."

He grunted. "Good."

She clicked off and went in search of Liv, who was drinking a cup of coffee in the kitchen and reading the paper. She looked up and asked, "Ready?"

"Yup. Anything in the news?"

"Stefan's murder," she said. "And a recap of how he was tied up early last week. The similarity between that attack and the attack on Christopher Ballonni."

"Great," she said without enthusiasm.

"And there's a paragraph about Jake's accident."

Accident. September set her jaw. No accident.

Liv's gaze lingered on September's face and September could read what she was thinking. "I feel better than I look."

"If you say so."

"You don't pull any punches, do you?" September said, cracking a smile.

"I just don't want you passing out on me or something and hearing about it from your brother later." She added, "And I do hope you feel better."

"I do." Marginally. But that wasn't going to stop her from getting to Jake.

The hospital was quieter when September arrived and she was able to show her ID and be directed to a waiting area on the second floor where she was told the doctor on duty would find her. She was a little taken aback when it turned out to be Dr. Denby, the authoritative physician who'd run afoul of Gretchen on a case earlier in the summer. But then, September told herself, she'd been at Laurelton General enough times in the past week that it would be a surprise if she didn't run into someone she recognized now.

Denby said, "It's Detective . . . ?"

"Rafferty," she reminded him, standing up to hold out her identification. The officious doctor with the slight build and blond, close-shaved beard leaned forward. His gaze scanned her ID but he kept his hands to himself. She wondered if it was because she looked ill. Based on the dispensers of hand sanitizer that were tacked on the walls, she thought it might just be standard policy to touch visitors as little as possible in order to keep the germ transfer down.

"Ah, yes. I remember you." His eyes moved past her, as if he expected Gretchen to appear.

"Detective Sandler isn't with me." September answered the unspoken question and he looked somewhat relieved.

"You're here to see about Mr. Westerly," he guessed.

"Yes. How is he?"

"He hasn't regained consciousness yet, so you won't be able to interview him."

September felt her legs quiver. She wanted to appear strong, but she was definitely feeling weak. "Has his family been alerted?"

"His parents are with him now. And his brother, I believe."

"Could you bring me up to date on his condition?"

He gestured for her to sit back down and September practically fell into the chair. Dr. Denby had resented them the last time they were there, but they'd been asking to interview a patient who was recovering from surgery and the doctor had been adamantly against the interview. This time he just laid out the medical facts without September having to go through the same rigmarole, the upshot being that Jake had actually gone through the windshield and into the wall. He'd apparently thrown up his arms to protect himself and both of them were broken, one at the wrist, the other at the elbow. The elbow injury was going to require surgery. There were lacerations on both arms and his face, but what the medical staff was watching the closest was the head injury Jake had sustained upon impact, the one that had created a swelling in his brain and was a direct cause of his unconsciousness.

September listened quietly, combating the spots before her eyes with long, deep breaths. She wasn't sure if her reaction was because of the virus or the feeling of helplessness that invaded her at the long list of Jake's injuries. Probably a combination of both.

You've got to wake up, Jake.

She noticed Denby kept talking about "if" he regained consciousness, not "when," and the distinction made anxiety swell inside her like a rising balloon. She spent several long minutes internally tamping down her fears, not speaking, and finally Denby got to his feet again, ready to move on.

"Thank you, Dr. Denby," she managed to tell him.

He nodded curtly and turned away, then stopped and glanced back as if he'd forgotten something. September was trying to keep him from guessing the extent of her fears and she just wanted him to get a move on before she lost professionalism entirely and went into hyperventilation or worse.

"Detective, if you wish to speak to Mrs. Cheever, I let her know that her daughter's body has already been taken to the hospital morgue. I'm sure she's already there."

Chapter Nineteen

Loni Cheever died when her chest was crushed by the steering wheel and her ribs punctured her lungs and heart. She might have survived if she and Jake had been found sooner, but too much time passed before her car was discovered by a couple taking an after dinner walk.

September didn't go to find Marilyn Cheever. She wasn't the crash investigator no matter what impression she'd given Denby. She was at the hospital in a personal capacity and that was all, and since she couldn't help Jake, and maybe could harm him, she didn't go into his room, either. Instead, she spent the rest of Sunday back at his house, recovering, calling the hospital and the doctor every hour, making a complete pest of herself, but unable to stop doing it. She needed to know that Jake was going to be all right, that he wouldn't suffer the same fate as Loni. She was out of control and out of her mind with worry.

Late in the day she put a call in to Jake's parents. The Westerlys were holding it together—just. They told her Jake's arm surgery was scheduled for later in the week. Everyone was just waiting to see when he would wake up. She called Colin next and was told more of the same, then spent the next few hours fielding calls from her own family as they each heard the news. She told them, "Thanks for calling. No, there's no change. I'll let you know when there is," too many times to count.

It was one of the longest days on record.

The only respite from her worries about Jake were her conversations with Wes, who'd managed to stay at the department for a couple of hours before throwing in the towel and going home, too. With Maharis's help, he kept the department running—sort of—and even got some work done.

"Gloria del Courte called you back," Wes told her the first time they spoke. "The one Ballonni's wife thought was hot for him."

"Yes, I know," she said impatiently. "What did she say?"

"That she was *not* hot for him. Actually, she thought he was kind of skeevy."

"In what way?"

"Del Courte thinks she caught him with some child porn pictures. Wasn't sure, because he swept them up before she could get a good look. It was after that, though, that he kinda came on to her, like he was trying to deflect, make her think he found her attractive, that kind of thing."

"She thinks it was his way of covering up."

"Yup. Like he was interested in her, a grown woman, not little girls."

For just an instant an image of Jake, throwing up his arms, the wall rushing toward him, ran across the screen of her mind. She squeezed her eyes closed to shut it down. She couldn't think about him. Couldn't. "Do you think . . . that . . . Ballonni may have hinted about his 'attraction' to del Courte to his wife? Maybe saying things about how great one of his coworkers was, how nice, how much he liked her?"

"Talking her up, you mean?"

"Yeah. Like that."

"Better to let the wife think you're interested in another woman," Wes said.

"Exactly." September swallowed against a dry throat. With difficulty, she was keeping her wandering mind on the case. "Janet saw that television show, about autoerotic asphyxiation. She put that together with her husband and del Courte and thought his being tied to the pole was sexual."

"You don't think she suspects, then, about his possible interest in young girls."

"Uh-uh," September said.

She ended the phone call by asking Wes to follow up on Shannon Kraxberger by finding the Kraxberger's new address, but when Wes called back he said he was still working on it, but he was about to head home.

Just before he hung up on their last call, he said, "Your brother located Bill Quade. I don't know what he said to him, but Bill just gave up his brother. Said he's back in Oregon, somewhere on the coast. Even coughed up an address."

"Way to go, Auggie." September infused some enthusiasm into her voice with an effort.

"You sure you're okay?" Wes asked. "This bug is a nasty motherfucker."

Best day of my life. A guy she'd dated briefly would answer any question like Wes's with that answer. She wanted to say it now just to prove that she was her old self, but she couldn't quite manage it. Instead, she said, "Maharis said Stefan's van is being checked out. Ask him to call me if anything comes out of that."

"Won't be for a while yet."

"Is he there?"

"Working on that missing person case. Said he was going to Gulliver's later."

Fast losing focus, September let Wes go. She went into the kitchen and looked into Jake's refrigerator, hoping for anything that looked appealing. Not a damn thing.

* * *

Monday morning she got up, went through her morning ablutions like an automaton, then headed to the hospital. Still no change in Jake's condition. This time she dared to go into his room, but she hung back in the doorway, not touching anything, in case she was still contagious. She was glad to look into his face but was struck silent by the paleness of his skin beneath his dark beard growth, and the IV drip that seemed so fragile a lifeline to his return to health.

She felt weak as she left, and she forced herself to stop at the small coffee counter and pick up a cup of tea and a bran muffin, which she ate in the car before she headed to work.

She arrived at the department ahead of time but Lieutenant D'Annibal was already there. He looked a little peaked himself, but he was all business.

"Bring me up to date on the Harmak case," he ordered her.

With Wes not in yet, D'Annibal was looking to September for answers. Or, maybe he knew how much she'd been involved already against his direct orders. Diffidently, she reminded him, "I'm on the Ballonni case."

He just waved her into his office and she entered and sat down in one of the chairs across the desk from him. She decided to cut through all the protocol bullshit and immediately launched in about the case from start to finish.

By the time she was through Wes had arrived and so had Maharis. George was still out.

D'Annibal walked out of his office and September followed. "This damn virus has decimated this department," the lieutenant grumbled. "Cleaning crews went through here last night doing an extra-thorough scrub." He turned to Blake Maharis. "Thanks for helping out."

"Thank you, sir."

"I'd like you to stick around for a while."

Blake brightened. "I'd like to, sir."

D'Annibal asked him, "Where are you on that missing person case?"

"I went to Gulliver's, the bar where Gillian Palmiter's roommate dropped her off last Thursday. The staff told me to check with a bartender named Mark Newsome. He's the main man on Wenches Night, which is every Thursday."

"Wenches Night?" he asked, then dismissed it with a hand.

"I've called his cell, but he hasn't picked up yet," Maharis added.

"I know Mark," September put in. "Sandler and I interviewed him on our last case." Do Unto Others was the case where she and Jake had reconnected and her thoughts automatically turned to him. She'd listened to his last message to her over and over again. Sometimes she worried that it would be his ultimate last message, but *no*. She *could not* think that way.

She realized she'd missed some things while her mind went on its journey of fear. Maharis was saying, ". . . names and numbers of Jilly's boyfriends. Got through to one of them, who was out of town last week, and a phone message into another. There might be some more. She was . . . playing the field."

September thought about Gulliver's, remembering the interview she and Gretchen had conducted. "Wait a minute. The Mark I remember was a waiter, not a bartender. One of those workout guys. Not exactly the brightest bulb in the fixture."

"Doesn't sound like the same guy. This Mark's a bartender," Maharis said again.

"Nine, follow up with Maharis, whatever the case," D'Annibal said. Then he turned to Wes. "Nine briefed me on the Harmak/Ballonni case and I want you on it full time. Find this vigilante and shut her down."

September's chest immediately tightened. "And what do you have for me?"

"I learned this morning that Pauline Kirby's been calling for you," the lieutenant responded. "If you're feeling ready, take the interview. We want to get the word out that we're looking for a woman. See what shakes out after you mention that's what your stepbrother revealed before he died."

Ex-stepbrother. "Can I meet with some other reporter?" she asked.

"Pauline seems to feel she has a relationship with you."

September bit back her feelings on the subject and said instead, "When I'm done with the interview, I still want to be on the case."

"You'll both be working with Wes," he said to September and Maharis, which made Blake happy and September worry that she was being subtly pushed out either because of her relationship with Stefan, or because she was sick with worry over Jake.

When D'Annibal retreated to his office, and Maharis was seated at Gretchen's desk, she looked over at Wes, who was looking back. She silently signaled him to meet her in the break room.

Once they were both there, she said, "What the hell's going on?"

"I'm thinking D'Annibal's just trying to ease up on you," Wes said.

"You think I need that?"

"You want the truth?"

She stared into his dark, liquid eyes and saw soberness and compassion. Immediately, fear welled up in her chest. *Jake . . .* Eyes burning, she turned away and said hoarsely, "See you after the interview. . . ."

Graham was struggling through the first periods of the day. He taught social studies, as a rule, but with cutbacks he'd been assigned a class of remedial math that was a last-gasp attempt to get the lower IQs of the school to actually learn something before they were moved on to junior high. Most of the students were male with a sprinkling of girls who wore too much makeup and had dull eyes and smart mouths.

After he got through that hell, it was lunchtime, and he wanted nothing more than to go outside and watch the lower grades at recess, though it was still raining like a sonofabitch and no one would be out there. With the blasted weather, he was forced to sit inside with the rest of the faculty at reserved tables. He bought himself a crappy turkey sandwich from a vending machine and a Diet Coke, then made his way to the reserved table, wishing he could avoid the admiring look on Mrs. Pearce's face. Pearce was a widow and even older than Daria. God.

But that girl with the rosebud lips was in her class and he found himself dreaming about her in a way that was thoroughly X-rated. No, he reminded himself. *No.*

He tried to shut down his mind, knowing what he felt would be misconstrued. He didn't want to hurt her. God, no. He just would like to get to know her a little. Just a little.

By the time he got to sixth period, he thought he'd gotten himself under control, but this was the class with Molly and he could feel his anticipation rising in spite of himself.

And there was Molly, seated in the back, sweet and lovely, mostly ignored by the rest of the class, which was filled with rowdy jocks and simpering sycophantic *women*—they just couldn't be called girls with those huge racks and loud, braying laughter.

He had a difficult time keeping his mind on any kind of lecture, so he had them open their textbooks and work on the questions at the end of the chapter on the Renaissance, a period of rebirth after the Dark Ages. His favorite author and statesman from the Renaissance was Machiavelli, whose actions and thoughts had coined the term *Machiavellian*, which was still in general use today and described in Wikipedia as *the employment of cunning or duplicity in statecraft or in general conduct.*

Duplicity . . . showing one side while another was underneath. He had to live a duplicitous life himself, didn't he? What a sad comment on society that he'd never be able to reveal his true, loving self. So what if his desire ran to younger girls. Was that really so wrong?

But even as that thought crossed his mind, fear pushed it away. He had crossed a line with Jilly there was no coming back from. Murder was a real crime. One which could send him away for the rest of his life, if he wasn't careful.

A thrill shot through him as his mind touched on Jilly again, the way her skull had crumpled in. He could get hard just remembering that one moment.

Wrangling his thoughts back with an effort, he cruised around the room, stopping behind Molly's desk. She was diligently writing down the answers to the questions, and he stared down at the shining hair lying like silk on the back of her head. He thought about laying a hand on her crown but had to hold himself back. His heart was slamming into his rib cage. Such a lovely girl.

And then he saw that she'd been texting on her phone. Leaning down, he whispered in her ear, "No cell phones in the classroom, remember?"

Immediately she blushed and switched hers off. "I forgot it was on, Mr. Harding."

"Uh-huh."

"I'm really sorry."

"I'm going to have to take it to my desk. You can pick it up after class." He grabbed the phone, then walked away. Being that close to her was exquisite torture. The phone felt warm in his hand as his mind tried to figure out how to be with her. What could he do? How could he have her? Where could he go?

Dad's house.

The thought had been moving around in the back of his mind. His father was growing dottier by the day. Graham had already taken his car. He could damn near move into the place now, except that the neighbors all shared in his father's care whether Graham wanted it or not, and they were nosy as hell. The house was a decrepit sty, too. Ever since he and his father had suffered a falling-out the place had gone to shit. Even worse, when the old man finally died, the place was going lock, stock, and barrel to Graham's sister, a superbitch with a rod up her ass. Luckily, she lived in New York and never visited. Her relationship with their father was primarily by phone.

Graham had been subsequently working his way back into his father's good graces and was almost there. But no lawyer in his right mind would ever believe his father capable of making the decision to put Graham back in the will. That ship had sailed.

But . . . the house had a basement with its own door. He might not ever be able to own the place but, if he played his cards right, he could still make use of the property.

He was deep into dreaming and planning when the bell rang and the students started filing out. Molly came up and asked if she could have her phone and he handed it over, letting his hands wrap around hers as he made the transfer. As she left, he watched her move to the door, his heart heavy. How was he ever going to be with her?

Especially with HER waiting for him. Her unexpected return had really thrown him for a loop. *Surprise, surprise! Here I am!* But luckily she was leaving again for San Antonio tomorrow. Tomorrow. It was barely soon enough.

He hated Daria. Loathed her. Despised her. Thought of ways that he could dispose of her and still keep her house.

She thought she knew all the answers. *How to Beat the Recession and Not Let It Beat You, my ass.*

If only he could kill her. He'd liked the feel of the Maori figurine in his hands. The weight. The power.

You can't kill her. You need her.

Graham ground his teeth together. He needed her respectability. With his job and hers, there was no way anyone would believe he was behind Jilly's disappearance or any future one, for that matter.

And what about that last encounter at that airport motel?

He broke out in a cold sweat, tried to push the memory aside, but it stayed with him, as persistent as a bad odor. He didn't know how old *that* girl was, but she sure as hell wasn't eighteen. Still, their sex was completely unsatisfactory because she'd been around the block a time or two already, even though she was very, very young. Little more than a child, really. Undoubtedly an underage prostitute. If she ever was caught and could finger him . . .

But no. He'd given her a false name and shortly after that encounter he'd hooked up with Daria. On purpose. To gain respectability.

His mind then touched on Jilly, lying beneath the raspberry vines. A chill fluttered inside his heart, part thrill, part fear. He should be more worried about her than the prostitute, he supposed, but he only had good thoughts when it came to her. The figurine crashing into her skull replayed in his memory. He could damn near have an orgasm without even touching himself. In fact—

"Mr. Harding?"

He was sitting behind his desk, thank God, his hard-on camouflaged by the top surface though he could feel his face flush. He looked up, registering that it was a woman's voice, not a girl's, as he said, "Yes?"

Then his heart slammed to his throat as he realized it was Molly's mother. "Mrs. Masterson," he said with difficulty.

"Oh, it's Livesay. I took my maiden name back after the divorce."

Like Molly she was petite and blond, and she was a lot younger than Daria. A lot younger . . .

"Ms. Livesay, then," he said, forcing a smile.

"I wondered if I could talk to you about Molly."

"Oh?" He could hear his heart beat in his ears. Had Molly said something about him? Had she guessed?

"Is now a good time?"

He realized she was dressed a little nicer than he'd ever seen her before and there was a light hint of perfume. Was he imagining it, or was she looking at him with extra interest? Maybe this really wasn't about Molly after all. . . .

"I was just leaving. I've got a date with *Monday Night Football* and a beer," he lied.

"Oh, I love football." She smiled and a dimple showed, just like Molly's.

He found himself somewhat entranced. "We should watch together some time," he said lightly.

"I could do that," she answered, her smile growing.

"When would you like to talk about Molly?"

"Some time tomorrow, if you're free?"

The way she said it, he was pretty sure she was coming on to him. In a flash, he thought about Daria leaving and maybe putting Ms. Livesay in her place. It would be a lot safer than his thoughts about Molly and the girl in Mrs. Pearce's class. A lot safer.

Maybe she would even invite him to her place . . . where Molly might even be.

"I've got some time tomorrow evening, if that works for you," he said. He got up from the chair and came around the desk, resting his thigh on the edge. His hard-on had relaxed but he felt a little twitch of interest. If she looked . . .

She looked. Then her eyes came up to his. "Tomorrow

evening would be great. My name's Claudia." She reached out a hand and he shook it warmly.

"Graham. Would it be wrong to suggest meeting for a drink?"

"Would it be wrong of me to suggest dinner and wine at my place?"

He knew women liked his slow smile and now he deliberately let it slide across his face. "What time?"

Lucky stood outside her car in the Twin Oaks parking lot wearing her jogging gear and baseball cap. She'd positioned herself closer to a green Ford Fiesta than her Sentra, just in case anyone should remember her, and turned her back to a biting wind. At least the rain had stopped, though the amped-up breeze was swirling loose rust and gold leaves in a whirling eddy. The front window of the school was covered with paper jack-o'-lanterns grinning out at the parking lot.

Her quarry's Chrysler wagon was two lanes over. She'd followed him to the school—hell, it felt like she'd been following him forever—and now she was anxiously waiting to see if anything would happen after school even though it was dangerous, even though someone could recognize her. But the woman he was living with had wished him good-bye this morning with a big kiss; Lucky had hidden herself by the neighbor's hedge again, having realized no one appeared to be living in that house, so she'd been able to get up close and personal.

She'd followed after him on his way to school, but since she'd expected this was his destination, she didn't worry about losing him if he got too far ahead. She'd managed to wheel into the lot just as he was letting himself into the school, and after a few minutes of making sure he was truly in for the day, she turned out of the lot and drove back to Mr. Blue's, waiting until school was out in the afternoon to pick him up again.

Things were changing all around.

When she'd returned to Mr. Blue's, she'd walked through the garage to her room, just like always, but this time she'd noticed that half his jars and tins and boxes of herbs and medicines were gone. She asked him about the missing stash when she saw him returning from the direction of the hot springs.

"I'm moving them to the storeroom," he'd said.

"Is there a problem?" A sense of foreboding feathered across her skin.

He considered his answer for a long time, which only increased Lucky's awareness that time was passing, the sands slipping through the hourglass.

"I believe in being prepared," was all he finally said.

"Should I leave?"

"If he has brought trouble to my door, you may not want to be here."

"You're talking about the man you mentioned earlier." Lucky glanced past him to where she knew the hot spring pools were, a quarter mile further on.

"I told him to deal with Juan, but he's not one to listen to anything but his own desires. Desperate people do foolish things."

"What's he desperate for?"

"An escape from reality. He wants to be high all the time." There was an unusual tone of censure in Mr. Blue's voice. Most often he didn't concern himself with the whys and wherefores of other people's motivations. "He is catching me in the trap he's made for himself."

"Can I keep the car, just until I'm finished with what I have to do?" Lucky sensed this was a real breakup, not a temporary split, and it made her feel low.

"The car is yours. Do with it as you will."

They'd stared at one another then, and it was Lucky who had finally been the first to break eye contact. She'd been overwhelmed. Mr. Blue was the best friend she'd ever had. Maybe the only friend. "I can be gone by tomorrow," she'd said, her throat tight.

"Come inside."

And he'd had her sit at the table while he went into his rooms. When he returned, he had a tight roll of bills that he placed into her hand. She could see a Benjamin wrapped around the outside. If they were all hundreds, she wasn't sure how much cash it was, but it was a lot.

"Buy a cell phone and call the house, so I have your number. I don't think it will be long before the authorities come looking."

"Will they arrest you?" she asked, alarmed.

"No. But he is reckless and they will find him and they will come to my door and try to look inside the house. It is better if the curtains are open and they can get a clear view, so no one feels they need a search warrant." He smiled faintly. "This isn't the first time I've been through this. It won't be the last. Maybe I'll invite them in and offer them herbal tea."

She'd started to feel better after that. Maybe it was just temporary.

But then he said, "If things go wrong, you know how to get into the storeroom, if you need to."

She almost said, "Things won't go wrong," but she didn't. It wasn't in her nature to offer false hope and panaceas.

Instead she'd said, "Good-bye, Hiram," and awkwardly shook his hand.

"I'll see you before you leave," he'd told her, and then he'd gone back into his rooms.

She believed when she returned tonight that the rest of the jars, tins, and boxes would be moved as well.

The thought of leaving him filled her with fear. She would be on her own again. Totally alone.

Momentarily she let her thoughts touch on her sister, but she pulled them back and shut them down. Her sister had abilities, too. Not the same as hers, but something. They'd come from the same strange mixture of genetic brew and though their meeting a few years earlier had been brief, she'd known Gemma had an extra vibe that told her things about people, a bit of precognition different from Lucky's.

A group of preteen girls came out of the school together, and Lucky was brought back to the present. They said their good-byes to each other, then split apart. One of them started heading straight toward Lucky's direction, so she opened her purse and pretended to be searching through it for something.

She was surprised when the girl slowed near the Fiesta. She was wearing skinny jeans and a raincoat over a red sweater with a deep vee that showed off an impressive set of boobs. She'd already pulled out her phone and was texting. Lucky moved a little bit away from the Fiesta, still searching through her purse.

"Can't find your keys?" the girl asked, climbing onto the hood of the green car.

Lucky slid her a look out of the corner of her eyes. The girl couldn't be more than twelve, as Twin Oaks only went through sixth grade, but she looked like she could be in high school. "Uh, no . . ."

"My mom loses hers all the time. God, I hope she gets out here soon. If it starts raining, I'm gonna be really pissed."

"Your mom's a teacher?" Lucky guessed.

"Sixth grade. I was like dying that I would get her as homeroom teacher, but they don't do that. But then, I got Ugh, so that's no better."

"Ugh?"

"He's like a lech. No one believes us because they all think he's so hot and all, but he's nasty." She gave a mock shudder. "He likes the nerds, though, so I get a pass. I wish I'd gotten Mr. Tarker. He's pretty cool. Owns one of those amphibians, you know?" Lucky shook her head. "They can drive on land

and into water. He takes some of the kids sometimes, but oh, no. I had to get Ugh."

"Why do you call him Ugh?" Lucky asked.

She gave her a sharp look. "Do you have a kid here?"

"I'm just waiting for a friend and then we're going to jog around the track," Lucky improvised.

"Oh, there's my mom now. . . ." She scooted off the hood. "And there's Ugh, talking to Molly's mom. Yuck." She made a face of supreme disgust.

Lucky glanced over to see her quarry smiling at a petite woman whose daughter was walking a few steps behind them. As she watched, "Ugh" slid a look toward the daughter that sent Lucky's radar into overdrive.

"Why is he called Ugh?" she asked again.

"That's his name. Ulysses Graham Harding, but all the parents call him Graham. They think he's cool, but believe me, he's just wrong."

The girl's mother was approaching, a trim, middle-aged woman with a tense expression and short black hair that was undoubtedly dyed. She gave Lucky a look and, taking her cue, Lucky tucked her purse under her arm, not wanting to give away which vehicle was hers, and jogged in the direction of the track. Halfway there she glanced back and saw Ugh still lingering with the woman and her daughter, Molly. Molly was as flat chested as the girl she'd been talking with was buxom.

If she could have, Lucky would have shooed the teacher and girl out of the parking lot as fast as she could so she could concentrate on Ugh. As it was, they seemed to take an inordinate amount of time getting into the Fiesta and driving away as Lucky waited by the side of the building, jogging in place, pretending to be looking for someone. Of course, what jogger would carry her purse with her, but she hadn't dared put it back in the car.

Finally, the Fiesta drove out of the lot and when Lucky was

completely sure they were gone, she stopped jogging in place and walked back toward her car. Ugh and Molly's mother were still getting pretty chummy, so Lucky had more than enough time to get back to her Nissan without him noticing her.

She could catch snatches of their conversation, and she heard him apologizing for the station wagon. The woman waved it away as if it didn't matter at all. She was well and truly hooked.

When he finally climbed into his car, Lucky had already switched on her ignition.

She watched him turn a corner, then put her car in gear and slowly followed after him. She half expected him to meet up with the woman; it looked like they'd made plans, but it didn't take long for her to realize he was heading home.

When he took the turn into the streets of his neighborhood she drove on by. Clearly, whatever plans he'd made with the woman, if any were made at all, were on hold. He was heading back to his roommate and the house on the outskirts of Laurelton.

Ulysses Graham Harding.

"Ugh . . ."

Chapter Twenty

The interview with channel seven's Pauline Kirby was shot in front of the police station, at the bottom of the three wide steps that led to the front door. It was September's second one-on-one with Kirby. The first interview had been several months earlier, but it felt like a lifetime ago. Then, September had been new to the department and nervous and blindsided by some of Pauline's tactics. Now, she was so distracted she didn't really give a damn.

Pauline was thin to the point of gaunt, dark haired and laser eyed. She gave September the old evil eye and it made her review her own appearance. She'd combed her hair, added blush and lipstick to make herself appear less haggard, and now she was waiting for the reporter's cameraman to set up, her gaze off in the middle distance, her mind with Jake even while Pauline assessed her from head to toe. September had called again to learn, once more, that there was no change. She'd demanded to talk to the doctor, wanting to know if this was a bad sign. How long could he be unconscious before his prognosis was downgraded? Right now everyone was cautiously optimistic. Cautiously optimistic. Bullshit. She didn't want to know what the euphemistic terminology would be if things went south.

"We're almost ready," Kirby assured her.

September nodded vaguely. Lieutenant D'Annibal had asked her to be the face of the department and that's what had led to the first interview. September hadn't wanted it then, and she didn't want it now, but what the hell. At least she didn't care as much this time, even if the reason was because she simply didn't have the time to waste energy on the likes of Pauline Kirby.

"Okay . . . Darrell's got us in frame," she said as she moved up to September, microphone in hand. "I'm going to start asking questions."

"Have you already done your introduction?" September asked. This was a sore point as last time Pauline had interviewed her, she'd done a separate piece with the two hikers who had stumbled across a dead body. She'd never told September about that interview and when the news had aired, with the hikers' interview placed directly in front of the one with September, the effect somehow made September, and the whole department, seem lost and inept. It had pissed September off but good.

"This time it's just you and me, Detective."

"Okay." September's tone suggested how little she trusted the reporter.

Apart from a tightening of lips, Pauline let it go. Darrell motioned for Pauline to go ahead, and the reporter immediately put a look of concern on her face and said, "I'm here with Detective September Rafferty of the Laurelton Police Department, who's been investigating two murders that may very well be connected. Detective"—she turned to September—"just last week a man named Stefan Harmak was first stripped down and tied to a pole in the yard of the elementary school where he was employed as a teaching assistant. There was a sign hung around his neck written in his own hand that said I WANT WHAT I CAN'T HAVE. Now that man is dead, gunned down in his home, which is just a stone's throw from the school where he was employed. It seems like the killer didn't finish what he started. What can you tell us about it?"

"That may very well be the killer's motive. We're working on several theories." Dazzle them with noninformation unless there's something you want to get across. With that in mind, she added, "We have reason to believe the victim may have been targeted by a woman."

Pauline blinked, surprised. "A woman. Really. Is that—do you have new information?"

"Mr. Harmak indicated to us that a woman was involved."

"Mr. Stefan Harmak—the man who was shot by an intruder?"

"That's correct."

"A man who just happened to be your stepbrother, isn't that right?" she added in a calculated tone.

"Yes, that's right. He was my stepbrother before my father remarried." September met the reporter's gaze coolly. *Bring it on, Pauline.*

If Kirby was surprised by September's quiet challenge, she took it in stride. "Is there any connection to your department?" Pauline asked. "Some kind of grievance against the police that may have instigated this attack?"

"The similarities between this case and the one last February would make that unlikely."

"You're talking about Christopher Ballonni, who was also stripped down and tied to a pole in front of his place of work, a local office of the US Postal Service. Are you saying the two crimes are definitely connected, Detective?"

"The MO would suggest that."

"Not a copycat?"

"There are pieces of information we purposely withheld that we believe only the same person would know. Our working theory is it's one killer."

"And a woman."

"Yes."

"Who went to Mr. Harmak's house and finished what she'd failed to accomplish at the school, namely his death?"

"The crime scene is still being evaluated." September slid away from a true answer.

"It's surprising that the killer is a woman," Pauline said in a voice that implied September was giving her a load of bull. "How is she attacking these men, and why?"

"As soon as we have some answers, we'll let the public know."

"Do we have some deranged serial killer in our midst once again? Should we be locking our doors against this woman?"

She was digging away. Trying to worm any information from September that she could. But there wasn't much more to say. The vigilante, whoever she was, seemed to be targeting suspected pedophiles; at least that was the prevailing theory. But unfortunately September was running more on feeling than fact, and how this woman targeted her victims was still a mystery. And she wasn't planning to say anything about any of it to Pauline Kirby.

When Pauline shut down the interview, she had a look of disgust on her face. "If you'd told me about this 'woman' ahead of time, I could have fashioned a better set of questions."

"Let's call it a draw. You wanted to blindside me about my relationship to Stefan Harmak."

Kirby's brows lifted. "The young detective has teeth."

"I'm going back to work."

"Keeping us all safe, eh?"

September didn't bother answering as she turned away from Pauline Kirby and her cameraman and climbed the front steps of the station. Guy Urlacher looked up as she entered and she lifted her index finger to stop him from speaking. "Not today."

"I saw you with that reporter," he said by way of explaining why he buzzed her in without demanding to see her ID.

Bully for you.

"How'd you do?" Wes asked when she entered. He was drinking tea and eating some saltine crackers. Lunch had been chicken soup that Kayleen had sent with him and September had wished she felt any appetite. Between her worry over Jake and her own uncertain stomach, she could scarcely look at food. However, when Wes held up a saltine, she decided she needed something so she accepted five or six of them and managed to munch them all down. A good sign.

"At least the interview's over," she told him. "It'll be on the evening news."

"I've got the Kraxbergers' new address for you," he told her. "The daughter's at school and the husband's at work at a car dealership, but the mom's home."

"Great. Let's go talk to her," September said, glad that Wes had waited for her.

Maharis looked up from notes he was writing on Gretchen's desk. "Thought the lieutenant said you should go with me to interview the bartender."

"What time does he start work?" September asked, checking the clock. It was nearly five.

"Six."

It was after day-shift hours and Maharis's face said as much, but that was just too damn bad in September's opinion. "I'll meet you at Gulliver's later. I'll call you when I'm on my way."

"Okay," he said glumly.

"If you've got something to do, I'll go with Nine," Wes said.

"Nope, nope. I'm ready."

Wes grinned and as he and September headed for his Range Rover, he said, "Newbies. Always want it both ways."

"Technically, I'm still a newbie."

"Nah. You got stabbed and damn near ran the department the last few days. You're one of us now."

"Thanks." As ever, September's thoughts turned to Jake again. *Wake up,* she told him silently. *Be all right.*

Ten minutes later they arrived at the Kraxbergers' home, a two-story split entry on a winding road at the edge of Portland in the West Hills. Wes had called Mrs. Kraxberger, who was clearly waiting for them as the front door opened before Wes had even set the brake.

September and Wes walked up to the front door together. Mrs. Kraxberger was a woman in her forties who wore her light brown hair in a short, stylish cut and had a sharp line between her brows. As soon as September drew near, the woman sized her up in that way some women did automatically, as if every other female was a potential rival. "Detectives," she said flatly. Her gaze slid from September to Wes, taking in his lanky, slow-moving way.

"Hello, Mrs. Kraxberger," Wes said. "I'm Detective Pelligree and this is my partner, Detective Rafferty."

"Come inside," she said. "You said this was concerning the postman who killed himself, but I don't see how that has anything to do with us."

Wes took the lead after she led them up a half flight of stairs to the living room, which was divided into two sitting areas. She invited them to sit down and perched on one of the ottomans. September sat on the edge of the couch and Wes took a chair.

"Before you moved, you lived on Christopher Ballonni's mail route," Wes began.

"I didn't know him though," she denied immediately. "Who knows their mailman?"

"One of your neighbors, Mrs. Bernstein, made a formal complaint against Mr. Ballonni. She claimed that Ballonni gave her daughter a stick of gum and was too familiar with her."

"I don't know this Mrs. Bernstein," Mrs. Kraxberger said stiffly, her hands clasped together tightly.

Wes paused, sizing her up. She clearly didn't want to talk, so September tried with, "Do you know Mr. Ballonni's son, Christopher Jr.?"

"No."

"He was a classmate of your daughter, Shannon," September pressed.

At the mention of her daughter's name, it was like Mrs. Kraxberger had been jabbed with a pin. "I don't think that's right."

"Would it be all right if we spoke to Shannon?" Wes asked.

"No." She was firm.

"Christopher Jr. suggested I speak to her," September said.

Her head swiveled around and she stared at September as if she'd started speaking in tongues. "That can't be true. You're making that up!"

"I wouldn't make it up," September assured her as color washed up Mrs. Kraxberger's face, then leached right out again.

"What are you trying to say? That the mailman was too personal with my daughter, too? Well, he was. Always giving out sticks of gum. Trying too hard to be friendly. Do I think he had a problem? Yes. Am I sorry he's dead? No. But it has nothing to do with Shannon and I don't want you saying anything ugly to my daughter to give her any ideas that it does." She jumped to her feet and stalked to the top of the stairs, waiting for them.

Wes and September rose to their feet. "We're investigating another homicide that may be connected to Mr. Ballonni's," September said in an effort to bring down the tension.

"I don't care what you do, as long as it doesn't concern my daughter."

Wes pressed a card into her hand on the way out and said, "If you think of anything."

"I won't. Thank you." She practically slammed the door on them on the way out and when they were back in Wes's Range Rover they looked at each other and Wes said, "Well."

September nodded. "There's something there, but she can't face it. I mean, I get it. We're talking about her daughter and she's only twelve or thirteen now, so how old was she when Ballonni got too friendly?"

"The guy was a pedophile," Wes said, his expression grim. "That I believe."

"And that's why he was killed. I'm with you. But how do we prove that? How do we find the woman who's doing this?"

He reached for the file that he'd stuffed between the front seats. "Who else lives on that route?"

"I've got the names of the two women Rhoda Bernstein said defended Ballonni. Maybe we should talk to them."

"Which ones are they?" he asked, looking at the list, and September pointed them out. "I wish I could talk to Shannon herself, or even Chris Jr. again. I want to know what that generation thinks about Ballonni."

"We could drop in on the Ballonnis after school," Wes suggested.

"I need to stop by Laurelton General and see Jake."

"You want me to do it?"

September pictured Wes Pelligree walking up to Janet Ballonni's door and changed her mind. "She doesn't like me, but it would still be better if I interviewed her."

"She's gonna object to a black dude showing up."

"She's gonna object to the law showing up again. Especially since we want to talk to Chris. I'll go see Jake later."

When they arrived at the Ballonni house a boy and a girl in their early teens were standing at the end of the driveway. *Chris Jr. and maybe his girlfriend,* September thought, wondering if she could really get that lucky.

As she and Wes stepped out of the Range Rover, she

called, "Chris. Hi. I'm Detective Rafferty and this is Detective Pelligree."

The boy stepped away from the girl as if she'd burned him and September saw a section of blinds, which had been opened for a peek, snap back into place.

"Janet's seen us," she warned Wes.

The words were barely out of her mouth when Janet Ballonni came flying out the door and swooped in on her son like a bird of prey. Chris's eyes cast a silent good-bye to the girl, who turned a shoulder to them and began walking away.

"Haven't you hurt us enough?" Janet challenged them as she grabbed Chris's arm. Her gaze raked over Wes as if he were the devil incarnate.

"Mrs. Ballonni, Chris, we just want to talk to you about Shannon Kraxberger," September said.

Chris threw September a wild, accusatory look, but let his mother drag him inside. Janet slammed the door with a *bang*.

September's gaze then swiveled to the back of the girl who was quickly walking away from the scene at the Ballonnis.

"Jamie?" September called.

The girl hesitated, then looked over her shoulder at them.

"Chris mentioned you to me," September said.

She stopped and turned fully around. She was pretty enough with straight dark brown hair and wide blue eyes, but she had that sullen look so often adopted by tweens. "He did?"

"He told me you were his girlfriend when I talked to him on the phone the other day." September was moving toward the girl but Wes hung back, letting her talk to the girl without overwhelming her.

"He said he talked to the police. Janet doesn't know."

"I figured."

She cocked her head to one side. "You're kinda pretty for a cop."

"Thanks."

"I can't believe Chris told you about Shannon. I mean, he knows what a sick psycho his dad was, but he won't ever talk about it. Like never."

"Chris knew his father was a sexual predator?" September asked.

"Well, I don't know about that. But yeah, he knew about Shannon. And you know why? Because I'm the one who told him about her."

Chapter Twenty-One

Jamie tossed back her hair and warmed to her subject. "Chris's dad was always trying to get too close. I stayed out of his way whenever I was at their house. Mostly, Chris comes over to my house. His dad just would look at me weird, y'know, and I knew what he was thinking, especially because of what Shannon told me." She stuck her tongue out and made a gagging sound. "Shannon told me about him 'cause she knew Chris and I were friends. This was a few years ago, before we were going together. She'd gotten kinda weird and we didn't know why. Then she told me. She was like having a real hard time because she'd always thought Chris's dad was cool 'cause he shared his gum with her, but then once he got out of his truck and pretended to hug her but then he felt her up, and she didn't even have *anything* up there. She tried to get away, but he stuck his hand down her pants before she could run into the house." She made a face and shuddered. "She was really, really scared to tell her mom and dad, so she never said anything, until she finally told me. I told Chris his dad was like a sex maniac. We had this really big fight. But then Shannon's parents were leaving and she was glad and she told me not to tell anyone else. She was kinda upset that I told Chris. After she left, Chris and I didn't really talk about it anymore, especially after his dad died, but I always kinda thought it happened because he was a sexual predator, like you see on TV."

September had suspected as much but hearing Jamie baldly call Ballonni a sexual predator made it very real. "Do you know of anyone else, besides Shannon, who might have had contact with Chris's dad in that way?"

"Maybe you should ask the day-care lady," Jamie said.

"Day-care lady?"

"The one who had the day care on the end of Shannon's street."

September turned to Wes, who was within earshot, and they stared at each other in mute horror. *A day care?*

"Ask Shannon about her. She'll remember."

"Thank you. I'll do that."

"You won't tell Chris that I told you all that, will you?" She darted a fearful look back at the Ballonni house. "That would really be bad."

"I don't know if I'll be talking to Chris again," September said.

They left Jamie and the Ballonnis and climbed into Wes's SUV again. "Back to the Kraxbergers?" he asked.

"We need to talk to Shannon."

"How are you gonna get past the mom?"

She shrugged. "I don't know. I'll think of something on the way."

He turned the Range Rover around as September consulted the names on the map of the mail route again. The street the Kraxbergers lived on ended in a cul-de-sac. There were two houses at the final curve. The one facing toward the north was owned by a family named Maroney; the one toward the south was owned by the Francos. She dialed the Maroneys' number first and got voice mail. She left her name and number, then she called the second number and the Francos' voice mail answered as well.

"Damn," September said after she'd clicked off, not liking any of it.

"Yeah."

When they arrived at the Kraxbergers' again, it looked as if Mrs. Kraxberger had just picked up Shannon from a dance class as the girl was just getting out of a car, dressed in a leotard and tights with a big jacket thrown over the outfit.

Shannon glanced over at them as September and Wes got out of their vehicle. She still didn't have much in the way of breasts and there was something very childlike about her body.

"What are you doing here again?" Mrs. Kraxberger practically screeched, grabbing hold of Shannon's arm.

"Who are they?" Shannon asked her mother.

"We're detectives with the Laurelton Police Department," September said loudly as Shannon's mother was hustling her up the front steps to the door. "We wanted to talk to you and your mother about Mr. Ballonni." September knew she was stepping over the line a bit, engaging the minor without her parent's permission, but she honestly didn't much care.

"Get out of here!" Mrs. Kraxberger yelled at them.

Wes said in a calm voice, "We're trying to solve a homicide and could use some help."

"Don't talk to them," she told her daughter.

Shannon glanced over at September, who said, "We just talked to Jamie."

Shannon's eyes widened and her mouth dropped open.

"Who?" her mother demanded. "Leave her alone!"

"She said there was a day care at the end of your street," September pressed, as Wes said for her ears only, "Careful with mother bear."

"I'm calling your superiors!" Mrs. Kraxberger opened the

door and tried to pull Shannon into the house, but the girl shook herself free.

"He's dead, isn't he?" she called down to September. "Mr. Ballonni?"

"Yes," September said.

"Do you know what he did to me?"

"Yes," September said again.

"Shannon!" her mother cried, appalled.

"The day-care lady was Mrs. Vasquez," Shannon said. "I think she moved because of him, too. You should talk to her."

"Shannon," her mother said again.

"Thank you, Shannon," September told her.

The girl nodded gravely. "He was a sick man. That's why he killed himself."

Mrs. Kraxberger had had enough. This time she managed to yank her daughter inside and slam the door.

"Or, that's why somebody killed him," Wes said, speaking September's thoughts.

"Who do you think this Mrs. Vasquez is?" she asked. "It's not a name on either of the houses at the end of Fir Court, the Kraxbergers' street."

"Maybe it's a different house?"

"Or, one of them's a rental?"

She was silent as they drove toward the Kraxbergers' old neighborhood.

"What're you thinking?" he asked her.

"My brother, March, has a ten-year-old daughter, Evie. A lot of times March works at my father's house and he often brings Evie. Stefan lived there for years."

"Oh."

September exhaled heavily. "Maybe I'm borrowing trouble."

More silence as they drove away, then Wes said, "Maybe you should talk to your niece."

"Maybe I will," she said solemnly. She glanced at the time. It was after five.

Fir Court was a dead end that went for several blocks and then jogged at an angle into the cul-de-sac. They drove past the old Kraxberger home, now owned by a family named Cordelle, according to the name on the mailbox, and then took a right into the cul-de-sac. The house toward the south, the Franco's, had aging plastic play equipment in the backyard, faded from the elements, along with a swing set and slide.

They chose it first. Wes knocked on the door and there was a sudden gallop of feet from inside and then a boy of about ten opened the door.

"Hi," he said.

"Hi," September answered. "Is your mom, or dad, home?"

"Mom's upstairs. I'll go get her. Mom!" he yelled, running back up the stairs he'd obviously just run down, leaving the door wide open.

A few minutes later a woman rushed down, shooting a damning look up at her son. "Carl, the *door!*" she yelled in a reminding tone. Flustered, she asked September and Wes, "Yes?" Her hand was on the door as if she were about to slam it in their faces.

September had had enough of that for one day. Pulling out her identification, she introduced Wes and herself, and asked, "Are you Mrs. Vasquez?"

"Heavens, no. She moved away years ago. We rented the place from the Francos after her. I'm Karen Webster. Did she—why are you looking for her?"

"Do you know her new address?" September asked.

"No, but she moved to the east side of the river. Still has her business, though, I think. Calls it Tiny Tots Care."

"You don't know why she moved, do you?" September tried.

"She didn't like that mailman. That's what the owners of the house told me. Left right before he killed himself."

"Mom!" came from up above.

"She left the play structures behind and that's what sold us on this place," Karen said. Then, "What, Carl?"

"Come upstairs now!"

Ignoring him, she asked, "Is there some problem with her?"

"No. Thank you," September said, and she and Wes left as Carl yelled, "Right now, Mom!" and Karen Webster shut the door, but not before they heard her scream, "Just hold your horses!"

Wes asked September, "What now?"

"It's after six. I don't have time to go to the east side and find Mrs. Vasquez. I have to meet Maharis."

"I'll drop you off at your car and look into Tiny Tots Care."

September nodded. "Marnie Dramur and LeeAnn Walters live a couple of blocks over on Candlewood, the same street as the Bernsteins."

"You want to stop in?"

What she wanted to do was get to the hospital, but she could see her time slipping away. Maybe it was better, anyway. Once she got these interviews out of the way, she could go to the hospital and stay all night, if they let her. "Hell, we're here. Maharis can wait," she said.

Wes quickly drove to the first house—the Walters'—but no one was home. The Dramurs' home was around the corner and the lights were on, so they parked in front of the modest ranch style house with its wrought iron fence and walked up the drive together. Once again, Wes knocked on the door. It took a while before it was opened by a harried woman wiping her hands on a towel.

"Yes?" she asked suspiciously, then held the hand with the towel to her chest in surprise when she realized they were officers.

"Are you Marnie Dramur?"

"Y-e-e-s-s-s . . ."

September explained that they were looking into Christopher Ballonni's death and brought up Rhoda Bernstein's complaint against him. Marnie's lips tightened in disapproval. "I never agreed with Rhoda. She told you that, didn't she? She always thought her Missy was so perfect that no man could look at her without desiring her, and my God, she was just a kid. It was sick. Ask LeeAnn about Rhoda, if you don't believe me. LeeAnn Walters. Lives right around there." She pointed to the corner they'd just driven around. "She'll tell you." She pressed her lips together. "Chris Ballonni was our mailman for years. Rhoda made that complaint and then he committed suicide. What does that tell you?"

"We don't believe it was a suicide," Wes said, and she gave him the elevator eyes, assessing him.

"There was a similar staging of the crime last week," September said.

"I saw that, but you know, you just give somebody an idea, and the next thing you know, they're doing it, too." She sniffed.

"Evidence suggests the same person is responsible for both crimes," September said.

"What are you saying? That Christopher Ballonni was murdered?" She looked from Wes to September as if they were both bonkers.

"We've already spoken to a family named Kraxberger who lived along your route and whose daughter was inappropriately approached by Ballonni. We believe he was targeting girls, not boys."

"You're saying Rhoda Bernstein was *right?*"

"Could you think of anything, any other girl who might have lived along the route and who may have been approached by Ballonni?" she asked.

"Oh, God. Oh, God. No. There was—I don't know anyone. I just know LeeAnn and . . . well . . . we have boys, so . . . no."

She paused, wrapping and unwrapping the towel over her hands. "But there was that day care, of sorts, I suppose."

"Tiny Tots Care. Run by Mrs. Vasquez?" September asked.

"You know it. Yes. But she moved a while back." She shook her head. "Oh, God, is that why?"

"Not that we know of," September said truthfully.

"Oh, my *God,*" she said again.

"Thank you," Wes said, effectively cutting her off.

They left her standing at the door, watching them walk across the street and get into Wes's Range Rover again. He drove September to her car and then they said good-bye to each other and he went back into the station. For a moment September debated on taking a quick trip to the hospital but it was almost six already, so she texted Maharis and said she was on her way, then called the hospital again to learn if there was any change, which there wasn't.

Depressed, she arrived at Gulliver's at six-thirty to find that Maharis hadn't showed yet. The bar was fairly quiet with only a few patrons leftover from happy hour. When September entered she watched several departing customers pat the suit of armor by the door—a tradition for good luck—and she did the same, touching the knight's cool metal visor. She could use some good luck and so could Jake.

Sidling up to the bar, she dropped her messenger bag on the smooth, laminated wood surface. Her gun was inside the bag, not at her hip, but her ID was in her pocket and she flipped it out for the woman bartender to see.

"I'm looking for Mark," September told her.

"Bartender Mark or Waiter Mark?" she asked.

"Bartender Mark."

"He's around." She glanced over her shoulder. "Probably on break. I'll go find him after I serve these people."

These people were a man and woman sitting at the bar, facing each other and rubbing each other's thighs. The bartender handed them each a drink, what looked like a cosmo for her and a glass of straight Glenfiddich for him, then she lifted up a section of the bar and turned through a door into the kitchen area. A few minutes later a serious young man came out to where September was standing and introduced himself as Mark Newsome as she showed him her identification.

"I remember you," he said, looking past her. "You came in with your partner and talked to Mark Withecomb about Emmy Decatur."

"Waiter Mark."

"Yeah, Waiter Mark."

"I have a new partner." September answered his unspoken question. "He's on his way."

"Did you want Withecomb?"

"Actually I wanted to talk to you. You were working last Thursday night?"

"Oh, yeah. Wenches Night. We all were. It's fucking nuts around here on Thursdays." Hearing himself, he said, "Sorry."

"That's all right. A young woman who was dropped off here on Thursday is missing. Gillian Palmiter?"

"Jilly?" He looked stricken.

"You know her?"

"She's a regular on Wenches Night. Dresses the part." He made a face. "She's one of the vodka whores."

"Vodka whores," September repeated.

"Girls looking for a guy to buy them a few drinks. Sometimes they go home with them. More often than not it's the same group of guys."

"I heard she has a number of boyfriends."

"I guess you could call them that."

"Was she with her group of guys on Thursday?" September asked.

"I think she left with Tom. He's one of her regulars. Drives a BMW."

At that moment Blake came through the front door. He

glanced at the suit of armor suspiciously before walking up to September and Mark.

Mark said, "You're the cop who called me?"

He nodded and introduced himself, "Officer Maharis."

September noticed how he scrupulously kept from calling himself a detective. She remembered those days. Wanting it so badly, wondering if it would ever happen.

Blake asked, "So where are we?"

"He remembers Jilly," September said, then filled him in on the "vodka whore" label and that it looked as if she'd gone home with someone she knew named Tom.

"Thomas Eskar," Maharis said. "I just talked with him. That's why I'm late. He took her to his place but she was puking and he left her in the car. She never came upstairs."

What a guy, September thought. By the look on Maharis's face, he felt the same way.

"He thought she might've come back here," Maharis went on. They both looked at the bartender, who shook his head.

"Mark." The female bartender jerked her head to indicate the back of the bar where she stood.

"I gotta get back to work," Mark said to September and Blake.

"Any of her other regulars talk to her that night?" September asked.

"Nah. She was trolling." He walked around and lifted the same section of bar the female bartender had and let himself in beside her, sidling around her as she refilled the drinks of the couple who couldn't keep their hands off each other.

Mark suddenly looked at September as if he'd had an epiphany.

"What?" she asked.

"There was this older guy. In his late forties, maybe. Jilly was coming on to him pretty hard and he was going for it, buying her drinks, thinking he was going to get lucky. I warned him off her. Kinda to protect them both. I don't know."

He shrugged and shook his head as if in wonder at his own altruistic motivations. "Anyway, he left and then she hooked up with Tom and a few hours later she went out with him."

"Know anything about this older guy?" September asked.

"Never seen him before."

"What did he look like?" Blake asked.

"Hungry," he said after a moment. "Jilly was really laying on the 'little girl' bit. Calling him 'Daddy,' shit like that."

"I mean his physical appearance," Blake said officiously.

"Wait." September cut in. "What else did she do?"

"Uh . . ." Mark caught a glare from his coworker and lifted a finger to September and Maharis as he poured the impatient guy at the end of the bar a draft beer. When he was finished he came back and said, "Jilly's legal, okay? Twenty-one. I've seen the ID and it's hers. But she looks like five years younger. Ten years. I don't know. She's proud of it. Likes to play little girl with guys and some of 'em get all hot and bothered and just go ape-shit. Her regulars don't care. But this guy liked it. Wanted a big slice of Jilly pie. That's kinda why I warned him off her. I told him she was with lots of guys and he got all pruny and left."

"Pruny?" Maharis asked.

"Disgusted. Left in a hurry like he could pick up a disease just being around her."

"Physical appearance?" he asked again.

"Light brown hair. Big smile, but fake-like. I guess you'd say he was decent looking. Kinda reminded me of that actor."

"George Clooney?" the female bartender suggested. She hadn't appeared to be paying attention but she'd apparently been avidly listening in.

"Nah. I know his name. . . ." He struggled, but couldn't come up with it.

This older guy liking the little girl act set off warning bells in September's head. "Did he pay by credit card?" September asked hopefully.

"Nah. Cash. I remember because he was careful with it. Some guys just don't want to part with a dime even when they're paying with big bills. He wanted Jilly to think he was loaded." He shook his head. "That's all I got." Then he snapped his fingers. "Kevin Costner. Like in *Dances with Wolves*."

September thanked him, then she and Blake headed outside into a dark, crisp night, the rain having let up and left pinpoints of stars peeking through scudding clouds. There were several cornstalks outside the front door but one of the jack-o'-lanterns that had clearly once been a part of the tableau was now smashed into mushy orange pieces against the nearest curb.

"What do you think?" Blake asked her.

"The last anybody saw her was when Tom left her in his car."

"The guy calls himself Thomas. He corrected me."

"Well, naturally," September muttered. "Because he's so goddamned proper that he'd leave his girlfriend out in the car, puking."

"Didn't sound like she was such a great girlfriend," Blake said.

"Don't be an asshole," September warned him.

He looked at her in surprise, then added insult to injury by saying, "Everyone told me you were the nice one."

"Yeah, well, don't believe them," September stated flatly. Gretchen's reputation as a bitch preceded her. She'd come by the label honestly, but September was starting to think it wasn't such an awful moniker after all. Maybe channeling her inner bitch might not be that bad an idea. "We're not here to judge Jilly. We're here to find out what happened to her."

Somewhat chastened, Maharis said, "You think this Costner look-alike's got something to do with it?"

"Chase down the other boyfriends and recheck with *Thomas*. Find out if anyone saw Jilly after he left her in the car. Make sure he did leave her in the car and he's not lying about that. See if there are cameras around."

"Okay."

"I don't know if the Costner guy has anything to do with it or not, but maybe," September mused.

"You gonna run with that, then?" he asked her.

"Yeah, I'll see what I can do. Maybe he trolls other bars."

Or maybe I'm just too sensitive to the issue, she thought, which reminded her to put a call in to March, which she did as she walked to her car. The line rang and rang and when her brother's voice asked her to leave a message, she said, "Hey, March, it's September. I know Verna's at the house and July told me that the memorial service for Stefan is coming up on Wednesday. I'll be there, but I'd like to talk to you beforehand. Call me back when you get a chance. Bye."

She clicked off and climbed into her Pilot.

Chapter Twenty-Two

By the time September got to the hospital it was after eight. She'd done a pretty good job of pushing her deepest fears aside while she was working, but now, walking through the hallways of the hospital, smelling the underlying odors of astringents and cleaning supplies and maybe even sickness, she could feel her anxiety return as if she'd suddenly opened a box and released it.

"Pandora's box," she muttered.

Her steps slowed as she drew close to Jake's room, and for one moment she sent up a desperate prayer for him to be all right. Auggie had texted her earlier, wanting to know how she was doing, but she hadn't responded. She hadn't wanted to stop and allow herself to *think*.

But she could no longer escape from her new reality.

Pushing open the door, she stopped short upon seeing the woman sitting in the chair, her head bent forward in abject misery. September had seen the same thing in Verna after Stefan died. Hearing her enter, the woman's head lifted and she stared at September through dull eyes.

"You're her," she said. At the same moment September thought: *Loni's mother.*

"Mrs. Cheever," she greeted her.

Marilyn Cheever swiveled her eyes toward Jake and said in a voice dry with grief, "I'm so sorry. . . ."

Lucky woke up in the dark on Tuesday morning feeling chilled. Outside her bedroom window there were no hummingbirds. It was still too dark for them to be flitting about but she felt they wouldn't be there anyway, that they might feel, as she did, the need to scatter and hide.

She'd packed up all her belongings and stowed them in her car the night before. Now she turned on her light, stripped the bed and threw the sheets in the washer, then she ran wet wipes over all the furniture in both her bedroom and bathroom. She glanced around the garage and saw that all of Mr. Blue's jars and tins and boxes had been moved. The place was empty and smelled stale and only the faintest hint remained of the musky, earthy odors that had permeated the air, nothing anyone would be able to discern.

She hadn't seen Mr. Blue the night before. He'd been in his rooms. He and she had said their good-byes already, so maybe he just wanted her to go.

Taking the box of wet wipes into the kitchen with her, she switched on the interior lights and blinked against the sudden brilliance. She was about to scrub down the table, cabinets, and counters, but was arrested by the sight that met her eyes. In the center of the table was a box containing items from Mr. Blue's vast supply, a cornucopia of drugs and herbs and exotic extras with a note that read: *You may need these.*

Picking up one particular bag, Lucky stared through the plastic at the dried item within. The wheels in her mind started turning. Quickly, she gathered up the box and stowed it in the trunk of her car along with the thermos that she'd used to tote sweet dreams.

Back inside the house, she finished rubbing off any sign

that she'd ever been there, then she picked up the pencil Mr. Blue had left beside the note and wrote: *Thank you.*

Taking the pencil and plastic container of wet wipes with her, she then drove through the early dawn to a gas station to refuel first, then back to Ugh's house, parking in one of her usual spots. She was going to have to find a new home base. Some No-Tell Motel where the manager wouldn't blink when she paid in cash. A place, in fact, that might actually prefer cash to a credit card. A place where no questions were asked.

She watched the end of the driveway, her mind wandering. After a while, she decided to walk along the neighbor's hedge again and see if she could get a closer view of what was going on. Ugh would probably be getting ready for work and—

Her attention suddenly snapped back as the nose of the black Lexus appeared at the end of the drive. The car pulled out with Ugh at the wheel and his roommate sitting in the passenger seat. Lucky turned over the ignition and followed, keeping far back from the vehicle. By the time they'd crossed the Willamette River and were heading east on I-84 she'd decided they must be heading to the airport. Maybe the girlfriend was going on another trip?

Fifteen minutes later her suspicion was answered in the affirmative when they turned onto Airport Way. She followed the Lexus onto the upper level drop-off zone. When Ugh squeezed the Lexus to the curb in front of the United counter, she drove on by, pulling over at the far southern end, slipping into a spot in front of Alaska Airlines and hoping she wouldn't be hassled by the airport traffic cops.

Luckily, Ugh's drop-off was fairly quick. In only minutes the Lexus slipped past her and headed back down to Airport Way eastbound. She followed at a discreet distance as he took the curving ramp to 205, figuring he was now on his way to Twin Oaks and, apart from his quick jog into a Starbucks drive-through, that's exactly what he did.

So, the wife, or girlfriend, or whoever she was, was on a trip.

Maybe it was time to make his acquaintance, and, on the heels of that thought, wondered just how young she could make herself look.

September had planned to be at work early but could barely make it out of bed by eight-thirty and only then because her cell phone forced her up. Yesterday had been horrendous. The bug had gotten her down and just wouldn't release its grip on her. This morning her headache was gone, but she still felt achy and stiff and uncoordinated, as if her limbs were reluctant to respond to the messages her brain was sending them.

It hadn't helped that Marilyn Cheever had been half out of her mind with grief, alternately apologizing for what had happened to Jake and almost blaming him for her daughter's death, praising him for all the hours he spent trying to help her get better and railing at him for failing at the task. September had listened without saying anything; she'd had to tune it out to keep from saying hurtful things back. Her eyes kept turning away from Marilyn and back to Jake, taking in his bandaged head, his growing beard, the closed eyes, the drip of the IV, his arm in its protective sling.

At times she'd wanted to snap at Marilyn Cheever for her unfairness, but she'd held herself back. And truthfully, she'd also been just too damn tired and sick with worry to engage her, so she'd let Loni's mother do her worst and simply said nothing.

Eventually, the woman had taken in a last deep, shuddering breath and closed her eyes.

Then September turned all her attention to Jake and just ignored her. She still didn't want to get too physically close to him. She didn't want to risk infecting him with the virus, but at least she could look at him from across the room. She'd let herself wonder when the surgery on his arm was scheduled, but she couldn't think about his head injury and what that might mean.

She'd left his room about an hour after she'd entered it, and Marilyn had roused herself and followed September out of the room as well.

"I'm sorry, too," September told her at the elevator and she'd nodded, accepting September's words, though Marilyn could have just as easily launched into another diatribe about Jake, his relationship with September, and what that had done to her daughter.

She'd driven home and fallen into the bed she shared with Jake, pressing her face into the pillow, drinking in his scent. In the darkness she'd completely broken down, feeling the soft scratch of the pillow against her cheek, recalling how it felt to be wrapped in his arms, remembering the way his mouth curved in amusement at things she said, the sweep of his lashes, the feel of his lips.

She'd awakened slowly, not wanting to leave the bed as dawn stretched its gray fingers across the room. Then her cell phone rang by her ear and she reluctantly plucked it from the nightstand to hear July's voice asking her how she was doing.

"Fine," she'd told her, seeking to get off the phone as quickly as possible, but not before July extracted a promise from her that they would go to Stefan's memorial service together.

Just what she wanted to do.

Now she wheeled into the station's back parking lot and entered the building through the side door, which was generally unlocked during the daylight hours. She could hear the babble of voices, hushed through the walls, and the sound of the furnace and the squeak of desk chairs as she entered. The place sounded as if it were almost back to capacity, and as if to prove her right, she rounded the corner into the squad room and there was George, still a bit peaked, back at his desk.

She set her fears aside with an effort and said, "You look like you've lost a few pounds."

"Well, I should. Couldn't keep anything down till last night." A small, opened bag of Fritos sat by his left hand, and he reached into it without looking up from his computer, placing several chips in his mouth.

Blake Maharis was already at Gretchen's desk, talking on the phone, and September fought back a wave of annoyance. She liked Maharis. But she didn't like the way he usurped her partner's desk. Auggie might have left, but Gretchen was coming back.

"Where's Wes?" she asked.

"Break room," George said. "He got here just before you did. I was early."

That's a first, September thought.

Wes appeared at that moment, looking loads better than the day before. "I left a message on the Tiny Tots Care voice mail last night and got a call back from Mrs. Linda Vasquez this morning."

"What'd she say?" September asked.

"Well, she didn't say she moved because of Christopher Ballonni. Said it was because of a lot of other things: her husband's job, the cost of the Laurelton rental, a chance for a lease option, like that. But she did remember Ballonni. And yeah, she thought he was a little too friendly, but her day-care kids were always in the back if they were outside, on the equipment. Not in the front by the mailbox."

"That's a relief."

"We might take a trip to Tiny Tots Care," he said. "She was distracted when we talked. People dropping off their kids. Maybe she'll say more if we're actually there."

"All right."

Maharis looked over at her. "Jilly still hasn't shown up."

"No calls from her picture?" she asked.

"Not so far. I talked to Thomas and he's finally worried."

"What a guy. Did you connect with her other boyfriends?"

"One of them was out of town last Thursday. I checked and he's telling the truth. The other one finally answered his phone. When I mentioned Jilly's name, he was kind of rude about her, but in an affectionate way."

"How do you do that?" September asked coolly.

"Said 'my little slut' and stuff." Maharis was slightly embarrassed. "He said he hasn't seen her since before Thursday, though."

September nodded, her lips tight. She didn't really want to talk to Maharis anymore and it must have shown on her face, because he protested, "Hey, I'm not trying to be an asshole, here."

"Try harder," September suggested, and out of the corner of her eye she saw Wes fight a smile and turn away so that Maharis wouldn't see him.

"What about that older guy who was interested in her?" Maharis asked now, a bit belligerently.

"I haven't got to him yet, so check with some other bars. See if he's been trolling for young girls elsewhere," September suggested. "Gulliver's probably isn't the only place."

He nodded curtly and turned back to Gretchen's desk.

September looked over at Wes, who was on the phone. He caught her eye and held up a finger. A few minutes later he hung up and said, "If we get to Tiny Tots around four, some of the kids'll be gone."

"Isn't Tiny Tots the name of a brand of sardines?" George put in.

September turned her attention back to him, thinking his weight loss might be very short-lived. "I'm going out for a while," she said.

"Where to?" George asked, and September could see Maharis cock his head, listening for her answer as well.

"Gotta talk to my brother about something," she said.

"I heard he's moved to Portland PD full time," George said.

September didn't bother to answer. For one thing, she wasn't interested in talking about Auggie right now. She was still wrapping her head around the fact he was leaving and she didn't feel like sharing. Yes, she knew Auggie found the work more fulfilling in the larger arena, and she also knew she would slowly forgive him. She just didn't feel like sharing that with the others yet. He was her twin, and he was there for her when she needed him and she would get over feeling left behind.

But the other reason she hadn't responded to George's comment was because she hadn't meant that brother. Where she was going was Castle Rafferty to talk to March, her oldest brother. March was as stiff and remote as Auggie was accessible. She was planning to broach a delicate subject with him, one she had no earthly idea how to go about—their ex-stepbrother's suspected pedophilia and the long periods of time he'd been in close contact with March's daughter, Evie. And it wasn't going to be easy.

The Creekside Inn was located near a culvert that had a dirty stream of water moving behind it, runoff from I-5 mainly, which, Lucky supposed, in the widest sense could be considered a creek. It rented rooms by the day, week, or month, and that was all she cared about. She wore a sloppy shirt and her loosest jeans, unlaced shoes that she could clomp in, her hair in a low, untidy ponytail with strands falling around her face, and a pair of big, round sunglasses. She'd specifically adopted a vacant look, dropping her mouth open a little, when she asked the day manager—a young man still fighting acne—for a room for a week. He was reading an erotic novel that he slid under the counter when she walked in, and he was apparently so distracted by it that he took in her sloppiness in a glance and simply had her fill out a form. Paying with cash in advance didn't phase him, either. As she headed to the car for her bag, he was already back deep into the book.

She had several bags but she only hauled in the one that held most of her clothes and makeup, and the box Mr. Blue had given her, which she hid in the back of the motel room's closet. Ugh's partner was out of town and it was unlikely she would be back this evening, which meant he was footloose and fancy free. She'd bet her last dime that he would take advantage of the time alone and pick up a date for the evening. And she would be there to make sure the date was of legal age.

Beyond that, Lucky had a plan forming for Ulysses Graham Harding. With Mr. Blue's help once again, she would neutralize him once and for all.

The pseudo Bavarian-style rambling mansion where September had grown up, Castle Rafferty lay under a slate gray sky looking blank and foreboding. As a result of the fire, the siding was still missing around newly installed garage doors, and September could hear hammering as she climbed from the Pilot, which she'd parked on the wide apron in front of the house next to Verna's car.

She rang the bell and listened to it peal sonorously through the house at the same time she tried the door. Locked. A few minutes later it was opened by Rosamund, the lady of the house herself, looking ever more pregnant and a little flushed.

"September." It wasn't exactly a big welcome and September guessed her current stepmother blamed her, as well as Auggie, for foisting Verna on them.

"Is March here?" she asked.

"Oh, no. He and your father have some meeting in Portland. But Verna's here," she said with false gaiety. "Maybe you'd like to pay her a visit. Oh, and Evie's here, too. But steer clear of her. She's sick. She's in the corner bedroom, vomiting, I believe. I told Braden that if I get that thing, I'm divorcing him. You'd think her mother could do something for her, but her days with Evie are set in stone, apparently. March has to take care of her on his days, whether she's sick or not." She smiled tightly. "That's not the kind of mother I'm going to be."

She'd stepped back from the door a little as she delivered this speech but still September had to practically bully her way inside. She hadn't expected to see Evie herself and it was an opportunity she was going to take regardless of Rosamund, who, with her shining dark hair and imperious ways, looked surprisingly beautiful in her last trimester.

The hammering, which had briefly stopped, started up again, coming from the kitchen area. Rosamund threw a dark look at the closed door behind which work was clearly being done. "The cabinets. Finally. The noise is about to drive me insane!" She turned back to September, narrowing her eyes, as if recognizing she'd wormed her way inside. "What do you want with March?"

"Nothing that can't wait. I think I'll check on Evie and then I'll go."

"But I just warned you!"

"I know."

"Fine," she snapped. "Then take her some dry toast. Suma was supposed to be here by now, but she's late, and I'm not going near Evie." She bypassed the kitchen and turned to the butler's pantry where a toaster and microwave sat on a granite shelf. Two pieces of wheat toast were sitting in the toaster. Pulling out a plate from the overhead cabinet, Rosamund plucked out both pieces of toast, plopped them down, then thrust the plate at September.

Verna appeared at that moment, looking frail and beaten down. She placed a hand on the wall separating the living room from the dining room. "September," she said in a dry whisper, as if all the energy had been drained out of her. "Will I see you at the memorial service tomorrow?"

"I'll be there with July," she said, feeling awkward. She had no idea how to deal with Stefan's broken mother, especially with what she suspected about her son.

Verna nodded and Rosamund said to her stiffly, "Did you want something, Verna?"

As September carried the plate down the long hallway that led to the bedrooms, she heard Verna respond with a bit of her old spunk, "I wouldn't dream of imposing on you, dear. Unless there was some coffee made . . . or maybe some of that toast . . . ?"

The room Evie was in lay at the farthest corner of the house. September hesitated outside the door, knowing she should really talk to her brother first, completely aware she wasn't going to. March was difficult at the best of times. Better to ask forgiveness than permission. Her brother always said no first, no matter what the issue, and she didn't think she could stand that right now.

Raising her hand, she knocked lightly on the solid core walnut door. "Evie? It's September. I have some toast for you."

"Come on in," was the muffled reply.

Twisting the knob, she let herself into the darkened room, the only light coming from a small gap at the base of the blinds, though the gloom of the day didn't penetrate much of the cavernous room. On the bed, Evie was working herself into a sitting position as September entered. A glass of water sat on the nightstand and she reached for it, allowing September to set down the plate of toast.

"I don't feel hungry," the girl admitted.

"Rosamund said you've been throwing up."

"Only all the time." She made room for the glass next to the plate, then sank back into the bed, her blond tresses fanning out on the pillow. "Rosamund doesn't want to come in here because of the baby."

"She's not wrong. I just got over what you've got. It takes a few days."

"It takes forever!"

"Feels like it . . ." She drew a breath. "Evie, I don't really want to bother you when you're sick. I came here today to talk to your dad, actually, but he's not here and this has to do with you, too."

"What is it?" she asked.

"Uncle Stefan."

She jerked with surprise and then her gaze dropped to the coverlet. "They said some lady killed him."

"It looks that way," September agreed, trying to think how to go on.

"Why?"

"I'm trying to figure that out."

She looked up. "Was she mad at him?"

"Maybe. We don't know her reasons yet. That's kind of why I wanted to talk to you. You were around him a lot when he lived here, and I think maybe he took care of you once or twice?"

A long moment passed, and then she said, "You want to know if he was weird with me."

"Umm . . . yes."

"He took pictures of me in the bathtub," she said. "He tried to act like he didn't, but I saw him. And he was always trying to touch me. I mean, sort of. Like get up behind me when I went into a room, touch my arm and head. I told my dad about it, but he said I was just making things up."

September fought back her own horror. "Did you tell your mom?"

She shook her head. "She might not have let me see my dad anymore, and then I couldn't have come over here."

"If that kind of thing happens, ever again, you need to tell someone."

"I just wanted to stay out of his way," she admitted.

"I understand. But you need to tell someone. That's the thing. It needs to not be secret. You should tell your parents."

"I can talk to my mom, I guess. . . ."

"Good. Do that."

She chewed on her lip. "Will you tell me what really happened to him, when you find out? I want to know."

"I will," she promised.

"I hope he didn't hurt any other girl."

"Me, too," September said grimly.

She purposely steered the conversation away from Stefan for a few minutes before she said good-bye. Whatever else Stefan had done, it appeared he hadn't physically harmed Evie.

On her way out she avoided both Verna and Rosamund, and as she passed the hammering and pounding coming from the kitchen, she thought of the fire and the boxes in the garage that had belonged to both Verna and Stefan.

Maybe July was right all along, she thought. *Maybe the arsonist was Stefan. Getting rid of evidence of his perversion that Rosamund had inadvertently sent to the storage unit. Pictures of Evie and God knew what else.*

Shuddering, she plucked out her cell phone as she climbed into her SUV, hitting the button for Auggie.

He answered on the first ring, as if he'd been waiting for her. "I was just gonna call you," he jumped in before she could say anything. "I talked to Bill Quade, brother of Dan, Carrie Lynne Carter's ex-boyfriend. You and Wes musta put the fear of the law into him. He told me his brother's not in California, if he ever was. I'll bet that was a cover story they concocted between them. Anyway, Dan's in the Seaside area."

"That's great, Auggie. Maybe you can tell Wes. I've got something else going, and—"

"Just let me finish. Because of Dan, Clatsop County Sheriff's Department's on to some guy who sells and trades all kinds of herbs, drugs, whatever. And get this, he's *blue.* His skin is apparently actually blue. He's drunk some kind of silver shit for years and it permanently changed his skin color."

"The alien drug dealer," September said, drawn out of her thoughts in spite of herself.

"You got it. Clatsop County's on their way, so my work here is done. Tell Weasel."

"I will. And thanks."

"What are you onto?" he asked as an afterthought.

"I'll fill you in later."

Chapter Twenty-Three

September stopped for a sandwich at Bean There, Done That. The coffee shop didn't have much of a lunch menu and everything they did was heavy on vegetables and shy on meat, which was just what she wanted ever since her bout with the virus. On a whim she called Gretchen as she was walking into the place.

"I'll be there in ten minutes," her ex-partner told her.

She was already seated when Gretchen breezed in. With her untamed, tightly curled hair, swarthy skin, and catlike blue eyes, she turned heads even without the authoritative strut that was purely her. Slim and taut in a pair of tight jeans, boots, and a black leather jacket, she owned any room she walked into. She looked at the line of people waiting for coffee, said, "Fuck that," then took the chair opposite September. "Couldn't get a booth?" she asked.

"Not today."

"How's Westerly?" she asked, eyeing September's sliced egg and tomato sandwich on wheat bread.

"You want half?" September asked.

"Looks too healthy."

"It's good. Here." She slid her plate with her untouched half Gretchen's way, holding on to the remains of her half. "I'm stopping by the hospital before I head back to the station. He hasn't regained consciousness."

Gretchen carefully bit into the sandwich, her gaze on September. "That doesn't sound good."

September had put the last bite in her mouth but suddenly found it hard to swallow. Reaching for her bottled water, she took a long drink, and said, "They expect him to at any time."

Gretchen nodded. "I saw your interview with Kirby. You held your own."

"Thanks." She nodded, wrestling her fears about Jake down with an effort. "I've been working on becoming the bitch around the squad room."

"I leave for a few weeks and this is what happens?"

"I kind of like it."

Gretchen snorted, but smiled faintly. "So, who's this woman who shot your stepbrother?"

"Ex-stepbrother. Don't know her name, but she seems to be hunting down pedophiles."

September's cell phone rang and she pulled it from her messenger bag and looked down at the screen. Her chest tightened as she saw the name and number—*Jake's brother*.

"What?" Gretchen asked, but September waved her off as she said, "Hey, Colin," in a tight voice.

"It's good news, Nine," he greeted her, his voice full of relief. "Jake's awake."

"Thank God!"

"He's wondering what the hell happened to him. Kind of pissed about it."

"Oh, that's great. I'll be right there." She clicked off and nearly knocked over the table in her hurry to leave.

"Hey." Gretchen stood up and blocked her way, shocking September when she placed both of her hands on her shoulders and looked her in the eye. She was a long way from the touchy-feely type. "Take a moment. You're crying," she said.

"Oh. Thanks." September brushed off the unexpected tears, gave Gretchen a smile, then hurried out.

Lucky wasn't much of a shopper. She'd been a fugitive most of her life, in one way or another, and clothes were merely a method of camouflage.

As she looked around the racks in a local Target she searched for something youthful and girly. She had a jog bra already, which would help strap her breasts down. Not that they were overly huge, but the less obvious the reminders were that she was a woman, not a girl, would be helpful when she was up close and personal with Ugh, which she hoped would be tonight.

Maybe it wouldn't work. Maybe Ugh wouldn't look at her no matter what. Stefan Harmak wouldn't have; she'd sensed that in him.

But she'd also seen Ugh flirting with Molly's mother, and he'd been kissing his girlfriend in front of the window not so long ago, so she suspected he might at least engage with her a little, if she played her cards right.

She picked up a light pink shirt and short black and pink plaid skirt. The skirt would barely cover her ass.

And shoes . . . ?

Wandering over to the shoe department, her eye fell on a pair of black flats until she spied a pair of pink-sequined ones. Checking the price, she quickly snatched them up, thinking of the roll of bills in her pocket.

Thank you, Hiram.

The hospital parking lot was full of cars, and September chafed as she circled for a spot, finally finding one just as a spate of rain suddenly poured from the heavens. She didn't give a damn and ran through the deluge bareheaded. She reached Jake's room just as his mother, father, Colin, and Colin's wife, Neela, were saying their good-byes to him, promising they'd be back soon.

She barely said hi to them, but it didn't matter. His mother shooed her inside, a huge smile across her face. It was the best thing September could have seen and she slipped into the room, running a hand over her wet hair, her gaze pinned on the bed and Jake.

He smiled crookedly upon seeing her. "There you are."

He was still bandaged and bruised but he looked wonderful. "Here I am," she said. "Maybe I should stay on this side of the room. I just got over that damn virus that goes through places like this hospital like wildfire."

"Get over here."

She smiled and moved forward to stand by his bed. "I'll stay right here."

He wouldn't listen to her and reached out and clasped her hand. She squeezed back, staring into his eyes, relieved to see the intelligence alive in their gray depths.

"Tell me what happened," he said.

"You don't remember?"

"No. And no one seems to want to remind me." Lifting his right arm, he touched the bandage on his head. "The last thing I recall, Liv and I were moving your bed and you were at work."

"Have you talked to the doctor? Maybe I shouldn't say anything—"

"Tell me," he ordered. "Please."

"Okay." She chose her words carefully. "Marilyn Cheever called you about Loni, apparently. Because Loni had left you a message."

Jake stared into space for a few moments, clearly trying to dredge up the memory. "So, I went to find her . . . and there was an accident . . . ?"

"Yes . . ."

"Nine . . ." he said softly.

"Loni drove her car into the back wall at Sunset Valley. You were in the passenger seat."

His eyes widened. "Oh . . ."

"You remember?"

"No . . . not really . . . but she's been reminiscing about high school. What do you mean, drove her car into the back wall?"

"We don't really know what happened yet."

"Yes, you do," he said, watching her.

"No."

"Everyone's tap dancing. Don't do that to me."

"It looks like . . . she may have hit the gas . . . on purpose."

Jake closed his eyes, his mouth grim. "Okay."

"Nothing's certain yet."

"Where is Loni? Is she okay?"

September didn't respond and his eyes opened. He stared at her for long moments. "Oh, no . . . no . . ."

"She killed herself, Jake."

"Oh, God."

"Marilyn was here, in your room, last night. She wanted to be near you."

"Oh, my God," he murmured.

Dr. Denby and a nurse came into Jake's room at that moment and September reluctantly released Jake's hand.

"We have surgery planned for that arm tomorrow morning," Denby told Jake, pointing to the one in the sling.

Jake's eyes were reaching for September. "I'll be back," she told him. She hoped she hadn't said too much.

Jake threw a look at the doctor while the nurse was checking the bandage on his head. "I'll be right here," he said with a faint return of humor. As she left, September touched her fingers to her lips and blew him a kiss, her eyes extra bright.

She was more together by the time she reached the station,

and when Lieutenant D'Annibal called her into his office, she was able to hide her feelings.

"Take some time off," he told her. "I understand you were here even when you were sick. Don't know how you did it."

"I'm fine. Really. I want to stay and check out a lead on the Ballonni case with Wes."

He looked like he was going to argue but let it go. She didn't add that she wanted to keep working until Jake was out of the hospital. Then she'd take some down time.

"All right. But you've been working too many hours."

"I'll take some time at the end of the week."

He waved her off and she returned to her desk, writing up reports on her interviews over the past few days, cleaning up the busy work.

At three-thirty she and Wes took off in his Range Rover.

"Why are you smiling?" he asked her.

"It's been a pretty good day," she said, then told him about Jake as they crossed the river to the east side.

The TINY TOTS CARE sign sat in the front yard of a two-bedroom house with a wide driveway and a large, fenced backyard. As September and Wes got out of his vehicle, they both looked over the top of the fence that surrounded the property to a group of about four kids playing in the muddy grass and the newer plastic play equipment that looked very much like the setup Mrs. Vasquez had left behind in Laurelton.

They were walking around to the front when a side door opened and a woman waved them toward the kitchen. "You're the detectives, right?" September nodded, and Mrs. Vasquez asked for their identification before she allowed them inside.

She was a small woman with a round face, dark eyes, and hennaed hair. The kitchen was scrubbed and neat and there was a picnic table-cum-day-care dining table that was covered with a plastic tablecloth and laid out with paper cups of water, banana halves, a bowl of crackers, and a wedge of cheese.

"Just about snack time," she said, eyeing her charges

through the kitchen window. Three of them were climbing on the equipment and the fourth one was just standing and watching. "I'm on my way to bring them in, and we're heading down to the basement with those muddy boots. Just sit yourself down. I'll be right back."

They chose to wait at the top of the stairs as she herded them inside, stripped them of their boots and jackets and had them wash up at a large downstairs basin before collectively tromping back upstairs in the shoes that had been waiting for them on the bottom step.

Once they were seated around the picnic table and munching away, she gave Wes and September her undivided attention. "I'm not sure I can help you, but I'll try. What are you looking for?"

Since Wes had already talked to her about the Ballonni case, he looked to September, seeing if she had something specific she wanted to ask. Taking her cue, September said, "As my partner told you, we are investigating two separate incidents where the victim was drugged and tied up to a pole outside their place of work."

"Chris Ballonni, my old mailman, and that new guy," she said.

"Stefan Harmak. Yes. We think the two crimes were committed by a woman who may have thought her victims were pedophiles and decided to exact her own kind of vigilante justice."

"I heard that you thought it was a woman." She wagged her head slowly from side to side. "I've been thinking about that."

"You said your move to this side of the river had nothing to do with Christopher Ballonni."

"We moved because we could afford this house," she said, "but I can't say I was sorry to leave. I didn't like Ballonni around my kids. He asked a lot of questions about them. Too many, really. A couple of times, when Grace Vandehey's mother picked her up early and he was delivering the mail, I just got a bad feeling about the way he looked at her."

Wes had his notebook out and wrote down the name.

"Is Grace still one of your charges?" September asked.

She shook her head. "When I moved, my Laurelton clientele didn't move with me. It's too far."

"What does Grace look like?"

"Long blond hair and a big smile. A sweet little girl. She was starting kindergarten the fall I left." She glanced at the kids at the table and had to move forward and take the banana away from one of the boys who was aiming it at the others like a gun and making popping noises.

She added, "If you're looking for hard evidence that he was a pedophile, I can't help you, but I think you're on the right track."

"We're trying to figure out who this woman is," September said. "The one we think killed them both."

"Could she be someone on Ballonni's mail route?" she asked.

"Maybe, but Ballonni and Harmak worked and lived in different parts of the city," September said.

"I was just wondering because there was a woman, a jogger, who stopped by my day care once. I'd seen her running by before, and she stopped to specifically ask me what I thought of the mailman. I wasn't sure who she was, so I didn't say anything at first, but she said she had a daughter and she thought he was overly friendly with her. I said he made me uncomfortable for the same reason. After that, I saw her run by a couple of times when he was delivering mail, and I thought, 'she really watches him.' It seemed kind of intense."

"Did he notice?" September asked.

"I don't know. I doubt it. I wouldn't have if she hadn't stopped by and talked to me about him."

"What did she look like?"

"Mmm. Light brown hair in a ponytail. Baseball cap.

Maybe around thirty? About five seven or eight. Nice looking. Sort of stiff-shouldered like she was tense, or something."

One of the kids knocked over his cup of water and it ran in a line across the plastic table top where a little girl, the one who'd been hanging back on the playground, gasped and shouted, "Mrs. Vaz, Mrs. Vaz!"

"I'll get it, Rachel." She was already moving with a dish towel in hand to catch the errant water.

"So, you think she lives on the mail route?" Wes clarified.

"I never saw her other than jogging, so I don't really know."

They left her a few moments later as parents started picking up their kids.

"What do you think?" he asked September when they were on the road.

"I like the woman jogger angle. Chubb talked to all the people on the route and we've rechecked with them and haven't turned anything up. The jogger's a piece we didn't have before, and it sounds like she was monitoring him."

"Think we should have Mrs. Vasquez meet with our sketch artist?"

"Works for me," September said.

Graham had watched the minutes crawl around the clock face of his wristwatch throughout the day. He'd been short with Mrs. Pearce at lunch, wanting to shout at her to do something about that dyed black hair. Even in sixth period, with Molly right there, her shining face looking at him across the room, he'd had trouble keeping his thoughts from straying to the evening ahead.

Daria had texted him that she was staying two nights in San Antonio and then possibly moving on to Louisville for a smaller venue if the promoters could ever get their collective heads out of their asses. *Go,* he'd thought. *Go!*

But no matter what, he had tonight with Claudia Livesay

and he was looking forward to the evening with a mixture of anticipation and dread. He wanted to have dinner with Molly and her mother. He even wanted to have some conversation with Claudia. She'd told him she wanted to discuss Molly, and he sure as hell was interested in every detail about her.

When class was over, he couldn't stop himself from saying to Molly, "So, is your mom picking you up?"

"No, I'm going to my dad's tonight. He's going to help me with my report on climate change."

Graham's disappointment was so keen he could hardly keep his smile in place. "Mrs. Pearce's class," he said, the words sharp despite his control.

"Yeah . . ." She darted him a quick look, then scurried from the room.

So Claudia had planned for Molly not to be there. Of course. It made sense, but he was furious with her all the same. Sure, she was youthful looking and attractive enough—a helluva lot better than Daria the cow. But he'd pictured an intimate meal with the three of them and now that was not to be.

He could kill her for that.

It took serious effort on his part to drive home and get ready for the evening. He stepped under a cold shower to take some of the heat off his anger, then dressed in a pair of chinos and a white shirt topped by a tan pullover sweater. Dressy casual, Daria called it, but he hated her. HATED HER.

He took HER car when he was ready to go, stopping by a store and buying a medium-priced bottle of wine with some of HER money. He imagined dropping the Maori figurine atop HER head and it brought on a massive boner.

That was the first good thing that had happened all day, he determined. He would keep crushing Daria's head in the forefront of his mind in case things got intimate between Claudia and him and he found she didn't do it for him.

She was waiting for him eagerly when he showed up

promptly at six. When he presented the bottle of wine to her in both hands, like a practiced waiter, she giggled like a schoolgirl and said, "Ooh la la."

The sound was a turnoff in someone her age. And in her black sheath that showed off the bones at her throat there was something skinny and dried up and gristly about her. He could tell she worked out and was proud of her body, but there was the faintest hint of varicose veins running below the surface of her legs.

She took his coat and hung it on a wooden hall tree that sat beside the glass and wrought iron console table in the entryway. Upon the table's clear surface sat a heavy metal bowl that currently held the car keys to a Porsche.

He was damn glad he'd driven the Lexus. Sure, she'd seen the wagon but he could fob it off as a work car.

Grabbing his hand, she led him inside to a small living room with expensive furniture, then she guided him to the couch and the coffee table, which held a chased silver tray full of gourmet cheeses, sliced salami, and dried fruit. Soft, instrumental music played from speakers atop a bookcase that lined one wall. As he sat down he tried to dredge up the image of him slamming the figurine into Daria's head. It worked some, but it was sort of fading in and out of his thoughts.

She took the wine to the kitchen and opened the bottle there, talking so much in a loud voice that he didn't have to utter a word, even when she returned with two healthy glasses of red wine. He'd known when he bought the bottle that he was going to have to pretend to drink the stuff, but he realized quickly that Claudia was going to swill her own glass down so fast that he wasn't going to have to take more than a few swallows before she might not notice.

Finally, she finished in the kitchen and sat down beside him on the couch, but she kept up the magpie chattering so much that his throat constricted and it felt like he was choking.

"You wanted to talk about Molly," he broke in to a particularly revolting discussion of her job as a geriatric nurse that reminded him of his father and the damned neighbors who wouldn't leave him alone.

"Oh, well, yes . . ." She smiled, her dark eyes—just like Molly's—regarding him impishly. "That might've been just an excuse to talk to you," she admitted, giggling again and rolling her eyes. "I've been working up to this"—she moved her index finger back and forth to include him and her—"since school started. Unless, of course, there's something you want to say about Molly," she added, growing more serious.

His blood froze. "Like what?"

"Like, is she having trouble in your class? She told me that you had to take her cell phone away yesterday. I say, go ahead. One of the best things we can teach our kids are boundaries."

Graham nodded and picked up a small piece of cheese. He had to look away from her or his distaste would show on his face. He'd so looked forward to tonight and then she'd sent Molly away. Bitch!

His gaze fell on the bookshelf and the picture of Molly—with her head tilted and a sweet smile on her face—that was tucked into its corner. Abruptly he got up and walked toward it, pretending interest in the paperbacks jumbled beside it.

"Let me put the finishing touches on dinner," Claudia said, and he wanted to say, *Don't bother.* He didn't think he could work up an appetite.

Except maybe for her daughter. But no, no . . . he knew better. . . . He'd be damned, if he were caught. He had to leave things be. Keep his thoughts hidden and not act on his desires.

She'd made a chicken dish with herbs and more dried fruit over rice. He pretended to really enjoy it, and the constant gabbing, but it was damn near impossible. How come he hadn't noticed her diarrhea mouth when she'd come to his room?

Because she kept it from you. She didn't want you to know. No wonder the husband left.

After dinner, she refilled her glass—was that for the third

time?—linked her arm through his and they strolled back to the couch. Graham had managed to pour out two-thirds of his drink when she'd taken a trip to the bathroom and now he held it in one hand, like her, as if he were relaxing and letting the night go where it would go.

She was gazing at him with heavy-lidded eyes and he could practically smell her desire for sex. Well, he'd done this to himself, hadn't he? Showing off yesterday. Getting her to look down at his dick.

When she leaned closer to him, he had to fight the desire to push her away. He shut his eyes and gritted his teeth, and then he thought of Molly and as his arms tightened around Claudia and she leaned in for a kiss, his gaze flew to Molly's picture and he thought of her instead.

Suddenly he was clawing at Claudia's dress and she was going with it, telling him to hurry, and giggling, and wriggling out of the dress and damn near jumping on his crotch, legs splayed, while he was still unbuckling his belt. For a moment, reality intruded, but he concentrated on Molly's picture, then the thought of crushing Daria's skull, then the remembrance of the soft *crunch* of Jilly's as she tumbled to the entryway floor and he was suddenly driving into Claudia Livesay and she was gasping and hanging on for all she was worth.

"Oh, baby. Oh, baby, come on," she was shrieking.

Graham, with his eyes on Molly's picture, was miles away from the woman beneath him as he spilled into her with a deep groan.

Suddenly she was squirming and swearing beneath him. "Good God. No condom? You're crazy! I'm crazy. Oh, shit . . . oh, shit . . ." She was half laughing. "Oh, my God. I've never done anything like this. I can't believe it! Oh, my *God* . . ."

He couldn't take his eyes off Molly's picture. Claudia's

words buzzed like gnats around his head. He just wanted to swat them away.

And then there was silence and it felt like a long time later before he finally tore his gaze away and looked down at her, seeing the deep lines etched between her brows. She was only half drunk, he realized, and her eyes were still on Molly's picture where she'd obviously followed his line of sight.

Now her eyes met his. "What the fuck were you looking at?" she breathed in shock. *"Molly?"*

"What? No."

She tried to scramble out from under him. She tried to get away, and without thinking he immediately grabbed her hands, holding her down.

"Let me up!" she cried, afraid.

Graham came back to himself with an effort and released her, but she shot to her feet and ran for the bedroom, naked. Maybe he could have reasoned with her. Maybe. But all he could see was that she knew. She knew, and she would tell. Yanking up his pants, he went after her.

There was no lock on the door but she was holding it closed and crying. He slammed into it, throwing her off her feet.

"What's wrong with you?" he demanded, looking down at her as she huddled on the floor. "We have a good time and then you run away?"

She blinked back tears. "I don't know. . . . I . . . thought . . ."

"What?" he demanded impatiently. She was really pissing him off and he was starting to worry that she was going to run down to the school and tell someone the first moment she could.

"I'm sorry," she said, cowed.

Graham suddenly just wanted to escape. He stepped back into the living room, wondering what to do about her. She knew. She knew his thoughts. She'd seen him staring at Molly while he was having sex with *her*.

And then suddenly she ran past him, toward the door, buck-ass naked. She was going to run outside and scream for help. He could *feel* it!

With hardly a conscious thought he lunged forward, grabbed the metal bowl and swung it at her head as she scrabbled with the lock. *Plunk.* The sound of her skull cracking was music to his ears as she crumpled to the floor, just like Jilly had.

He leaned over her. She was alive but her eyes were staring blankly and there was blood where the skin had broken, dampening her hair.

Instantly he started to shake. Who knew that he was coming over here? Had she told anyone? Molly? Her ex-husband? Mrs. Pearce? *God!*

Running to the hall, he threw open the door to what he suspected was the linen closet. His eyes fell on a thick comforter. Grabbing it up, he hurried back to Claudia. She was still staring but her breathing had slowed. With any luck at all she would die.

He snapped his fingers in front of her face but she didn't react. Nobody home.

As quickly as he could he wrapped her in the blanket, covering her from head to toe. Cautiously, he opened the front door. There were other houses nearby but most of them had garages jutting out like pig snouts, blocking their windows from a view of Claudia's house. Directly across the street was a park.

If he was lucky, and careful, and smart, he could move her out the back door through Claudia's garage and then around to the Lexus, which was parked right in front.

What would he say if someone caught him?

It didn't bear thinking about.

Pulling out his keys, he unlocked the Lexus with his

remote from inside the house. Then, slinging the heavy bundle inside the blanket over his shoulder, his nerves jumping at the rasping gasp of her breaths, he hauled her into the garage, feeling his way through the dark. He carried her all the way across to the man-door on the side and stepped into a cold but dry night, hugging the side of the garage rather than risking opening the garage door with its big, wide maw.

He grabbed the Lexus's back door handle and wanted to scream when the overhead light burst on. Leaning in, he switched it off as soon as he'd laid her along the seat. Quickly, he shut the door and then relocked the car. Glancing around, he hurried back to the shadows, watching the neighborhood. He could hear rock music throbbing inside one house, but the windows that he could see were curtained. Vaguely, through the curtains of another house, he saw a television set's flickering colors.

He hurried back through the garage the way he'd come in, then grabbed up the tray of crackers and cheese and dumped it down the disposal. The dishes and wineglasses he hand washed and put back in the cupboards with shaking fingers. The flatware he stuck in the dishwasher. The pan with the chicken he decided to just take with him.

The entryway tiles didn't have much blood but he found the bleach and poured it on the tiles, recognizing dimly that this was becoming a habit with him. He'd set the metal bowl back on the console table and he realized with a start that there was a small circle of garnet-colored blood pooling beneath it. Grabbing up one of the dish towels hanging on a hook, he wiped that up, too, then threw the towel in the pan with the chicken.

She'd made a salad, and he threw the remains of it down the sink and rinsed out the bowl and put it in the dishwasher.

How long had it been since he put her in the car? The kitchen was clean. The entryway wiped up and spotless. The console table and bowl wiped down.

Did he leave any fingerprints anywhere?

The bedroom doorknob and panels.

Quickly he grabbed another towel and wiped them off. His heart was pounding. He ran the towel over the knobs on the door to the garage, then, shouldering his way through, he cleaned the man doorknob as well, carrying the pan with the chicken in his other hand.

At the car he put the pan in the front seat foot well, slid into the driver's seat and inserted the key. Claudia's breathing was ragged and deeper, like maybe it would stop altogether.

Reversing onto the street, he put the car in drive, touched a toe to the accelerator and disappeared. He met no one en route as he drove carefully all the way back to Daria's house.

Chapter Twenty-Four

George called September's cell as she and Wes were crossing the Marquam Bridge on their return from Tiny Tots Care. "We got a call from a Mr. Dorcas, who just happens to live right next to the Harmak house," he told them. "Last Friday the Dorcas's daughter, Diane, was out with her boyfriend, Keith Collier, and they had just come back and were saying good-bye to each other when this woman came barreling out from the backyard. Damn near ran into them. She was stuffing something in her pocket that they didn't quite see. Coulda been a gun, but they didn't think that at the time cuz they didn't hear the shots. She just ran off."

"She ran out from Stefan's neighbor's backyard?" September questioned.

"That's what I said."

"The shooter?" she asked with repressed excitement.

"Sounds like it's the right timing. Guess it wasn't till Sunday that the girl realized that her neighbor was dead. She overheard her parents talking about hearing something that night that they thought was a car backfiring. Then they saw the news and wondered if it was the shots from the Harmaks'. The daughter was scared and called her boyfriend, but they didn't come clean until today."

"She didn't tell her parents?" September asked.

"The kids were making out by the road when the woman appeared. The parents hate Collier. The daughter was supposed to be with her girlfriends that night, but snuck out and met him instead. She didn't want to confess, so it got delayed. Typical stuff."

"How well did they see the woman?"

"Close up. Security light came on and the place was lit up like day, apparently."

"Was she wearing jogging clothes and a baseball cap?"

"Don't know. The Dorcas family's coming down to give us a description."

"Okay."

"What?" Wes asked, when September had clicked off.

"We might have a description on our vigilante."

The Dorcases arrived at the station about an hour after Wes and September returned. They were utterly uncomfortable being at the police station and their daughter, Diane, felt the same. They did not invite the boyfriend along, so September put a call in to Keith Collier's voice mail and asked him to get in contact with her.

Diane's description of the woman avenger was very generic but she said Keith could probably tell them more. From September's point of view it was a win, whichever way you looked at it, because one of the first things out of Diane's mouth was the fact that the perpetrator had indeed been wearing a baseball cap and jogging clothes. *Bingo,* September thought in jubilation. Things were turning around. The case was coming together and Jake was awake and going to be okay.

She drove to the hospital to see him as soon as the Dorcases left. He was dozing most of the time while she was there, but held on to her hand again. Though she wasn't certain he really heard her, she told him all about the investigations she was working on. In that regard, he was the best kind of listener. No interruptions, questions, or distractions. Finally, she ran out of things to say and with exhaustion creeping in, she took her leave. And this time when she snuggled into the bed they shared, she fell asleep cradling the pillow to her face, a smile flickering on her lips even in sleep.

Wednesday morning September leaped out of bed and apart from a sharp twinge of protest from her neck wound, did a quick check of her body and decided all systems were a go. Today was Jake's surgery and Stefan's memorial service. On the work front, she hoped Keith Collier had called back, and if he hadn't she was going to hunt him down and get his input on the description of the woman who'd nearly run them over.

She was at Bean There, Done That picking up an iced coffee—her summer drink and now her fall one, too—when her cell rang. Wes, she saw. "Good morning to you," she said.

"Cheery. Where are you?"

"Getting coffee. D'Annibal told me to take some time off and I'm starting by showing up late today."

"We're getting traction. You got a minute."

"Sure."

"Your stepbrother's van," he said. "It was wiped clean but there was a long hair, possibly female, found inside it. Not sure whether they can extract DNA yet, but it jibes with the woman vigilante theory. If we catch her, we might have something to put her in the van."

"When we catch her," September corrected him.

"Second, the Clatsop County Sheriff's Department caught up with Daniel Quade, per your brother's intel from Bill

Quade. He coughed up the name of one Hiram Champs, Mr. Blue to those who know him, as his skin is apparently blue."

"Just like Auggie said."

"Quade said he got the ketamine from Champs, so Clatsop County checked out his place. Anyway, they found nothing. It was almost like he was waiting for them. In fact he invited the deputies in for herbal tea."

"What do you make of that?" September asked, sipping her cold drink. She didn't give a damn that the weather was dropping in temperature and there was talk of bitterly cold rain and hail for Halloween.

"Quade's getting the stuff wherever he can. Maybe he got it from him, maybe he didn't. There's a hot springs on Champs's property that Quade and his new girlfriend like to use. Sounds like he and Champs had words about that, so maybe Quade's getting payback. He spread the lie that he was moving to California, but he didn't go that far."

"Does it look like Champs gave him the ketamine?"

"The deputies weren't sure. Champs is kind of like a mystic. Believes in all sorts of herbal remedies. He could be the dealer, or he could be someone Quade found it convenient to blame. At least Quade's admitting he gave it to Carrie Lynne, for recreational use only. He just happened to then move on to the next girl and Carrie Lynne used it to take her life. I don't like the guy, but I believe him."

"What about Champs?"

"I'm gonna keep an ear to the ground. Keep checking with Clatsop County."

"Okay, is that it?"

"Uh-uh. We've got another missing person. A sixth-grade girl spent the night with her dad—part of a custody arrangement—but when he dropped her off at the mom's, Mom wasn't there. He left without checking and the girl called it in. Wasn't Mom's usual MO."

"Maharis on it?" September was walking through fits of

wind-driven rain to her car, her coat practically ripped from her fingers where she was holding it together with her right hand.

"Yeah, but get this. The girl, Molly Masterson, goes to Twin Oaks."

That caught her up short. "It's barely been a week since Stefan was left tied to the pole."

"Which is another thing. Stefan had gunshot residue on his right hand. Latest theory is he might have shot himself by mistake, maybe wrestling for the gun. If we catch our vigilante, it may be hard to prove murder."

"*When* we catch her, Wes. And I'll worry about proof then." She climbed into the Pilot. "Jesus, Wes. Is that all? I was going to say we haven't heard from Keith Collier yet, so I might have to track him down."

"Maybe you won't have to," he said breezily. "I could have all our cases wrapped up by the time you get here."

"Bull. Shit."

She hung up on his rolling laughter.

Lucky followed Ugh to school and waited in her Sentra while he went inside. She'd trailed him to a cul-de-sac the night before and had waited impatiently for him to come out, hoping he was just making a stop off before he went to a bar. She'd been afraid to turn into the cul-de-sac in case someone saw her and so she'd parked outside of that tight circle, settling in to wait along the cross street. She had dared to take a stroll along the sidewalk in front of the houses and duck into a park across from the house Ugh's Lexus was in front of, but she couldn't see through the curtained windows, so she'd had to go back to her car. Fairly early in the evening she'd seen the Lexus come out of the cul-de-sac, and she'd thought maybe he would head for a bar, but instead she followed him all the way to his driveway. She'd thought about sneaking along the neighbor's fence again, but too many cars were passing by at that time and a woman with a German shepherd was out walking her dog, so she stayed put. By the time she dared to sneak along the hedge and spy on him, the Lexus was parked by the station wagon and the house was dark save for a light in the back that might have come from the kitchen.

He was in for the night. He'd clearly met up with whoever lived at the house and that had been enough. A woman? The one he'd been flirting with in the school parking lot on Monday? Someone else? Someone *young*?

No. She didn't think so. She sure as hell hoped not. If he'd actually hurt someone on her watch . . .

She inhaled and let out her breath heavily. She was going to have to intercept him, but where? Not here.

Did she dare just go to his house? Show up with some sweet dreams in a thermos and dressed in her short, short skirt and say what? *Hi, Mr. Harding. I'm here to give you what you want. . . .*

It would be so much easier if he would just hit a bar. Alone. Without the woman from the parking lot or anyone else.

Discouraged, she turned back to the Creekside Inn.

The service for Stefan at Rigby House, a venue for memorials, meetings, and octogenarian birthday parties, was blessedly short. Apart from the Rafferty clan and a smattering of the Twin Oaks staff, it was very poorly attended. September sat between July and Evie, who'd insisted on going, though March, clearly annoyed and baffled by his daughter's request, had tried to talk her out of it. Throughout the service, Evie clutched September's hand, and September squeezed back, silently letting her know that she understood.

Auggie made an appearance but stayed in the back of the room, acknowledging September with a nod. She would have liked to meet with him and tell him about Evie, but that was for the future. Clearly Evie hadn't confessed what she knew about Stefan to her father; September hoped she'd been more forthcoming with her mother. Time would tell.

Verna cried throughout the service, while Rosamund, tucked close to Braden in a black sheath that showed her growing bump, looked properly serene, stoic, and sympathetic, playing the part for all it was worth.

"She glows," July muttered in disgust. "Look at me. I've never looked worse."

July's skin was several shades paler than normal and her blue eyes were a bit sunken. September decided not to say anything one way or the other, so July snorted. "Thanks for trying to make me feel better."

"You don't look that bad."

"Gee, thanks."

As soon as it was over, September was outside, dialing her cell phone. She called Jake's mother, who told her the surgery was over and went well.

July caught up to her, her own baby bump barely visible, though she did look like it was a hellish pregnancy. "You okay?" she asked.

"Best day of my life."

"What the hell does that mean?" she asked crossly.

"Jake's through his surgery and he's going to be okay."

Graham's head was not in the moment. Teaching was such a painful task, and the blank stares of his students, as if they were all stoned, generally made him want to slap them silly and scream at them to wake up. Today, however, it felt like all those eyes, row upon row of them, were staring him down, like they *knew.*

It had taken him well past midnight to get Claudia Livesay in the ground. The wind had been fierce and those sudden buckets of rain chilled him to the bone. Afterward, he'd stayed in the shower until he'd run the water heater out of hot water. Even then he was shivering—from the cold and so much more.

When he'd gotten to school the news was already out. Ms. Livesay wasn't home when Molly got dropped off by her dad! The girl had to call 911 herself! Where was she? Did something happen to her?

Mrs. Pearce grabbed his arm when their third-period classes were letting out. "Oh, my God, Graham. What do you think happened?"

The girl with the rosebud lips had filed out of her room behind the rest of the children, throwing a worried look over her shoulder at her teacher.

"What's her name?" he asked, lost in his own world.

"What? Whose?"

He tried to focus on Pearce. Her forehead was puckered, her lips pinched. "Umm . . . Molly's mother. I can't think of it."

"Claudia. Livesay. She goes by her maiden name. You know it," she chided. "Oh, my. I feel just awful for Molly. Where is she? I mean, you don't just leave your child unless something terrible's happened, right?"

He'd moved on from her as soon as he could, but then it was lunchtime and the staff was abuzz with rumors. But even in the midst of it, while he felt like he was having an out-of-body experience, deep inside he was laughing his ass off. They were all so gullible and unaware. Maybe even a little titillated by Claudia's complete lack of responsibility.

But later, he'd made the mistake of walking to the front of the building where there was an impromptu meeting being held by Principal Amy Lazenby, the battle-ax of all battle-axes with her short gray hair and mannish style. A pair of diamond stud earrings winking in her fat ears, a gift from her boyfriend, someone had said—though he didn't believe for a minute that she had anything to do with men and vice versa—didn't help cut that image, either.

And David DeForest's simpering wife was there, too. Graham could feel her gaze touch on him, even while she clung to her husband's arm.

"We should get the police here," DeForest was saying, and his wife agreed on a gasp, "It's like someone is targeting Twin Oaks!"

Lazenby said, "Hopefully, Ms. Livesay will have already returned home. The Laurelton PD and Detective Rafferty, whom I've personally met, are on the case. I've asked them to let us know the moment Claudia Livesay is found."

"Detective Rafferty? The one in the interview?" Patti DeForest asked.

Lazenby nodded.

"Is she the one who was Mr. Harmak's stepsister?" Patti pressed.

Graham's heart clutched at the mention of the police. "Who is that?" he asked.

"One of the Laurelton PD detectives," DeForest snapped, dragging the attention back to himself. "I say we have a meeting. Get the parents involved, too. Talk to the people who knew her. Who are Ms. Livesay's friends at the school? Does anyone know?"

Mrs. Pearce was hurrying up to join them and caught that last remark. It was the break before their last period class. She looked at Graham. "You walked out with her the other day. What were you talking about?"

"Molly," he said shortly. "She's in my last period class."

"How did she seem?" Pearce asked.

"Fine." Graham was irked and a line of sweat had formed down his back.

"Molly was talking to her friends about how you might come over and have dinner with them," Pearce went on blithely. "I didn't know you knew the family so well."

"I don't."

He wanted to smash her teeth in. She had a bland look on

her face, but he knew she was paying him back for not paying attention to her. "Molly has tried to set me and her mother up before. Man, I hope Claudia turns up soon," he added dolefully for good measure.

They all expressed the same desire and the meeting broke up. Graham went back to social studies class and felt a pang of loss that Molly wasn't in her seat. He had to learn the name of that other girl. The one in Mrs. Pearce's homeroom. She'd looked so lonely.

But first things first. He needed to make sure his grave-digging the night before wouldn't give him away in the light of day.

As soon as school was out he hurried to his car. HER car, really, but he was beginning to think of it as his.

As if she knew she'd crossed his mind, his cell phone rang and he saw it was Daria. Reluctantly, he put it to his ear, hoping to hell she wasn't coming home early.

"Hello," he said stiffly.

"Well, what kind of a greeting is that?"

"I'm in the car. Can't drive while I'm talking to you."

"Turn on the Bluetooth, dummy," she teased. "It looks like I'm going to be here for at least tonight, maybe tomorrow, we'll see."

"I thought you weren't coming back until Friday." He tilted the rearview mirror, checking his appearance. He'd been a little scattered this morning. Hadn't been able to think.

"Well, I don't think I'll be able to get away tomorrow, but I'm working on it. They've got me at an extra breakfast meeting tomorrow morning, and it really annoys me that they think they own me for every damn hour I'm here. I told them that it was for only one meeting, but they don't listen. . . ."

Graham tuned out. He'd heard it all a thousand times already. As he readjusted the mirror, his gaze touched on the backseat. His heart stuttered. Was that a smear of blood on the black leather? Had Claudia bled through the blanket?

He glanced in the mirror again. His blue eyes were wild.

". . . I told James that this was the last time—"

"I gotta go, Daria. Sorry." He snapped off the phone. His hands were shaking.

With an effort, he stifled the panic and took a long, shuddering breath. No reason to worry. None at all.

He just had to get home and clean the backseat. That's all. And make sure the body was buried deep enough.

And then . . . then he would make the most of his night, just in case she did come home tomorrow.

Keith Collier strolled into the station late Wednesday, apologizing for not answering his voice mail. He had a slacker mentality, September thought, viewing him with disappointment, so she was pleasantly surprised when he gave a much more detailed description of the female avenger, even to offering up ways to improve the composite drawing already done with changes in jawline and cheekbones. He worked with the sketch artist for nearly an hour and then pointed at the drawing and proclaimed: "That's her."

"That's her?" September repeated.

"Yeah. That's her."

September gazed down at the picture. The girl in the picture was pretty, with large eyes and wide lips and a ponytail resting on her shoulder. Keith had wanted to put the baseball cap back in, but September told him the public needed to see her without the distraction of a costume.

She thanked Keith and as he left, she said to Wes and George, "Let's get it out there *toute suite.*"

"Hope it works better than Jilly's picture," Maharis said glumly from Gretchen's desk.

"Yeah," September agreed, as she headed for the break room for her coat and messenger bag. She hoped it did, too.

Chapter Twenty-Five

Lucky watched Ugh drive into the lot of Bad Dog Pub a little after seven P.M. Once again she drove past the bar and looked for a spot on a side street. It took a while to find a place where she could fit the car in with its nose out, facing toward the road, just in case she was in need of a quick getaway.

Her pulse was running light and fast. She'd practically willed this meeting with him, but now that it was here, she was feeling light-headed and jazzed.

Her thermos of sweet dreams was in the glove box along with the stun gun and several other gifts from Mr. Blue. Beneath the passenger seat was an empty placard with twine looped through two holes. It was questionable whether she would actually be able to get him to write out his sins, but it didn't hurt to be prepared. Her mission, by necessity, often had to be altered at a moment's notice.

She was in her black and pink plaid skirt, the pink sequined flats with white anklets, and the pink blouse. She'd plaited her hair into one long braid and tied a pink ribbon around the end of it, and she'd dusted on a light coating of makeup, emphasizing her lips with bubble-gum-pink lip gloss.

Now, throwing on a long, black raincoat, she walked into

the bar, carrying only a small wallet in her pocket that held her fake identification, ID that said she was Alicia Trent. She had to leave her stash of "self-defense" equipment in the car, but she intended to wangle Ugh out of the bar anyway.

Inside the door, she turned directly to the restrooms, which were marked POINTERS and SETTERS. It took her a moment before she got it, so tense were her nerves. She went into a stall, took off her coat and folded it over her arm. Then she flushed and walked back out, checking her appearance. If she didn't get carded it would be a miracle, though maybe she looked like she was play-acting. Maybe that wasn't what he was looking for.

Tough. She was here. So was Ugh. It was time to make contact.

The bouncer proofing patrons at a podium said, "ID," in a bored tone. She handed it over and he did a serious check on it, but she knew it was probably good enough for him. If the police caught her, and a background search were done, well, that was another story, but here she felt confident he wouldn't find anything amiss.

Her eyes searched past him and she located her target sitting at the end of the bar. A television tuned to a news program hung from the ceiling directly in his sight line, but his attention had been drawn to his right by a couple seated at a nearby table. The guy looked pretty young but the girl beat him by a mile with her baby face, slim build, and tiny stature; she couldn't be more than five feet. Height was another thing Lucky had against her. Five foot seven was just too tall for a man like Ugh.

She would have to give the performance of her life.

"Okay," the bouncer said, eyeing her short skirt and length of bare leg.

As she moved in on Ugh, his odor enveloped her, chokingly

thick. She had to fight down an urge to gag and steeled herself with a cold mind and laserlike focus.

"Hey," she said, moving up beside him, startling him. He reared back as if caught in a nefarious act.

"Hey," he said after a moment.

"Oh, sorry. I thought you were someone I knew. . . ." She glanced around the room, feigning confusion.

"He's not here?" Ugh asked, his interest rising.

"Apparently not." She turned to meet his gaze directly, her stomach quivering.

"His loss."

She smiled. "I guess so."

"What are you drinking?" he asked.

Swiftly she glanced at his drink and saw that it was a mug of steaming coffee. She didn't catch a hint of rum or whiskey and thought maybe it was devoid of alcohol. "I'm not really much of a drinker," she said. "Maybe some white wine?"

He signaled to the bartender and ordered her a glass of Chardonnay. "That okay?" he asked.

"Perfect. I see you've got coffee."

"Nothing can take the place of good strong java," he said, his gaze all over her face and body. She was glad she'd smashed her breasts down.

Laying her coat on the bar, she searched the pocket for her wallet as the bartender came back with her glass of wine.

Ugh's hand reached out and dropped over hers. "My treat."

"You don't have to."

"I want to."

"But you're not drinking."

He picked up the mug with his free hand and leveled a gaze at her. "That's not how I take my pleasure."

His smile was pure evil, at least to Lucky's way of thinking. It was an effort not to react with revulsion. He hadn't lifted his hand from hers and her skin felt like it was moist and blistering beneath his touch.

Pulling back her arm, she eased away from his touch, but covered up the move by turning more toward him. "I really was supposed to meet someone else, but he's not the most reliable guy."

She spun the stem of her glass meditatively on the bar and he watched her with such craving that she had to look away, toward the television, just to break the intensity. "My name's Lucky," she said.

He sucked in air and laughed silently, loving it. "I'm Graham."

Her mind was racing. She could probably get him to leave with her right now. But how to finagle him to some rendezvous where she was in control? He might be unaware of her plans for him, but he was still dangerous and unpredictable.

And then a picture came on the television. A drawing of, oh God, *herself*! The volume was turned down and the noise from the bar was too loud to hear, but she knew that was her.

How? How did they know?

The teenagers.

His hand had stolen around the small of her back, resting lightly there. Was it her imagination or was the bouncer staring at her again? Had he seen the picture? Did he know?

She had to leave. Immediately. Had to get out of the spotlight.

Leaning into Ugh, making sure she kept his attention off the television until the bulletin passed, she whispered, "I'll be right back."

"Where are you going?"

She put a finger to his lips to stay any more questions, then she swept up her coat and sauntered toward the front door, giving him a good look at her swishing ass, hoping that was what imprinted on his memory, not her face.

Once outside she sprinted toward her car. Leaping inside, she jammed the key into the ignition and threw the Sentra into gear. She slammed hard into the bumper of the car ahead of hers, but managed to get out without further incident. Then she drove as fast as she dared, little trills of anxiety running up and down her spine, and when she got to the Creekside Inn she buried herself inside, shoving a nightstand in front of the door, shaking and gasping from exertion and fear.

What if the desk manager saw the sketch and knew it was her?

She switched on the television in the room and chewed on her nails as she waited for another news break. God. She needed more time.

What if Ugh saw it later and remembered?

Graham waited forty-five minutes and when the girl didn't return rage boiled up inside him. "Lucky, my ass," he muttered, stomping out of the bar and turning around in the parking lot, seeing if by some chance she was outside, waiting for him.

But no. The bitch was gone.

He went back into the bar, his mood black, but no one else caught his eye. He'd liked the look of the girl with the guy who'd been seated near him, but they'd left shortly after Lucky did and he'd never really had a chance with her anyway.

He wanted to cry with frustration. He knew he should be lying low after what had happened with Claudia, but instead of slaking his desire, her death just made him want more of the same.

He had to leave. Head to his father's basement. He couldn't be under Daria's thumb any longer. She was cramping his style. Worse, she seemed to think she owned him, like they were meant to be together forever and ever.

But could he leave the bodies at her place? There were two of them now. Claudia had finally stopped making that ugly rasping sound, but if she hadn't, he would have put her in the ground anyway.

No. He had to move them to his father's. Maybe he should head over there now and start digging into the earthen floor. He couldn't just take the bodies there if the ground wasn't prepared. His father, though nutty and weak, was still ambulatory and could take it into his head to have a peek in the basement if he sensed Graham were there.

But he didn't want to move them tonight. He wanted to fuck that tight piece of ass that had *walked out on him.*

Damn!

Trying to calm himself, he thought about his collection of porn and drove home with his mind on his favorite videos. But even so, he couldn't get the chick in the little skirt out of his head. He could already hear her cooing his name as he slipped his hand up between her legs.

Bitch! Where did she go?

Around midnight he fell asleep in a chair in front of the TV, paying no attention to the "actors" groaning and screwing and screaming on screen. In the wee hours he heard something that sent him bolt upright, instantly awake: a door opening. Immediately he switched off the television, though the DVD was long over. It was still in the player, but he didn't have time to remove it and stash it away.

Instead he looked around for a weapon. Nothing.

Creeping toward the hall, he thought he saw movement in the mudroom. Darting quickly, he grabbed the Maori figurine and then jumped into view, holding it high over his head.

Daria snapped on a light at the same moment, her mouth opening and closing like a fish. "Graham!" she shrieked.

Out of the corner of his eye he saw, through a gap in the curtained window, the glow of red taillights from the departing cab, lights that winked out as the vehicle turned the bend in the driveway.

"Fuck, Daria. What's with this sneaking in? You trying to get yourself killed? Give me a goddamn heads-up next time!"

"I'm sorry. I'm sorry." She looked ready to cry. "I wanted to surprise you."

"I hate surprises! GODDAMN HATE THEM," he roared.

"I know. It's my fault. I'm so sorry."

It took everything he had—*everything!*—for him to put down the figurine and slam back into the den. Quickly, he ejected the DVD and slipped it into a nondescript jewel case, stuffing it behind one of the tomes in her bookcase temporarily.

About a half hour later, he heard her tentative knock on the den door.

"What?" he barked.

"Are you coming to bed? It's really late."

"I'm sleeping on the couch," he said through his teeth.

"Okay."

Sneaky old hag, he thought, hearing her footsteps head back to the bedroom. No consideration for the fact that he had to get up in the morning and teach those fucking whiny brats. Maybe Molly would be back; that would be a plus. But probably not, he thought, falling into despair.

It was all Daria's fault. He hated HER. He wondered if he could keep sleeping in the den until he made the move to his father's. But he hated his dad's place, too. Hated the old, musty, broken down wreck of a house, hated his father's constant throat clearing and whining.

But he couldn't stand being with Daria anymore at all. He loved her house, the grounds, the whole place. If it were his, he could be happy here. He wouldn't need anyone. He could maybe keep his thoughts away from the dangerous paths they wanted to follow and just live.

Daria had money socked away in bank accounts, too. There was online access. All he had to do was learn the codes and maybe he could wheedle those out of her. If there was enough money, maybe he could even quit his job.

He just had to get rid of her. That was all.

Staring into the dark, he let himself fall asleep again and was dead to the world until his eyes suddenly flew open, attuned to his internal clock. It was early morning and he needed to get ready for school.

He'd barely gotten any sleep and that made him cross. It was still dark outside so he had a little time, but he was sick to death of the daily grind, sick to death of everything.

The idea of walking through HER bedroom to use the en suite bathroom made his stomach turn. He had to think about that for a while, so instead he pushed the button on the coffee maker that he'd already prepared for the morning. His full strength stuff. She could just make a face when she drank it or not drink it at all.

Swallowing down his first cup, he felt better, more resolved. All he needed was a solid plan and then he would be good to go. The next time Daria went on a trip—and he sure as hell hoped it was going to be soon—he would move the bodies. In the meantime, he would figure out how to access her accounts and then he would decide what to do about her. He couldn't get rid of her yet, much as he might want to. He would have to wait until everything was in order.

"Graham?"

She came out of the bedroom in her bathrobe, looking worn and tired, and there were smudges of leftover makeup beneath her eyes.

Play nice, play nice, play nice.

"Good morning," was all he could croak out.

He could see the relief cross her face and she sighed and came over to him, wrapping her arms around his waist. He was still in his clothes from the night before and he suddenly wanted to rip them off and get in the shower. But she gazed up at him with that *look* on her face, the one that sent warning bells off in the back of his head. She wanted to make love and he was not in the mood. Would never be in the mood again.

"I can't," he said. "I've got to get ready for work."

"Oh, come on. It won't take long."

"Yes, it will." Seeing her hurt, he added, "You know how we are when we get going."

She smiled. "Yes, I do." Her hands started unbuttoning his shirt and he wanted to clamp down on those old fingers and rip them away from him. Instead, he allowed her to pull his shirt free of his pants, take the coffee cup from his hand, and set it deliberately on the counter, then grab his hand and tug him a step forward. "Come on," she whispered.

No. He couldn't do it. It wasn't in him. There was nothing there.

But you need her. Just a little while longer. Turn your mind around. Think of something else. . . .

His mind flew to Molly. Her shining hair. Her sweet ways. But that was no good. No. He needed to quash that and think of something else. Something he could have.

Lucky.

In his mind's eye he saw the way her short skirt flipped when she walked, the little anklets, the tight ass.

He let Daria walk him to the bedroom, blind to everything but the scenario running through his head. Where the fuck had Lucky gone? Why had she left?

Daria was taking her robe off, but Graham was lost in another world. He had Lucky down and she was fighting him. He felt her hands on him and he threw her down on the bed and pinned her wrists. She was pretending to want him, making all the right noises, her hands roaming his body, but he knew she was playing some kind of game.

Well, fine. He could play that game, too.

He spread her legs with a hard knee and slammed into her, pounding as hard as he could, loud growls issuing from his throat, the sound of his burning frustration. She was going to *pay* for walking out, *pay* for leaving him hard and dissatisfied, *pay* for playing a game that only he could win!

"Ulysses! Goddammit. Ulysses! *Graham!*" He came to slowly to realize Daria was pounding on his back with impotent fists. "What the fuck was that about?" she demanded.

His heart was racing. He felt completely amped up. "You didn't like it?"

"No, I didn't like it! What's going on with you? That's the second time you've been too rough."

Conversely, now that she didn't want him, he wanted to take her again. Grabbing her shoulders, he held her down and she twisted and tried to jerk a knee up to hit him in the balls.

"Don't," he said through tight teeth, and then abruptly he was done with her.

He hated her too much to take her again.

She scrambled around and grabbed up her robe, breathing hard, half mad, half scared. "I really don't like where this is going," she told him, slamming out of the bedroom and stalking down the hall.

Well, fuck her. Graham headed into the shower and turned his face into the hot spray. His black mood from the night before had returned. How long could he keep this up? Not much longer. All he really wanted to do was grab her by the neck and smack her head into the wall until it was a bloody pulp.

He dressed in slacks and an open-collared shirt. He had no enthusiasm for the job, but until Daria was out of the picture he had to keep going.

Walking into the kitchen, he saw that she was staring out toward the garden, a cup of coffee in her hand, her face set. To his shock, she suddenly went to the kitchen drawer that held her business supplies, rooted around inside and came up with a handgun.

"Whoa, Daria! What are you doing?"

"I'm just going to scare him," she said tautly.

His gaze followed hers out the window and he saw the coyote tugging on something under the raspberry vines. *Holy shit!*

She ran outside, yelling at the top of her lungs, the bathrobe tie tearing loose and exposing her white sagging skin. As Graham watched in shock, the animal dropped the human hand that was in its mouth, unable to pull the whole corpse from the ground.

"Get out!" Daria screamed after him as he loped away.

She turned back, too mad at the coyote to look at what he'd uncovered. "Beasts," she snapped as she came back inside and pulled the French door shut behind her.

"You scared him away. I didn't know about the gun. Wow. But you scared him off."

He was babbling and he had to stop himself. He felt high and weird. For a moment he thought he had gotten away with it, but then she glanced back through the window toward the raspberry vines.

The Maori statue was still on the kitchen counter where he'd left it the night before. He didn't wait for her to think too hard. He snatched it up and swung it at her head with all his might. She half lifted the gun, some inherent last sense of self-preservation, but he caught her in the temple hard. She went down to her knees and pitched forward.

It felt great. Powerful. Better than sex.

"Daria?" he asked after a few moments.

She just lay there, face down.

Then he looked at the statue in his hand. He couldn't believe he'd done it.

But you needed those access codes!

"Daria?" he tried again. She wasn't dead yet, but she was as good as, he thought. "Damn!"

Well, there was nothing to do now but bury her with the others. Jesus. What a lot of work. He would barely have time before school to bury her, he thought as he headed to the garage for the shovel and rake. What time was it? He was going to be late. There was no getting around it.

He took off his shoes and donned his boots, then looked down at his pants. He would ruin them but, Christ, he had to get moving.

As he was coming out of the garage he thought he heard something. A sharp noise from inside the house. He glanced around wildly. Was someone here? He took several steps toward the front of the house, then turned back to the job. He had to hurry.

He went through the breezeway to the garden and shuddered when he saw Claudia's hand and arm poking through the mud. Fucking coyote. He slammed the shovel into the ground beside the body, deepening the hole, shoving the body down in it with the toe of his boot, then covering up his ministrations. He'd already worked up a sweat even in the cool morning air, and he hadn't even started on Daria's grave. He was going to have to move all of these bodies and soon and it pissed him off.

He glanced at his watch. He couldn't go to school. He couldn't. He was going to have to call in. Dropping the shovel, he stalked back to the house, yanked off his boots and padded sock-foot through the mudroom.

Immediately he saw that Daria had dragged herself around the counter and into the center of the kitchen. There was blood on the floor, blood on the cabinets, blood on the counters, and the knife drawer was open. Bending down, he grabbed her hands, searching for the weapon. A small knife clattered to the floor.

Her glassy eyes stared at him.

"Trying to kill me?" he snarled.

When she didn't answer, he picked up her limp wrist and tested her pulse.

A moment later he flung it back down.

"Too late, bitch."

Hurrying to the den, he snatched up his cell and called the school. He'd hardly started in with his excuses when that ugly woman with the bad knees, Maryanne, insisted she was putting him through to Lazenby, who answered flatly, "Mr. Harding."

"I can't come in today," he snapped at her.

"Are you sick?" she challenged him.

"I'm not feeling well, that's true," he said, surprised that she would dare to talk to him in that tone.

"I've asked for someone from the police to come and speak with us, and I'd like you to be here. You have Molly Masterson in your class and you know Claudia Livesay. I think it's important you attend."

"I just told you I can't." Should he manufacture a cough? No. Might sound too forced.

"Try to find a way," she said unreasonably, and then hung up.

Graham was incensed. How dare she! She couldn't do that. He would report her to the union. See how she liked that. High and mighty bitch.

But then he thought how everyone else on staff would be there, kowtowing to Lazenby's wishes, sucking up for all they were worth. And if he wasn't there, it would be noted, and not just by Lazenby.

He had to go. Had to.

In a flurry of fear and indignation, he grabbed a tarp from the garage and wrapped Daria's body in it, then hauled her across the breezeway and into the garage, laying her on the concrete in front of the Lexus. The burying would have to wait.

He returned to the kitchen, scrubbing up the streaks of blood on the floor, wiping down the Maori statue, setting it back on the mantel. He poured the rest of his coffee down the sink and automatically filled up the coffee maker with water, replaced the filter in the basket and measured out tomorrow's grounds, then put the carafe back in its slot.

He went into the bedroom and made the bed, then cleaned up Daria's toiletries in the bathroom. His heart jolted when he saw her bag still half filled with her clothes and he ripped out the remaining items and threw them in the wash. Then he stowed the bag in the hall closet. He wanted no evidence that she'd recently come home from a trip.

Satisfied with the bedroom, he went to the den, found his porn CD and tidied up the couch. He took the CD into the spare bedroom and shoved it behind the knickknack shelf she had filled with collectibles. They were probably worthless but he would look at them later, when he had time to sort through and sell them.

Finally, he glanced down at his clothes—drops of blood and splattered mud were everywhere. Ripping off his shirt and pants, he threw them into the already running wash that held Daria's clothes, not caring if they were ruined forever. Then he redressed, adding the touch of a tie this time, just to up his game. He practiced in the mirror until he'd perfected a somber expression. His color was still high from the physical exertion and he looked damn good.

Chew on that, Lazenby, you old cow.

He prowled around the house a few more times, making sure everything was in its right place, everything was perfect. Daria's body was a problem, but there were no windows to the garage and he was going to lock it up tight after he took out the Lexus. It was his now, he figured. She wasn't going to need it any longer.

With a rich feeling of ownership heightening his mood, he backed out of the garage and hit the remote, watched the door slowly close, wiping Daria's remains slowly from view, almost like a magic trick.

"How to Beat the Recession and Not Let It Beat You!" he crowed.

Hah!

Chapter Twenty-Six

September had barely gotten in to work when George, who'd arrived before her, said, "There's a detective from the Winslow County Sheriff's Department on his way."

"Winslow, not Clatsop?" she asked, thinking of the investigation into Hiram Champs.

"Detective Will Tanninger from Winslow County. I wrote it down."

"Oh, all right."

As she settled into her desk, Wes arrived. "George says a detective from Winslow County SD is on his way. Have anything to do with you?"

"Nope," Wes said.

"Maybe he wants to meet with the lieutenant," she posed.

"D'Annibal's coming in later," George said.

"Whatever," September said, turning her attention to the day's work. "Nothing on our vigilante sketch yet?"

"A few calls came in," George said without much enthusiasm. "Dispatch sent over the list and I looked it over. I put it on your desk if you and Wes want to check them out. Did you talk to the principal at Twin Oaks?"

"Yeah. Yesterday," September said, irked that George seemed to be checking up on her.

"She called again today. Wants to have some kind of forum at the school. I told her one of us would come," he said.

"Which one of us?" September asked.

He merely lifted his brows and she was pissed all over again. "Fine," she said, then asked, "Is Maharis still working with us?"

"He's got two missing persons now," George said.

September felt a twinge of conscience. D'Annibal had asked her to help him with the Gillian Palmiter case, but apart from going to Gulliver's, she'd left it all to Blake. "I'll check with him on those."

A few minutes later, the door opened into the squad room and a man and a woman walked in. The man was wearing the tan uniform of the Winslow County Sheriff's Department but the woman was just in jeans, a black ribbed, turtleneck sweater, and a black jacket.

September got out of her chair and was in the act of offering her hand for a handshake, when she met the woman's eyes directly.

Holy Mother of God . . . !

She was their vigilante!

"Who are you?" she asked, her gaze on the woman as the man shook her outstretched hand and introduced himself as Detective Will Tanninger.

"My name's Gemma LaPorte," she said, "and when Will and I saw the news last night, we realized you're looking for my twin sister, Ani."

"What?" September asked.

"We've been looking for her for four years," Tanninger said.

The squad room was dead quiet. Both Wes and George were staring at Gemma LaPorte as well.

"Ani," September repeated. "Why are you looking for her?"

Tanninger said, "The same reason you are. Because she has a sixth sense about sexual predators and targets them for death."

Seeing the blank looks on their faces, Gemma said, "We need to give you some background."

"Yeah." September looked around. "There's an interview room down the hall. . . ."

By the time Lucky pulled herself out of the safe cocoon of her room she figured Ugh had been at school for hours. She hadn't had the nerve to follow him to Twin Oaks again and make sure. Even the parking lot was off limits now.

Mr. Blue had been right to ask her to leave. If she were found at his place with that sketch of her all over the news . . . It didn't bear thinking about. She owed him her life.

But now her timetable had shrunk. There was no more time left. If she was going to get Ugh she was going to have to do it today.

With that in mind, she put on her black jogging pants and her baseball cap and placed a money band around her waist, stuffing in the rest of the cash Mr. Blue had given her and her room key. She drew her black V-necked Lycra shirt over her head, hiding the money band, then slipped on her matching black jogging jacket. From a hiding place among her clothes, she rolled out a flat felt case that held four small narrow pieces of metal, a set of homemade lock picks she'd asked Mr. Blue to find for her. She put the felt case in her jacket pocket and zippered it in. Then she grabbed up her wallet, which contained her fake ID, and shoved it along with the other items Mr. Blue had given her into the small backpack she used on her forays. At the car, she added the items from her glove box into the pack along with the placard that she'd had under the seat.

She would go to his house and wait for him.

* * *

"The first time Ani crossed our radar was when she ran down a man named Edward Letton in her car," Will Tanninger told them. "Letton was a sexual predator. He had a van equipped with ropes, chains, handcuffs . . . child pornography, and he was in the process of trying to abduct a girl from a soccer field when Ani drove straight at him."

"She saved the girl from capture," Gemma added soberly.

September absorbed that and asked, "What happened to Letton?"

"He died from his injuries," Tanninger answered. "Regardless of her motives, she killed him."

"He deserved to die," Gemma said.

"She's your twin," September said, not wanting to get into that gray area, though she felt very similar to Gemma.

"I thought it was Gemma behind the wheel," Tanninger continued. "We didn't know Ani even existed."

"You didn't know?" September asked Gemma.

"We were separated. Cleaved apart, actually, as we were conjoined. I've done some research in the town of Deception Bay since Ani appeared in my life. Our birth mother was known to all the locals as Mad Maddie. She was a seer, of sorts, and she apparently passed on that ability to both Ani and me. She named us Gemma and Ani for the sign of Gemini. The doctor kept Ani as a kind of payment while our mother slowly lost all touch with reality. I was luckier with my adoptive family.

"But I didn't know any of this when Ani began killing. A psychologist would tell you she's killing the doctor who abused her over and over again."

"Letton wasn't her only victim," Tanninger said. "But Ani was also being stalked by a killer who thought she was a witch and tied her to a burning funeral pyre. She escaped somehow, then stole a woman's car from the town of Quarry. That car was found in the ditch on a side road deep in the Coast Range about a week later. There's been no sign of her since."

"Actually, she was handed over the keys to that car by the woman's developmentally handicapped son," Gemma said. "I know she has to be stopped, but if there's any way to save her . . ."

A long moment passed and then September said, "Some might say she's doing the world a favor, but our job as members of law enforcement is to keep her from harming anyone else."

"You sound like Will," Gemma said, smiling faintly. "I've been thinking about her for years. I just want to be with her again."

Wes spoke up. "You know we'll take every precaution to bring her in unharmed."

"Yes," Tanninger said firmly. "But she is dangerous. She shot my partner and it was touch and go for a while."

"Okay," September said, a little boggled by everything they had laid down.

Gemma added, "She goes by Lucky. I don't know why, but that's what she calls herself."

Tanninger put in, "I don't know what her timetable is, but she may have already targeted someone else."

After Tanninger went into the specifics of the cases Ani had been involved in four years earlier September asked, "How does she find her targets? I mean, choose one specifically."

"No easy answer to that," Tanninger said, looking to Gemma.

Gemma said, "You won't believe me. I can tell already, but that's fine. There is no explanation other than she just knows. It's a kind of precognition. I have something like it, too, but it doesn't work the same way."

September stared straight at her, afraid that if she turned even the slightest toward Wes or George that she would hit them with a "can you believe this?" look.

Instead, she again went over the facts of the cases that Ani had been involved in four years before, keeping things on a level that made sense. Wes and George both asked questions, too, but in the end they didn't know much more about Ani's methodology than when they'd started.

As they rose from the chairs, Tanninger said, "I want to be kept in the loop."

"Of course," September told him, shaking his hand and Gemma's once again. Wes and George echoed her sentiment. Knowing Tanninger was from Winslow County, she almost told him that she'd had some dealings earlier in the year with one of the deputies from his office, Danny Dalton, but decided against it. She hadn't thought much of Dalton and Gretchen had considered him a complete moron.

It was gratifying to realize that in Will Tanninger, the county had someone who appeared more than capable.

After they walked Will and Gemma back through the squad room and the door closed behind them, September exhaled heavily and looked at Wes and George. "Well," she said.

"Yes, 'well,'" Wes said.

"Do you believe that shit?" George sank into his chair and it squeaked familiarly beneath his weight. "At least we know her name."

"Two names," September reminded him. "She goes by Lucky."

"All right—Lucky," George said. "How does that help us catch her?"

"Is she setting someone up?" Wes asked. "There was quite a bit of time between Ballonni and Harmak."

"Let's forget all the woo-woo and get down to basics," September said. "Someone will have seen her." She picked up the list George had left on her desk and saw the note that he'd scratched about Principal Lazenby's request. "Let's start calling and see what we come up with."

Wes reached over and took the list from her hand. "Won't take long to get through these."

"Go ahead and do it. I'll call Amy Lazenby back and see what I can do for her," she said dryly, shooting George a look.

He lifted his hands. "She asked for you. So sue me."

When Lucky got to the end of Ugh's drive she found a spot on the street in her usual area. Drawing a deep breath, she climbed out of her car, slipping the small backpack over one shoulder. A man drove by in a car and gave her a wave, freezing her where she stood. Then she realized he'd recognized her from all the time she'd spent recently on this street. The houses were spaced far apart and back from the road so he'd probably seen her jogging, maybe even thought she lived on the street.

But if someone got a good look at her, and put two and two together . . . ?

This is your last time, Ani.

She took a hard look around. Should she sneak up through the neighbor's yard and scale the chain-link fence again, or should she boldly march up the driveway? Ugh should be at school and his roommate was still gone, as far as she knew. In the light of day, trespassing on the neighbor's property didn't feel safe anymore, but then, ever since she'd seen her face on television, nowhere felt safe.

Her own indecision disgusted her. In the end, she walked up the driveway, cautiously coming around the bend that opened up to the front of the house.

Ugh's station wagon was still parked in front and the garage door was down. He must've taken the Lexus to school.

She breathed easier. The girlfriend must still be gone if he was driving her car. If all went well, with her skill set, she should be able to break in to the house and lie in wait for him. With that plan in mind, she cautiously moved into the breezeway, taking a look at the back doorknob. She tested it, just to be sure it was locked, and then pulled out her picks, placing two into the tiny hole of the lock, listening for the sounds that meant she'd tripped the tumblers. She wasn't as adept as she'd once been and it took long minutes before she gained ingress. When the lock popped, she quickly slipped the picks back to her zippered pocket, then moved stealthily through a small room that entered into the kitchen.

The place smelled of disinfectant. Checking the sink, she saw traces of cleanser in the basin. She opened the cupboard beneath and plucked out a green can of Comet. The outside was slippery and damp. Was the roommate back after all? she wondered. Ugh just didn't seem like the kind of guy who would go into full-on cleaning unless he had a really good reason.

Worried about the girlfriend, she did a careful reconnoiter of the house but found no sign of anyone. She was alone. But there were more signs of cleaning. The master bath had a woman's toiletries all shoved together in a tight circle on the counter. No one had used them recently.

What was he cleaning up?

Back in the kitchen, she unzipped her backpack, the small ripping noise sounding like a cacophony in the tomblike silence of the house. She grimaced, listening hard, even though she knew she was alone. The loudest noise was her own thundering heart.

As a final precaution, she slipped back across the breezeway and turned the knob on the garage, finding it locked as well. Once more she plied her picks to the lock and this one took even longer to open. If she survived this, she was definitely going to have to work on her breaking in skills.

Opening the door, she was relieved to see that it was as she had suspected: no Lexus.

But there was a rolled up tarp on the floor.

Oh, God. Was that a *body*?

Had he *killed* someone?

Lucky tiptoed across the floor and stared down at the tarp

a long moment before placing her hands on it and slowly unrolling it. It was a body. She could tell by the feel.

Mouth dry, she unfurled it until a woman's body lolled out, eyes open to a vacant view. Her frosted hair drenched in blood.

She had to fight a scream. He'd killed the roommate.

With extreme care, she rolled the woman back into the tarp, hoping it looked undisturbed. Ugh had grown even more bold, more dangerous. Carefully relocking the garage and returning to the house, she glanced around the kitchen, her eye falling on the coffee maker. He liked strong coffee. He'd told her that.

Flipping open the top, she saw it was already set to make another pot. With determination she pulled out the stainless steel carafe and slipped the contents of one of her plastic bags inside.

Then, grabbing up her backpack, she looked around for a good hiding place, settling on the second bedroom closet.

At three o'clock, September grabbed her coat and messenger bag and said she was on her way to Twin Oaks.

"You should send Maharis or another uniform," George said.

"Seems she wants me. Besides, Maharis is out canvassing bars, looking for someone who remembers the older man who hit on Jilly. I'm good with it."

Actually, she was frustrated that they weren't getting any further traction on the investigation. The phone calls she and Wes had returned didn't seem to be going anywhere. To a one the call-ins had been people looking for more information than offering it. She already felt like she'd dropped the ball with Maharis. She wasn't going to fob some new task off on him.

As she pulled into the Twin Oaks parking lot she ran into a blockade of parents picking up their kids. A line of cars snaked around the building. She sensed this was not the norm.

With everything that had gone on the last week, the parents were being proactive in transporting their children safely back and forth to school.

Amy Lazenby was already standing in the hall outside the front offices when September walked in. "Thank you for coming, Detective. We're meeting in the gym. There are a lot of people with a lot of questions."

"Lead the way."

As they entered the room, September noted that only a smattering of chairs were taken, but within ten minutes it was standing room only. She looked out at the faces and waited as Lazenby addressed them all, introduced her, and then went straight to a Q & A. Parents peppered September with questions, most of which she couldn't answer. They already knew most of what she did from the news: Stefan had been killed by a gunshot wound. A woman was involved. The same woman who they believed had tied him to the pole days before. The same woman suspected in the murder of Christopher Ballonni.

About Claudia Livesay, she had even less information. "We've been gathering evidence on her disappearance, talking to family, friends, neighbors, anyone who might offer up a clue," she assured them.

"But you think it's foul play?" one earnest man asked.

"It's too early to say."

A woman raised her hand. "I'm a friend of Claudia's. I spoke to an officer and told him that she would never just leave Molly. Never."

There was a murmur of agreement. September really wished she had more solid information, but it was too soon. The tech team had gone through Claudia's house but the results weren't in yet.

After another twenty minutes the meeting broke up. September was introduced personally to some of the faculty and staff. One woman came up to her and said, "I'm Bette Pearce.

I teach sixth grade. I've talked to Claudia many times as her daughter, Molly, is in my home room. Graham knows her, too. . . ." She indicated a man who was hanging back, talking to another teacher who'd introduced himself to September earlier as Evan Tarker. "He has Molly for sixth period. No one's interviewed any of us yet."

"The investigation is just getting started," she assured her. In truth, she and others in the department had hoped Claudia Livesay might turn up on her own, which often happened, but as time elapsed that scenario was looking less and less likely.

Fifteen minutes later, September was saying her good-byes to Lazenby and the front office staff when the raised voices of a man and a woman could be heard coming from one of the back offices.

Lazenby looked over with an annoyed glare. When a man and a woman appeared, she said, "Dave?" sounding surprised. The man moved ahead of the woman and came from behind the counter to shake September's hand.

"David DeForest," he introduced himself. "Vice principal. We appreciate everything you're doing, Detective."

The woman followed him out, her face flushed, her mouth determined. She shot him a baleful look, then also turned to September. "I'm Patti DeForest."

Lazenby clearly wanted to ask them what had been going on, but stayed her tongue, probably not wanting to air dirty laundry in front of September, whom she ushered toward the door. "If you learn anything, please tell us. We all need answers."

"I will," she assured her.

As she was heading down the steps, she heard behind her: "Detective Rafferty!"

Turning, she saw it was Patti DeForest. Her husband burst through the doors after her, perturbed and flushed, but Patti was bent on getting to September.

"Dave doesn't want me to say things I shouldn't," she said

with a bite as she hurried down the steps. "But I have to go with my conscience."

"What is it?" September asked her.

"That picture you had on television. The woman you're looking for? She was here at Twin Oaks. Said her name was Alicia Trent and she was checking out the school to see if it was right for her son."

"Patti." David DeForest's voice was soft and disappointed, but he looked like he was about to blow a gasket.

"It was her, Dave," she insisted, rounding on her husband.

September turned to DeForest, who said, "Well, sure. There was a similarity. But the woman you're looking for is obviously not Alicia Trent."

"Why 'obviously'?" she asked.

"Because you're looking for a killer," he said, as if that explained everything.

"Do you have her address or phone?" September asked him, gratifying Patti and sending his face even redder.

"She hasn't filled out any forms yet. She came to our Fun Night last Friday. She really wanted to know what the school was about before she committed."

"And you haven't seen or heard from her since," Patti said smugly.

"It hasn't even been a week!" he sputtered.

"And she didn't bring her son to Fun Night, and that's what it's all about. Bringing your kids. I don't even think she has one," Patti declared. "It was her," she said again to September. "She's the one you're looking for. She didn't kill Mr. Harmak the first time, so she came back looking for him."

"He wasn't at Fun Night," DeForest snapped.

"So she found him at his home later."

September listened to them fight for a few more moments, then said soothingly, "I'll look into Mrs. Trent."

"Don't tell her I was the one who told you," Patti said, scared.

"It's a waste of time!" DeForest declared.

"I'll be discreet," September assured him, extricating herself from both of them. At some level, she thought Patti might be on to something, though Ani/Lucky going to Fun Night in search of Stefan seemed unlikely. If Ani had picked him up at Valley Mall, then left him tied up at his place of work, wouldn't she have already known where he lived, especially since it was so close to the school?

So, if Alicia Trent were truly Ani, what then would be her reason for attending Twin Oaks' Fun Night?

Her next target?

Was it at all related to Claudia Livesay's disappearance?

It was nearly five when Lucky heard the sound of an approaching car. She dared to sneak out of her hiding spot long enough to peek through the curtains and see the tail end of the black Lexus slipping into the garage. She'd had all day to come up with a plan to approach Ugh and had failed to think of anything more effective than simply charging him and hitting him with the stun gun. Once he was incapacitated, she would be able to tie him up, get him into the backseat of the Lexus and drive him away. Better to use his girlfriend's car than her own.

But could she really leave him tied up in front of Twin Oaks like she had Stefan? No. That method had been played out. It was a shame, because she liked the humiliation angle, but she was probably going to have to come up with a secondary plan.

She heard him come in and pressed herself into the closet as he stalked down the hall to the master bedroom. In her mind's eye, she pictured the room. If he were on the other side of the bed she might not be able to reach him with the stun gun before he could defend himself.

It would be better if she waited until he came back out. Maybe she could follow him down the hall.

Ten minutes later he did just that, but as Lucky started after him, one arm of her backpack got hung up on the closet door. It rattled in its frame, but at the same moment there was a loud *thunk* from Ugh's direction. "Shit," he muttered, then picked up whatever he'd apparently dropped and walked out through the kitchen, slamming the door behind him.

She hesitated, then tiptoed to the hallway, peeking out. There was no one there.

Cautiously, she moved toward the kitchen, stun gun in hand.

A flash of color came through the French doors. She pulled back out of sight as she saw he was outside, carrying a shovel toward the raspberry vines, wearing jeans and a sweatshirt and a pair of boots.

He was going to bury the girlfriend.

Could she come up behind him?

Maybe.

She waited, holding her breath, until his back was to the house and he was digging, then she racewalked to the kitchen, realizing he'd inadvertently swept a metal vase off the counter when he'd walked by. He'd placed it on the table where it hadn't been before, a dent in its side. She squatted down behind the counters, in the center of the kitchen's *U* and sidled toward the back door.

Opening it cautiously, she carefully stepped into the breezeway, looking toward the garage door where the body in the tarp had been positioned just inside the threshold, ready for easy pick up.

"Who the hell are you?" his voice boomed, causing Lucky's hair to stand on end.

He was standing at the end of the breezeway, shovel in hand, his boots mud caked.

She wanted to charge him. She wanted to take him out. Right here, right now.

As if sensing her thoughts, he lifted the shovel menacingly.

"Who are you?" he demanded again, his voice vibrating with tension. Then, "You're the girl from the bar!"

Lucky broke and ran. Her car was at the end of the driveway. She was in her sneakers and he was in boots. She could beat him.

She got three steps before the shovel hit her in the back like a spear, knocking her down.

He was on her in an instant, wrenching off her backpack, grabbing her hat and hair, slamming his body atop hers.

"What the fuck's that?"

The stun gun was still gripped tightly in her outstretched right hand. With everything she had, she twisted around and zapped him.

He squealed and flopped around. She threw him off her, scrambling to her feet.

The zip-ties. The backpack.

His hand tangled with her ankle and she tripped. Smacked onto the concrete. The stun gun went flying.

Momentarily dazed, she staggered upward with an effort. He was still recovering. She didn't have a lot of time. Her fingers found the zipper on the backpack and she pulled it down, agonizingly slowly. Seeing stars, she put her hand to her head just in front of her temple and it came away bloody.

"Bitch . . . bitch . . ."

He had one knee under him.

Shit. Shit. Shit.

Her hand was inside the pack when he hit her, knocking her sideways. She scrabbled for the ties, the thermos, anything, but before she could grab onto those items he bowled her over with the weight of his body.

His hand was around her throat. "Who are you?" he rasped, glaring down at her. "Who the fuck are you?"

"Lucky," she said, then was choked unconscious.

Chapter Twenty-Seven

"... so I don't know if she's Ani, or if she's legit," September finished telling her story to Jake. She'd pulled a chair up close to his bed, as ever, and had laid out all she knew about the vigilante who called herself Lucky.

"How long ago was it that she did this before?" Jake asked. His arm was wrapped from shoulder to wrist. The blood that had drained beneath his skin along the side of his face from his head wound had turned his skin brown, green, and yellow, making him look like an extra from a horror movie. September decided to keep that observation to herself.

"About four years."

"And you think she might be this Alicia Trent?"

"I put Wes on it before I came here. He said he'd call if he learned anything."

"So far no call," Jake said.

"So far no call."

He thought that over, appearing more sober than he had the last time she'd seen him. Catching her concerned look, he said, "I was just thinking about Marilyn . . . and Loni."

"Ah."

They were both silent a moment, then he reached out his

good hand and recaptured her hand, threading his fingers through hers. "I'm glad you moved in," he said.

She smiled. "I had to rewash the sheets because they were a wrinkled mess. I haven't got the last of my stuff yet, but it's at the top of my list."

"I'll try to stop worrying about you," he said. "I know you don't want me to. And anyway, I'm the one who got in harm's way, not you."

"Well, I don't mind a little worrying," she said softly.

"Okay." He smiled.

Lucky awoke slowly and realized she was strapped in to the passenger seat of the Lexus. Ugh was driving. Her hands were zip-tied in front of her and the car was barreling through a dark night to some destination of his choice.

He had her stun gun mark under the right side of his jaw and he looked kind of wrung out. Good. Her throat was on fire from where he'd half strangled her.

"Okay, who the fuck are you?" he demanded again.

She wondered where the backpack was. Had he left it on the ground? If he'd looked in it, he might not be asking that question. "I told you," she rasped out. "Lucky."

"Cut the bullshit. You're the one who tied Harmak and that mailman to poles and made them write out those messages."

So, that answered the backpack question. She'd had a lot of time to come up with various stories while she'd waited for him, so now she put one in play. "They treated me badly and I wanted payback."

He threw her a wary look. "People were saying they were . . . sexual abusers of children."

"I know, but I'm telling you the truth. I had a stepdaddy once who showed me love . . . that way."

"You're lying."

"No," Lucky said truthfully. She didn't have to tell him that her memories of the abuse were what drove her to stop men like him.

"What were you doing in my house? How'd you find me?"

"I followed you last night."

"Jesus."

"I would've come in last night, but I didn't know enough. I didn't know if you lived with someone, and there was that station wagon in front. I decided to wait and see if I could catch up to you today."

"You broke in to my house."

"The door was unlocked."

"That's a *fucking* lie."

"The lock wasn't caught. I jiggled it and it opened, I swear."

"I tested it! It was locked."

She shook her head. "I was going to wait for you outside, but when I could get in, I just did."

They drove in silence for a while, west on Highway 26. She didn't know exactly where he was headed, but he was going toward the coast, toward the area she was most familiar with.

But right now they were passing by the town of Quarry, which always gave Lucky the heebie-jeebies. When he suddenly turned onto a road on the western edge of Quarry, her nerves jumped to attention. People knew her in Quarry, people knew her sister. She couldn't be seen here at any cost.

"Where are we going?" she demanded, the words wrenched from her.

"My dad's place," he said, and the smile on his lips boded of bad things to come.

They drove past farmhouses until they came to a narrow driveway that wound through rows of hazelnut trees. "Not Dad's," Ugh said, his mouth turning downward. "The stupid bastard sold off all the property that mattered. Lost it all . . . in a Ponzi scheme."

Lucky wasn't sure what that was, but she could feel the

anger and injustice inside him. His "scent" was damn near overpowering her and she had to struggle to keep up with the conversation, keep him talking.

He cut the lights as they drew close to the house. "We don't want him to know we're here, so if you make a sound, I'll kill you."

"I'll be good."

He shot her a look and she managed a faint smile.

"Maybe I'll try some of your stuff on you," he said, inclining his head toward the rear seat. She glanced behind them and saw her opened backpack with a number of items spilled over the backseat. There was a black smear in the middle of the seat. Blood?

"Why'd you kill them?" he asked suddenly. "Harmak and the mailman."

"I told you. I wanted payback. I didn't mean to kill Chris. I was just trying to teach him a lesson. So he would be nicer to me."

"You killed Harmak with a gun," he reminded her.

"He shot himself. Yes, I had the gun. He'd hurt me, too, and I was angry. But he grabbed it from me and must've pulled the trigger. I heard the shot and just ran."

"I don't believe a word out of your mouth."

She shrugged and said bitterly, "You and everyone else. I've spent my whole life kicking around in the shadows. I've grown accustomed to living on the edge. And when someone hurts me, I hurt them back. But if they're good to me, I'm really, really good to them."

He'd switched off the ignition and now he stared at her through the darkness. "We're going through that basement door," he said, inclining his head toward the house. "If you make one sound, I will squeeze your throat until you're dead."

"You like to live on the edge, too."

He didn't answer, just climbed out of the car and came around to her side, opening her door and putting his finger on her lips. She kissed that finger and gazed up at him in silence.

He pulled her out by her tied hands and then gently closed the door. With a sideways glance at the house, he suddenly pressed her against the car, his dick hard against her leg.

"How'd you find me?" he rasped out.

"You told me not to speak," she reminded him softly.

"How'd you find me?" he snarled in her ear.

"I'm lucky."

One of his hands found her neck. "Give me a straight answer."

"I liked the way you looked," she said. "I saw you before at Bad Dog. I wanted a chance with you, so I kept coming back there until you showed up again."

"I never was at Bad Dog."

"Yes, you were. A few days ago. I guess you didn't notice me. I'm crushed . . ." She moved then, settling him between her legs. The hand at her neck drifted downward and she lifted up her arms and gently wrapped them around the back of his neck. In the way she'd taught herself years before, she went to some other place. Somewhere safe. Far removed from the terrible moment.

But she couldn't go completely away. Couldn't totally forget where she was. She needed to be cognizant to get the upper hand.

He dry humped her against the car, then slid her down to the cold ground and climbed atop her. She could tell by the tenor of his breathing that he liked the danger. He ripped down the zipper of her jacket and yanked off her jogging pants. She was afraid he'd feel the lock picks in her jacket pocket with such intimate, frontal contact or find the band of money at her waist.

But no, he was too intent on getting his dick inside her to take much notice of her clothes.

A light came on over the basement door and Ugh froze in the act of undoing his belt and ripping down his pants.

Immediately he was yanking her arms from around his head and scrambling away from her, grabbing at his trousers.

A door opened and a man's quavery voice asked, "Who's out there?"

"It's me, Dad," Graham yelled back. "I'm just coming in."

"Ahh . . . okay . . ." Lucky could see the older man head back inside.

"How the fuck did he hear?" Ugh muttered. He looked down at Lucky and for a moment she thought he might go for it again, but then he pulled her up hard by her zip-tied wrists. "We'll wait until we're in the basement."

"Untie my hands so I can touch you."

"You wish." He laughed.

He dragged her along with him and she stumbled because her pants were still at her ankles. She fell once and he swore, releasing her for a moment. "Pull those up," he ordered tautly.

She did as she was told, bending over to grab her pants, unzipping her jacket pocket in the process.

"What's that?" he asked, alerted to the sound.

"The zipper at the bottom of my pant leg."

He made a move toward her but she'd gotten her hand in the pocket with the picks. "What are you doing?" he demanded.

She yanked out a pick and lunged for him. He turned his head at the last second and she jabbed the pick down, down into his left ear as hard as she could.

He screamed and yanked back from her, grabbing at his ear. She went head down and barreled into him, tripping on her pants, falling hard atop him as he flew backward, his head coming down with a crack.

Quickly she scrambled back, grabbed her pants, pulled them up. Glancing down, she saw he was remarkably still. Leaning over, she saw his head had hit a flat stone and he was out cold. She checked his breathing, hoping against hope that she'd killed him. No such luck.

She straightened. She had to get out of here. She had to get these ties off her hands, but first . . .

She ran lightly to the car, opened the back door. Her belongings were strewn about and she returned them quickly to the backpack. She had more zip-ties, however, and she brought them to Ugh and bound his legs, then rolled him over and bound his hands behind his back as well. It was her turn to take him to a location of her choice, but to get him to the car she was going to need her hands free of her own bindings. After a moment of thought, she ran to the basement and down a set of concrete stairs. The door was locked.

"Shit."

He'd been heading that way, so he must have a key, she realized. Quick as she could, she returned to him, searching his pockets to no avail. She sat down, breathing hard, thinking, worrying.

The keys were still in the ignition.

Climbing to her feet, she hurried to the car once again. Sure enough, the keys were dangling down. There were a number of extra keys attached to the ring. Grabbing them up, she ran to the basement door and on the third try it opened.

She groped around for a switch and her face ran into a hanging string from an overhead bulb, causing her to gasp before she caught herself. Pulling the string, she looked around in the sudden illumination. In the center of the large, rectangular room a set of stairs led to the upper floors. She hoped the old man wouldn't hear her.

Along the back wall were tools and she hurried toward them. Her eye scanned the wall. A box cutter. Snatching it up, she sawed away at the plastic until it gave. She dropped the box cutter, thought better of it, picked it up again and added it to the picks in her pocket.

Switching off the light, she hurried to the outside door

just as the one at the top of the stairs opened, throwing a square of yellow light into the blackness. "Ulysses . . . ?" he quavered. "Eleanor called. She heard you. . . ."

Lucky ran out the door and up the stairs. Ugh was groaning awake. With a strength born of fear, she hauled him to the Lexus and into the backseat. Slamming the door shut behind him, she circled to the driver's door, stuck the keys in the ignition, and threw the car into reverse. Mud flew from the rear tires and as she slewed around and finally got aimed the way she'd come in, she saw a series of lights flick on in the nearest house. Eleanor, most likely. The house was set well back from the road but within easy earshot of Ugh's father's place.

Then she was on the main highway, driving with control and determination. She was going to get out of Quarry and over the mountains to the beach. The Pacific drew her like a mother.

And she was going to send him directly into mother's arms.

September stopped into the station before heading home. George was already gone, naturally, but Wes was still at his desk. "Crime techs found blood spatter in the Livesay entryway," he said. "Looks like it might be Livesay's."

"So, she was attacked," September said, disheartened.

"That's what it looks like. A lot of shit happening in a short time at one school," he observed.

September nodded. A lot of shit, she thought. Stefan sure as hell wasn't responsible for Claudia Livesay, so maybe she was on the right track when it came to Lucky after all. Maybe she had found another target at Twin Oaks. Someone who Ani/Lucky felt needed to be permanently removed.

Ugh woke up before Lucky was halfway to the coast and started flinging himself around in the backseat. She wished she had her stun gun, or even Mr. Blue's .38. Something, to get him to calm down, but her hands were on the wheel and she was laser-focused, her sight narrowing to the ribbon of road in front of her, dark as pitch through the mountains except for the occasional light outside a far-off cabin or along a curving bridge.

He swore at her, a string of filthy epithets that went on for miles. Then suddenly he slammed his head into hers. Pain exploded inside her skull. She held the wheel with an effort, the tires sliding, and screamed as she crossed the asphalt to the other lane and back again.

"You want to die? You want to kill us both?" she shrieked at him.

"My ear," he cried, then swore some more before finally, mercifully, lapsing into silence. She could feel his rage. It wasn't an aura like his lust, but it was dense and hot and filled the car.

She turned south off Highway 26 to 101 and drove steadily toward Deception Bay. She wasn't exactly sure what she was going to do when she got there, but it felt right.

Just as she slowed at the entrance to the jetty, Ugh suddenly reared up and grabbed her face with one hand, his fingers digging at her eye. "You think I didn't have a knife, bitch!!!!" he screamed, pulling the weapon out with his other hand.

She lurched forward as he struck downward, freeing herself from his grip, jerking the wheel back and forth, flinging him away as the knife grazed her shoulder and plunged into the seat. The Lexus tore through the gate. A piece of painted white metal flew into the window, scarring it all the way with a *bang* before it flew off.

"Stop!" he shrieked, struggling to reach her as she wrenched the wheel one way, then the other, aware of the dangerous edges of the jetty on either side, the wheels spitting up rocks, the car careering like a drunken beast.

The end of the jetty was in sight. It was all she could see. All that was there. Ugh was struggling to grab her. She felt his hands digging at her, undoubtedly grasping for the knife again. But all she saw was the ocean.

The Lexus roared toward it like a rocket.

At the last moment a figure appeared in front of the car. Lucky gasped in shock. Dr. Parnell Loman. Her stepfather. Her abuser.

She drove right at him.

And then suddenly she was airborne, the restless Pacific rushing up to meet her.

Chapter Twenty-Eight

Ulysses Graham Harding had always imagined he was meant for great things. He couldn't believe someone as insignificant as this woman would have the brio to try and take his life.

As the Lexus smashed into the waves and rocks below, he was thrown into the front seat beside her at the same moment the windshield burst open and water rushed in, engulfing them.

He was swept out in a back flow and found himself floating in frigid water, relatively unhurt. His would-be killer was floating out of the vehicle also, a limp rag. Probably dead. Good.

He let the tide take him out, away from the shoals and the Lexus that was being tossed by waves and slammed into boulders. Poor Daria. Her baby was being beaten to death.

There were lights on the jetty. Headlights and flashlights. They'd been seen crashing into the surf.

He ducked into the frigid water, knowing he wouldn't last long in its deadly cold, but also knowing he had to get far, far away. He couldn't be found. Couldn't be associated with Lucky, whoever she was.

Eventually, he hauled himself from the tide and across

rocks and sand to a stretch of beach that led to two oceanfront cottages, neither of which was occupied. Shivering so much he could hardly function, he managed to scrounge up a decent sized rock and hurl it at what looked like a bathroom window. It crashed through and he stripped off his shirt, wrapped it around his hand so he could reach inside the shards of glass and find the latch.

Once the window was open, he squeezed himself inside, heading straight for the shower to warm his hypothermic body. His damn head hurt now that he was out of the cold, and his ear ached excruciatingly, but otherwise he was in one piece.

He checked the closets. Though there were clothes, there was nothing even close to his size.

But there was a washer and dryer.

Stripping naked in the dark, he put his shirt, pants, socks, and boxers in the dryer. He'd managed to hang on to his shoes by some minor miracle.

While his clothes were drying, he considered his predicament. It wasn't quite as dire as it could be. There was Beth out there, living in Cannon Beach. She could pick him up in twenty minutes, if need be.

There was no phone at the cabin and he wouldn't want to use one here anyway.

As soon as his clothes were dry, he put them back on and then went into the bathroom and examined his face. Not too bad. A scratch by his eye and that damned mark from the stun gun. He turned to look into his ear and thought he saw more blood.

Bitch!

His shirt was a mess of stains but it couldn't be helped.

Before he left he wiped every surface that he'd touched, then he let himself out the front door, locking it behind him.

He was in the town of Deception Bay, he realized, and he walked into the center of the town and into a pizza parlor called Sammy's. Approaching the counter, he said to the teenaged girl behind it, "Dropped my cell phone in the water, looking at that wreck off the jetty. Any chance I could use the phone?"

"Is it a local call?"

"Yep."

She considered a moment, but waved him behind the counter and to the wall where a phone was mounted. "Don't talk long. We get orders."

"I'll be quick." He winked at her and she half smiled.

His luck was holding. Beth was home and said she would be more than happy to come and get him. She had to be over forty, a little on the old side, but his imagination could turn her young again. It would have to. He didn't have any little blue pills, and Beth was going to want payment.

Thirty minutes later she was walking into Sammy's. Ten minutes after that he was giving it to her in the back of her car with her hooting and hollering and saying how long it had been since she'd been a backseat babe. Graham had his mind fixed solely on Lucky. It was Lucky beneath him, and she was screaming for mercy. He damn near smashed his hand over Beth's mouth, like he'd done with Daria, but he just managed to balance on the knife's edge between fantasy and reality, holding himself back until the deed was done.

Then she was driving him back to Laurelton. It was no problem, really. She wanted to take him.

It was problematic that she knew where he lived, but then, he was good at problem solving.

By the time he finally got Beth to leave, it was damn near dawn. He'd shoved Daria's body back into the garage before she could see and locked the door, but he still had to bury her in the garden. But it was Friday. A school day. If he tried to take off another day it was bound to look suspicious. It was going to be hell getting through all his classes, but after he did, no one would dare to think he could have anything to do with the crash off the jetty.

Switching on the coffee maker, he went to the bathroom and took another shower. When he got out, he dug through Daria's makeup drawer and found a tube of flesh-colored makeup. Putting a dab on his finger, he smeared it on the stun gun marks. It took a few tries to cover it up, and if someone looked closely they'd realize he was wearing makeup. Better that than the marks, though. He also covered up the scratches on his face, too, and in the end was pleased with the results.

Back in the kitchen, he opened the refrigerator and pulled out the carton of half-and-half. Pouring himself a cup of coffee, he added a liberal dose of cream and then sat down at the table, drinking the coffee, enjoying the moment, staring outside at the raspberry vines, a smile creeping across his face. He'd done it! He'd fooled them all. All he needed to do now was move the bodies and no one would ever suspect.

"I got away with murder," he gloated to the empty house, swallowing down the rest of the cup.

September walked into the station with a smile on her face that just wouldn't quit.

"What now?" Wes asked.

"Nothing."

"Not nothing. You were at the hospital with Jake," he said.

"He's being released today."

"And?"

She shook her head, unwilling to reveal what had been said between them, how Jake had leaned forward, grabbed her with his good hand and tumbled her over the bed until she was half lying on him.

"What are you doing?" she'd demanded.

"Kissing you," he'd answered, and then had made good on that promise with a long, lingering kiss that reached down to September's toes.

"You taste minty," she'd said, when it was over.

"You think I'd kiss you with mung mouth?"

"I considered it a possibility, but you notice I didn't stop you."

She'd tried to pull back then, but he'd held on to her and she'd lifted her brows, gazing into his gray eyes, questions in hers.

"Do you remember what you said before?" he asked.

"I say a lot of things. You gotta give me more."

"You said you would say yes when I asked you."

September had thought about playing dumb, but had immediately scratched that idea in favor of getting to the truth. "So, are you asking?"

"September Rafferty, will you marry me?"

"Detective September Rafferty," she'd corrected him, fighting to keep a straight face.

"Detective September Rafferty, will you marry me?"

She'd been shocked, thrilled, scared, but in the end had said, "All signs point to yes. . . ."

Now, remembering, she just couldn't wipe the smile from her face. She was thinking of heading home, making sure the place was ready for when she went to pick him up. D'Annibal had already told her to take time off.

As if hearing her thoughts, the lieutenant came out of his office and said, "The Tillamook County SD wants someone to check on one Daria Johannsen, the owner of the black Lexus that took a dive off the Deception Bay jetty last night. They've been calling her, but she hasn't answered."

"I'll do it on the way home," she offered.

He nodded and added, "They found some things in the car. Some zip-ties and what looked like a water-logged placard with twine looped through two holes."

"Holy . . . mother of God. Ani? " September stared at him. "Is she using the name Daria Johannsen?"

Wes called from his desk, "Uh-uh. I'm looking at the

picture on Johannsen's driver's license from the DMV data bank."

Both September and D'Annibal went to Wes's computer. A middle-aged woman with short, frosted hair and a wide smile stared back at them.

"Did anyone survive the crash?" September asked.

"No bodies yet. Probably one or more'll wash up sooner or later," the lieutenant answered grimly.

"An eyewitness puts a woman at the wheel," Wes said. "TCSD is giving us updates, but my money's on Ani going off the jetty."

"Maybe you should go with her," D'Annibal told Wes.

"I got this," September said. "If there's a problem, I'll call."

She left the station, thinking about making a stop at the market as well. Maybe she should pick up steaks again . . . show Jake she wasn't half bad at barbequing herself.

She was lost in pleasurable thoughts about the night ahead when the Johannsen drive appeared on her right. The house was situated down a long, curving asphalt driveway and she wound down it slowly, pulling up to the sprawling ranch next to a station wagon already parked in front.

Slipping her gun from her messenger bag, she placed it into the holster at her hip. She was lax about carrying it when she was with a partner, something she'd been reprimanded on and always swore to do better. But when she was on her own she was more careful. Grabbing her cell phone, she stuffed it in her jacket pocket, then she stepped out of the car. She realized her heart was beating hard in her chest. What if Wes was wrong about Ani going over the edge and she was here, lying in wait?

Cautiously, September walked toward the breezeway that separated the garage from the main house. At the back door, she peered through a small window that looked across a mudroom into a bright, yellow kitchen.

A man's trousered legs were splayed on the floor beyond the counter's peninsula, his upper torso blocked from her view.

Her already pounding heart speeded up. Something odd there. Looked as if he'd passed out and lay in the position he'd landed.

She tried the knob and the door opened beneath her hand.

Grabbing her cell phone, she called Wes and said softly, "There's a man lying on the kitchen floor. Maybe unconscious. I can see him through a window."

"At Johannsen's? Don't go in. I'll be right there."

"He might need help."

"Damn it, Nine. Listen to me."

"You sound just like Auggie," she said. "I'm just going to check on him. Hold on . . ." She shoved her cell into her pocket, then pulled out her gun. Pushing open the door, she led with the Glock, moving cautiously into the kitchen, aware that she was ignoring all protocol, all senses heightened. If Ani was here . . .

She hesitated a moment, counting her heartbeats, waiting, listening. The man was either unconscious or dead, she thought. He wasn't making any sound. Stepping in as quietly as she could, she hugged the cabinets, moving further inside until she could dare a glance over the counter at the man. A chair was knocked over and he was lying on his back, his eyes wide open, staring at some nameless horror.

She blinked in recognition. He was from Twin Oaks. Something Harding. One of Claudia Livesay's daughter's teachers.

She inhaled on a soft gasp. And he sort of looked like Kevin Costner.

The hairs on her arms lifted. *He'd* been Ani's target. That's what it was. She *had* been Alicia Trent, and she'd gone to the school looking for him.

Immediately she went on red alert. Was she here? Was she?

Grabbing her cell phone, she asked in a whisper, "You still there?"

"Yeah, and I'm on my way, goddammit," Wes snapped back.

"Call 9-1-1. Looks like we've got a dead body. Male. I think it's a teacher named Harding from Twin Oaks."

"Shitfire, Nine."

"I know. But there's nobody here but him and me."

She clicked off and looked at the scene. He'd apparently fallen out of the chair, she thought. A cup lay shattered on the floor beside his head and a small amount of coffee had spilled onto the floor. Had he had a heart attack, or had there been something in the coffee? Something Ani had given him? Roofies or worse? One of her special cocktails?

Looking down at him, it dawned on her that he'd probably kidnapped Gillian Palmiter. Bartender Mark had said he'd wanted Jilly that night at Gulliver's, and it looked like he'd found a way to have her and secrete her away. Probably followed her to the boyfriend's apartment parking garage, picked her up there, brought her here, possibly?

And maybe he was responsible for the missing Ms. Claudia Livesay as well.

She got right down, looking him over closely. He'd been through some kind of fight. There were scratches on his face, and was that a stun gun mark? She inhaled sharply. It looked like he'd already tangled with Ani.

Her eye caught on something else: a faint line of what looked like blood on the toe kick beneath the cabinet that ran around the end of the peninsula. On hands and knees she followed it into the main *U* of the kitchen and saw, scratched into the wood, the word GARDEN.

She stood up fast, staring through the French doors to the garden beyond. Whose message was it? Daria Johannsen's? And was that the beginnings of a casket-sized hole being dug just past the raspberry vine? She longed to go out and look, but decided she'd broken enough rules already. It would be far more prudent to wait by the body. Let the techs do their job outside.

Moving back to the dining area, she glanced down at him again. Her gaze stopped on the coffee spill once more. Turning her head, she zeroed in on the stainless steel carafe of the coffee maker.

Had Ani put something in the coffee? Hemlock or foxglove . . . ?

Grabbing up a paper towel, she carefully picked up the carafe. She could hear liquid sloshing so she carried it to the sink, holding it with one hand while she searched through nearby cupboards for a vessel to pour it into. Finding a bowl, she set it in the sink, then poured the coffee into the bowl. Something was pressing against the lid, so she pulled off the top and dumped whatever was inside into the coffee in the bowl.

Something sank, then floated to the surface.

A dead salamander.

Huh, September thought. *Now what the hell is that all about?*

Epilogue

She woke slowly, her ears recognizing the sound of a match striking, her nose registering the familiar burning scent at the same moment. Opening her eyes, she saw the glow of the flame as it touched a wick inside a hurricane lantern, dispelling the room's darkness in a warm circle of light.

She was lying on a hard bed in a fir-paneled room. Years of caution kept her from asking the first question that crossed her brain: *Where am I?*

But the woman lifting the lamp from the bedside table answered her as if she'd spoken. "You're with us now."

Lucky blinked several times and stared at her. She was middle-aged, blonde, her hair pulled back into a bun, and she wore a long, old-fashioned nightgown with a high-necked, lace collar. She gazed down at Lucky in a stern way, as if she found her lacking, which maybe she did. Lucky had run into that all her life.

"Who are you?" Lucky demanded in a raspy voice which ended in a deep, rattling cough. *The ocean. The frigid water*. She remembered the sense of soaring as the car flew off the jetty.

And she realized, vaguely, that the clock inside her head had stopped.

"I'm Catherine. And you're one of Madeline's daughters," the woman said. "Which makes us family."

I'm at Siren Song, she realized with a jolt. Inside the gates . . . inside the lodge.

"You can stay here until you have your strength back, but then you'll have to leave."

"How long do I have?" Lucky asked with an effort.

"As soon as you're better you'll have to leave. You're not finished with your work."

How did she know? *Did* she know? Lucky could only stare mutely at her, afraid to give too much away.

"I'll give you as much time as I can," Catherine promised her, walking to the window and gazing into the black night. "But we can't have the authorities at our door."

"No," Lucky agreed quickly.

She turned and looked at her, her expression softening the tiniest bit. "Welcome home, Ani."